Titles by Kathryn Shay

PROMISES TO KEEP
TRUST IN ME

TRUST IN ME

KATHRYN SHAY

BERKLEY BOOKS, NEW YORK

TRUST IN ME

A Berkley Book / published by arrangement with
the author

PRINTING HISTORY
Berkley edition / February 2003

Copyright © 2003 by Mary Catherine Schaefer.
Cover design by George Long.
Cover illustration by Franco Accornero.
Interior text design by Kristin del Rosario.

For information address: The Berkley Publishing Group,
a division of Penguin Putnam Inc.,
375 Hudson Street, New York, New York 10014.

ISBN: 0-425-18884-1

BERKLEY®
Berkley Books are published by The Berkley Publishing Group,
a division of Penguin Putnam Inc.,
375 Hudson Street, New York, New York 10014.
BERKLEY and the "B" design
are trademarks belonging to Penguin Putnam Inc.

PRINTED IN THE UNITED STATES OF AMERICA

10 9 8 7 6 5 4 3 2 1

*To Mary Jane Brooke,
treasured friend and trusted confidante,
for more than thirty years!
Thanks for always being there.*

PROLOGUE

———

Spring 1983

"WHERE the hell are Joe and Annie?" Margo Morelli asked as she took a long drag on a homemade joint and passed it off to Linc.

He leaned on his Harley, feet braced on the blacktop of the deserted parking lot of The Downtown Diner and took the joint from the girl who was his world. Inhaling one last stream of smoke, he crushed the butt under his foot like his stash hadn't cost a cool hundred. "He said they'd be here at two."

Linc's eyes narrowed on Margo's neck. He slid his hand inside the collar of the leather jacket he'd bought her. She had to keep it at his place—her mother would have thrown a fit if she'd known her daughter owned it. Linc wore a matching one. "When'd I do this?" he asked of the red brush burn just below her jaw.

She moved in close, her breasts straining big-time at the tight white T-shirt she sported under her coat. "Last night." She nuzzled his chest.

His body jerked to attention, even though they'd just screwed a couple of hours ago. "Sorry." He sounded like a freakin' frog.

"I'm not. I like having your mark on me." Her voice was pure sin, and at seventeen, he fell headlong into it.

"Mmm. Maybe we should ditch this plan. Go back to my room . . ."

Margo shook her head, sending waves of dark auburn hair everywhere. Her hazel eyes blazed with defiance. Though Linc would never tell her, sometimes she scared the shit out of him. Her urge to rebel went way beyond even his, and that was saying something. "We're going ahead with this." She threw back her shoulders. "Just as soon as Joe and Annie get here."

A giggle drifted out from the woods at the end of the parking lot, and from the trees stepped Linc's sister, Beth, and Danny Donovan, one of his best friends. Even in the dim light, Linc could see Beth was a mess. It didn't take Einstein to figure out what they'd been doing.

He stiffened. "Shit."

Margo's laugh was sultry. "You're such a prude sometimes, Grayson."

"They been humpin'."

"Well, as my mother would quote from her scripture, people in glass houses shouldn't throw stones." Margo edged in even closer and stood between his legs. She rubbed up against him, and for a minute, he was afraid he might go off like a pimply-faced kid.

"She's my baby sister," Linc said.

"She's sixteen, my age. What'd you think, she'd stay chaste?"

"I don't have to like it."

Margo's expression softened, making her seem young and vulnerable. "You always look out for all of us."

"The Outlaws was my idea. I look after what's mine."

"Yeah, Jesse, you do."

Though Linc started the gang, Margo had researched famous criminals and they'd all had a blast picking out role models. He was Jesse James, the leader. Margo was Ma Barker—strong, competent and utterly ruthless.

"Hi, guys," Danny said as he and Beth approached. His hand was draped over Beth's shoulder and there was a shit-eating grin on his face. The kid had dark hair and eyes, like Linc, but his features were more . . . patrician. Came from being so rich, Linc guessed.

"Hey, Clyde." Linc eyed his sister. Tall, pretty, with the curves of a Playboy model, Beth smiled, too. "Fix yourself up, Bonnie." Even her makeup was smeared and her clothes askew.

Danny did it for her. He straightened her shirt and wiped the black stuff from under her eyes. He always took care of Beth; it was the only thing that kept Linc sane about their relationship. In the middle of the night, ghosts haunted Linc, accusing him of corrupting his sister, his girlfriend and his best friends. He didn't take the onus for Annie Lang, as she was a baby compared to the rest of them—a goddamned freshman and barely fourteen. Their other friend, Joe Murphy, aka Billy the Kid, had dragged little Belle Star into the gang as an honorary member.

Speak of the devil. Joe's Harley, huge, black and more powerful than either Danny's or Linc's, roared into the parking lot. As always, Joe was going too fast.

When he drew near, Linc saw that he was alone. The monster machine screeched to a halt, and Joe eased off like he wasn't about to participate in a robbery, but instead was moseying into the town's ice-cream social.

"Ready to party?" he asked.

Linc nodded.

"Where's Belle?" Margo asked Joe.

Joe's face hardened. "I took her home." He drew out a cigarette and lit it, then fished a bottle out of his pocket and uncapped the Jim Beam. After taking a swig, he offered the liquor to the others. "Annie won't be part of this."

"Why?" Margo's belligerent tone drew a scowl from Joe.

"I don't want her to." His fist curled. "She's too fuckin' young."

Linc started to say something, but held his tongue at the last minute. His buddy could be violent. Linc had seen Joe take apart guys in the school yard, rip rooms to shreds and mutilate his own hand in a fit of temper. Linc also had an ugly inkling, from Joe's frequent black eye or swollen lip, that his old man—the elder Joe Murphy—had taught his son well. But the only time Linc had brought it up, Joe had gotten madder than a caged animal. So Linc had never tried to talk to him about it again.

Hell, they all had their problems. He and Beth were orphans, supposedly cared for by grandparents who didn't know squat about what to do with teenagers who didn't toe the line. Danny was pressured by his hoity-toity parents to cut loose from the gang; they'd also forbidden him to pursue his one true love, race car driving, the main industry of this hick New York state town. And the girl beside Linc probably had the worst of it because

what had been done to Margo had been done in the name of God
and religion.

If there was a God—and, funny thing, he believed there
was—Linc knew in his heart He wasn't that kind of Supreme
Being.

"We gonna do this?" Margo grumbled. "Or we gonna stand
here all night and chat?"

"We're gonna do it." Linc straightened. "I want me the dough
that's in the safe."

He'd sweet-talked a baby-faced waitress into coughing up the
information he needed about when deposits were made, the loca-
tion where the money was kept overnight and any security the
diner had. They were going to blow the safe.

"Everybody ready?" Linc asked, again seized by a twinge of
guilt. Though they'd stolen before, they hadn't gone after anything so big. If they got caught, they'd be in deep shit.

Which just made it all the more fun.

The Outlaws nodded.

"Let's go." Linc headed to the diner, his posse following him.

A half hour later, they stalked back out, pissed as hell. What a
crock the waitress had given them. There'd been no money in the
safe. Just as they reached their bikes, they heard sirens and saw
flashing red lights.

THE jail was a pigsty, like most of the town. Though Glen Oaks
housed one of the nation's premier stock-car tracks, for as long
as Linc could remember, the town had been on a downslide.
Every season it was overrun by rowdy race fans who got their
rocks off by tearing the streets up, landing in this stink hole and
making an even bigger mess of it. The cells smelled of day-old
piss and vomit, and the only light came from a grimy window
where gray dawn was just peeking through. The blankets on what
passed for cots were threadbare; Linc sat on one, listening to
Margo swear her head off in the cell next to the boys.

"She's in a mood," Danny said nonchalantly. As always, he
didn't seem to have a care in the world.

"Fucking son of a bitch."

"She swears like that when she's nervous."

Joe's head snapped up. His dark hair brushed his collar and
his gray eyes were cold and flat. "Why she nervous?"

"I heard the cop say her mother's on the way."

Danny shook his head and Joe swore. Virginia Morelli was a loony, and she was mean, too; that made her dangerous to the sixteen-year-old she controlled.

Loud voices came from the main office. Expecting their parents or guardians, the guys glanced over at the entryway. In walked Annie Lang, looking tiny and fragile in a baby-pink sweatshirt and jeans. Her long blond braid was rope thick and hung down her back. "Joey?"

"Jesus Christ." Joe bolted up from the cot. "What are you doing here?"

Annie backed up a step at his tone. "I . . . I had to see you were all right."

Joe crossed to the bars. "Get over here!"

Again, Annie hesitated. Then she took baby steps to him. When she was close, Joe reached out and snagged her wrist. She startled. "Joey!"

Linc started toward Joe, but his friend dropped Annie's arm immediately and hooked his hand around her neck. "Aw, baby, I'm sorry. But I worry about you. You shouldn't be here."

Annie pouted innocently. "I should have been with you."

"Like hell."

She whispered something to him, then he whispered back. Linc eased away and dropped down next to Danny, watching the other two talk and inch up as near as they could get.

Danny said, "They're all right."

"Yeah, I know. I worry about Joe, though."

"Why?"

"He's got it tough. That old man of his . . ."

Linc heard another commotion from the outer office. "If you don't do as I say, I will sue your ass."

Danny rolled his eyes. "Oh, shit, dear old dad."

Linc shook his head. Did Danny have any idea how lucky he was to have parents that cared? None of the rest of them had that.

He revised his assessment, though, when Carl Donovan strode into the cellblock with Angus Anderson, the night cop. Donovan always played King Shit and treated everybody else like peasants.

Annie edged away, and Joe said, "Go, honey, now." She scurried out.

Donovan's face was mottled red. "Daniel, what's this all about?"

Danny stood, a cool, defiant gleam in his eyes. "I didn't do nothin'."

Donovan took a bead on Linc and Joe. "It's them again. They've corrupted you. First the gang. Then racing."

Linc heard a moan from the next cell. Beth. The Donovans hated her with a vengeance.

"What happened, young man?"

Facing his father cockily, Danny said no more. Donovan tried staring him down, but it didn't work. So he went for his son's Achilles' heel. Striding over to the next cell, he addressed Beth. "I hope you're proud of yourself. Now you've turned my son into a criminal, not just a juvenile delinquent."

"I . . . I'm sorry, Mr. Donovan."

"Don't apologize to the asshole," Margo spat out.

Danny had gripped the bars. "Dad, don't. Leave her alone."

"You're pathetic." Donovan swept them all with a mocking glare. "You're hoodlums, all of you. You should be shipped off to some desert island."

So the town doesn't have to deal with us. Linc knew the drill.

"Well, I've tolerated this long enough. I've put the wheels in motion, Daniel, to get you out of this and away from *them*." He stood before his son again. "This time, you're not staying in town. We're sending you to that prep school in Vermont. Maybe you'll forget all your glory dreams about racing." He glanced toward Beth. "And about them."

Beth gasped. Margo swore. Donovan stood back while Angus unlocked the door and Danny exited the cell. Donovan turned on his heel and stalked out, expecting his son to follow.

Instead, Danny rushed over to the other cell. "Bethy, they can't do this. They can't keep us apart."

Beth started to cry. Danny talked quietly with her.

From the office, they heard an angry growl. "Daniel? Now!"

After a few more murmured words to Beth, Danny left.

The Donovans weren't gone five minutes when Virginia Morelli marched in with two of the Fearsome Fanatics, as he and Margo had dubbed the members of her religious commune, Holy Waters. "Mary Margaret Morelli, shame on you." Her mother stood before the cells, tall, bulky, with frizzy hair and glazed eyes. Linc crossed to the bars so he could see and hear more.

Margo said nothing. For all her piss and vigor, her mother could shut her up with a stare.

"The good Lord is crying, I'll tell you. Right, Sister Susan?"

"Right, Sister Virginia." Her companion was equally as hefty and dressed in the same drab green dress which was the garb of the whole fucking commune.

Virginia Morelli took a step toward the bars. "And what's that you have on?"

No answer.

"The devil's clothes." Margo must still be wearing her leather jacket. "Hand it over to me."

There was a rustling, then Linc watched her cherished coat drop into the hands of her crazed mother. Virginia tossed it off to her cohort. "Burn it, Sister Susan."

Angus came back in. Virginia faced him. "Unlock her. Holy Waters posted bail and assumes responsibility for this sinner."

"Well, the juvy people might have something to say about what she done," Angus murmured. "But you can take her now."

The jangle of keys. The scrape of steel. Margo stepped out into Linc's vision. Her shoulders seemed slight in the T-shirt, and every single one of her pretty features were tight. "On your knees, sinner," Virginia Morelli said. "On your knees in front of your friends."

Margo snagged Linc's gaze. He lurched into the bars, ready to tear them apart.

Joe came up behind him and put a hand on his shoulder. "Easy, buddy. You know you'll only make it worse if good old Mama notices you."

"On your *knees,* I said."

With Sister Susan and Sister Teresa each pressing on a slender shoulder, Margo sank to the floor.

"Ask God's forgiveness."

Margo raised her chin but said nothing.

"Ask his forgiveness."

Still, nothing.

A loud crack—flesh against flesh. Margo swayed backward like a small sapling blasted by February wind, but kept her balance.

Virginia stepped away. Sister Susan took her place. Then Sister Teresa. *Smack. Smack.* Still Margo was silent, but angry red welts were already forming on her face.

Angus intervened. "That's enough."

"Don't worry, Sister Virginia," one of the others said, "we'll take her home and discipline her properly."

"The hell you will." Linc's hands curled around cold, unyielding steel. He screamed at Angus, "Do something about this!"

Angus shook his head. "Should've thought about that before you tried to pull off a felony, Grayson."

Like a vulture sensing meat, Virginia Morelli strode up to Linc. There was a wildness in her eyes that made him shrink back. "You will never have her."

"Oh, yes I will. I'm going to take her away from you, far away from this town, and we're never coming back."

The words echoed ominously as the three "sisters" literally dragged Margo out of the jail. Rage, pure and simple, coursed through Linc, and he pounded the bars till his hands started to bleed.

Joe tried to soothe him. "There's nothing you can do, buddy. Nothing any of us can do." His tone was full of despair; they'd had a shit load of conversations about the future. Whereas Linc and Margo were bound and determined to escape the town, Joe saw himself literally rotting here. What made it worse was that his friend was the smartest guy Linc knew, though everybody only saw the *hoodlum.*

Beth was the one to knock sense into Linc. "Please, Linc, we're in real trouble."

And then, as if summoned by the words *real trouble,* Joe Murphy Senior stumbled into the jail. Crossing to Angus, he grabbed the keys, unlocked the cell door, and stepped inside. A cloud of stale whiskey and cigarettes accompanied him. Joe straightened, and for the first time, Linc spotted a glimmer of hope on his face. "You getting me out, Pa?"

"Like hell." The man raised his fist and rammed it into Joe's jaw. Joe staggered backward and hit the cot, then the wall, then he went down. Murphy walked out of the cell, weaving, and threw the keys to Angus. "Let him rot in here for all I care. Don't let none of those do-gooders get him out. Ya hear?"

Even Angus looked disgusted. Murphy left, and Linc looked at Joe. His friend's lip was split and his eyes were murderous. Linc bent down, and Joe said, "Don't." He seemed embarrassed. "I'm all right."

Linc had never heard more false words.

* * *

MID-AFTERNOON, Linc and Beth and Joe were still behind bars when they heard voices in the office again. Had Linc's
grandparents finally come for them? Instead, Tony Scarpino, The
Downtown Diner owner, shuffled in. Linc had seen the guy in the
diner, and around town. Middle aged, with no kids, he was small
and wiry and had a quick smile for everybody. Guilt, thick and
ugly, assaulted Linc. He wished he could do all the bad things he
routinely did and not feel so bummed about it.

"So," Scarpino said, coming right up to Linc. "I understand
you're the leader of this little excursion."

"Yeah, I am." Bravado fell easily from his lips.

"Got your sister involved, too, huh?"

That stole his thunder. Linc's shoulders sagged.

"The town don't do much for you guys." Scarpino threw a
disgusted look at Angus. "Kids need help staying on the straight
and narrow."

Linc wanted to say they didn't need the town . . . but they did;
he kept seeing Margo slapped up by the commune people and
Joe's father using him as a punching bag. Somebody should do
something about that. If Linc was in charge, he'd help kids like
him.

"Your parents died a bit ago, didn't they, Linc?"

Linc nodded.

Scarpino studied him. "Them grandparents of yours? Where
are they?"

"Probably napping."

"Nobody called them?"

"Yeah, I did," Angus put in. "Said they didn't feel good
enough to come down here this morning."

Sighing, Scarpino shook his head, a wealth of meaning in the
gesture. "I got me a proposition, Linc. Listen up. I'm gonna get
you out of here. And you're gonna make amends. You're gonna
work at my diner, report to me and keep your nose clean. If you
do, I won't press charges for breaking and entering. You didn't
get no money, anyway."

"Go to hell," Linc said, unable, unwilling, to accept charity.

Then he heard Beth start to cry. *Aw, shit.* "Please, Linc, let's
do this. I'm really scared."

Linc expelled a weary breath. His tough-guy instincts warred with his brotherly concern. And, to be honest, he was wrecked most of the time, being responsible for everything. Sometimes, he wished an adult *would* take him in hand. He thought about his girl; if he did this stupid stuff with Scarpino, he'd be able to get Margo out of town quicker. He had another year of school left, she had two. If they could just finish . . .

He heard a rustle behind him. Joe was restless on the cot. Linc said, "Murphy, too?"

Scarpino shrugged. "Sure. Why not?"

"No can do." Angus sounded sorry. "His father said nobody's to bail him out for a while. Legal guardians have say."

Linc faced Joe. His friend's expression was so damn bleak it broke Linc's heart. "Do it," Joe said. "I'll be all right."

"I won't leave you hangin'."

"You got to."

"Joe . . ."

"Go, Linc. You got a chance." The unspoken *And I don't* hung heavily in the air.

Torn, Linc nonetheless nodded. He turned to Scarpino. "All right."

Angus unlocked Beth first; her face was streaked with tears. Then the jailer opened Linc's cell.

Beth flew into his arms, and he held onto her. "Oh, Linc."

"Shh. It'll be all right." He'd never lied worse in his life. As he looked back at his friend, sitting on the ragged cot in the dismal jail cell of Glen Oaks, his face swollen from his father's fist, Linc knew in his heart things wouldn't be all right for any of them.

He also knew that it was mostly his fault. And he'd have to live with that forever.

ONE

———

THE silver Jag sat low and sleek, hugging the curb in front of Zip's Bar and Grill. Ron Donovan's eyes narrowed on it, then glanced up the street to his mother's place, The Downtown Diner. At midnight, the storefront was dark. She'd split for home hours before, but he could still see her disappointed face, hear her fed-up tone and angry words. *No more hanging out with those guys, Ronny. I mean it.*

He kicked one of the rocks at his feet; it flew off the cement sidewalk into the road. Taking a drag on his Marlboro, he blew the smoke out in tiny little rings; the familiar tobacco scent calmed him. As he watched the puffs disappear into the March darkness, he remembered another night ten years before. The night his father, Danny Donovan—way cool dad, stellar husband and up-and-coming race car driver—had been killed.

His mother hadn't been yelling at him then. Instead she'd crept into his room and sank onto the edge of his bed where he lay, facedown. She'd gently turned him over, dried his freakin' baby tears with the sleeve of her pajamas and cuddled him to her chest for a hug. Then she gave him the hot chocolate she always fixed when things were tough. As he drank, she whispered, *You got me, buddy. We'll be okay, I promise.*

Because the words stung like a son of a bitch—they'd been anything *but* okay thanks to Ron himself—and because the memory was an emotional knife twisting in his gut, he ground the cigarette under his boot, yanked up the leg of his jeans, and slid out the blade he'd bought in the city at Violence, Inc. His buddy Loose had introduced him to the seedy little shop in the Village. The metal was cold against Ron's fingers—cold, slick and potent.

The heavy feel of the weapon gave him courage; he stalked across the street toward the hotshot car just begging for his attention. The goddamned window was down, and its rich, expensive exterior was wide open—tempting a saint. Familiar fury built with each step Ron took; by the time he reached the car, a red haze of rage was ready to eat him alive.

Memories of his grandmother's scrapbooks fueled his anger. In them were pictures of his dad, not tall but muscular as hell, in his NASCAR helmet and racing suit. His mother's dark hair had flowed down to her waist then, her big brown eyes twinkling at the camera. Wrapped up in his dad's arm, she looked happier than Ron ever remembered seeing her. There were corny snapshots of him and his dad together, too. When Ron looked at them, sometimes he could still feel the heavy weight of his father's arms hugging him tight. Ron was the spitting image of his dad, Grandpa Carl always said, right down to the curly brown hair, stubborn chin and dark eyes.

Cursing the bastard who'd ruined it all, Ron jerked the knife up to hover over the Jag. Cocky and self-assured, that's how the guy had been described in the newspapers—Tucker Quaid, aka The Menace, owner of this little baby and three-time Winston Cup champ. So sure of his dick-brained self that he left his car unlocked and the windows down. So sure of himself that he'd dare come back to Glen Oaks all these years later.

Emotion clawed to get out of Ron. When it did, he cut the knife through the air. The sharp blade ripped the convertible top, meeting some resistance, but Ron got the job done. The soft gray leather of the driver's seat with its rich new-car smell was an easier mark, the knife's slice as smooth as a boat's hull cutting through water. Ron only had to lean over to tear up the passenger side. Then, he squatted down and dug into the tire at his left. He stole around the car and made quick work of each one.

With each righteous stroke of the blade, some of the haze

lifted. Some of the defiance faded away. When he was done and surveyed the torn leather and shredded tires before him, he almost couldn't remember making the dozens of cuts. Straightening, he went to stuff the knife in his boot when an arm like wood locked around his neck; fingers like steel encircled his wrist. His weapon clattered to the pavement with a rickety thud. Ron was slammed back against a rock-hard chest.

"Damn fool kid," the guy who cornered him barked out. "What the *hell* makes you think you can get away with this?"

Ron had heard that sissy Southern drawl on TV; he knew whose voice it was. If he circled around, he'd see the big rangy body, the cropped blond hair and the cold green eyes of Tucker Quaid.

The man who'd killed Ron's father.

TUCKER Quaid prowled the police station waiting area, a stark twelve-by-twelve room smelling of stale coffee and furnished with sticky orange vinyl chairs. He was more keyed up than he used to get before a big race. With each step, he cursed a blue streak.

He should've known that coming back to Glen Oaks would be bad news all around. But shit, he hadn't planned on *this*. He'd been poleaxed when he'd learned the snot-nosed brat who'd slashed his Jag was Danny Donovan's son. Tucker had jerked the knife out of the boy's hand, smashed him facedown on the hood, then pinned the kid there with his knee and chest. He'd whipped out his cell phone and punched in 911, only to hear, upon the arrival of a Lieutenant Pratt, who the vandal was. Damn it to hell. Couldn't anything go right with this friggin' family?

Drawing a cup of coffee, he sipped the brew, wincing at its bitterness, scowling down at the scarred wood floor. As always, the guilt came, as clear and cold as a mountain lake—and just as sobering. Searching hard for his alter ego, *The Menace*, Tucker tried to block the images. But the kid looked so damn much like his daddy that the memories were impossible to backstop.

This time Tucker was bombarded by one of the zillion headlines from the newspapers. Big, bold, accusing letters declared, *Menace's controversial blocking takes life of young driver. NASCAR investigation to follow.*

Remorse had dogged Tucker like a rabid fan as he followed

the racing circuit and climbed the slippery ladder of success until
his own crash three years before had left him with a bum knee
and no desire to race again.

Yeah, hotshot, what're you doing here, then?

Tucker sighed. Good question.

Before he could answer it, the door to the waiting area flew
open and people hustled in. Aw, shit! It had to happen someday,
since he was back in town, but he hadn't expected it so soon, or
when he was so raw, or when he'd had a couple of bourbons
under his belt to lower his defenses. He tried to marshal them
fast.

Danny Donovan's widow, and the guy with her, froze just inside the room. At a loss for words, Tucker simply stared at them,
feeling like a Class-A bastard.

Breaking the freeze-frame first, the man approached him. To
Tucker's surprise, he held out his hand. "I'm Linc Grayson, Mr.
Quaid. Ronny's uncle. We're . . . sorry about this."

Uncle. Grayson. He had to be Beth Donovan's brother, then.
Though Tucker hadn't ever talked to her personally, he knew
something about her family. "I reckon I'm sorry, too," he said as
he shook Grayson's hand. Tucker tried to stifle the shame and
stigma of his actions of ten years before, but they surfaced like
topped-off gasoline when he stared over Linc Grayson's shoulder
into the rounded eyes and troubled face of the man's sister. It
about tore him up all over again.

Dressed casually in jeans, a red sweatshirt and a windbreaker,
she'd changed in the ten years since he'd last seen pictures of the
grieving widow, as the papers had played it out. She'd been in her
twenties then, with long dark hair and smooth, clear skin. No
worry lines had marred her brow. No creases had framed her
mouth. The wear and tear of raising a son alone, supporting herself, and dealing with *her childhood sweetheart's death* had taken
its toll on her. Though there was a womanliness about her now
that could make a guy ache deep in his gut, she'd aged. And
toughened up.

In a rusty voice, he mumbled, "Mrs. Donovan. I'm sorry." In-
adequate words. Goddamn it, he'd waxed eloquent in interviews
after winning at Daytona and Darlington, but he was as tongue-
tied as a teenager on his first date in front of these two strangers.

She crossed the room, tall and graceful, and smiled sadly at
him. Close up, her brown-as-chestnut eyes were bloodshot and a

little puffy, like she'd been crying. Free of any cosmetics, her skin was spattered with freckles. "No, Mr. Quaid, *I'm* sorry. For what Ronny did."

Honesty made him say, "Understandable."

"Unacceptable," she answered. "He had no right . . ."

Tucker held her gaze, dumbstruck by what he saw there. No blame, no bitterness that he'd ruined her life. There was only cold acceptance.

Grayson broke the tense stare-off. "Shall we sit?"

Crumpling up his cup and tossing it into a rank-smelling trash can, Tucker dropped into a chair.

"Want some coffee, Bethy?" Grayson asked.

Beth Donovan nodded. "I think we'll be here awhile."

Her brother had poured her a cup and one for himself, when the door to the holding room opened. The muscle-bound lieutenant with a jaw made of stone nodded to Beth. "Good, you're here, Beth." He glanced at her brother. "Reverend."

Surprise ambushed Tucker and he blurted out, *"Reverend?"* He studied the man, seeing a boxer, or even a construction worker, in the solid wiry form that sported jeans, a flannel shirt and a quilted vest. His face was stubbled with a growth of beard, and his dark hair brushed his collar; he didn't look like any minister Tucker had ever seen.

Despite the circumstances, all three people smiled, even the stand-at-attention lieutenant. "A common reaction," Grayson said. "I don't look the type."

"It's 'cause you're not," Beth told him affectionately. This, at least, brought a sparkle to her eyes.

Lieutenant Pratt quelled another smile and nodded. "I'm glad you're here, in any case. Ronny's more surly than usual."

Beth drew in an anxious breath. Linc reached for her hand and pulled her up. "We'll deal with this, honey. Let's go in."

"You, too, Mr. Quaid." The cold reserve of the lieutenant made the Graysons appear downright cozy with him. Doc had warned him that even though the town council had literally begged Tucker to come to Glen Oaks, some people would treat him like a leper.

Which was just fine with him. He'd lived the last ten years in an emotional wasteland, and he planned to keep it that way. Especially while he was in Glen Oaks.

The holding room was smaller than the waiting area. The air

bore the faint scent of sweat. Straight-back chairs were pushed up to an old wooden table; one seat was already occupied by the young man of the hour—knees spread, head bent, hands linked together. When they entered, the boy looked up. Tucker expected the insolence Pratt had mentioned and which he'd seen earlier. Instead, when Ron Donovan's eyes landed on his mother, there was only sadness in them. He said nothing, though, just stared at her.

Linc spoke first. "You okay, buddy?"

Transferring his gaze to his uncle, the boy nodded.

After a moment, Beth crossed to her son and squeezed his shoulder. She bent down and whispered something to him, making his head droop lower. He rubbed his eyes with his thumb and forefinger. Gently she kissed his hair.

Averting his gaze, Tucker took in the white walls covered with WANTED posters, the overhead fluorescent lighting and a phone on the square table; he looked anywhere but at mother and son.

Beth asked the lieutenant, "What's going to happen now, Mike?"

Small towns. Tucker had forgotten what they were like. He'd buried all memories of the backwater village in South Carolina where he'd grown up almost as deep as he'd buried his recollection of that life-altering day here in Glen Oaks ten years before.

Pratt dropped his file on the table and indicated they should sit. When all five were settled, the officer said, "He's had his last chance, Beth, you know that. When he ripped off those boots." The cop's gaze hardened. "And his grandparents aren't going to pull strings this time, like they did before."

"I know." She stared at her son, but again not like he was some alien creature, whose behavior was foreign to her. It was as if she *understood* him. Felt bad for him. Tucker didn't get it.

"But that was a year ago." This from Uncle Linc. "He's been straight since then."

"I realize that." Pratt shot a quick glance at Tucker. "But I also know he's been in trouble at school since the end of February."

When The Menace had returned to Glen Oaks. The cause of the boy's backsliding was obvious. Tucker wanted to squirm on the hard chair like a kid in the principal's office, but forced himself to sit still. Nobody spoke.

Then Pratt focused in on the mother. "I'm going to arrest him for this, Beth."

Her little gasp knifed Tucker low in the belly.

"He just turned seventeen." Her voice was close to a whisper. "He'll have a record as an adult if you do that."

Blowing out a frustrated breath, the officer shook his head. "He knew all this, didn't you, Ron?"

The boy ran his finger over one of the scars in the table. "I knew."

"You want to go to jail, Ronny?" Linc asked.

His gaze still lowered, Ron shook his head.

"Then why'd you do this?"

The boy's head came up fast, and this time his face *was* surly; he looked loaded for bear.

Grayson told him, "It's gotta come out, Ron. You gotta see it."

"I *see* it." He spat out the words.

The minister surfaced from inside the uncle. "You're having trouble with Mr. Quaid's return to Glen Oaks, aren't you?"

"I don't give a shit about *Mr. Quaid.*"

"I wish you wouldn't swear in front of your mother, bud."

Ron actually bit his lip. "Sorry."

Man, this whole thing was out of kilter, Tucker thought. The kid had just committed a crime, and they were on him about swearing. But it wasn't just that. There was no animosity among the three of them.

"Look, I did this," Ron admitted. "I gotta pay."

"You don't know what you're in for, honey," Beth said with surprising strength. "There'll be a heavy penalty this time."

The grim resignation in her voice moved Tucker to action. "What if I don't press charges?" he asked, unplanned, and maybe unwisely.

Four heads snapped around to look at him.

Bitter hate flared from the boy's eyes. "Don't do me any favors."

Pratt scowled. "It isn't that easy, Mr. Quaid. He committed a crime. The damage was thousands of dollars. I can't let it go."

"Why would you *want* to, Mr. Quaid?" Beth asked. "He destroyed your car."

Tucker was stunned by the question. "How can you ask that?"

A kaleidoscope of feelings bounced crazily around them, rearranging the emotional landscape too fast to follow. Tucker scraped back his chair, the sound loud in the suddenly quiet room. "Obviously my comin' here has brought on a fall from grace in the boy."

The reverend gave a wry grin. "*From grace* is a pretty big stretch, but you've got the gist of it."

"Look, I don't condone what he did. But there seem to be extenuatin' circumstances."

"That's an excuse," Pratt said, shaking his head. "I won't let him off scot-free."

Linc's eyes narrowed. "How about having the Council make a recommendation to the court?"

"The what?" Tucker asked.

"The Community Youth Council. An organization comprised of the police, the school, a community representative, the Social Service agency in town and a member of the clergy." Linc smiled sadly. "Glen Oaks has a long-standing problem with the youth of this town. It has something to do with the influence of the race track and our proximity to New York City. We've established a council to set up programs to keep the kids straight, and our own kind of lay court to deal with minor transgressions. We also make recommendations to the judge."

"This crime is more than minor," the lieutenant put in.

"But the circumstances are unusual. And since Mr. Quaid has indicated an understanding, maybe this is the best route to go."

"I don't like it." Pratt's face was implacable.

"You've been pleased with Ronny's turnaround this last year."

"I have."

"At least let the committee meet. You're on the Council. You know we don't let the kids off scot-free, Mike."

Pratt jangled the keys attached to his belt loop and stared at the floor thoughtfully. "All right. Try to call it for Friday night." He faced Tucker. "You think about this, Mr. Quaid."

"Sure." Tucker had no intention whatsoever of thinking about whether or not he was gonna hurt this family again.

Glancing at the clock, Pratt stood. "Take him home, Beth." He zeroed in on Ron. "It's not over, kid."

Ron stared sullenly at him. Everyone rose.

Beth said, "Linc, take Ronny out to the car, will you? I'd like to talk to Mr. Quaid for a minute."

Her brother gave her a sideways glance, and her son glared at her.

"Stay here." Pratt headed for the door with Linc and Ron. "I'll walk you two out."

Tucker's heartbeat speeded up like he was about to circle around a hairpin turn. His palms began to sweat. He'd been staying out at the lake with Doc and avoided this woman since he'd come back to Glen Oaks three weeks before; he'd planned to keep his distance for the six months he'd be here.

They were alone all too soon.

Tucker swallowed hard and faced her.

Huge brown eyes stared up at him. Again he was surprised there was no anger in them, no blame.

Having grown up with animosity as a daily diet, Tucker didn't know how to digest Beth Donovan's attitude at all.

"WHAT'D you wanna talk to me about, Mrs. Donovan?" As in the pictures she'd seen of him, before and after the accident, Beth noted how hard Tucker Quaid's face was. His jaw was granite-edged, his mouth stern and unsmiling. But she knew a living, breathing man suffered inside the expensive leather jacket and tailored pants and shirt he wore. In the weeks following the crash, a few of the photos had captured a tortured look on his face. There'd also been the letter he'd written her, full of remorse. He'd offered financial assistance, which she'd of course declined.

Setting her purse down on the table, she straightened her shoulders and stuck her hands into the pockets of her nylon jacket. If nothing else since Danny's death, she'd gotten tougher. "I wanted to thank you for what you're doing for Ronny."

A quick glint of something—annoyance, or maybe just guilt—flickered in his green eyes. Right now they were hard and flat, the color of jade. "It's the least I can do."

"Many people wouldn't."

His gaze slipped from her to the WANTED posters on the wall. His sigh was evident in the movement of his shoulders.

"I just want you to know I appreciate it." When he didn't respond, she added, "And the whole town appreciates your coming back to help us out."

Still nothing.

"Why *are* you here?"

He faced her, almost against his will. The stoic mask was in place, though his light complexion was flushed. Rotely, as if he were reading from one of the publicity flyers, he said, "I'm here at the request of the town council to help revive the economy of Glen Oaks. My reputation as a driver, along with Doc Holt's as my former crew chief, has attracted the best NASCAR drivers in the world for an exhibition race in September. My comin' out of retirement, and the new car Doc's workin' on, are the lure—along with the track's refurbishment. Your town's hoping to recapture its status as one of the finest raceways in the world."

Patiently, she stared at him, waiting for a real answer.

The mask slipped. Digging his hands in his trouser pockets, he said in low, gravelly tones, "I *owe* you. I *owe* this town." His voice cracked on the admission.

"No, Mr. Quaid, you don't."

"Tell me that boy out there didn't get into trouble because he lost his daddy. Tell me he didn't backslide because I came back to town."

"Ronny's issues aren't your fault."

"Of course they are."

Wide-eyed, Beth cocked her head. "Is this how you've felt for ten years?"

A muscle leapt in his throat. "More or less."

She gave him a small smile. "Then maybe that's why God sent you back here."

"God had nothin' to do with my comin' back."

"You're here to pay a debt you don't owe, Mr. Quaid. It's not your fault Danny died."

"My car played chicken with your husband's for ten laps before his skidded off the track, causin' it to flip twice and crash into a stone wall. Everybody said my blockin' was too aggressive." His mouth thinned. "There was even an investigation."

The stark words resurrected a vivid image. For a minute, she relived the scene she'd watched from the stands: the high-pitched screech of the tires, the shattered glass, the thud of Danny's car crashing into the concrete wall. Ten years had blurred the memory, but sometimes it still had the power to shake her. In a hoarse voice, she told him, "The NASCAR sanctioning body declared the collision an accident of indeterminate cause." She frowned. "Auto racing is a dangerous sport. Everyone out there is at risk. It's why I don't want Ronny involved."

The man's face clouded with naked emotion. "Your son wants to race?"

"Yes. But he won't. Not just for me, for his grandparents. Julia and Carl are horrified at the thought, just like they were about Danny. They have a fit when Ron even goes to the races held at the track now."

"He should do something else. It's a tough life."

Beth remembered Danny's high every time he climbed out of the car. His unshakable belief that he was going to be the best. His refusal to even listen when she expressed the concern every person who loves a driver feels when he gets into a race car. "I know. I don't want that life for my son. He's good in art; I wish he'd pursue that. I need to keep him on the straight and narrow."

"A parent can only do so much."

"You couldn't be more wrong about that, Mr. Quaid. A parent can save a child's life."

"Or destroy it."

"What do you mean?"

"Nothin'. Look, for the record, I don't want any thanks for this. As I said, it's the least I can do." He looked away. "Besides it was a good excuse to spend some time with Doc after his heart problems."

"I heard about that. How's he doing?"

"Fine. Ornery as ever."

She crossed to him; Tucker Quaid was unusually tall for a driver, and she had to look up at him. This close she could smell some woodsy scent on him. "Well, *for the record,* I don't blame you for Danny's death; if it makes a difference, I wish you wouldn't blame yourself." She reached out and squeezed his arm; he looked like she'd given him a gift. "Anyway, I appreciate your wanting to keep Ronny out of jail. I'll see you at the Council meeting."

"What?"

"You'll have to go when the case is presented."

"Can't I just send a statement?"

"I'm not sure. They'll want to talk to you, I'd guess."

He seemed resigned to that. She wished she could help, but she had a hundred and sixty pounds of trouble waiting for her outside that door. Right now her son needed her.

And truthfully, she was shocked to realize she wanted to help this man. Though her own past, and having a minister as a brother, had helped her to forgive Tucker Quaid, she'd never envisioned feeling sorry for him.

With that strange emotion in her heart, Beth turned to leave the police station.The door creaked as she opened it.

His words stopped her. "Mrs. Donovan?"

Circling around, she faced him. "Yes?"

"Can I ask you a question?"

"Of course."

"There's somethin' different about your relationship with the boy. I can tell you're as mad as a hornet at him. But there's no animosity there. It's as if you *understand* him."

She smiled serenely. "I do understand him. I know exactly where he's coming from."

"How?"

"Because, Mr. Quaid, by the time I was Ronny's age, I'd done a lot worse things than steal some boots or slash up a car."

AS if performing a sacred rite, Beth poured the whole milk into the pan, turned on the gas and watched it flicker. When she was young, she and her best friends Annie and Margo used to make hot chocolate to soothe themselves if things got really bad. All three of them still kept up the ritual.

Willing her hands not to shake, she told herself that this, too, would be all right, that God would watch over them once again. He'd certainly carried them through scrapes before.

This is more than a scrape.

She swallowed hard. Her baby boy was in trouble. That little dark-haired infant with the brown eyes and dimples in his cheeks was in for it this time. Beth knew just how long it took to make the law throw up their hands.

"Hi."

She glanced up. He filled the doorway, looking so much like his father in jeans, socked feet and one of his blasphemous T-shirts; Danny had loved sacrilegious T-shirts, too. Usually she found them entertaining. Not tonight. She cringed at its message. *I feel much better now that I've lost all hope.*

"Hi, buddy."

His grin was the little-boy expression he'd donned when he had frogs in his pockets or a stray cat stashed away in his room. "That for me?"

"Of course."

When the milk began to boil, she stood on tiptoes to get the chocolate—the expensive Swiss kind Ronny loved. She couldn't reach the shelf. He must have put it there himself.

"I'll get it."

She poured the milk in mugs and took them to the table. He joined her and dropped into a seat adjacent to hers. When she added the chocolate, its rich smell soothed her. The crowning touch was tiny marshmallows. She remembered when Ronny couldn't say the word clearly.

And, as always, when it was ready, they clanked cups. "I love you, buddy," she said hoarsely.

Tears formed in his eyes. "I love you too, Mom."

"We'll get through this, Ron."

"I'm sorry."

"I know you are."

"I'll do better this time, if I have the chance."

"God will give you the chance, honey. I know it."

"Then I'll do better."

"I believe you." Behind him, a picture of his father grinned out at her from a silver frame. She swallowed back the emotion. "We'll talk more about this tomorrow." *When I can do it without crying.* It was important not to cry.

"All right."

He seemed relieved as he finished his drink, kissed her on the cheek and headed upstairs.

Beth sat alone in the kitchen, thinking about her son. At least he had a mother to stand by him when he did stupid things. And she'd be there forever, no matter what, because she loved him and because she'd gone through this kind of thing alone.

That would *never* happen to *her* child.

She picked up Danny's picture and stared at it. God, she just wished she had someone to share this with.

TWO

—

IT was almost one A.M. by the time Linc returned to his apartment. As he traipsed up the rickety steps to three small rooms over the church's garage, weariness accompanied him like an old familiar friend. He'd been up since six in the morning, grappling with his sermon for Sunday, visiting Mrs. Temple in the hospital, and taking care of the hundreds of other details that were his sole responsibility in the congregation.

They were blessings, he reminded himself, not burdens. And he had a gift for being a minister here in Glen Oaks. His ability to handle the odd church, with its interesting and sometimes eccentric assortment of parishioners, was one of the reasons God had sent him here, Linc was sure. Sometimes, he wished he knew the rest of God's plan, but that mostly remained a divine enigma.

With a sigh, he unlocked the door and dragged himself into the living room. He cursed softly as he stumbled on his baseball glove, bent over, and tossed it onto the frayed chair. He'd played catch with some of the boys in the empty lot earlier that night. Like many of the kids in Glen Oaks, they needed a role model. When Linc had needed someone to emulate at a critical point in his life, God had sent former diner owner and all-around savior, Tony Scarpino, who'd rescued both him and Beth. Now Linc was paying back some dues. For that and for other things.

Just as he collapsed on the worn but comfortable couch, he

caught sight of the blinking light on the phone. *Messages.* Lord, give him strength, he wasn't up for this. Church members called at all hours, and Linc met their needs no matter what the personal cost. But before he went to sleep that night he'd wanted to think about this newest development with Ronny and how he was going to help his sister. Stretching out flat on the sofa, he pressed the answering-machine button, closed his eyes, threw his arm over his forehead, and listened.

"Reverend Linc, it's Connie Smith." One of the more active members of the church. "I wanted to remind you the Ladies' Aid Society is meeting tomorrow morning at nine in the fellowship hall. We hope you can start us off with a prayer."

He could do that.

"And please," she said stiffly, "ask Mr. Portman *not* to clean during our meeting."

Poor Henry. He was one of the volunteers who helped keep the church running. Many of them made more work for Linc, but he'd never deny them their contribution. He made a mental note to watch for the silent, but dedicated, man before nine.

Be-ep.

"Reverend Grayson, this is Rosa DeMartino." Rosa sounded sad tonight. "I won't be at the women's group meeting tomorrow. Something's come up."

Damn. Linc could guess what that was. Her husband, Sam DeMartino, had openly opposed Rosa's involvement with the newly formed women's self-esteem group that Linc had begun. And Linc was worried about the situation between the couple. He was afraid of missing the signs, like he had with his friend Annie. His guilt over Annie's situation still haunted him, mostly in the early morning hours like now when you saw your mistakes, distorted and magnified as if you were looking through a fun house mirror. Sometimes, he ached with the need to share his insecurities with a partner, to have someone to help him clarify things and make the hours of doubt less lonely.

No, not somebody. Margo. Eve to his Adam.

Another beep. "Hi, handsome. It's me. Um, it's midnight. Either you're out taking care of your flock, or you're dead to the world asleep. If it's the former, call me when you get in." Linc frowned as Margo's voice quavered on the last word. "No matter what time it is."

Fully awake now, he sprang up from his supine position and punched out her number. She answered on the second ring.

"Hi, honey," he said casually. One of the first things he'd figured out early on about Margo was that she spooked easily. "What're you doing up at this hour?"

"I could ask you the same, Rev." It was good to hear the sass in her voice. That husky teasing tone had driven him nuts as a teenage boy.

"Saving souls, as usual." He fingered the nubby couch fabric. "What's going on with you?"

Ignoring his question—she did that whenever she wasn't ready to talk—she asked, "Anything I should know about?" Their shared history made the question normal.

"Yeah, as a matter of fact. I was gonna call you tomorrow. Ronny's in trouble again."

"Oh, no. Tell me."

Briefly Linc sketched out Ronny's newest escapade to his mother's best friend.

"Damn that kid's behavior."

Linc chuckled. "Pot calling the kettle black, Mary Margaret?"

Use of her full name made her laugh. "I guess. How'd Bethy take meeting Quaid face-to-face?"

"Like a trooper. She's too strong." He grinned, though the circumstances were dire. Somehow, Margo always made things better. "Beth told Quaid about our checkered past."

Margo sputtered, "She *what*?"

"Apparently he asked why there was no animosity between us and Ron. Beth came right out and told him."

"He'd find out soon enough." A brittle edge slipped into her voice. "The sanctimonious Glen Oaks grapevine is still milking that, I'm sure, even after all these years."

Complaints about the town, and the church, were a familiar part of her catechism. Rightfully so, he knew. Her mother's skewed view of God and Christianity had almost destroyed Margo.

"I don't know how you put up with it," she added.

"My personal penance." *That and hearing about you with other guys.* "So, why'd you call this late?"

"We missed Sunday's phone call." Since they'd parted company when they'd graduated from New York University fifteen years before, they'd spoken on the phone every Sunday night—

all through his divinity school training, her move to the Midwest to get away from *him and his God,* she'd said heatedly, and even after she got married; that had been the hardest time for Linc.

The hardest period in their relationship for her had been when he'd accepted this ministry in their hometown. She'd come to New York unexpectedly for his graduation. After the outdoor ceremony, he'd taken her and Beth to dinner in the Village and when they were finally alone, Margo had begun to tell him what he'd prayed for years to hear. *I left Guy, Linc. I'm moving back to New York. Maybe we can . . .*

He'd stopped her words with his fingers against her lips. It was the most difficult thing he'd ever done, telling her he was returning to the town she despised. To embrace religion, which she saw as a curse upon mankind. She'd refused then, to finish what she'd begun to say. In his lowest spiritual moments, Linc still argued with God about the timing of her change of heart. Naturally, like every time he squared off with his Maker, God won. Linc never had a prayer of beating Him out, but it didn't stop him from trying.

"Linc, did you doze off? I asked you a question."

On cue he yawned. "Nope, I'm here."

"Christ, that church is draining you."

"Don't swear, honey. It makes me mad."

In a serious tone she said, "I hate to make you mad."

"Then tell me why you called." He hesitated. There were a lot of minefields between them, most of which they were both pretty good at sidestepping. One, Linc always skirted the most carefully. "How was your business trip to Boston?"

A long, thoughtful pause, giving Linc time to picture her. He could imagine her stretched out on her five-hundred-dollar bedspread in her expensive co-op on New York's Upper East Side, maybe a little jazz crooning softly from her stereo in the corner of her bedroom. She was probably wearing her favorite bedtime outfit—silk pj's or nightgown. In college, she'd often worn his T-shirt and boxers, as they were roommates—and more—all four years. Deep red hair, the kind found in a Renaissance painting. Big cat eyes that got almost green when she was angry or aroused. A body that, in his street days, he'd called stacked. Thoughts of her body made him uncomfortable. As usual. No doubt about it, Margo was more tempting than all the scarlet women of the Bible put together.

"The trip was interesting."

She said no more. Always a clue to her state of mind.

"Did Pretty Boy wine and dine you?" Linc usually tried to hide his dislike of Margo's colleague, Philip Hathaway; in meditative moments, he even admitted to himself and to God that he was jealous. Tonight, he was whipped, so he wasn't as quick to camouflage his un-Christian feelings about the jerk.

For eight years Margo had sung Hathaway's praises. As Executive Vice President and right-hand man of the CEO of CompuQuest, the computer firm where she worked, Hathaway had escalated her career fast and a little too carefully for Linc's taste. If the guy hadn't been married with two daughters, Linc would have been more concerned. But with her background—Margo's father had been legally wed to another woman when her mother had gotten pregnant—Margo would never become involved with a married man.

"Linc, did you hear me? I said Boston had a lot of nice restaurants and things to do."

Not what I asked. "Oh, good." After waiting for her to say more, and she didn't, he asked, "Did you get the account?"

"Yes, Philip handled it beautifully. Laufler's gave us the whole shebang."

"Wonderful." He asked God's forgiveness for lying. Sinking back down onto the couch, he stared at the ceiling. He could hear a tree limb bat against the window outside. "So you'll be busy?"

"Yes, but I was hoping to see you soon." A long pause. "I miss you."

A chorus of angel voices couldn't have sung sweeter words. "I miss you, too."

"Can you get away for a weekend and come up again? I loved having you here after Christmas."

"Not right now, honey. That was only a few months ago. A minister can't be gone on too many Sundays." Especially one in his circumstances. He'd taken this job with a ragtag congregation ten years ago knowing he'd be minister, mechanic and all-around handyman; knowing what the demands on him would be. Though most of the time he believed it to be an opportunity from God, tonight, tired and alone, everything felt like an obligation.

"Ah, yes, of course. Mother Church. She sucks you dry, Rev."

Margo said *church* like most people said *cancer*—with horror and a lot of fear. Though she loved Linc, she despised anything to do with religion. Understandably so, after her mother turned born-again and took her twelve-year-old daughter to live in a cult-like commune just outside of Glen Oaks. When Virginia had died ten years before, Margo had still been estranged from her.

"No rest for the wicked," he joked, trying to lighten the pall that was cast over their conversation every time they discussed his calling and spiritual beliefs.

Again, there was a confessional-like silence on the other end. Finally, Margo spoke. "You're the only truly good man I know, Linc."

Linc sat up straight and hiked the phone to the other ear. "Margo, something *is* wrong. Tell me."

"I'm just tired . . . and lonely tonight."

"Come home, then."

She snorted. "Glen Oaks is *not* my home. It's just the place I grew up."

Very fast, Linc knew, since he'd been partly the cause of her quick rise to adulthood. He'd given her her first cigarette, her first swig of Jim Beam, her first joint.

And, God forgive him, her first taste of sex.

"Bad choice of words. Come to see *me,* then." When he got no response, he said, "And Beth. The Council's meeting Friday night; she could use your support. You know how Ronny adores you." Still no answer. So he asked for God's understanding and added, "Annie told me the next time I talked to you to tell you to call her. She's tried to reach you several times."

"Is she all right?" He heard the distress in Margo's voice, shared it. They were both protective of Annie Lang after what she'd gone through. Of all of them—the kids of Glen Oaks who'd been hell on wheels in their teens—Annie had suffered the most from her disastrous past.

"As right as she ever is."

"Linc, Annie's problems are *not* your fault."

Yeah, sure. "Well, why don't you come to Glen Oaks this weekend and see how she's doing in person?"

"Are ministers supposed to use blackmail?"

No, and they're not supposed to lust after old girlfriends, either. "My God will understand."

Unfortunately, Margo didn't believe his God existed. And if there was anything Abraham Lincoln Grayson knew without a shred of doubt, it was the reality of his God.

"I wish I believed that," she said flippantly.

"I wish you did, too." After an uncomfortable silence, she said, "I'll think about taking the train up on Friday." They chatted for several more minutes, until Margo yawned and so did he. "Well, talk to you Sunday, I guess."

"Unless I see you first."

" 'Night, Linc. I love you."

"I love you, too."

And that, he told himself, as he plunked the phone down into its cradle, was precisely the problem. Linc did indeed love her. But not as she'd meant the declaration, as a friend. Nor even the love-everybody type his Christian doctrine professed. No, Linc loved Margo in a carnal, passionate way. He loved her like a man, with bloodlines tracing back to Adam, David and Lot. The devil could taunt him all he wanted with that frailty, but nothing would change it.

Still enervated, Linc rose from the couch and wandered over to his desk. It was old and scarred but served its purpose. He dropped down in the flea-market chair, propped his feet on top of a pile of paperwork, linked his hands behind his neck and closed his eyes. He was bone weary but he knew if he went to bed, he wouldn't sleep. He never slept well after he talked to Margo.

Nope, he'd lie there in bed or on the couch and remember. Sometimes it was the radiant sparkle in her eyes when she discussed her latest project. Sometimes it was the long span of her legs encased in black stockings. And sometimes he went to the past. It was then that his sins haunted him, emotional bullies that took on a life of their own in the middle of the night.

"Damn!" he said aloud. If only he could undo what he'd done all those years ago—starting with introducing his sister and his friends to street life. Linc had been their leader and couldn't bear to think of the criminal activities he'd instigated for the Outlaws, as they'd pretentiously called themselves.

He glanced up at the wall over his desk. Hanging on it was a hand-carved oak cross. Margo had given it to him when he'd graduated from divinity school. It meant so much to him because he knew how she felt about religion, yet she'd transcended those feelings to buy him the gift. How appropriate—this wooden symbol of atonement. Because where Margo was concerned—and Beth and Annie—Linc had much to atone for.

Deciding he needed some focused prayer tonight, he stood,

found his way in the dark to his bedroom, stripped off his clothes and lay on the bed. Its springs protested his weight loudly as he sank in, closed his eyes and linked his hands behind his neck again.

Once Linc had discovered that prayer was simply having conversations with God, he'd settled into comfortable and frequent dialogues. Though a few of his professors at Union Divinity School would have been outraged at this definition of prayer, others would have expected it from Linc, their most unorthodox graduate student.

Margo thought he was crazy.

Speaking of which, buddy.

Yeah, I know. She's on my mind too much.

No, not too much.

You aren't upset about the, ah, the fantasies, are you?

Sex doesn't upset me, Linc. I invented it, remember. And when it's loving and good, it's fine by me. You know that.

Well, I'm just making sure. They're pretty prevalent lately.

As usual, you're too hard on yourself. You've done a lot of good this week.

Not with Rosa.

Ah, Rosa.

What's going on with her?

That's why I sent her to you. To figure that out.

You still won't give me any answers, will you?

No, but I've given you the heart and soul and mind to find them on your own.

Should I go over there tomorrow?

What do you think?

I think it would be a mistake. She's afraid of her husband and I'd make it worse.

There are other ways to help her.

She needs someone to listen to her, mostly.

Yes, just like Margo.

Back to her again.

You never leave Margo. You carry her around in your heart wherever you go. You always have.

Remember Wuthering Heights? *Where Catherine says she is Heathcliff? Sometimes, I feel like that. That we're a part of each other.*

You are. I don't throw people together by accident, you know.

Yeah, I know. That's why you sent me back to Glen Oaks, right? To make up for all the sins I committed here.

Linc, Linc, Linc. Now you're making me angry. Guilt is the devil's instrument, not mine. What you were at seventeen made you the man you are now. You've got to find a way to deal with that.

Help me.

Always.

But help Margo first. Even though she thinks you abandoned her.

I never abandoned Margo.

I know that.

And there are no "firsts" up here. I'm God. I can do more than one thing at a time.

AFTER she hung up from talking to Linc, Margo stared at the phone as if it were a mechanical problem needing to be solved. Its navy color fit the decor of the room perfectly. Greens, blues and a touch of mauve made her favorite room picture perfect. The entire co-op, its furnishings and closets full of designer clothes were exactly what Margo had always wanted in life. That and her job as an executive in a fast-rising computer firm.

And Linc Grayson, a little voice nagged.

Well, at age thirty-six, two out of three weren't bad.

She sipped the hot chocolate she'd made when she couldn't get Linc earlier. But the drink didn't calm her tonight. Rising, she crossed to the windows. It was pitch black out and when she placed her hand on the glass, it was cold. Her breath left a circle of fog on it.

Margo felt cold inside, too. Because of Philip. She could still see him standing at the connecting door of their hotel rooms dressed like he'd walked off the pages of *GQ*. She could still smell the citrusy scent of the aftershave he always used. She could still feel his strong fingers grip her arms and pull her close to kiss her. She'd sent him away, of course, but the sense of betrayal and disappointment that had swamped her was deep. The next morning, professional concerns had arisen. What did his actions mean in terms of her working relationship with him? She'd admired his business savvy and respected his expertise for seven years. He was the main reason she'd joined CompuQuest. She'd even spent time with him and his family: business dinners, holiday parties and some social events. He had two beautiful daughters in high school. Damn it, why had he done something so stupid?

She thought back to that morning; he'd been apologetic but not . . . really sorry. . . .

"Margo," he'd said when he'd come down to the coffee shop for breakfast. "I obviously upset you last night. Forgive me."

His perfectly styled blond hair was brushed back from his forehead, and for a man of forty-four, almost no wrinkles marred his classic brow. Pale blue eyes held her gaze unflinchingly. For a minute, their coolness frightened her. Then they warmed a bit and he'd grasped her hand. "I misread the signals. I take full responsibility. Please forgive me."

What could she say but yes? He'd done more for her than any man in her life—except Linc—and if nothing else, Margo was loyal. She'd smiled weakly and told him she'd forget it ever happened. His eyes had flickered with emotion that told her . . . what? That he wouldn't forget it?

She'd wanted desperately to talk to Linc about this, but she hadn't. He didn't like Philip and had cautioned her against the man. *I don't trust him, Margo. He's too smooth. Too glib. And he looks at you like a man looks at a woman.*

Margo had told Linc he was overreacting, that his obsessive protectiveness was leaking out and spilling onto her. After that, Linc only asked pointed questions once in a while. . . . *Oh, was Pretty Boy's wife there? . . . Are you sure you have to go on this trip with him? . . . Aren't you spending an awful lot of time with this guy?*

No, she *shouldn't* share any of this with Linc, though she wasn't sure she could hide it from him. He was her best friend, her veritable Rock of Gibraltar, but she should try to keep Philip's pass from him. Just like she kept her feelings about Linc as a man to herself, and by tacit agreement, he did the same.

Margo shut off the lights and strode to the spacious foyer to secure the door and the alarm system for the night. Then she headed to the spare room she'd converted into an exercise area. It was connected to the guest room by a oversize bathroom with a Jacuzzi. She stretched briefly, then stepped onto the Nordic Trac, hoping to exorcise the sleep demons.

But this room conjured other images. As she stared at the

doorway, she remembered Linc standing there, two months before . . .

She'd been working out while he took a whirlpool bath. He'd
come to the doorway when he'd finished, clothed only in brief
navy gym shorts, his skin glowing a rosy hue from the hot water.
Droplets dotted his broad shoulders and chest. That boyish shock
of chestnut hair fell around his always-mischievous eyes. Watching him, the desire she'd kept for years in an emotional container
marked NO ACCESS had threatened to erupt. She'd gripped the
exercise machine bars and picked up her speed.

"That felt great," he'd said.

"Good."

He'd shot her a puzzled look but hadn't said anything else. . . .

Angry at giving in to the temptation to wallow in the sensual
images of Linc, Margo swore, purposely using words which
would offend his minister morality. It helped to remind her that
no matter what happened in their past, they had no future together.

They were at opposite ends of the salvation scale. Lucifer
himself might rejoice in his taunting of them with their lustful
feelings but no benevolent deity was going to bless their union.

By morning, she'd convinced herself.

PHILIP Hathaway's office was a palace compared to Margo's.
Next door to the CEO—they shared a reception area which
housed the executive assistant, Geraldine—it was the size of two
junior executive offices, had a row of windows facing Sixth Avenue and a chrome and glass desk with a reclinerlike chair behind
it. Bookcases lined the walls, sporting many of the awards he'd
earned in his career at the company for which he was now second in command.

As Margo entered the plush surroundings, Philip sat off to the
side at the conference table, seven of the upholstered chairs occupied by him and the department heads. Since Mark Listrom
had retired, she was filling in for the engineering department. If
she took his place and became VP of Engineering, she'd attend
this level of meetings regularly.

"I thought I'd shit when that bear came outta the woods," the
vice president of Sales quipped.

"You and me both, buddy." Philip shrugged out of his cashmere sportscoat and Margo glanced down at her outfit.

One of the few business concessions she refused to make was dressing like a man. Today she wore a light green sheath with a multicolored scarf at her waist. As with everything, she preferred heels.

He noticed her in the doorway. "Oh, hello, Margo."

"Hi guys." She entered casually and she circled around to the empty chair.

Philip glanced pointedly at the clock. "We're all here, I guess we can get started."

Eight fifty-five. "Am I late?" she asked, knowing she wasn't.

"No, no." Jonathan Norton, from Research and Development, smiled. "You gave us time to rehash our *Deliverance* experience."

"*Deliverance?*"

"Margo's young, Jon. She doesn't know the movie."

"I know the movie." Margo was irritated but careful not to show it. "I just don't know what you're referring to."

"We spent some time at Philip's cabin on Glenora Lake this weekend," Bill Smith, the head of manufacturing, told her. "It was . . . an experience." He grinned a Burt Reynolds grin.

"So I see." And she did. She'd come across this in the company where she'd worked before CompuQuest. "Just some good old male bonding."

Philip flashed her a puzzled look.

She smiled sweetly, ignoring the question in his eyes.

As the work discussion began, Margo threw herself into the meeting. She was bothered by their exclusion, not that she was at their level yet, to be included, nor would she have even wanted to go to some ridiculous out-in-the woods weekend. It was just so *male*.

As Philip talked about new programs they were designing, Margo's mind drifted to Linc and how tired he'd sounded on the phone Tuesday night. There were marked traces of fatigue in that baritone voice of his . . .

"Margo, where are you?" Philip asked. "I need a final update on the design for Jamison's energy-management program."

"Sorry." She opened her folder before it hit her. "A *final* update? You told me to have the prelims for today."

"No, I asked for a design. And the prelims for Laufler's."

He hadn't. She studied him, rolling her Waterman pen between her fingers. "There must be some confusion, then." Which both of them knew was false. Margo was organized and efficient. Everyone teased her about her Type-A personality. "I've only got the prelims on the Jamison account and haven't started Laufler's. I was waiting for the specs on the latter."

Silence. Then Philip smiled, and shrugged. "No problem. You can work on it today."

As they went on to the production schedule, Margo wondered what had just happened. She stayed behind at the end of the meeting to find out.

As the others exited, every one of them clapped Philip on the back and made some reference to the weekend. The Ol' Boys Network at its best.

When they were gone, Philip faced her. "Something I can do for you?"

"Did you have a nice weekend?" she asked. Actually, he looked like he'd had a hell of a time. His eyes were bloodshot and his skin a little pale.

"Uh, yeah, sure." He cocked his head. "Did you?"

She nodded to the door and crossed her arms over her chest. "Tell me Philip, did Martin go, too?"

"Martin?"

"T. J. Martin." Her competitor for VP of Engineering.

"Sure, he came up."

Now, that complicated matters. It was an obvious preference over her.

Philip stared at her. "Something wrong, Margo? You're not still upset about Boston are you?"

"No. That's behind us." She stood. "And I'm not upset." Circling the table, she made to walk past him.

He grasped her arm. And didn't let go. "About Laufler's?"

"What about them?"

"You'd better get to their account."

"Oh, I will. As soon as I get the last of the specs I need."

"You have them."

"No, Philip, you didn't give them to me."

"Yes, I did."

God, this was odd. "When?"

"Last week. I had Geraldine put them in your in-box."

"I'll check with Gerry. But your secretary doesn't usually make these kinds of mistakes."

"Neither do you."

She raised her brows. "I didn't this time, either." She shrugged to release his hand. He held on for a moment longer, then let go. "I'll be in touch."

Her heart beating at a marathon clip, she walked out of the office, a million thoughts racing through her head.

THREE

———

ANNIE Lang's breath hitched in her throat as her son Matt's color rose and his voice hiked up a notch. He paced around the cozy kitchen in his jeans and performance fleece, his Nike high-tops clomping on the tile. "I'm too old for a baby-sitter. Why can't you just go to that stupid meeting and leave me and Faith here alone?"

It's a normal adolescent reaction. Don't blow it out of proportion.

"Oh, honey," she said reaching out and grabbing his hand. He stopped in front of her, and she feathered back his dark hair. His shoulders were broadening and he'd topped her meager five-foot height months before. Every day he got to look more like Joe, except his eyes were more blue than gray, though they had the Murphy shape. Maybe the resemblance was why she worried so much lately. "We agreed that when you were twelve, you could stay alone. Less than a year to go."

His brow knitted. "Johnny's parents leave him alone."

"Just your luck to end up with the Wicked Witch for a mother."

As usual, humor did the trick. Matt's features softened and he shot her a half-grin. Her heart turned over in her chest at the look. "Yeah, sure. Every girl in school loves you." Sometimes, owning

DanceWorks, Glen Oaks' only dance studio, had its advantages. "They say I'm the luckiest kid alive."

Turning away, Annie bit her lip and swallowed hard. The last statement zinged her mother's heart. She picked up the soup pot draining in the sink and dried it as an image from six years before surfaced, imprinted on her mind like a movie scene you couldn't forget. Only this was all too real—five-year-old Matt, his body still bearing baby fat, diving in front of her, so afraid he was crying; but he confronted his father with determination. *Don't, Daddy. No more.*

"Mom? Did you hear me? I said it was okay."

Annie sighed. There it was again. The anxiety in his voice that she dreaded almost as much as any sign of violence. She circled around. "No, Matt, don't do that. If you're mad, say it out loud. It's the best way to deal with anger."

"I'm not mad." He shrugged one shoulder. "I'm *embarrassed.*"

"Aunt Suzie won't tell anybody she's watching you. And she's fun to be with, isn't she?"

"Yeah, sure, I love Aunt Suz."

Suz. It was what Joe had always called his sister.

The back door creaked open as he said the words, and a curly brown head poked in. Again, Joe's eyes stared at her from under thick, dark bangs. "Did I hear my name mentioned?"

Annie smiled over at the twenty-nine-year-old woman. Since Annie's parents—neglectful at best—had moved to a warmer climate, Suzanne Murphy was all the real family Annie and the kids had. Suzie slipped inside, her long, lean body muscled and fit from years of teaching dance. "Hi, sis." Sniffing, she said, "Hmm, I smell minestrone. Save me some?"

Annie laughed. "In the fridge."

Suzie hugged Annie briefly, then pinched Matt's cheek. "Hey, guy, you grow another inch since last week? Geez, you're big."

"I'm eleven." Matt grinned. "I'm supposed to be growin'."

Eleven. As she stored the dishes and Suzie teased Matt about his oversize feet, Annie shook her head. It was hard to believe that Annie herself had been only two years older than Matt when she started *dating* Joey Murphy. And only three years older than her son when she and Joe first had sex. Annie shuddered at the thought of something like that happening to Matt.

"Hey, the kitchen looks good." Suzie scanned the freshly

painted cream walls and rim of blue stenciling around the top. Along with a new hardwood floor and gleaming white appliances, the room was a showcase. "You do this alone?"

"Nope, Wick's Lumber put in the floor. Linc and the Donovans came over and helped with the rest." She smiled. "Ronny did the stenciling." Annie tried not to beam with pride over finishing off another room in this house. Six years before, while pregnant with Faith, she'd taken the savings she and Joe had managed to put away—if nothing else he was a good provider—and she'd bought this dilapidated property because it was so cheap and because she couldn't stay one more night in the apartment she'd shared with Joe. Linc had said the house was a metaphor for Annie herself. She'd been beaten and broken, just like this place, and had healed herself as she'd renovated the house. He'd been right. Her goal was to provide a safe retreat for her family, an oasis from the stresses of their daily lives. All that was left to remodel was the upstairs.

Matt had taken a chair at the table and tossed a baseball up in the air; its rhythmic thud as it hit the glove was soothing to Annie. Suzie perched on a stool and questioned him about his team.

Soon, a high-pitched voice rent the air. "Aunt Suzie!"

Five-year-old Faith burst into the kitchen, a human tornado on pink-sneakered feet, and threw herself at her aunt. Faith's thick, waist-length blond hair was the exact color and texture Annie's had been at that age; it bobbed in a jaunty ponytail.

Slowly, Annie's hand crept to her shoulder, where loose locks that turned curly when she cropped it replaced the heavy strands that she'd sheared—again, six years before—because Joe would never allow her to cut it.

She frowned, wondering why her ex-husband was on her mind tonight. After the divorce, she could go for days without thinking about him, even though, within two years of their divorce, a monthly reminder began coming like clockwork—the child support check that grew larger as time went on. As she finished cleaning up supper dishes, and the kids entertained Suzie, Annie remembered getting the first check. She'd rushed right to Linc . . .

"What does this mean?" she'd asked, distressed over seeing Joe's bold masculine scrawl on the envelope.

"Apparently he's decided to start paying child support."

"It's from the city. He's only an hour away?"

"I guess. Look, Annie, if he's left you alone for two years, it's not likely he's coming back."

"Oh, God. What if he does?"

"What if he does?" Linc had asked simply.

She'd sat in Linc's cramped apartment over the church garage, taking deep breaths, trying to silence the alarm bells going off in her head. Finally she calmed enough to say, "I can handle it. I can call the police, or a friend. I can get another restraining order. He won't hurt me unless I let him."

"Good girl."

Two years of therapy had done wonders; Annie had won the battle with what used to be incessant anxiety. . . .

Suzie was talking to her. "What time do you have to leave?"

Annie looked over to see Faith nestled on Suzie's lap, examining her aunt's blue metallic nail polish. Annie knew she'd come home to find Faith's finger- *and* toenails the exact color. Though she was an angelic child worthy of her name, she loved to try different things.

"Linc's picking me up in ten minutes."

"How come you have a midweek council meeting? Aren't they usually on Friday?" Annie was the community representative on the three-year-old Glen Oaks Youth Council which, thank God, Linc had started to help kids in trouble. Like she'd been. Like they'd all been.

Her mind on business now, Annie wiped her hands on a towel, gathered up her purse, dragged a fleece jacket out of the closet and threw it on over her green sweater and jeans. "The new Social Services guy is coming tonight. This is to meet him."

"I thought he wasn't due until the end of the month."

"He wasn't. Haven't you heard? Marnie"—the head of the Youth Council and director of Glen Oaks Social Services—"had a baby girl early—the day before yesterday."

"No kidding." Suzie looked at Annie. "Who's the new guy?"

"Somebody from the city division. Apparently, he asked to come to Glen Oaks. Must have wanted a change of pace."

"Hmm, new blood in town. How old is he?"

"I don't know anything about him. No one does, since he wasn't expected until April." Annie grinned and ruffled Suzie's hair on her way to the door. It was thick and silky—like Joe's used to be. "I'll check him out for you, though, kiddo."

"Check him out for yourself."

Annie turned as she opened the door. "No way. The last thing I need in my life is a man." Though the thought no longer made her stomach queasy, it'd be a cold day in hell when she'd trust a guy again. Surveying the kitchen, she added, "I told the kids you'd make hot chocolate."

"Mommy's favorite," Faith commented idly.

As well as Beth's and Margo's. Annie smiled at the thought. "Lock up and put the alarm on. It's getting dark."

Long ago, she'd accepted the fact that she might never feel completely safe, but, with the necessary precautions, she could live with that. Smiling, she stepped out into the cool night air.

JOE Murphy sat in his brand-new Bronco, staring at the Social Services building, his new place of employment, starting in a couple of minutes. A compact little brick structure, it was attached to the town hall and new to Glen Oaks in the last six years. Nestled across the street was the high school, which brought back bad memories.

Better get used to it, buddy. The reminders are going to be popping up at you like jack-in-the-boxes.

But he could handle it. He could handle anything. Once you'd lost all you had, once you'd hit bottom hard enough to knock some sense into your head—and survived—you could handle whatever came your way. That lesson was one of the many things he'd learned in the years since he'd hopped a bus out of this town on a snowy February night, the reality of what he'd become slapping him in the face harder than the cold raw wind.

You're not that man anymore.

No, he wasn't. But sometimes he'd wake up sweating in the middle of the night, worried that monster still lurked inside of him, like Hyde to Jekyll, and someday would claw his way out.

"You can beat Hyde, if indeed it's true," Pete, his counselor in the recovery program, had said. "You're one of the strongest men I know, Joe."

Strong enough to face Glen Oaks tonight? Strong enough to face Annie? Linc?

Yes.

Grabbing his briefcase from the seat behind him, along with his tweed sportcoat, Joe exited his car, donned the jacket and took a deep breath. But setting foot on Glen Oaks soil again caused another spurt of anxiety to race through him. What if this wasn't the right way to reenter? Should he have let them know he was moving back here?

Pete had asked him the same question. As Joe strode up the sidewalk and approached the door, he soothed his nerves by recounting why he'd opted for his return to be a surprise. . . .

"I'm going back to see Matt. If I let them know I'm coming, Annie could take him somewhere, keep him from me. Even get a restraining order. But if I take this job, publicly show her I've changed, she might reconsider doing anything hasty. Also, if I'm established in a respected position, she might not be able to keep him away from me."

Pete had scowled. "Sounds risky to me."

"All that matters is I get to see my son."

"Your health and happiness matter, too, Joe."

"I need to see my son. To . . . make sure he doesn't end up like me. You know the statistics."

Pete had nodded then, and wished him luck. . . .

Slowly, Joe pushed open the heavy aluminum door to the agency. In his head, he enumerated who would be there tonight. The new high school principal, Sandra Summers. A police lieutenant named Mike Pratt. A probation officer, Jim Tacone. There was a secretary, Jane Meachum, to take notes. Then five people he knew, Mayor Al Hunsinger, Roman Becker, attorney-at-law, and retired teacher Janice Breed. Of course, his former best friend, Linc Grayson, whose brainchild this Council had been.

And, last, his ex-wife, Annie Lang. She'd dropped his name with the divorce.

Taking in another cleansing breath when he reached the meeting-room door, he stepped inside. The area was about fifteen foot square, wallpapered with muted colors. The scent of strong coffee dominated the room. Carpet covered the floor. Two people were sitting down at a rectangular oak conference table. Four others were gathered by a coffeepot, chatting. Two more were off to the side in intimate conversation. It was those two who drew him like a lodestone. But he couldn't focus on them just yet.

Scanning the group, pasting on a smile full of false bravado, Joe said, "Hi, everybody. Sorry I'm late. There was heavy traffic coming out from the city."

Eight heads turned toward him.

Don't look at her.

A tall, balding man rose. He approached Joe. "I'm Al Hunsinger."

"I know who you are, Mr. Hunsinger."

The man cocked his head. "Have we met? You look familiar."

Here goes. "It's because I grew up here, but I left town six years ago. I'm Joe Murphy."

A small gasp drew everybody's attention, including Joe's. His ex-wife—all compact five feet of her—had frozen like a trapped animal. Next to her, his ex–best friend gripped her arm.

Linc hadn't changed much. He was still stocky and muscular and had the irrefutable aura of a gangster. Of an Outlaw. It was Annie who looked different. She was still as slender as she'd been six years before, with the long muscles and lean lines of a dancer. But all that glorious hair was gone.

A memory assaulted him. Pete had told him to be prepared for these ambushes. *Over my dead body you'll cut your hair. Now get over here and shut up.*

He nodded to her.

With grim resolve, he scanned the others. "I know some of you," he said with a smile that cost him. "I'm sure my presence here is a surprise to you, but I've been working in the Youth Division of Social Services in New York for a while now, and I asked to be sent to Glen Oaks." He gave them a self-effacing grin. "You're probably surprised to see me in this role, so if you want to get coffee and take a seat, I'll pass out my résumé. You'll be able to tell that I'm fully qualified to be Director of Social Services here. I'm confident I can facilitate this worthwhile committee, and I hope you'll accept me for who I've become."

Several people got up to get coffee; all of them shot concerned looks at Annie and Linc, who remained rooted to the spot by the window.

Joe set his briefcase down on the table, took out copies of his résumé, shook hands with the still slick-looking Roman Becker, the Council's lawyer, and with the probation officer with the tired eyes. The secretary, Jane Meachum, was a pretty, innocent type, who gave him a shy smile. Then he distributed the papers to the six people near him, introducing himself and shaking hands as he went along.

His heart beating like a drum, he forced himself to head for the window. *Remember the plan. If you could recover, you can do this.* Too soon, he stood in front of them.

Linc's arm slid around Annie's shoulders. God, she was so little Joe had to keep himself from wincing. He topped her by a foot, and had close to a hundred pounds on her.

She'd never stood a chance against him.

Viciously pushing the thought away, Joe looked her straight in the eye. "Hello, Annie." He glanced to her left. "Linc."

Annie straightened and moved away from Linc. Her warm amber eyes were frosty, and her mouth a grim slash in that beautiful porcelain-skinned face. "Joe." She cleared her throat. "What are you doing here?" Her voice was strong. He was glad she'd gotten some backbone.

"I came home, Annie. I want to see my son."

Her gaze flew to Linc's, panicky. Before they could say any more, Joe added, "I hope you two will look at my résumé. I think it'll help to calm your fears." He shrugged. "It'll be a start, anyway."

Annie shook her head.

Though he'd expected this, it still made his heart trip in his chest. "Linc, will you try to convince Annie to give me a chance? I'm back to stay, and I promise I won't do anything to hurt anybody. But I want to see my son." He handed them his résumé. "Read this."

With that he turned and walked back to the table. He could feel their eyes bore into him, could still see the traces of fear in Annie's. Rightly so.

Unbidden, the ghosts came. The last time he'd seen Linc, they'd been in a shadowy waiting room at Glen Oaks Hospital, where Annie was having a miscarriage. His friend's face had been mottled red, his voice condemning as he grabbed Joe by the collar and yelled, *Get the hell out of Glen Oaks and never come back.*

The last time Joe had seen Annie, she'd been on the floor of their apartment, her lip split, her shoulder dislocated, and cradling her abdomen protectively, she'd pleaded, *Don't kick me again, Joey, I'm pregnant.*

*   *   *

FORCING her hands not to shake—she had control here, if she took it—Annie stared woodenly at the papers in her hands. Still by the window, she read the résumé.

Education: Three years at NYU in an accelerated Social Services program. Graduated 2000. Two years in a Masters of Social Work program, graduating Magna Cum Laude in 2002. Pursuing a doctorate in Clinical Psychology at Columbia University.

Work experience: Interned summers, vacations and weekends at: Forty-Fifth Street Youth Services, VOA Children's Center, Catholic Family Center for Troubled Youth. Spearheaded Times Square Save-the-Kids Project

Employment: Center for Family Services, 2001 to present.

Runs support groups for Children of Alcoholics, Children of Batterers, Recovered Batterers.

The last stopped her, like walking into a wall in the dark. Disoriented, she couldn't take the whole thing in. It had to be a bad dream that she'd awakened from. But like all those other times, her contact with Joe Murphy was an all-too-real nightmare, and needed to be dealt with.

So, fine, deal with it. He might be back, but that didn't mean he'd get access to the kids.

Kids.

Oh, no. He'd spoken only of Matt. Didn't he realize . . .

Her thoughts were interrupted by his clear, controlled voice. "Now that you've had time to peruse my credentials, perhaps you could come to the table and we'll talk about this Friday's Council meeting." Absently she noted how different his vocabulary and even his speech patterns were.

Nudging Annie, Linc said, "Come on, kid, we can do this."

She leaned on his shoulder for a moment, taking comfort in the strong, muscled feel of him. Then she crossed the room and took a seat at the opposite end of the table from her ex-husband.

"Can we ask some questions first, Joe, before we start talking about the newest case?" This from Janice Breed.

Joe grinned. "Of course, Mrs. Breed. I just hope I can answer them better than I could in your English class."

Some of the tension was broken by his levity.

"Are you permanently assigned here?"

"It's still up in the air. Marnie Smith has a year's maternity leave, so I'll be in this job for at least that long. But honestly, I'd like to move back to Glen Oaks permanently."

Annie's insides turned cold. She'd read stats on batterers. Relapse, when thrown into the old situation, was high.

He spoke again, and smiled, calling attention to those dimples she'd once loved. For the first time, she allowed herself to take in his appearance. Though he was only in his late thirties, he'd aged dramatically. His dark hair had turned salt and pepper. He'd donned wire-rimmed glasses, accenting the lines around his eyes. His clothes were neatly tailored—a gray sportcoat under which he wore a pristine white shirt and tie, with black slacks. She shivered as she glanced at his hands. They were big, still capable of great pain, even though they were bordered by starched cuffs now. Expensive dress for someone who had worked in Social Services.

She recalled the large child support check she received every month. Where did he get his money? Drugs? Though they'd done pot when they were young, they'd quit in their twenties. He drank like a fish then, but never touched anything else.

She tuned in when Roman Becker asked, "Why'd you leave Glen Oaks in such a hurry, Murphy?"

Joe swallowed hard and his gray eyes flashed with something—not anger, something self-directed. "For personal reasons, Mr. Becker. I can assure you, I've changed since I last walked the streets of this town. I hope you'll all give me a chance to show you that."

They didn't have a choice. But Annie did.

"Now, if we can get down to business." He glanced at the clock. "I understand the Council meets on Fridays. I've acquainted myself with the procedures of the group—which, by the way, I believe is a sound, well-run committee." He picked up a folder. "And I've read the file on Ronny Donovan."

"You gonna be able to be objective about the kid, Joe?" Mayor Hunsinger asked. "Wasn't his father a good friend of yours?"

Joe glanced at Linc. Annie saw Linc's expression soften. He was always the most sentimental, the most forgiving, of them. The vise around her chest tightened. What if Linc sided with Joe?

"We knew this would be an issue on the Council in general," Linc said. "Because Glen Oaks is a small town, members would know or may be related to the teens who come before us. We haven't had a problem with it before. And any time there was a question, we've worked it out."

"But Murphy's in charge of this committee, like Marnie was. He has a lot of power."

"I think I can be objective, Al. My past experiences and training have taught me that allowing someone's bad behavior to continue is not in their best interests. The old concept of tough love." After more questions and a brief discussion of the case at hand, he glanced at the clock again. "If there's nothing else, we can adjourn until Friday. I don't intend to prolong meetings when it's not necessary."

Everyone agreed. In minutes, the room emptied of all but Linc, Annie and Joe, who stood and faced each other. Someone closed the door, its snick loud and meaningful. Annie felt Linc squeeze her shoulder, then he turned to Joe. "This is a hell of a thing."

Joe shrugged. "I know it's a surprise." He looked directly at Annie. "I did it this way on purpose. I didn't want to give you time to take off, or get a restraining order, without giving me a chance to show you I've changed."

Annie flicked her fingers against the résumé she'd picked up from the table. "A few degrees and some jobs working with kids isn't proof you don't hit women anymore."

Her comment had found its target. His face flushed and he cleared his throat. "No, it doesn't. But I spent a full year in a Batterer's Recovery Program in the city. I've also had three years of private counseling."

"You're still a wife beater," she said starkly.

Raising his chin, he held her gaze. "I'm a *recovered* wife beater."

Linc leaned over and whispered, "Annie, you have options."

She blew out a heavy breath. "There's no way I'm going to let you see your children unsupervised, or be alone with me and them."

Joe said, "I don't expect—" He halted mid-sentence, stared blankly at her. Ludicrously his gaze dropped to her stomach, making her realize what she'd revealed.

"Children?" His shoulders sagged and his confidence visibly receded. "You didn't lose the baby that night?"

Sighing, she averted her face and scrubbed her fingers over her eyes.

Linc put a hand on her shoulder again. "He would've found out soon anyway, Annie."

Resignedly, she nodded.

Linc faced Joe. Very simply he said, "You have a five-year-old daughter, Joe. Her name is Faith."

BEFORE Joe could react, Roman Becker and Al Hunsinger came back in and asked to talk to him privately. Annie watched her ex-husband agree, turn and ask Linc and her to wait for him, then calmly follow the other men to the mayor's office. She was stunned by his composure. For a man who'd just been told he had a second child, he seemed as cool as a winter morning.

She and Linc tried to discuss the ramifications of Joe's decision to come back to Glen Oaks, but they were both shell-shocked and didn't have much to say. When Joe finally returned, she faced him, ready to do battle. Linc stood a little in front of her, as if to protect her. One of the side effects of what Joe had done to her was her best friends' guilt for not realizing Annie was being battered. Linc's was the worst. Though Annie had assured them she'd purposely kept it to herself, ashamed and afraid to let on what was happening—God, it had been such a cliché—her three best friends suffered over their ignorance.

Joe faced her, his jaw hard, his features taut; but his gray eyes burned with intensity. "I have a daughter?" His voice had cracked on the word.

"Yes." Annie crossed her arms over her stomach in remembered pain. "No thanks to you."

A muscle leapt in his throat. "Is she . . . is she all right?"

Annie knew what he was asking. A swift kick in the stomach during pregnancy could cause brain damage. Luckily, the blow had landed on the top of her thighs, not where he'd aimed; still, the hospital had been concerned about a miscarriage because she'd fallen. "She's fine. A lot smarter than you or I ever will be."

Which was a lie. Long ago, Annie had figured out that one of Joe's issues was his frustration over his intellect. No one else had known he was so smart, no one had encouraged him, and he'd seethed with a severely stifled brain. To top it off, all his adult life he'd worked a rote, mindless job at the local electronics parts plant.

His eyes closed briefly when she told him Faith was mentally and physically fine. In gratitude? She guessed it probably was, but Annie wasn't about to feel sorry for him.

"Does she dance? Like you used to?"

Annie only nodded. In truth, when she danced, Faith floated through the air as graceful as gently moving clouds, and had that indefinable quality that made the difference between a dance student and a potential pro. Annie herself had had it, too. Joe, of course, had been jealous of her dancing and had wanted her to quit. But by the time she reached high school, she was teaching dance and earning money, which she needed to live, so he let her do it. After they married, it was a necessary source of income.

"What do you want, Joe?" Linc asked.

"I want to see my son . . . and my daughter."

Linc zeroed in on him with his minister look. "Why now?"

Joe straightened to his full height, and Annie had to keep herself from flinching at those big hands and muscular arms that could inflict so much pain. "Because I'm better now. I'm not the man I was six years ago." He scanned the two of them, then focused on Annie. "I know I'm recovered, and it's safe for me to see my kids."

"*I* don't know that." Annie's voice was hard and cold.

"Yes, well that's why I'm moving back. To prove it to you."

"You're dreaming, pal, if you think I'll let you near Annie or the kids alone."

The corners of Joe's mouth turned up just a bit, despite the gravity of the situation. Every once in a while, the street kid peeked out of the minister, and showed that Linc was still as tough as nails. "I have legal rights, Linc." He turned to Annie. "But I don't want to go that route. I'm willing to do this informally, if we can." He opened his briefcase, fished out a manila envelope and handed it to Linc.

With a frown Linc took the folder.

"Here's some documentation that might help. Papers verifying completion of a year-long court-sanctioned recovery program, and evaluations by the counselors. Transcripts from the educational institutions I attended. Reports from the support groups I run." He shifted from one foot to the other, as if the subject made him nervous. "And there are phone numbers to call to check the facts, if you don't believe me." He stared at the file, then at Linc. "I thought maybe you could manage this whole thing."

"Me?"

"Uh-huh." Joe raked a hand through his hair. "Look, I know this is a shock, but as I said, I was afraid to do it any other way. Afraid you'd try to keep me from them."

Annie frowned. "I've never known you to be afraid of anything."

His eyes got so bleak, she was silenced by their expression. "I'm afraid," he said simply. "Of a lot of things." He drew in a deep breath. "I always was. All I'm asking for is a chance. If you'll go along with my request, I promise I'll do this however you say, but I've got to see my kids."

He was right. He did have legal rights, no matter what he'd done. After she got healthy, Annie had researched domestic abuse. Some batterers were even left in the home with their families while they went through a legally mandated recovery program, probably like the one Joe had been in. After six years of rehabilitation and counseling, then coming here as a cross between Doctor Spock and Sigmund Freud, any court in the world would let Joe Murphy see his kids.

So she said, "I'll think about it."

Linc sighed. "Annie, there's something else. This is a small town. By tomorrow, everybody'll know he's back. Matt and Faith will hear it at the corner store."

She nodded. "I'll tell them in the morning. I'd like to leave now."

Joe stopped her with his words. "I'd like to tell my mother and Suzie."

Who was at her house. It would be hard to keep Joe's arrival in Glen Oaks a secret from her sister-in-law. She loved Suzie like a real sister and valued her friendship, not to mention her partnership in the business.

"I plan to visit them tomorrow morning," Joe added. "It will be easier for them if I let them know I'm back."

She looked to Linc.

"I agree," he said.

"Fine. I d like to go now, Linc. I'm whipped."

Linc told Joe he would get in touch with him at the motel just outside of town where he was staying, and they both left without saying goodbye. Joe stayed where he was, and Annie felt his eyes bore into her as they left the tension-filled room.

FOUR

——

FOR one of the first times in his life, Ron Donovan was down-and-dirty scared. He glanced over at his mother, who sat like a stick in the chair, dressed in a dark skirt and fuzzy pink sweater, as she listened to the Youth Council members discuss his latest sin. Her pretty brown hair was pulled off her face in a knot, making her look fragile.

She hadn't laid a guilt trip on him, though. She'd just made him hot chocolate that first night, as she always did when things got bad, and tried to get him to spill his guts the next day. And that made him feel like pond scum. But he couldn't talk to her about this.

Catching him staring at her, she reached over and squeezed his arm. *No matter what, buddy, we'll get through this,* she'd told him a thousand times. But he'd heard her crying at night, alone in her room, like she hadn't cried since his dad died. That worried him more than anything. His mother was tougher than anybody he knew. What he'd done this time had really thrown her, probably because it concerned his father.

Or maybe because her only son could go to jail. His gut clenched. His only hope of reprieve, the eight people seated at the table in front of him, seemed about as sympathetic as a jury for Jeffrey Dahmer.

On the other side of him, his aunt Margo smiled at him, too, foxy as ever in cool black jeans, a black sweater and boots. Huge gold hoops dangled from her ears and matched the jangling bracelets on her wrist. He'd known he was in deep shit when she'd shown up from the city to go to the Council meeting with them; but he'd been glad to see her. About the only person in the world who understood him these days was Margo Morelli, his mom's best friend. Because she hated Glen Oaks as much as he did and there was something inside her, a streak of rebelliousness, that he recognized as kin to his own. However, the fact that she'd come home for this meeting was a wake-up call to Ron.

As the mayor droned on about his priors—truancy, vandalism, petty theft, possession of marijuana, underage drinking with a DUI—Ron checked out his uncle Linc. It was obvious that *he'd* been glad to see Margo. His eyes had lit up like the lights around the racetrack when she'd strutted her stuff into the room. Linc was a cool guy, and not afraid to show his feelings. He'd talked to Ron about sex a zillion times, and admitted his own needs as a man. For a minister, Ron thought that was pretty mag. Of course, Ron knew Linc had been hell on wheels when he was young, along with his mother and their friends. Hell, maybe his getting into trouble was genetic.

When the mayor finished his speech, the head honcho running the meeting faced Ron. Joe Murphy—the guy who'd stopped traffic when he'd walked into the town hall. Jesus Christ, he was Annie's ex. Ron didn't have a clue what had happened between him and Annie—it was hushed up like state secrets. Whatever it was, though, made the nicest woman he'd ever met glower at the guy all night and made his mom and even Margo gasp when they saw him. "Ron, we need to hear a few things from you."

Ron nodded at Murphy's comment. *Be respectful, kid, and don't let that chip on your shoulder show, or I'll beat the crap out of you,* Margo had told him.

"Yes, sir," he said politely.

"We can all guess why you did this. But tell us in your own words."

There was a low murmur of voices among the group when Ron didn't answer right away. He wanted to scream at them to leave him the hell alone. But this was too important to blow, so he battled back the urge. When he needed it, he had his mother's grit. Besides, he was scared shitless of going to jail. In halting words, he told them what he'd done and tried to explain why. "It was like this anger just took me over—kind of a red haze, making everything fuzzy."

Murphy's broad shoulders straightened. His intense eyes focused sharply on Ron. "Do you have a problem controlling your anger, son?"

No, Sherlock, I smile when I mutilate cars, vandalize the school and steal from stores. "Yeah."

Murphy nodded. "And your anger at Mr. Quaid has to do with your father's death?"

Ron's hands fisted.

Murphy glanced pointedly at them. "You have to say it out loud, Ron, to have any chance of controlling what you feel."

"Yeah. It's because of my father." Though his mother and Linc had talked of forgiveness, had said it was a twist of fate that had caused the accident that Ron had witnessed when he was seven, no amount of rationalization could acquit Quaid in his mind.

Murphy glanced behind Ron to the second row of chairs. Ron knew Quaid sat back there with Doc Holt, a wiry little guy with a brush cut and dark, knowing eyes. He was the mastermind of three Winston Cup cars that flew like the wind. Ron had studied every single car Holt had ever worked on. Five years before the man had had some heart problems and retired from the racing circuit, and had come to live in a cottage on Glenora Lake, twenty miles away. Quaid was here probably because, in an article Ron had read about him, Quaid had called Holt a father figure. In racing books, they'd been compared to Clark and Chapman—the famous Formula-One driver-and-crew-chief team.

"Mr. Quaid," Murphy said. "You've stated that you don't want to press charges."

"That's right." Quaid's voice was deep. "Considerin' what the boy just stated."

Murphy nodded. "Still, we can't let this go."

That uptight son-of-a-bitch Pratt leaned forward. "Legally, that's not an option. And Ron knows that. I'll listen to the Council's recommendation, but I'll put it before the judge only if it's acceptable punishment."

"Perhaps we should list our options," Murphy suggested. Man the guy was cool as a cucumber in this room full of people who hated him. He wasn't even sweating, like Ron was.

The retired teacher, Mrs. Breed, who'd always told Ron he

wasn't living up to his potential, stood and crossed to a board behind the table. "I'll list the choices as we brainstorm them. I miss this," she said picking up a piece of chalk.

For ten minutes Ron watched his future etch out on a freakin' blackboard. Trial and most likely prison was the first option. Fear hit him when he saw it so starkly written; it felt like a kick in the nuts.

Weekend jail, suggested by Pratt, was the second suggestion. Fuck, he couldn't do that. His mom needed him to work at the diner on weekends. The list continued with counseling, and a few other mamby-pamby things he knew would never fly; it ended with community service.

In another ten minutes, the panel members had narrowed down their choices. Pratt wouldn't settle for probation again, or nightly curfews or making monetary restitution, all of which Ron's grandparents had pulled strings to get him in the past.

"All right, let's discuss these four." Murphy had put on glasses and was staring at the board.

Mayor Hunsinger cleared his throat. "Weekend jail would hurt his family's business. Ron works there to help his mother."

Straightening, his mom shook her head. "I'll be fine, if it's an alternative to prison. I can take care of the diner myself."

She couldn't, Ron knew.

"No offense, Beth"—the straight-arrow lawyer glanced at her then turned to the others—"but in any case, should our decision be based on Mrs. Donovan's needs?"

The prick. Becker had dated his mom and she'd dropped him after a few months. It was payback time.

"We need to consider everybody's needs in this, Mr. Becker." Seemed this Murphy guy had his own opinions.

Ron sensed movement behind him. He knew Quaid was gonna say something and he braced himself. Goddamn it, he didn't want a murderer's help.

But instead, a rusty voice that sounded like it had a history with Camels and cheap bourbon boomed out, "Can I speak?"

"And who are you?" Murphy asked.

The man identified himself as Doc Holt and explained his relationship to Quaid and the town.

Murphy cocked his head. "Is it okay with the rest of you?" The members of the panel agreed. "Go ahead, Mr. Holt."

"I got a way for the kid to make reparation for the three-K-

plus damage he did and maybe learn somethin' in the process.
Assign him community service until September. To me and
Tucker Quaid. He can help us on the car."

Ron whirled around fast, but Margo grabbed his hand and dug
her nails into his palm, telling him to shut up.

"We're doin' this whole exhibition race for the benefit of the
town," Holt went on when nobody jumped at the offer. "So it'd
be genuine community service if the boy helped us. We'll work
his butt off." Holt glanced quickly at Quaid, whose face was
blank. But his green eyes burned fire. "And the kid'll have to
deal with the demons that chase him." Still, the stunned silence.
"Seems like a mighty big punishment to me. The devil inside's
the hardest one to face, ain't it?"

Things happened in a blur after that. All Ron knew was, by
eleven o'clock, a decision had been made by the panel and accepted by the cop to be presented to the judge: biweekly counseling sessions with this Murphy dude, weekend detention at the
county jail until Memorial Day, and assignment to Doc Holt and
Tucker Quaid for fifteen additional hours of community service
each week until September.

"WE ain't on the track, man. Slow the hell down." Inside Doc's
Mach I Mustang, the old man leaned against the passenger's
door. Tucker drove with Grand Prix concentration as he and Doc
headed home from the Council meeting.

"If I slow down, I'm gonna reach over there and strangle you
one-handed, old man." Tucker tried to make his voice take on the
cold hard tone of The Menace.

Doc cackled. "Yeah? You and whose army?"

Tucker gave him what passed for a smile these days.

Doc pulled out a cigar, sniffed its rich tobacco scent, and went
to light it.

"Put that goddamned thing away. Didn't you learn anything
from those angina attacks?"

At least that got to him. "I'll oblige, if you get off your chest
what's buggin' you. You're actin' like you did every time we lost
a race."

The dark night was broken by the headlights of an oncoming
car. In their cold glare, Tucker could see the angular planes of
Doc's face. "What the *hell* possessed you to do that tonight?"

Doc shrugged. "Like I said, time to get the monkey off the kid's back. And yours."

Tucker shot a sharp look Doc's way; the papers had called that expression "green ice," and it had shriveled grizzled mechanics, pushy newspaper reporters and the likes of Richard Petty. Doc, however, seemed immune to it.

"I wanna help the kid," Tucker said. "But this is nuts."

"Don't think so." Doc settled his bones into the chocolate-colored leather he'd ordered from New Mexico, obviously appreciating its fine, smooth feel. "The kid's on a fast track to the pen, Tuck. You and me both know it."

"Because of me."

"The NASCAR sanctioning board said you didn't do nothin' wrong."

"The NASCAR report was *inconclusive*. I was negligent in my driving that day. I drove like a bat outta hell and didn't care who I took out." The guilt still clawed at him.

Doc let loose his best curses. Then he said, "You really think that, then do somethin' about it instead of nailin' yourself to the cross in this godforsaken town."

"What can I do for the kid?" Tucker finally asked.

"Well, we talked them highbrow social workers and law people into keepin' him outta jail 'cept for the weekend. Which'll probably be good for him."

Tucker frowned, seeing again Beth Donovan's face when they came up with their verdict. "What will she do, you think?"

"Who?"

"His ma. I wonder if she really needs the kid to work at the diner. Between the weekend sentence and spendin' fifteen hours a week with us, he won't be able to help her out much."

"She'll be okay," Doc said with a dismissive wave of his hand. "She's got some people workin' for her. One—Gerty Stoffer—is a little batty, but they seem like good employees. And Beth Donovan has family and friends to help out."

"How you know all that?"

"Small towns."

"You don't live in town."

"I truck down *into* the place on occasion."

"I . . . worry about her."

"I know," Doc said gently. "But you tried to give her money

years ago, and she refused. The girl's a tough one. She'll come
outta this okay."

"At the police station, she told me she'd been in more trouble
than the kid by the time she was his age. You know what she
meant?"

"Yeah, some."

"What?"

Doc smiled. "Seems she was a real hellion as a teenager.
There was this group of kids in Glen Oaks that made up a gang
of sorts; called themselves the Outlaws. They weren't as bad as
the gangs in the city, but they got in a shitload of trouble. Her
brother was the leader."

"The minister?"

"Yep. They drank, did some drugs. Big-time vandalism. They
even got into scrapes with some thugs in the city. And there was
a robbery when she was sixteen that could've sent her to juvy."

"Didn't it?"

"Nope. Seems the owner of the diner took an interest in her
and her brother, and corralled them into workin' for him as punishment. I guess it turned their lives around."

"Why would a stranger do that?"

"The two kids were orphans. Grandparents raised them, but
they pretty much got to run wild. Like the rest of the town, the
diner guy felt sorry for 'em and wanted to help."

"So you tryin' to play savior like him?"

"That'll be the everlovin' day." He waited a bit, then confessed, "I just wanna help the boy, Tuck."

"Well, I hope your hair-brained scheme doesn't backfire and
make things worse for her."

"Nah, it won't."

"That, old man, remains to be seen."

JUST hours after the Council meeting, Annie stared hard at her
reflection in the beveled, free-standing oak mirror she'd purchased at a flea market and refinished. "You're thirty-four now,
not thirteen," she told herself over the soft rock that crooned
from her CD player. "You own a house, and a dance studio.
You've made a good life for your kids. He has no control over
you like he did then." She swallowed hard. "He can't interfere."
Light brown eyes, full of apprehension, peered back at her, call-

ing her a liar. By virtue of the fact that her children were biologically Joe Murphy's, he could, and obviously would, interfere.

But he wasn't going to choreograph the whole thing; he did not have *control,* and that's what it had all been about before— the isolation from others, the orders on how to dress, the battering. And the insistence on sex when, and in ways, she didn't want. She'd been a marionette for over fifteen years and only after intense counseling had she realized what a bastard had pulled the strings. And what a wooden doll she'd been to allow it. Six years ago she'd cut those ties and had no intention of tangling herself or her kids up in them again. None.

With renewed confidence, even if it was tinged with unease, she turned away from the mirror, made her way out of her in-the-process-of-being-remodeled bedroom and strode down the hall. Hardwood floors squeaked under her feet; unwillingly she took the past with her into Faith's room.

The child had kicked off all her covers, just like Joe used to, and was sleeping in the same position he always had, sprawled on her stomach, face half buried in the pillow, arm over her head. He'd taken up most of the bed, too, which was a symbol Annie had never recognized before. His needs, his wants, his views were the only important things. Thankfully, Faith was the opposite of him in every way that counted—she was the most giving child Annie knew.

Carefully, Annie settled down on the end of the white canopy bed, her legs crossed, her posture dancer-straight, and gazed at her daughter.

Faith stirred, and Annie leaned over and smoothed down her hair. The weight of the braid was heavy in her hand. Suddenly an image overwhelmed her. A flashback to the past struck as if she'd touched a live wire. Usually she kept the memories at bay, but tonight she allowed this one to come, to give her strength, to remind her just what Joe Murphy was capable of. Annie's hair had been braided just like this . . .

"Get over here, bitch." Joe had yanked on her braid when they'd reached his car after leaving the seedy bar on the outskirts of town. "I saw you come on to that guy." He'd jerked on her hair again and swayed drunkenly. He'd been downing shots of scotch all night. "I told you not to flirt with him. . . ."

She'd shrunk away from him. He'd never been this physical with her before. "You're hurting me, Joey."

He slammed her up against his battered old '77 Chevy. "Yeah, well it's gonna hurt a lot more," he said raising his other hand.

It *had* hurt more, but inside rather than out. Because it was the first time the love of her life, the boy who'd rescued her from neglectful and sometimes abusive parents, had slapped her, twice, across the face. It had stung like a whip, but the emotional scourge had hurt worse. And she'd been so shocked. Oh, she'd been slapped before, by her mother, her father. But never, never by Joey. He was her savior. He was the one who'd given her hope. And he told her over and over she had done the same for him.

Tears had formed in her eyes and she'd tried to sidle away from him. He grabbed her arm roughly and dragged her back. "Get in the car."

A noise from the bar distracted him. Three men exited and shuffled toward the van parked next to them, joking and singing one of the Country Western songs from inside. Joe saw them and let her go. He circled around to the driver's side and slid in, assuming she'd follow his orders like the good little girl she was. Instead she'd darted away, into the woods next to the bar. As she ran, she glanced over her shoulder. Blurry through her tears, she could still see the men go up to the car. One asked, "Hey man, what's goin' on?"

Once in the woods, she'd run and run, the low tree limbs scraping her face and arms, her lungs burning right out of her chest. She'd run until she couldn't run anymore and fell sobbing by a large oak tree on the other side of the woods that bordered a town playground. Dazed, she stared at the swings and teeter-totter, wishing she was six again, wishing back her childhood illusions for a knight in shining armor. But she was sixteen, all grown up now. And that knight had turned black and dangerous.

He'd found her there at six the next morning, shivering in the early June chill. She'd fallen asleep, never gone home. He'd been bleary-eyed, a rough beard shadowing his jaw, his clothes rumpled. And he smelled like stale booze. He'd knelt down, sober and sorry. "Oh, baby, I was so worried. I passed out in my car . . ."

Still afraid, she'd tried to scramble away from him. "Leave me alone." Her hand flew to her cheek. "You . . . you *hit* me."

His face crumpled with remorse. "I'm sorry. I'm so sorry." He gulped back the emotion in his throat. "I had too much to drink. . . . You know how jealous I am . . . I lost it when I saw that guy come on to you. . . ."

She cowered like a frightened dog kicked by its master.

Until he started to cry. She'd never seen Joey cry before. He was four years older than her, a man, and he was *crying* huge fat tears. Even his shoulders shook. "Please forgive me. I promise I'll never do it again."

She'd melted, and held him in her arms as if *he'd* been the abused one, as if *he'd* been hurt . . .

Of course, it *hadn't* been the last time. She didn't know then that they'd follow the same pattern over and over—the violence, then remorse, and weeks or even months of a honeymoon period until he lost control again and hit her again.

Annie felt herself shiver and sat upright. She left Faith's room quickly and fled to her own bedroom. In the doorway, she sniffed at the fresh paint she'd applied herself, in the house that she'd bought, to remind her that *this* was her present. Those memories were in the past; it was over. And it was never going to happen again. Six years before, when he'd almost killed their baby, she'd vowed never to let him hurt them again.

"And I won't." She crossed to the mirror again. Fingering her short hair, she told herself, "The braid's gone, the woman who wore it is gone, and that part of your life is over."

Joe Murphy may have some legal rights in this situation, but she had control; she had power, too.

And damn it, she was going to use it. To protect her kids, and herself.

RONNY Donovan had a bedroom that Margo would have killed for as a teenager. It took up the whole top floor of a little Cape Cod the Donovans had bought two blocks away from the diner and fixed up before Danny had died. With its peaked roof, warm pine paneling and thick carpet, his space was a secure, safe hideaway from the world. Most of the walls were covered with race car posters, and on the wall facing Margo were the drawings Ronny had made on his computer with the CAD program he'd learned at school. They were precise, professional and unique.

From one of the beds—he had two, for christssake, making Margo remember the lumpy cots in the commune—she tossed back the baseball he'd just thrown to her. Staring at the kid who was Danny's double, right down to his intense dark eyes and cocky grin, she asked, "You're scared, aren't you, buddy?" He'd been dealt a heavy blow tonight.

He started to deny it, but she gave him a don't-shit-me look and he nodded. Throwing the ball back to her, his face reflected a myriad of emotions. "You ever spend any time in jail?" he asked.

"Yep."

"When?"

Margo shook her head, making her earrings clink. She couldn't believe she'd ever been the young girl who'd stolen Mr. McFinney's car from the drugstore parking lot on a dare. "A couple of times. The last was when I was sixteen, I nabbed a car. They put me in juvenile detention for a few months. Finally, your uncle Linc talked my mother into getting me out."

"Was she pissed?"

"Are you kidding? They took turns at the commune beating the crap out of me, then made me pray on my knees for twenty-four hours straight, begging for God's forgiveness." Absently, she rubbed her knee and drew in a deep breath, battling back the chill that rode along with memory. "I never got in trouble with the law again." She arched a brow pointedly at him. "Luckily my last run-in with the legal system was when I was a minor."

"I know. I was stupid."

"You got it." She softened when she saw Ronny's eyes sparkle with tears just before he glanced away. Letting the ball drop to the floor, she sat up. "You'll be okay, kid. From what I hear, the weekend jail thing isn't with hardened criminals. Nobody named Butch is gonna make you his bride."

Ronny's jaw dropped. "Oh, God."

"Really. A guy from work's kid got assigned it a couple of years ago. You'll probably be in some minimum-security thing. Or a work program, so you're not cooped up the whole time." She nodded to the computer. "Wanna look the specifics up on the Internet with me?"

"Yeah, okay."

Margo slid off the bed and Ron stood too. When had he topped her five foot eight inches? When had his shoulders gotten so broad? Her heart turned over in her chest for the boy who was the closest thing she'd ever have to a son. Spontaneously, she enfolded him in her arms. God he even smelled like a man. That he didn't rib her about hugging him was a measure of his fear and anxiety. She patted his back, and for a while he just held on to her. When he drew away, he whispered, "I'm worried about Mom, Margo."

The kid was so good. Way down deep, he was a genuinely good person. "I'm glad to hear you're concerned about her." She left her hands on his shoulders. "We'll be here for her. I'll take your place at the diner if I have to."

Ronny gave her an adult look of scorn and jammed his hands into his jeans. "You hate this town. You hardly come back, even to see Uncle Linc."

A brief picture of *Uncle Linc's* face when she'd pranced into the Council room that night made her warm. His eyes had burned with heated intensity that she felt right down to her cowboy-booted toes. Then he'd given her that smile that had gotten him into her pants at fifteen, and into her heart forever. "When times are tough, kid, you do what you gotta do. Just like you will." She angled her head at the computer. "Come on, let's see what you're in for." As he sat down and the familiar bing of a computer booting up filled the room, she said casually, "I meant to ask you if you're staying away from LaMont and Anderson."

"Yeah, but you know, you and Mom and Uncle Linc don't make sense about that." His eyes glued to the screen, he didn't look at her. "They're my buddies, like you all were to each other."

Margo stared over his shoulder, watching the icons materialize. "No, *we* took care of each other. Sure we got into too much trouble, but we loved each other. Those guys would sell you down the river without batting an eyelash."

Her vehemence must have made Ronny back off, because he didn't answer; just the *click click click* of the keys filled the silence. Trying to defuse the moment, she cocked her head. "Any girls on the scene?"

A faint blush crept up the back of his neck.

She tugged him around. "*Are* there?"

"Well, there's one girl. Lily." His brown eyes danced, again reminding her of Danny. "She's different."

"Wanna talk about it to good old Aunt Margo?"

"Nah, not yet anyway." He turned back to the computer. "Here, I'm into the search engine. Let's do this."

When Margo left Ronny an hour later—this time blasting

imaginary enemies with simulated ray guns in a computer game—she felt better. According to the sites on the Internet, weekend jail was a milder experience than the real thing. Though she'd played the confident adult for him, she'd been terrified of what could happen to him in prison. She bounded down the steps, relieved.

In the living room at the bottom of the stairs, Beth was seated on a huge stuffed denim couch, sipping a beer. She looked exhausted, her pretty eyes smudged underneath with signs of sleeplessness. She'd kicked off her shoes, and had tucked her feet under her.

Across from her, sprawled on a stuffed chair, was Linc; Margo's eyes took in every detail of him: disreputable jeans, a red thermal shirt that made his complexion glow, ragged sneakers, propped up on an ottoman. As usual, his hair was a little too long, falling boyishly over dark eyes. He looked more like James Dean than Father Flannigan. "Hi, babe," he said catching sight of her. The gravelly quality of his voice always enervated her.

"Hi. I thought you were at Annie's."

"I was. We talked awhile, then she wanted to go to bed. I made sure the alarm was set and headed over here."

Margo glanced at her watch. "A minister's job is never done."

Usually he laughed at her barbs. Tonight, his smile was feigned. She knew he was worried about Ronny and Beth and Annie, and she wished she hadn't jabbed him. It was just that the goddamned church would eat him alive if he let it. "Sorry, cheap shot." Crossing to him, she kissed his cheek—it was stubbly like it always got at night—and took a sip of his beer. The tart taste stayed in her mouth. Plopping down next to Beth on the couch, she asked, "How you holding up, Bethy?"

"I'll be fine. Linc says we should be grateful that Pratt agreed to take the Council's recommendation to the judge."

"It could be worse. Ronny and I just looked up this weekend jail thing on the Internet. He printed off a copy for you." She gave Beth a brief rundown on their findings. "It's not too bad."

Beth blinked back tears. "Thank God."

"How is he?" Linc asked.

"Scared. Sorry. Worried about Bethy."

"I'll be fine," she said wearily.

Margo exchanged a look with Linc. His expression read, *Not tonight; she's too raw.*

Adhering to his silent admonishment, instead of analyzing the problem from all angles, listing the options, then choosing the best, which was Margo's style, she shrugged. "It'll work out. We can talk about you and the business tomorrow."

Beth glanced at the clock. "Speaking of which, I have to be at the diner at six. I'm going to bed."

"Don't you have people to open up?" Margo asked, worried about Beth's obvious exhaustion.

Standing, Beth stretched. "Gerty'll be in, but Nana's off." She smiled at her brother. "Lock up when you leave, would you, Linc?" She grinned. "*If* you leave."

He snorted. When Margo was in town, she and Linc were known to stay up all night talking.

Linc stood too, waited until Beth kissed Margo on the cheek, then took his sister's hand and walked her to the bedroom in the back of the house.

When he returned, and without speaking, he picked up his beer, took a swig, handed it to Margo and dropped down onto the couch. She drained what was left, then went into his arms like a long-standing lover. Cuddling against his chest, she breathed him in—no cologne, just that indefinable scent that was Linc. Simply the smell of him calmed her more than any words he could say. They lay back into the cushions, silently reveling in the other's presence.

Finally, he said, "You look tired. Bad week?"

"I worried like hell about Beth and Ronny."

"Worry won't help, babe."

"I suppose you prayed for them."

He grunted.

"Did that help?"

"The outcome wasn't too bad. Not as bad as it could be." Lazily, he rubbed his large, calloused hand down from her shoulder to her elbow, his heat penetrating her black lambswool sweater. His serenity seeped into her by degrees, and she found herself closing her eyes to savor him. To savor him.

"You gonna tell me about it?" he asked.

She stiffened, then cursed. Without saying a word, she'd given herself away.

"It's okay, honey." He brushed his hand down her hair, tangling it between his fingers. "I know something's wrong."

She buried her nose in his chest. "You always know."

"So tell me."

"Promise me you won't get mad."

His chuckle reverberated in his rib cage. "I gotta be the only person in the world you're afraid to piss off."

"You are."

"I won't get mad."

She said simply, "Philip hit on me during the trip to Boston."

Linc's whole body tensed. "The bastard."

She tried to pull back to look at him, but he held her close. He was *really* angry if he wouldn't face her. "I wasn't going to tell you, because of how you feel about him. But I haven't been able to stop thinking about it."

His heartbeat speeded up—she felt its thump under her hand. "Did you . . . I mean . . . the pass . . . did you *want* it?"

"Hell no. I hated it. And I told him so."

Linc's body relaxed.

This time Margo did pull away, summoning righteous indignation. "Jesus Christ, Linc, he's a married man. You know how I feel about that kind of thing."

But, as usual, Linc didn't back down. Which was one of the reasons he had that little scar just below his jaw. She'd witnessed the knife fight when he'd gotten it, could still hear the blades hit and his low moans in her nightmares.

"I know," he said sternly. "I also know how you feel about Pretty Boy."

Raking her hair off her face, she tried to get up. He yanked her back down so that she fell back onto his chest. His arms vised around her.

After a long moment, he kissed the top her forehead. His lips were warm and familiar. "You know why this is so hard for me."

Margo knew. Though they never verbalized it, not once in the eleven years since he'd come to Glen Oaks, Margo was all too aware of his feelings. As he was of hers. Which was why she shared as much as she could about her dates, and prodded him to tell her about his. There was no chance for them together, and they struggled to keep finding ways to keep themselves apart. "I know." She waited. "Don't say any more."

"I won't." A long silence. "What's the situation with Hathaway now?"

"He apologized the next morning. And at work he's been just like always. But it's been hard for me to forget."

"Do you have feelings for him, Margo?"

"Not like you mean. I care about him as a friend, that's all. I just wish this hadn't happened." She smoothed down his shirt. "It's over. I put it back in its compartment, but it still bugs me that he did it."

"Feelings aren't easy to compartmentalize, babe."

Ah, but he was wrong, she thought as he slid to the edge of the couch and eased her to the inside. She stretched out next to him, and he lay down beside her, propped up by pillows. One arm still snug around her, he reached over and clicked off the lamp on the end table. The room was plunged into darkness, except for a sliver of moon peeking through Beth's front windows. The only sound came from a ticking grandfather clock in the entryway.

Margo sighed. How many times had they slept this way?—on a park bench, at a bus station; even when they got their own apartment in college, sometimes they fell asleep together on the couch.

She hugged him tightly. The demons never came after her then, and he knew it. Linc Grayson could keep them away just by his even breathing and the feel of his arms around her. Closing her eyes, she treasured both sensations.

And felt safe once again.

FIVE

JOE knocked tentatively on the church office door. Annie opened it. Dressed in a short black skirt with leotard and leggings underneath, her stance, despite her petite stature, would have done Atilla the Hun proud. He scowled, though, at the smudges under her eyes that betrayed her sleeplessness. Once again, he was the cause of them.

"Hi, Annie."

She glared at him. "Be careful, Joe. I mean it."

"I will," he promised, more anxious than a convict facing the parole board. His heartbeat tripled as she drew open the door.

They made a picture perfect tableau, standing before the window, with the last rays of the sun muted behind them. Could that tall adolescent really be the small boy he used to swing up and carry on his shoulders? Wearing a hooded sweatshirt, jeans and sneakers, Matt looked so much like a Murphy it startled Joe. The boy's dark hair, square-cut jaw and broad shoulders came directly from him.

Joe's eyes dropped down to Matt's arm, which encircled a tiny little girl. She had hair like Rapunzel's. The braid draped over her shoulder caused his heart to constrict—it was as long and as thick as Annie's used to be. And how she was dressed mirrored her mother—same color tights and leggings and a bulky sweater over a leotard. But her face differed from Matt's and

Annie's dramatically. She was smiling. Oh, God, he had a little girl.

Off to the side Linc stood guard.

"Hello, Matt." Joe's voice was husky. "Hi, Faith."

As if she'd sensed his nervousness, Faith broke away from Matt and crossed daintily to him, already as graceful as a prima ballerina. Her expression angelic, she stared up at him. "Hi."

Squatting down, eye-level, he whispered, "How you doing, sweetheart?"

Annie turned her back on them and faced out the window. Belatedly he remembered why. *Don't call me sweetheart after you've slapped me, Joe. It's obscene.*

"I'm good," Faith said. Reaching out, she placed a small, cool palm on his cheek, as if touching him made him real. "You're my daddy."

Daddy. Briefly, he closed his eyes to savor the innocent gesture and precious words. "Yes, I am."

"Mommy said you came back to Glen Oaks last week but had to wait to see us. Till Uncle Linc said it was okay." She cocked her head. "Jimmy Docker had the chicken pox and couldn't see anybody 'cause he was 'tagious. Were you 'tagious?"

Joe swallowed hard and glanced at Linc. God bless him, though the man was angry at Joe for past transgressions, he nodded his encouragement. They'd all agreed on a version of the truth. "I was sick, Faith, like Mommy told you. But it was here . . ."—he pointed to his head, then clapped a hand over his heart—". . . and here. It took me six years to get better. But no, I'm not contagious." He stole a glance at Matt. *At least I hope not.*

When his son made no move toward Joe, Linc stepped forward. "Why don't we all sit down."

Chairs had been arranged around a small table. Annie took one, and Matt dropped down next to her, their shoulders touching. Linc flanked Matt on the other side. Like the little doll she was, Faith grasped Joe's hand and led him to a seat. The gesture meant more to him than that first college degree he'd earned.

Start out with an innocuous subject, he told himself, after they were settled. "So, Matt, I hear you like baseball."

Sullenly his son met his eyes. "Yeah."

"Maybe we can toss a ball around sometime."

Matt's look soured even more. "If Uncle Linc is free."

Joe knew the kid was asking in a round-about way why the restrictions had been placed on their time to together. "You probably want to know why Linc will be with us for a while."

Shrugging, Matt held his gaze.

"Tell me, Matt, did you ever lose somebody's trust? Do something so they didn't believe in you again for a while?"

Obstinantly, Matt shook his head. A lock of dark hair fell onto his forehead, shading what, up close, Joe could see as the Murphy blue/gray eyes.

Again Linc intervened. "How about the time you and your three buddies went to the gorge by yourselves and Johnny fell and got hurt? Remember how your mom let you see those guys only at your house under her supervision for a few weeks?"

His face flushed, Matt nodded.

"Well, that's kind of what we're doing with your father."

Mutiny surfaced, a tangible presence in the room. "What'd you do that you gotta be watched?"

Joe forced himself to remain calm. Worry about what the kid had witnessed and absorbed had plagued him for years.

Annie stepped in. "I told you, honey, it's personal between me and your father. There are some things that you don't need to know. At least not yet."

"I'm not a baby, Mom."

"I know. Still, this is what we think is the best."

Joe said, "Matt, maybe after we get to know each other again, everybody will feel more comfortable with what's happening here. Then we can talk about what I've done, if it seems appropriate."

The rest of the allotted hour was a dream come true for Joe, and he reveled in hearing about his children's lives. Faith's words bubbled out of her like a storybook happy child, while Matt's came in halting preteen sentences tinged with wariness. The time flew by and Joe was sorry to see it end.

THE next afternoon, Joe locked the door to his new apartment and shuffled down the steep flight of stairs. After looking around town the weekend before, he'd picked this place for the quiet—it was over a small mom-and-pop bakery, open only from six to ten A.M. Though the rooms were a far cry from the apartment he'd sublet to Taylor in the city, they were surprisingly spacious and airy. He'd purchased just a bed and dresser, but the place suited his needs—to be in town, near the house that Annie had bought, and close to his job. It was also in good proximity to Linc's church and Beth's diner, where he was headed now, at three P.M. on Wednesday, to meet with Ron Donovan. He'd given himself an hour to walk around town—to face the ghosts of his past and to let out some of his present pent-up energy with a little exercise. He made a mental note to find a gym in Glen Oaks, and he had to start running again in the mornings.

He had a lot to smile about as he breathed in the warm March day—nothing in the world smelled quite like spring in New York State. At the top of his list of blessings was Annie's decision to allow him to see his kids. Joe had felt as if he'd won the lottery on Monday night when he'd gone to the church where he was to meet them.

Picking up his pace, Joe realized he was in the center of town; he passed Kilmer's Drugs where he'd bought his first condom, the small shoe repair shop where his father took his old boots, and Zip's Bar and Grill, where he'd taken his first drink. Some of the places elicited good memories—sharing a soda with Annie at the diner, picking out a tux for his wedding at Hall's Clothing, and the quick kisses he stole from Annie in the balcony of the Fox Theater. Carefully avoiding DanceWorks straight ahead on Oak Street, he took a turn down Market Street and bumped into his sister coming around the corner.

"Hi, Suz." Grasping her shoulders to steady her, he tried to keep his voice neutral. The meeting with her had not gone as well as with his kids.

She shrugged out of his grasp. "Hello, Joe."

He scanned her outfit. "Are you working at the dance studio?"

"I own half of it. Annie let me buy in last year."

"Really? I didn't know that."

"You miss a lot in six years, bro."

Taking a deep breath, Joe stuck his hands in the pockets of his raincoat. "I told you last week I was sorry about that."

"You have a lot to be sorry about."

"I know. And you're not going to let me off the hook, like Ma did, are you?"

Oh, thank the Lord, my prayers are answered. Joey's back.

Suzie hiked her DanceWorks tote back to her left shoulder.

"She can pretend you're the prodigal son incarnate if she wants. I know a lot more than she does."

A fist formed in Joe's throat. "I figured as much when you wouldn't see me after Thursday when I came by." It had been one of the hardest things to do—to let Suzie distance him—but he'd learned the black side of control and had vowed to allow people to handle his return in their own way.

She glanced at a Chevy coming down the street. "Annie didn't tell me. I was dating an orderly and found out from him." She raised wounded eyes to him. "He said Annie claimed she fell down the steps. But the hospital was suspicious. Since you left town, nobody pursued it. There were a few rumors, but everybody lost interest quickly."

"I'd like to talk to you about it."

"Annie already has." At his surprised look, Suzie added, "I told her I knew what happened as soon as she recuperated from her last run-in with your fists. And feet."

Joe cringed.

"Look, I believe in second chances. So I'll give you a shot. Just don't expect me to welcome you with open arms." Her eyes got bleak and she pushed the curls, which she'd always hated but he liked, off her forehead. "I've seen what you can do." Then she gulped hard. "Just like Pa."

"I'm going to talk to Ma about all this. Just as soon as the dust settles from my return."

"She won't discuss it. I've tried."

"I'll try again."

"She blamed Annie for your leaving, and never let her forget it."

"Just like she blamed herself for Pa."

Suzie's face was grim. "I've got to go."

Reaching out, he squeezed her arm. He thought it a good sign that she didn't flinch. "I'm not giving up on you, Suz. That's a promise."

She shrugged her shoulders. "Your promises don't hold much water in Glen Oaks anymore, Joe."

I'll never leave you, Suz, I promise. I'll always protect you from him.

"I'm going to change that. I'm going to regain your trust and everybody else's."

"We'll see." Without a goodbye, she circled around him and headed down the street.

Watching her go, he was struck again by all he'd lost. He'd been ready for obstacles, had vowed to overcome them. Hell, he'd scale Mount Everest if he had to. Just because he hadn't expected Suzie to be one of them didn't mean he couldn't deal with her animosity. Just because he'd protected her from their father's wrath didn't mean she'd remember, or give him points for it.

With one last glance at his sister, he headed for the diner, but Suzie's contempt brought the demons back and they fell into step with him. What he had done to Annie wouldn't stay in hell, and surfaced in the brittle light of day. . . .

"Where's my breakfast?" he'd asked Annie after a particularly gruesome night of drinking. He felt like a prickly bear and was ready to growl at anybody.

Dressed in a nightgown, her long hair had been hastily tied back in a braid. "I . . . I overslept. Have some coffee first . . ." She'd been so nervous at his mood that when she brought it to the table, she'd spilled it on his hand.

"Stupid bitch," he'd said, throwing the chair back and raising his hand.

The bruise on her cheek had shown up immediately.

She'd retreated to the corner and begun to cry. Her tears had sobered him, as they often did. After a few minutes, he crossed to her and reached out. *I'm sorry, sweetheart.*

She'd yelled at him then not to call her sweetheart. It was one of the few times she'd defied him. Unfortunately, she'd paid for her defiance in a way that made him sick to remember now. . . .

Forcefully, he shrugged off the nausea, as the counselors had taught him to do, and struggled to keep the depression that hovered constantly on the outskirts of his mind at bay.

He'd changed, and he knew it. Now he had to convince everybody else.

THE Downtown Diner had changed, too, in six years; like many establishments in Glen Oaks, the place had gotten a face-lift in hopes of attracting a bigger racing crowd like it had in its heyday. The restaurant was still the same size, about twenty by thirty, but the row of windows that had replaced the two that used to be there brightened up the interior. Cedar walls had covered the outdated race car wallpaper, and newly upholstered booths in deep burgundy matched the fifteen or so stools at the counter. The burgundy and gray vinyl on the floor pulled the decor together. At the far end, a set of about ten tables and chairs created a new eating area. Beyond them on the wall were the racing pictures of Danny that Beth had put up after he'd died. Joe could hardly believe that when he was eighteen, he'd taken part in a robbery on this place.

It was about five minutes before four. Joe knew that until racing season started, the dinner crowd was thin here, and the diner closed several nights a week and Sunday afternoons. A lone man sat in a corner drinking a cup of coffee, and a waitress wiped up the counter. Dressed in a long flowing tie-dyed dress and several strands of beads around her neck, the woman's hair was long and frizzy and steel gray. She looked like a sixties hippie reincarnated. He sat down on a stool and she approached him. "Hi, what can I get you?" Her name tag told him she was Gerty.

"A cup of coffee. Cream and sugar."

Gerty's eyes focused in on him. "You're Grace Murphy's boy, aren't you?"

He gave her his best smile. "Yes, ma'am."

She laughed at the *ma'am*. "I used to live four doors down from you. You still got that motorcycle? The one that was as noisy as all get-out?"

"No, I left that behind in Glen Oaks." With a lot of other things.

The woman turned, retrieved the coffeepot and poured him a cup without missing a beat. "Good. Now all we gotta deal with is Reverend Linc's Harley. Young Ronny's got his father's bike, but he lost his license and can't drive it."

Joe didn't know that. So Ron had Danny's motorcycle. God, he remembered the three of them, burning rubber all around town, angering the homeowners and often playing cat and mouse with the cops.

She crossed her arms over her chest. "You back to stay?"

Carefully he stirred in the cream and watched the black liquid turn to pale brown. "I hope so."

"Not nice to abandon those two little babies of yours."

He felt his face flush. "I wasn't a nice man then, Mrs. . . . ?"

"Gerty." Sharp brown eyes focused on him through her granny glasses. "You a nice guy now?"

"Yes, I am." He sipped the coffee, its strong rich taste giving him the caffeine jolt he needed.

Gerty shrugged and said, "Hrrmph," just as Beth came out from the back.

Her face was drawn and she looked exhausted; she spotted him and glanced anxiously at the clock. Biting her lip, she came toward him. "Hi, Joe. He's not here, yet. I'm sorry. I know—"

Joe touched her arm. "It's all right, Beth. I'll talk to him about the importance of punctuality and responsibility. I made this first session informal to set ground rules and consequences, and get to know each other a little."

Her eyes glistened. "He's a nice boy, Joe."

"I'm sure he is. And I believe in second chances." His words were rife with meaning, and though she'd never gone to college, Beth was smart.

She gave him a half smile. "So do I. I had mine with this place and Tony Scarpino." She scanned the diner. "And you're getting yours. So Ronny will, right?"

"Why don't you sit and have—" His words were cut off as the door flew open.

Ron Donovan burst through it shouldering a backpack and wearing an anxious expression on his face. He checked the clock. "Oh, Christ, sorry I'm late." His eyes sought out his mother's and his expression softened. "Really, Mom, I had a reason. Mr. Johnson let me work after school with the CAD program."

She looked at him tenderly. "Mr. Murphy will talk to you about that."

"Joe," he said, standing. At least he was on firm ground here. He knew how to counsel teenagers. "I like to be on a first-name basis with my kids."

Ron's expression was wary. "Your kids?"

"Yeah, let's take a seat in one of the booths; I'll tell you about my background and you can tell me about yours."

"Want something, honey?" Beth asked as Joe picked up his coffee cup.

"A coke. Thanks, Mom."

Leaning over, she kissed his cheek. "Hang in there, buddy. Joe's an old friend, you remember."

Joe's heart warmed. Though she said it mostly for the boy, he vowed she'd view him again as a friend who could be trusted.

They settled in the most private booth they could find. After

Gerty delivered Ron's coke, Joe sipped his coffee and stared at Danny's son. This close, he looked so much like his father at his age that for a moment Joe just sat back and took it in. God, he remembered Danny—sitting in this very diner. *I'm gonna win the Winston Cup someday, Joey, I know it.* And on his and Beth's wedding day, Joe and Linc had teased him mercilessly. *Go ahead and rag on me. Your time's comin'.* And when Ronny was born, *Honest to God, guys, it's the best thing that ever happened to me.*

"What you staring at?" Ronny asked.

Joe smiled. "I was just thinking about your father. The day you were born, he told me and your uncle Linc it was the best thing that ever happened to him."

"No shit?"

Shaking his head, Joe said, "He was a wild kid, but he had a gentle streak, for you and your mother."

Ronny's eyes turned bleak. "Nobody talks about him anymore."

"Do you want to talk about him?"

"I don't care."

Joe recognized the teenage bravado. "Well, if you do, we can spend a little time in each of our sessions discussing your dad. I've got stories galore about him."

Ron looked down. "He'd be disappointed in me." He drew a ring on the table with the dew from his glass.

"Yeah, he wouldn't like the stuff you've been into. He'd ride your butt about it. But he'd understand, too."

"Cause he was a member of the Outlaws?"

Joe nodded.

"You, too."

"Yeah, we all were."

"Answer something for me?"

"Sure, if I can."

"Why does Mom pitch a fit about Loose and the other guys I hang out with when she was so wild?"

"Maybe it's because we *were* so wild. We weren't a good influence on each other and she knows what can happen."

"You all turned out okay."

"Maybe."

"Margo said you cared about each other and those guys don't give a shit about me."

Joe seized the opening. "Well, we all care about you, too.

Adult concern is something the Outlaws never had. And we'd like to keep you from repeating our mistakes." He smiled sadly.

Ron looked at the partially open backpack on the table. Joe tracked his gaze. A sketch pad with blueprints was sticking out. "Tell me about the things you like to do."

Swallowing hard, Ronny was silent.

"You said you were late because you were working with Mr. Johnson on some CAD drawings." Joe shot a glance at the pad. "Are those them?"

A spark lit Ron's eyes. "Yeah. I, um, like to draw stuff."

"What kind of stuff?"

He shrugged. "Mostly cars." He glanced over to the office door where Beth had retreated. "Mom doesn't like it. Grandma and Grandpa have a fit about it."

"Can I see your drawings?"

Again the shrug.

Joe waited. He knew kids, and he knew they succumbed to interest in what they liked to do better than anything. Finally Ron tugged out the pad.

For ten minutes, Joe leafed through his sketchbook and opened up the drawings. They were very good, very professional. He told Ron so.

"I guess," the boy said. "Mr. Johnson thinks so."

Joe made a mental note to talk to Mr. Johnson. "We never had courses like this in high school."

"I hear you were a terror there."

"I'm afraid I was."

"Why?"

This he could answer honestly. "A lot of reasons. One was I was pretty smart and everybody saw me as the thug I pretended to be. Nobody saw past it, so I acted out."

Straightening his shoulders, Ron's look was very adult. "I like Annie and the kids. Why'd you come back?"

"Because I want to spend time with them."

"She wasn't as happy as a pig in shit to see you."

Joe's heart constricted. "She's got reason."

"What?"

"Let's just say I wasn't a very good husband or father." He faced Ron squarely. "So you see, I need another chance, too."

"That why you're giving me one?"

"That, and I've read your file. I think you're salvageable. You need help, though. We need to talk about what you're feeling inside."

Ron sighed heavily. "I don't have much choice."

"Well, you can opt for real prison instead of weekend jail and community service."

Terror flickered across the kid's face. Necessary, Joe knew, to drive home the point.

"I don't want that."

Sipping the last of his coffee, Joe took an appointment book out of his pocket. "Okay, let's set up a schedule for our meetings." He checked the clock. "And we have time to set some ground rules today."

Again the terror. Joe recognized the fear that came from knowing you had to share your unprocessed thoughts. Because he'd been scared by it, too, he squeezed the arm of Danny's son. "We'll take it slow, Ron. It'll work out. I promise."

SIX

"CAN I see you a minute?" Margo looked up from her desk to find Philip Hathaway looming in the doorway. Dressed in a slick Armani suit and perfectly matched shirt and tie, he was the epitome of corporate success. For some reason, Linc's flannel shirt and worn jeans came to mind. Before she'd left Glen Oaks last weekend, she'd bought him three new pairs of denims and left them on the bed in his apartment.

"Yes, of course, Philip."

He glanced at his watch, a Rolex that he'd bought with his last bonus. "Let's go downstairs and have coffee."

Margo hesitated. Though they'd often shared breaks at the Starbucks on the ground floor of their firm's high-rise, she was uncomfortable going with him today. Things seemed fuzzy between them now, and she couldn't bring them back into focus.

Running his hand through his perfectly styled hair and making it even more attractive, he gave her an ingenuous smile. "Look, there's been a chill between us for almost two weeks. I feel bad, like I blew our friendship. I'd like to try to get back on track." When she still hesitated, he said boyishly, "Please, Margo."

She rolled her eyes. "Why not?" She was probably making too much of this anyway, and a good talk might clear the air.

Grabbing her purse from her drawer, she stood and circled around her desk.

Philip whistled. "Wow. New dress?"

She'd bought the black sheath when she'd gotten back to New York from Glen Oaks. Linc's psychological mind would have a field day with that. Paying the hefty price for a simple dress might just be the proof she needed that she was out of Glen Oaks, and the world that had taunted her in the name of *religion*, for good.

"Yeah." She adjusted the black and white silk scarf she'd bought to go with it. "I needed perking up."

"Well, baby, in that outfit you'll *perk up* any man you see."

She halted at the sexual innuendo.

"What?" he asked with choir boy innocence.

"Do you think that's an appropriate remark, Philip?"

"Oh, for Christ's sakes, I initiated the company's sexual harassment policy, reviewed it, made my own changes and gave the final okay. We *really* need to talk if you take offense at that. It's nothing I haven't said before Boston."

Was that true? Because he could be right, because Linc could just have spooked her about Philip with his suspicions and dire warnings, she shook her head and accompanied Philip downstairs. They made chitchat in the elevator about work, and found a table in a corner of the crowded coffee shop. Once she was seated, he ordered café au lait for them both from the counter without even asking if it was what she wanted. She wondered how long that kind of thing had been going on. It seemed intimate, and possessive. Damn, had she really given off mixed signals?

When he'd gotten their coffee and sat across from her, he stared over the rim of his cup with solemn blue eyes. "I'm sorry about that night in Boston. I can tell how upset you still are about it, and I don't quite know what to do to make things right between us."

"I'm not upset, Philip. Just disappointed."

Hot emotion flared in his eyes. "I'm human, Margo. And I misread the signals."

Guiltily she looked down at her coffee. She took a taste of the sweet confection. "If I've given them out, I'm sorry. I didn't mean to."

"Just as I didn't mean to scare you off." Reaching across the table he took her hand in his. His was big and warm from the mug. "I wouldn't hurt you for the world. I care about you, as a business associate and as a friend."

She frowned at their clasped hands. Again she realized his touching her like this was nothing unusual. Wondering how gullible she'd been, she squeezed his fingers, extricated her hand and met his gaze. "I care about you, too. I probably overreacted."

"Good." He closed his eyes briefly then, and drew in a deep breath. "At least that's settled."

"What is it, Philip?"

"There's something you don't know. Something that might relate to what happened."

Concerned, she set down her cup and braced her arms on the table. "Tell me."

"I'm afraid to, now."

"You can trust me."

His blond brows arched. "Of course I can. And you can trust me." His expression and tone were guileless, and she was beginning to feel like a fool for her behavior these past few days.

"I know," she told him honestly. "I've overreacted. Let's put it behind us. Tell me what's wrong."

Swallowing hard, he looked down at his hands and twisted his wedding band around nervously. "Things aren't good with Sally and me."

Margo pictured Sally Hathaway. She'd last seen the woman at the firm's Christmas party. Tall and statuesque, Sally had been a goddess in a shimmery gold dress and piles of blond hair. Philip's classic good looks had complimented her beautifully. "Since when?"

"For about six months. This time."

"This time?"

"We've had problems before."

"Over what?"

"I work too much. I don't pay enough attention to her. I travel a lot."

Margo hadn't a clue. In the years she'd know the Hathaways, they'd always appeared the ideal couple. "I'm sorry, Philip."

His gaze was profoundly intense. "You and I are a lot alike, Margo. You understand my work, you share my dedication to it. I find that very attractive. I'm not sorry for it. But I am sorry if I offended you that night."

He was hurting, she could tell. And he'd been so good to her. Really, she was being unsophisticated about all this. Reaching over, this time she covered his hand with hers. "We've forgotten that, remember? Now, let's talk about you and Sally."

He smiled warmly at her and squeezed her hand. If he held on a little too long, Margo told herself, it was because he was upset about his marital problems.

Like hell, Linc would say.

As Philip talked about his wife, Margo thought about Linc's hands, and how calloused they were from the work he did around the church. And how they felt in her hair, on her shoulder, kneading her back.

Suddenly, a bigger more graphic image assaulted her.

She'd been fifteen, and he'd gone to rub her back one day in his old battered car. She'd flinched and pulled away.

"What is it?"

"Nothing." She tried to keep stuff from him because he had a terrible temper in those days and she hated to see it spark.

His dark eyes narrowed on her. "Turn around."

"Linc, please."

"I wanna see."

She'd argued, but eventually he had her facing away and lifted her sweater. "Fucking son of a bitch," he'd said when he'd seen the strap marks. They were particularly bad that time.

"Why?" he asked tightly.

"I wouldn't pray before dinner."

"Margo, just do it when they ask you and avoid this."

"No."

He'd leaned over and kissed a spot—there weren't many— where there was no welt. "I'm so sorry. We'll leave this crummy town. As soon as you graduate . . ."

"Margo, are you all right?"

"Hmm?"

"You look like you're somewhere else."

I was. Back in Glen Oaks.

Where Linc lived. Where she could never, ever live again.

HENRY Portman was a big, balding man who walked with a pronounced limp and always smelled a little like mothballs. A Vietnam vet, he was disabled in the war and lived on a pension from the government. Linc had recognized the emptiness of the older man's life as soon as he took over the pastorship at Community Christian Church. When Henry had asked, in one of his rare verbal episodes, if he could volunteer as the custodian of the church—a position which they couldn't afford to hire for pay—Linc was unable to turn him down. Even if it did mean cleaning up after Henry, or chasing around in his wake to repair damage.

Today, the poor man's latest target had been the stove in the fellowship hall kitchen. Henry had tried to clean it with outdoor bug spray, mistaking the can for oven cleaner. As Linc stuck his head in the oven, he had to smile, though the sickeningly sweet smell assaulted him. "No internal damage, Henry. I'll just scrub it with some bleach and maybe the smell will go away."

Again Linc chuckled as he pictured Connie Smith's horror when the Ladies Aid turned on the oven last night and the unmistakable smell of Zap 'Em Bug Spray permeated the fellowship hall. She'd come screaming to Linc. They were still airing out the place.

Linc pulled himself from the oven and stood. Henry shrugged and gave him an *I'm sorry* look.

"Why don't you go set up the chairs for the women's group in the first Sunday School room? Six of them. And find the blackboard for me to use. I'll have this done in no time."

A squeeze on his shoulder made Linc's heart lurch. So many lonely people in this world who needed to be needed. Henry left, and Linc began the messy task of cleaning out the oven. Like everything else around here, the stove was a relic. The kitchen was old, the fellowship hall was old and the church proper was old. The whole place would have been sold off long ago if Jeremiah Jordan hadn't died and left in his will money earmarked to purchase the entire property, now held in trust for the congregation. If they'd had a mortgage to pay, the forty-family church would never have survived. Jeremiah's bequest was the miracle God had planned for this tiny place.

While he scrubbed and rinsed, and scraped his knuckles on the wall of the oven, Linc's mind drifted to Margo. It had been paradise having her home last weekend. She'd slept like a baby in his arms the night of the Council meeting, then come to him after spending the evenings with Beth or Annie. They'd shared pizza and beer late at night and long, involved discussions into the quiet hours of the morning. He ran on empty for days after she left, but the pure pleasure of her company had been worth it. She wouldn't attend church on Sunday, of course, but she spent the whole afternoon with him before he dropped her off at the train station. Her hug had been warmer and longer than usual, and he could still summon the feeling of her strong arms around him and the sexy scent of her expensive perfume.

Maybe it was time for another talk with God.

I'm missing her something bad.

I know. It's all part of the plan, son.

What, to torture your most avid servant?

You do look a little like a servant there.

Poor Henry.

Henry's fine. Because of you.

It took him an hour to clean the oven, but talking with God made it go fast. When he was done, he glanced at the clock and realized he had just enough time to shower and change. Hurrying out of the kitchen, on impulse, he checked the meeting room for his group. Eight chairs were out. But they were in rows. He'd told Henry a million times he wanted them in a circle, to facilitate discussion. If Linc left the rows, the women would sit down before he got back and the discussion among them was already like pulling teeth. There was also a huge room divider set up in front. On it was a note in Henry's scrawl, "No blackboard. Use this."

By the time Linc rearranged the chairs and found the blackboard buried in a storage closet, he only had time to wash his hands and face and tuck in his shirt in the small men's lav. He did, however, manage a short prayer that he'd be patient and insightful for these women who trusted him. At ten o'clock, five out of six of the women had arrived for their third meeting.

"Pardon my appearance, ladies, but the stove took precedence over the shower today." He gave them a self-effacing grin.

They smiled back and Linc was warmed by their affection. He'd never had motherly approval in his life, and wondered if he was searching for it here. "Shall we start with a prayer?"

Once seated, they bowed their heads and Linc gave a short prayer. Then he said, "This is our third meeting. Today we're going to brainstorm some topics for future discussion and set an agenda of sorts. Anyone want to write?"

Barb Mandarino, a slim woman in her mid-forties with lively green eyes, turned to Anita Camp. The town's hairdresser sported flamboyant silky leggings and a long hot pink shirt. It clashed vividly with her red hair. "Anita, you do it," Barb said. "You're good in front of people." The implication was that none of the others were. Except for Anita, the self-esteem quotient in this room hovered near zero.

"Sure thing." Anita stood and sashayed over to the board. "All set, kemosabe," she said to Linc.

He smiled. "Who would like to go first?"

Absolute quiet. Linc waited.

Anita rolled her eyes and tapped her foot, encased in three-inch mules. "Geez, Louise, do I have to start off everything?"

Joanie Jorgensen, who worked part-time at the bakery, raised her chin. "No, I'll start. I'd like to talk about loneliness." Her husband, Woody, had died two years ago in a fluke car accident, and since her kids were grown, she'd floundered. Plain but handsome, she dressed like Linc's kindergarten teacher in prim dresses and thick-soled shoes.

Again, silence.

Linc finally spoke. "I have an idea to keep the discussion going. How about whoever speaks gets to pick the next person to suggest a topic?" He reached over and snagged the eraser from the board. Gently he tossed it to Joanie, who giggled when she caught it. "Shoot this to whomever you choose to go next."

Finally one woman nodded, another agreed and at last he had consensus. Primly, Joanie threw the eraser to Patricia O'Brien, mother of six. She said, "Raising kids?" Plump, with a pretty heart-shaped face and warm blue eyes, Linc suspected she really wanted to talk about not having any more children. Demurely, she tossed the eraser to Anita, who caught it deftly.

"Growing old?" Anita put on the board. She fluffed her hair. "Not that it's happenin' to me, mind you." That brought smiles. At forty-something, Anita was pretty in a flashy way. Margo teased Linc that the divorcée was sweet on him.

Ona James, who helped her husband out at the hardware store he owned, and who had one of the two supportive spouses of this group, took the eraser from Anita and said, "Having money. Of your own." Hmm, Linc hadn't guessed that might be an issue with her. He watched the somewhat plain forty-year-old flush at his concerned look.

"How about getting along at work?" Barb said when she held the eraser. Again Linc was surprised. He thought she liked her part-time job at the drugstore. Her husband, friends with Ian James, also was supportive of this group, and seemingly of her.

"Anything else?" Linc asked.

No response. Finally he said, "I guess that's enough for now. Why don't we—"

He heard the door to the fellowship hall open. From the entryway emerged a petite woman with brown hair scrubbed back in a tight knot; she wore an anxious look on her face.

Rosa DeMartino. "Sorry I'm late." Unbuttoning a worn coat, she crossed shyly to the group.

"It's fine, Rosa." Linc gave her a warm smile. "We're just glad you're here."

"Whatsamatter, sweetie. Oversleep?" Anita teased.

Everyone chuckled; they knew Rosa was the hardest worker in Glen Oaks, cleaning houses and doing other odd jobs around town when her husband was out of work. In his employed time, he wouldn't *let* her work. Shaking her head, Rosa looked much older than her thirty-eight years.

Linc remained silent, trying not to be judgmental. But he could guess why she was late. Sam probably just left for the racetrack, which would be opening soon, and had recently called back its workers.

"It doesn't matter, Rosa," Linc said softly. "We're just brainstorming ideas for the group to discuss in the future. Grab some coffee, take a look at what's on the board and see if you have anything to add."

Forgoing the coffee, she dropped down into a chair next to Barb and stared at the board. After a long look, she said, "Freedom. I'd like to talk about having some freedom."

SEVEN

ROLLING up the sleeves of his denim shirt, Tucker loped down the stairs to the first floor of Doc's cottage, into the living room, which overlooked Glenora Lake.

And faced a ghost. Dressed in jeans and a black T-shirt which read, *In my world you don't exist,* was the son who resembled his father so much it was hard to believe the boy wasn't a figment of Tucker's imagination. Had Doc forgotten to tell him something? Tucker was going to wring the old buzzard's neck.

The kid stood by the trophies lining the bookcases on the side walls. Seething all over again at the display of their success— Tucker wanted no part of it—he watched Ron inspect him.

Tucker finally nodded. "Ron."

Ron nodded back.

Doc, who was fishing something out of the drawer underneath the bookcases, straightened. "Here they are."

Calling himself a mealymouthed coward, Tucker made a quick loop to the left and fled to the kitchen, pretending he wanted something to drink; he was really giving himself time to deal with the all-too-real specter in the living room.

He hadn't expected this kind of . . . unease at confronting Ron Donovan, Tucker thought as he popped open a can of soda. The cold liquid wet his suddenly parched throat. The first few times he'd seen the kid, his discomfort had snuck up on him like a rookie driver trying to pass, but after a few contacts, he thought he'd be used to Ron's resemblance to the man he'd killed.

Must be this was going to be his purgatory. Every one of those fifteen hours per week of community service would likely burn the fires of the damned right through Tucker's soul.

Quit cowerin' out here, he told himself disgustedly. *Face your sins.*

Crunching the aluminum can in his hand, he tossed it in the trash and ambled out into the living room, as if he were strollin' along the riverbank. Doc had what *Sports Illustrated* called their "spectacular new car" plans spread out on the coffee table, and the kid sat next to him on the couch. Tucker circled around and stood behind them; he tried to concentrate on the blueprints, but instead, he stared down at the dark head and the gray one bent close together. Beth Donovan's hair was lighter than Ron's, more chestnut than raven. It curled real soft and pretty around her face and shoulders.

"See here," Doc said in his perennially gruff voice. "This is one of the modifications we're makin'."

The kid nodded; he was either clueless about cars or he didn't give a shit about Doc's landmark designs.

Your son wants to race?

Yes, of course.

"Quaid thinks we can go even bigger and still fit the template. We'll get thirty to forty more miles a gallon outta it."

Ron said, "I seen Honda's new design. They aren't trying that."

"Honda don't know shit about stock-car design. When they entered the last . . ."

Tucker let Doc's words fade off. He crossed to the triple glass doors of the room and stared out at the lake. March had stirred up the frigid water so it crashed on the shore like an angry fist pounding out its frustrations. Countless whitecaps were visible— big teeth that ate up the surface of the lake.

"Whatdaya think, Tuck?"

"Sorry, I wasn't listenin'."

"Young Ronny here agrees with you about the gas lines."

"I didn't . . ." The kid started to protest. He sounded horrified, as if agreeing with Tucker was tantamount to making a pact with the devil. Christ, was the entire six months going to be like this?

"You're outvoted then, old man."

Doc grumbled and handed the boy the plans. "Take these home and study them. Be familiar with the whole set by the next time you come."

From his vantage point, Tucker could see Ron's face lit with pleasure. "Is the car here yet?"

"In production as we speak," Doc told him. "The chassis and roll cage'll be delivered next week. We start puttin' on the shocks, suspension, springs and wheels soon as we get it."

Trying to join in, Tucker said, "Then it's called a rolling chassis."

Ron raised disgusted eyes to him. "I know that. I been around tracks all my life."

Again Tucker turned his back on them. Danny Donovan's apparition was bitter and surly and, fuck it, Tucker didn't want to deal with him. He'd told Doc so.

Tough shit, the old man had said. *It's a done deal.*

Doc was talking to him. "Tucker, we gotta set up this week's schedule."

Circling around, Tucker said glibly, "I'm not goin' to any cotillions, Doc. My time is yours. Schedule the kid any time you want." And just maybe Tucker could arrange to be absent.

Ron's voice was noticeably less surly when he said, "I, um, go to jail on Saturday."

"Hrrmph." Doc studied the calendar. "How 'bout after school on Monday, Wednesday and Friday? We can get the hours in then."

Ron nodded, mumbled something about meeting with a counselor first, then set times with Doc.

Tucker thought about Beth Donovan, and how she needed her son to work at the diner. In a moment of whimsy, he wondered if maybe he and the kid could trade places. Oh, sure, all he needed was to see those sad brown eyes full of forgiveness three times a week. It was hard enough trying to avoid her when she'd dropped Ron off here. Damn fool kid had a DUI and couldn't drive for a while.

Doc peered closely at Ron. "You smoke, boy?"

"Huh?"

"Asked if you smoked."

"Uh, yeah."

Doc snorted. "Come on out in the garage with me. We'll have a smoke before you go." He looked pointedly at Tucker. "Can't even have a goddamned cigar in my own livin' room now that I got a houseguest."

"You'll die from it, yet, with that angina," Tucker said.

"I'm too mean to die." He shuffled toward the garage with Ron behind him. The boy banged the door shut without another word.

Tucker turned away and his gaze caught on the bookcases. He might be able to keep Doc from smoking around him—and by God he'd get him to quit if it was the last thing he did—but he couldn't keep him from displaying their accolades like they were religious relics. Slowly, Tucker surveyed the showy mementos. Three Daytona 500 trophies. Three Winston Cups. Engraved plaques from big tracks like Darlington and Dover to the lesser wins in Pocono and Watkins Glen. A lifetime of achievements. And what did he have to show for it? No kids. No wife. No family to speak of. Just one lone man who was as ornery as a wounded bear most of the time. He wondered how Ron Donovan was going to deal with Doc. The kid was long on rebelliousness and short on patience.

Shrugging, Tucker returned to the glass doors, but his thoughts stuck with him like flypaper. Ron was going to jail. He hoped to God the weekend situation was better than most prisons. Tucker wondered how he could find out.

His mind immediately conjured up Ron's mother again. How were those slender shoulders going to bear this newest trial? Resigned, and placid, she'd *thanked* him, for God's sake. Her touch had been firm, and her scent—she'd smelled like magnolias—had wafted up to him.

Again, he wondered if he could do something for her. She'd refused the money he'd offered years ago. What the hell else could he do?

You can help her kid.

Damn, he wished he knew more about the jail thing. Then he remembered something. He crossed to the closet and ferreted out the jacket he'd worn to the Council meeting last Friday. In the pocket was Joe Murphy's card.

We'll need to stay in touch about this community service, if it goes down like this.

Tucker had tried to foist the card and the responsibility off on Doc—it had been his frigging idea after all—but Doc had dug in his heels and said Tucker'd have to deal with the agency.

Just another part of the punishment, he thought, heading toward the phone to call Murphy. Jesus Christ, how had he become a part of the Donovans' lives?

LANCASTER Correctional Facility loomed before them, a hulking brute of a building, made of stone that had weathered to an ominous gray. Out in the middle of nowhere, twenty miles to the north of Long Island and a half hour from Glen Oaks, it stood four stories tall and reminded Beth of a fortress. Ronny gasped as soon as it came into view. The dreary March Saturday morning was a fitting backdrop to the gloom that had settled into the van.

On her son's left, in the backseat, Beth grasped his hand; on his right, Annie had linked her arm with his. From the front seat, next to Linc, Margo, who'd taken the train up from the city the night before, said, "It looks a lot better than Alcatraz, kid. I think you can handle it." Beth recognized the traces of concern in her attempt to lighten the mood.

Linc reached over and squeezed her knee. He glanced in the rearview mirror. "We know you can handle it, don't we, buddy?"

They'd all agreed Ronny needed some *Scared Straight* tactics, but they weren't going to leave him hanging out to dry, either, with no adult support. They'd had too much of that kind of neglect themselves. Her son was frightened to death of this experience, and by God they were all going to help him through it.

They halted at an entrance booth, flashed the pass the jail had sent in a packet of instructions, and parked in the small lot. Beth slid out of the right side, and Ron followed her. He retrieved his belongings—he'd been told to bring a change of clothes, sleepwear, towel and toiletries, a book, quarters for candy and soda, and any medication in its original containers. As he dragged the duffel bag out of the back, she was reminded of the little boy she'd dropped off at a week-long camp when he was seven. His chin had stuck out in false bravado just like now, and he'd faced her with the same dark, wary eyes. Though he was over six feet tall instead of four, and wore black jeans, a shirt reading *It's not a phase* and black boots, he seemed as young and fearful as he had in his silly Camp Tomahawk T-shirt, denim shorts and navy blue sneakers. She'd cried on Margo's shoulder all the way home that day.

When everyone had exited, Linc locked the car and put his
arm around Ron; they walked to the entrance marked INMATES.

Inmates.

Oh God.

An armed guard buzzed them in. Painted a stark white with
nothing on the walls, the reception area held a desk and a structure behind it that looked like a huge cage with wire baskets. A
second uniformed guard, with a brush cut and a scar just below
his ear, manned the area; his name tag read, T. WELLS, CORREC-
TION OFFICER. He scowled at them. The only other occupant of
the room stood when they entered.

It was Joe Murphy.

"Joe?" Linc halted halfway to the desk.

Beth stopped, too, puzzled by Joe's presence.

Annie froze.

Margo stepped back and slid an arm around Annie's shoulder.

"What are you doing here?" Annie asked.

"I came to see if I could be any help."

Before Annie could respond, Ron said, "Thanks." He seemed
relieved Joe was there.

Joe nodded to the officer. "You'll have to surrender all your
personal belongings, Ron—wallet, comb, et cetera." He glanced
at Beth, gave her a weak smile, then stepped forward and guided
them both to the desk.

"Name," the guard growled.

"Ron Donovan." Ronny's voice cracked, which it hadn't done
since he was thirteen. Beth's stomach somersaulted. It all seemed
surreal, as if the guard was an actor out of *The Shawshank Redemption* and the monstrous building was a stage facade.

"Empty your pockets, and put the stuff in here." He handed
Ron a basket. "You goin' to Intake with him?" he asked Beth.

"Yes."

He faced Joe. "You his father?"

"I'm his social worker."

The guard gave a clipped nod. "You goin' in, too?"

Ron said, "Come, please. For Mom."

Beth nodded, grateful beyond measure Joe had had the fore-
sight to come out here. Though he was a far cry from the knight
in shining armor Annie used to see him as, Beth welcomed his
support today.

The guard asked Joe and Beth to give up their belongings,

then buzzed again, and indicated a heavy steel door. "Through there," was all he said.

Her knees like jelly, Beth turned to the door and took a step toward it but stumbled; Joe caught her arm.

"Easy," he whispered out of earshot to Ron. "We'll get through this."

Leaning on him, she followed her son into the jail.

They entered a larger area with a battered desk and four chairs. Behind the desk sat a man in a severe navy suit. He was big and black and wore wire-rimmed glasses. His name tag read, J. BAILEY, INTAKE OFFICER. "Ronald Donovan?" he asked coldly.

Ron nodded.

"Mrs. Donovan?" Bailey's voice held a trace of warmth as he extended his hand to her, shook it, and motioned them to sit. She noticed his wedding ring and wondered if he had any kids, wondered if he knew the agony of watching your child go through something so awful. He nodded to Joe. "Murphy."

Before she could question their familiarity, Bailey turned to Ron. "I'll outline for you and your mother what will happen this weekend, Donovan. Then you'll be taken inside alone." He faced Beth. "He'll be safe here, Mrs. Donovan, but we won't coddle him. This program is for men like Ron who are this close to prison." He made an inch-size gesture with his thumb and index finger.

Men like Ron? But her son was a . . . Oh, Lord, he was man.

"You're lucky to get in here." Bailey focused on Ron with a glacial stare. "And you do one thing wrong, you're out on your ear and we throw you into the system. You got that?"

"Yes, sir."

"Every weekend until the end of May you're ours at exactly eight A.M. on Saturday morning. For the first two weekends, you'll stay in a cell till Sunday night at seven, when your mother can pick you up. You'll be allowed out only for meals and breaks. This time is for you to think about what you've done and how lucky you are to be here. You'll have no contact with inmates but meals."

Ron nodded. So did Beth. At least he'd be safe.

"After those two weekends, you'll work in a supervised program." He picked up a folder. "Right now, we're painting for the Lancaster County Housing Authority. You'll start at nine A.M. on Saturday, work until seven at night. Meals will be provided.

You'll spend Sundays going to church, meeting with counselors and returning to the houses to paint for the afternoon."

Ron nodded again, but he gripped the edge of the chair. Beth reached out and covered one of his hands. Though it was big and masculine, it trembled in hers.

"There are only two rules here. Do exactly as you're told, and don't get in any trouble. You don't follow them, you're out. Being assigned to Lancaster's Weekend Program is a privilege, and if you blow it, you're history." He stood and checked the clock. "Time to go."

Beth felt her stomach pitch as Ron stood and stared at her. His eyes were so bleak, she couldn't bear to look at them, so she stepped forward and hugged him. He held on tight, and ludicrously, she remembered that when he'd turned eleven he'd stopped hugging her in front of others.

"I'm sorry, Mom," he whispered in her ear.

"You'll be okay, honey, I promise."

When he drew away, his eyes were moist. Beth almost lost it then, but she held back for him.

Joe took Ron's arm and drew him aside, said something Beth couldn't hear, and patted his shoulder. Then J. Bailey opened the steel door and took Ronny inside.

The door banged shut with a loud clang that reverberated through the barren room. She just watched after her son, numb. Then the feeling started, rising up from her lungs into her throat. She thought she might be sick, and clapped her hands over her mouth. Her knees buckled. Joe crossed to her, and with only a slight hesitation, took hold of her shoulders and pulled her close. She held on to him, clutching his soft sweater, listening to the soothing words he uttered. After a minute, she felt stronger and drew back. "Sorry, I'm not usually so . . . weak."

His gray eyes were full of warmth. "You got good reason, Bonnie."

Despite the horror of the circumstances, she smiled at the old nickname. "Thanks, Billy."

"Ronny'll be all right." Joe's tone turned sober. "And the first time is the toughest. Seeing everything. Its starkness. You won't even come in after today. Just drop him off at the door."

"Really? How do you know that?"

"I'm familiar with the routine."

Her eyes narrowed on him. "You knew they'd let you come in with me, didn't you? You knew the officer."

His expression said *guilty-as-charged*. "Yeah."

"Do they always let social workers in?"

His face reddened. "I got a little pull here. I've dealt with this facility before."

"Thanks Joe, for doing this for me. And for helping my son."

After a hesitation, Joe squeezed her neck. "You're welcome." He nodded to the exit. "You ready to go?"

She glanced at the steel door through which Ronny had passed. "Yes. I'll be all right."

"Sure you will. The Outlaws are tough, remember?"

She touched his arm. "I remember."

WHAT *the* hell *was he doing here?* Tucker leaned against the wall of the souvenir shop and stared at The Downtown Diner, like the stepchild he'd been, looking in from the outside. It was dusk and Beth Donovan had put up the CLOSED sign. The last patron had left, followed by what must be the employees, one tall and thin, one short and stubby. Mutt and Jeff, Doc had called them.

Through the front glass, he could see her move around. She straightened menus on the counter, then she wiped it off. She checked the coffeepots and headed to the front booths. When she leaned over a table, she looked up through the window. And froze.

Shit! Too late he realized he was visible underneath the new streetlight that had been part of the downtown renovation. His heartbeat picked up like it did before a big race. She stared at him for a few moments, then turned away. He blew out a heavy breath. A reprieve. She'd seen him but wasn't going to make an issue of it.

Pushing off from the brick wall, he decided to go back to Doc's, stop this stupid vigil that he'd been compelled to keep all day—driving through the streets, passing the diner several times, walking around town till he got too cold. Disgusted with himself, Tucker took a step toward his car when the front door of the diner opened. She stood in the doorway.

Go home, he told himself. *Leave it alone.*

He edged toward the road.

She waited.

He stepped down the curb.

She watched him.

He felt snared like the rabbits he used to catch in traps. Calling himself a no good, selfish fool, he crossed the street. Five feet away from her, he stopped, jammed his hands into his suede jacket and stared some more.

In the faint light of the street, he could see the lines of stress on her face. She'd pulled her hair back in some kind of tie, and it made her look as fragile as the tiny glass figurines his mother used to collect. Arms wrapped around her waist, she shivered in the thin cotton sweater she wore. Like the one she'd worn the night of the Council meeting, it was pink and soft as down. "It's cold out here. Would you like a cup of coffee?"

"I don't wanna bother you."

"You were watching me."

"I'm sorry. I didn't mean to intrude."

She shrugged. "You didn't. Come inside."

Mutely, he nodded and followed her into the diner. The lure was too great; he felt as if he'd been stripped of his own free will. Closing the door behind him, he stayed by it. She crossed the room, her legs impossibly long in the dark gray slacks. Behind the counter, she went to the coffee. A pot still warmed on the burner. He could smell the rich brew. "It's high test," she said softly. "I don't drink the decaf."

"Me, either." He unbuttoned his coat but left it on, not sure how long he'd be welcome, willing himself to break the spell and leave her. Instead, he approached the counter and took in details as he went. Great decor . . . cozy walls, neat recessed lighting. "Your place is nice."

"Haven't you been here before?"

"Not since . . ." His words trailed off. "Not in a long time."

She nodded, understanding. "It got a whole new face-lift, like the rest of the town. When the plans were made for your return, we all sunk some money into renovation."

Dropping onto a stool, he watched her set the mug in front of him. Steam filtered up from it, warming his cold cheeks. "I hope this works out for Glen Oaks."

"It already has. The hotels near the track and the bed-and-breakfasts within twenty miles are booked the entire week of the race in September." She sipped from her own mug. "Ticket sales for regular races are up, too."

"It'll be just like Indy week," he muttered. Doc was going to the big race again this year and badgered Tucker to go, but he'd refused, like always.

"Danny wanted to go there; he would have loved that—the track started booking NASCAR in ninety-three."

Tucker's stomach tightened. How much had he deprived young Danny Donovan of?

"I hear it's like Disney World." Beth's voice was dreamy.

Tucker remembered thinking the same thing the first time he raced there. "I'm sorry he never made it."

"We went to Daytona once as spectators. We took Ronny to Orlando afterward, to the Magic Kingdom." For a moment, her sad face glowed with fond memories, then it darkened as if she remembered present reality.

It made him ask, "How'd it go today?"

She scowled. "You knew he was going this morning?"

I thought about it all day. "Yeah. He, um, he told Doc how it all shook out."

Indicating the street, she asked, "Is that why you were out there?"

He nodded.

She bit her lip. "It went as well as can be expected."

"I'm sorry," he said.

"It was just so hard to leave him there, alone." Her eyes filled with tiny unshed tears that sparkled off the lights above.

"I wish . . ." He didn't finish. What the hell could he say? I wish I hadn't killed your husband? Ronny's father?

The moisture receded. "Mr. Quaid, we've had this discussion. Ronny's problems aren't your fault."

"Please, make it Tucker."

"Then call me Beth." She gave him a shy small smile that tugged at his heartstrings.

His eyes darted to the wall at the end of the room, decorated with racing pictures. In the center was a big framed photo. The temptation was too great. He stood. Beckoned by the memories, enticed by the past, he crossed to it.

There he was, the ghost that haunted Tucker to this day, in living color. He stared at the man he'd killed, noting his small stature. Most NASCAR drivers were Donovan's height and

build—five seven or eight, one sixty. Tucker himself was more
Richard Petty's size, with his six feet and heavier frame. They
had to make the driver's windows bigger for him to slide
through. His eyes burned as he took in the pictures. Donovan
held a helmet under his arm, and was dressed in a black-and-
orange racing suit, backdropped by a Ford emblazoned with
Mobil Oil on the side.

A lump lodged in Tucker's throat as he felt Beth come up behind him. "That was when he qualified for the ninety-two race."

The race he'd crashed in.

"He was ecstatic." She smiled wistfully. "It took him a long
time to get a sponsor." Her voice held warmth. Love. Devotion.
For one brief moment, Tucker was swamped with regret for
never allowing a woman close enough to feel that way about
him. Staring at Donovan, awash with guilt and grief, Tucker
shuddered.

He felt a hand on his arm. "It wasn't your fault, Tucker."

The use of his given name was rife with forgiveness. He
looked down at her. Her eyes were wide and sincere. Her lips
held a faint blush of coral, and were smiling sadly. How could
she possibly be this good, this forgiving? "Thanks for that,
Beth."

She left her hand where it was. "You have to forgive yourself." She glanced at Danny. "We all do, for our past."

Tucker swallowed hard. "You really believe that, don't you?"

"With all my heart. If I didn't, I couldn't—"

From behind, Tucker felt a cold draft and heard a booming
voice growl, "What's going on here?"

He turned. So did Beth. Quickly she dropped her hand, but the
woman and man poised by the door hadn't missed the gesture.
They were about sixty, both gray-haired, dressed to the nines for
a Saturday night out. The man wore glasses and an outraged expression on his face.

Tucker had seen these people before.

They were Julia and Carl Donovan.

Danny's parents.

BETH edged in front of Tucker like a lion defending her cub.
The whimsical thought would have made her smile if the circumstances had been different—he had several inches and at

least fifty pounds on her. Still, she felt compelled to shield him from what she knew was coming. "Julia, Carl. What are you doing here?"

Danny's father, a big man with square-cut features and a glint in his eye honed by years of corporate success, straightened his shoulders; he was still trim and fit at sixty-two. "I asked you a question, Beth."

Lord, she was too tired for this. Usually she could tolerate the Donovans' imperiousness. Danny had called them Charles and Princess Di behind their backs, and as a young married couple, he and Beth had joked their way through their dealings with his parents. Tonight she had little reserve for anyone, least of all her *royal* in-laws. But she'd learned early on that to back down with these people had dire consequences.

It isn't that we don't like her, dear. She's just not right for you.

"And I asked you a question, too." Angling her chin, she watched them with hard-won determination.

"We've been upset all day about Ronny," Julia finally told her, snagging a tissue out of her purse and delicately patting her eyes. Beth didn't doubt she'd cried over Ronny's circumstances. Her fine-boned features and well-bred facade showed lines of strain. In their own way, they loved him.

I'm sorry, Mrs. Donovan, but I love your son.
You're only eighteen, what do you know about love?
Enough.

"I know you're concerned, Julia. I stopped by to give you a report when I got back from Lancaster, but no one was home."

"Carl took me shopping in the city to cheer me up. We just finished dinner at the Country Club and drove by your house, but you weren't there."

"Beth, why is that man here?" Carl glared at Tucker.

Beth heard what might be a groan behind her. Remembering his green eyes so dark with remorse gave her strength. "We've been over this a hundred times. Mr. Quaid isn't the enemy, Carl. If you must cast blame for Danny's death, blame the sport."

"How Christian of you." Julia wasn't too upset to get that little dig in.

That brother of hers, he'll last as a minister about as long as snow in April.

Tucker shifted and came around beside her. "I'm sorry if my bein' here upsets you, Mr. Donovan. Mrs. Donovan." His voice was gritty with emotional strain. "I saw Beth in the diner and stopped to see how Ron was."

"You stay away from Ronny," Carl spat out, his face reddening. "He's to have nothing to do with that damned sport."

Beth drew in a deep breath. "You know that the court assigned Ronny community service with Mr. Quaid."

"You should have let us call our judge friend." Again, Julia sniffled.

Let us send Ronny to that prep school in Vermont where his father went . . . Ronny should be firmly disciplined . . . maybe he can stay with us. . . . Beth, you're just not capable of handling this kind of thing, especially with your background. . . .

"No, that wouldn't have been right." Getting Ronny off, as the Donovans had done in the past, only seemed to have made her son's rebellious streak worse. But Beth held on to her patience. The two people before her still suffered greatly over the loss of their only child; their grandson's decline into crime had almost leveled them.

"Is it right that you've allowed this man into your lives?" Carl asked accusingly.

"I'm leavin'." Tucker's stark words were clipped. When she stole a quick glance at him, she saw his mask was back in place.

Gripping his arm, she said, "No. I think we should all sit down and talk about this. Clear the air."

Julia tossed back her hair. "I have no intention of sitting anywhere near this man. If we'd had our way, he would never have been allowed to set foot in Glen Oaks again." Though Carl was on the town council, even his inimitable power and money couldn't keep them from voting for Tucker's return. "As a matter of fact, we've decided to go to Europe for several weeks just to get out of this town while . . ." Julia stared at Beth. ". . . well, you know." She faced her husband. "Let's go, Carl."

But Carl wasn't finished yet. He grasped his wife's arm and leveled angry eyes on Beth. "Danny would be very disappointed in you, Mary Elizabeth." With that, the couple swept out the door, full of righteous indignation and misplaced fury.

Beth wilted. The day had already been too hard before this onslaught of Donovan rage. She crossed to the counter and dropped down on a stool. Picking up her coffee, she sipped it. It was cold, and bitter, like life had gotten. She set it down and buried her face in her hands. Tucker came up behind her. Instead of leaving, he sank onto the seat next to her.

The tears came. She tried to battle them back but she couldn't, not after taking Ronny to that awful place that morning, not after the attack by Danny's parents. The flood broke through, and she was powerless to stop it.

Tucker's hand went to her shoulder; he moved in close, and his arm encircled her. Then she really cried, deep wrenching sobs that wracked her whole body. Dimly she was aware of his soothing motions on her back, of nonsense words of consolation. Strong fingers stroked her hair.

When her sobs abated, she sniffled and drew back. So did he. She glanced over at him. "Sorry, I'm not usually so emotional."

"You got the right." He tugged a handkerchief out of his pocket and handed it to her. She wiped her cheeks and blew her nose.

He sat back, picked up his cold coffee and sipped. Finally he asked, "Mary Elizabeth?"

It made her smile, which she suspected was his intent. "My real name. I'm Mary Elizabeth, my best friends are Mary Margaret, and Mary Anne. We got a big kick out of it when we were young."

"Ah." He waited, then angled his head to the door. "Are they always like that with you?"

Closing her eyes, she saw the Donovans the day Danny told them she was pregnant and they were getting married. She'd insisted on going with him to his house on the hill. *The palace,* he'd called it.

There are other ways to deal with this, son, you don't have to marry her.

But I want to marry her. I'm happy about the baby.

First her brother gets you into that gang. Now this . . .

"Yes, they always have."

"Why?"

She sighed and scrubbed her hands over her face. "The classic story. Girl from wrong side of the tracks corrupts fair-haired boy. It was my fault he raced. We lured him into the gang. I shouldn't have gotten pregnant before we were married." She shot him a self-effacing smile. "I could continue the litany, but the thing about it is . . . they were right."

"No."

"Yes, they were. Danny was pretty straight before he got involved with Linc and me. At first his falling in with us was an act of rebellion. But he got tight with Linc, and then me." She didn't hide the smile. "He fell hard and fast, and I kept him there."

"Did you love him?"

"Right up until the day he died, I was crazy about him. He was nothing like his parents. Money meant little to him. Prestige nothing. All he really cared about was me, Ronny and racing. He had all of it until he . . ."

Tucker stiffened.

She swiveled around and faced him. "Don't say you killed him, Tucker. You didn't."

He angled his head to the door. "They think so."

"They're into blame. Their world is full of it."

"I'm sorry."

"For them?"

He shook his head. "That you have to deal with them."

"I . . . care about them."

Tucker's jaw dropped.

"I do. They stopped their pressure a few years after Ronny was born. It only started again when he got into trouble." She was still facing him, her feet on the rung of the stool.

He swiveled around to watch her and crossed his arms over his chest. The position accented his big shoulders and long, lean frame. "When was that?"

"In ninth grade. Just like me." This time she glanced at the door. "They think it's genetic—that Ronny gets into trouble."

"Oh, Christ."

"Don't swear."

He arched a brow. "This from a former member of the Outlaws?"

"You know about the Outlaws?"

"Sorry ma'am. Word travels fast in these parts."

His humor made her tell him about the nicknames they had. He smiled broadly.

She returned it. "You have a nice smile," she said watching the corners of his mouth turn up.

"So do you."

She averted her gaze because she thought, for one crazy second, he was going to touch her again. The hum of the refrigerator turning on filled the silence.

"And you're a good person," he added.

She stared at the door. "They don't think so."

"Well, I do." He slid off the stool. "I'm goin'."

She nodded.

"Thanks for the coffee." He glanced around the diner. "Want me to wait till you close up?"

She chuckled. "No, I'm pretty good at taking care of myself."

His eyes burned with some emotion. Something that had nothing to do with what they were talking about. "Yeah, I can tell." He held her gaze. "Thanks again, Beth. Maybe I'll see you when you drop Ronny off on Monday."

Nodding, she whispered, "Good night, Tucker."

He reached over and squeezed her hand. "Good night."

Then he walked out of the diner.

Beth stared after him for a long time, the imprint of his touch still warm on her skin.

EIGHT

ANNIE waited by the window, watching for Joe. Faith was so
excited that he was coming, she didn't have the heart to put a
damper on it. Though inside, she churned with fear, and anger,
she forced herself to be cheerful about this first visit. Trying to
think of something good about him, she remembered taking
Ronny to prison Friday and how Joe had come for Beth.

Her friend had been alarmingly pale when they came out of
the interior of the jail, but she seemed calm. Immediately, Linc
rose and crossed to her. "You okay, kiddo?" he'd asked.

"I'm fine."

Margo shook her head and stood. "You're not fine." The
fringe of the suede vest she wore with jeans and cowboy boots
shimmied with her movement. Annie had been reminded of their
gang's title. The five of them were so different now. Who had
those kids been?

Annie stood, too. "You don't have to be strong with us."

Beth gave a small smile. "I'm not. I almost fell apart in there
with Joe."

Annie's eyes had narrowed on her ex-husband. His tan
sweater looked expensive, as did the creamy brown leather jacket
he'd thrown over it. She'd noticed the designer logo on his jeans.
Turning away, she grabbed her fleece jacket, shrugged into it and
said, "Let's go."

Margo and Linc entwined arms with Beth, and Annie was forced to fall into step with Joe next to her. Immediately her breath seized up in her throat; she was once again dwarfed by his size. She struggled to take in air.

As if he sensed her anxiety, he moved away when they got outside, walking parallel but not close. When they reached the van, they all faced each other.

Beth spoke first. "Thanks Joe, for what you did in there."

He patted her shoulder. He'd always been a toucher. Very physical. *Too physical.* "I'm glad I could help. Would you like me to come back with you Sunday night?"

Annie had bitten her tongue to keep from saying they didn't need him. Ultimately she wanted what was best for Beth and Ronny.

"No, thanks." Beth smiled. "This was more than enough."

He fished in his pocket and took out a card. "I'll be in the city if you change your mind. Here's my number."

Beth thanked him again, and Linc shook his hand. "I appreciate this, too."

Begrudgingly, Margo echoed the sentiments. Annie said nothing, thinking if she remained stone-faced and mute, she'd *feel* nothing inside.

Joe's expression was somber when he faced her. "Could I talk to you before you leave?"

Fear fluttered in her stomach.

It must have shown in her eyes, because he added, "Right out here. The others can watch you from the car and I'll stay back." His tone made her agree. It was so sad, it penetrated the wall she'd built up against him.

"All right."

As the others climbed into the van, the wind picked up, and she shivered in the light jacket and simple denim dress.

"Button your coat," he said automatically. "It's cold."

She arched a brow. "I can take care of myself, Joe. I've done it for six years and I never plan to stop."

"Sorry, it was reflex." He drew in a heavy breath. "I'd like to know the setup for tomorrow."

Linc had scheduled him to see the kids Sunday afternoon. "Setup?"

"Where will I meet with Faith and Matt?"

She bit her lip. "We should do what's best for the kids. When is Linc free?"

"One to five."

"You could take them out somewhere. But it's hard to find something to entertain both of them at once. There's such an age difference."

He grinned then, an old familiar smile that used to wrap around her heart. She'd seen it when they'd first had sex in the backseat of his Chevy and he'd said, *I'll always love you, baby.* She remembered it from when he asked her to marry him on that warm summer night with the stars twinkling above him. And it had been there when he used to stoop to take Matt out of his crib in the morning and nuzzle the baby's neck. "They're great kids, Annie. Faith's a beautiful child. You've done a good job with them."

She ignored the compliment. He was too dangerous to encourage. "Maybe you and Linc could take them to lunch at Beth's place."

"All right. And after?"

"You seem to have an idea."

"No, this is your call."

A hunch told her he was lying, that he had something in mind. The old controlling Joe was just clawing to come out.

What's best for the kids? she reminded herself.

"Maybe you should come back to the house afterward. That way, if you do something with one of them, the other will be in familiar surroundings. You can divide your time between them. And Linc might be able to get some work done, or even rest up. God knows he needs it."

"All right."

"I'll expect you and Linc at one." She focused on him. "Don't come without him."

He recoiled at the emotional slap in the face. "I won't." He jammed his hands in his pockets. "But for the record, I'm recovered. I'm not going to hurt you or them ever again."

Annie straightened. "Sometimes, when I dance, my shoulder still bothers me from where it was dislocated twice. By you." With that she turned, refusing to buy into the agonized look on his face. Head high, she got in the van and slammed the door shut.

As they pulled out, she caught a glimpse of him, standing in the dismal morning, backdropped by the foreboding jail, all alone.

Which was exactly what he deserved. . . .

From her vigil by the window, she saw Linc's car pull into the driveway, bringing her back to reality. Her heartbeat automatically sped up at the thought of letting Joe into her house.

"Mommy," Faith called out excitedly. "Daddy's here."

Annie swallowed back her fear. For her daughter's sake, she'd pull this off.

"Yes, honey, I know." She swallowed hard. "He's here."

"YOU look like a martyr on his way to the Colosseum." From the other side of the car, Linc's voice was filled with humor and good-old-boy razzing. Joe was reminded of the nights he, Linc and Danny had caroused around the city on their bikes without the girls. Sometimes he missed that kind of camaraderie so much it stung. Other than Pete and Taylor, Joe had no good friends.

"Nope. Martyrs don't get what they deserve." Joe's tone was dry.

As he shut off the car, Linc said, "They're good kids. It'll be fine."

Silent, Joe stared at her house. It was a moderate-sized, older two-story with a high, pitched roof. A jaunty little weather vane perched on the peak. Sided in white aluminum with black shutters, the early afternoon sun sparkled off the exterior. "It's nice," he said simply. "She's done well."

"She has."

"No thanks to me."

Linc sighed heavily. "You sent money—"

Joe interrupted him. "Forget I said that. I swore not to put you in the middle of all this. You're on her side and that's the way it should be."

"I'm not sure there has to be sides."

"If there does, she needs you."

"What do you need, Joe?"

He swallowed hard and glanced at his old buddy. "A chance with the kids. That's all."

"Then let's go. I think I see pink ribbons at the front window."

Joe's head snapped around. Peeking out between the drapes was a tiny heart-shaped face; blond hair was indeed pulled back with ribbons and there was a huge smile on her face. For a moment, Joe was dumbstruck by her innocent acceptance. "I don't deserve this."

"It's for God to judge. If you'd come to church this morning, you'd have heard that in my sermon."

"Really?"

Linc smiled easily. "Seems to me everybody in this town could use a reminder of the need to do unto others . . ."

"I didn't want to upset anybody by coming to church."

"Were you back? I had the impression at the jail you spent the weekend in New York."

"I had business in New York yesterday, but I came back last night." He reached for the door. Linc's arm shot out and gripped his sleeve. Joe faced him.

"Sorry I have to ask this, but the business you had in town? You're not into anything you shouldn't be, are you?"

Joe cocked his head in question.

Linc scanned Joe's leather jacket, pressed jeans and open cream-colored shirt. They were in stark contrast to Linc's cheap jeans and denim shirt. "Pretty nice duds for a social worker."

Ah, he got it. It shouldn't have hurt so much; he should have been prepared for it. He needed to be ready for these emotional ambushes. "I'm not into anything illegal. Occasionally, I have a second job."

"Occasionally?"

Joe battled back a grin. *This* was not something he wanted to share with the man who used to razz him about the kind of underwear he wore. "It's a long story. But it's harmless."

Linc waited. "All right. I'll take your word for it." Softly, he added, "You could think about trusting me, Joe."

Ever the minister. "Thanks." He drew in a deep breath. "Let's go face the lions in their den."

More like a friendly cub, Joe thought, as Annie opened the front door and a little bundle pounced from the other side of the room, throwing herself, literally, into his arms. "Daddy!"

He grabbed her and held on tight, closing his eyes to savor the feel of her sturdy little body. She smelled like chocolate. "Hi, princess." When he glanced up, Annie was watching them, her face grave. Dressed in paint-splattered jeans and a long T-shirt, she looked fifteen again. From behind her, Matt leaned against the archway to the dining room. Every line of his body—from his damp hair to his Yankees sweatshirt to his blue jeans—was taut with adolescent mutiny. "Hi, Matt. Hello, Annie."

"Joe." Her tone was cold; he studied her face. There were lines of fatigue on her brow and around her mouth again today. He had a flash of her coming home from hours of dancing, absolutely depleted. When he was sober, and sane, he'd rub her down for a long half hour, draw a bath, then put her to sleep with tender sex. The image stunned him for a minute. Years ago, he'd forced himself to stop thinking about her that way.

Faith scrambled out of his arms and down to the floor. She grabbed his hand and tugged him inside. "Come on, Daddy." She seemed unaware of the tense dynamics filling the air. "I maked you lunch."

"I thought we were going out." He stepped inside and Linc followed. From the corner of his eye, he saw Annie kiss Linc's cheek and thank him for coming. Jealousy sparked inside him but he didn't allow it to kindle.

"You're not. Faith wanted to fix you lunch." Annie gave him a challenging look. "Think you can handle that?"

"Of course. I'll put my best foot forward."

"What does that mean?" Faith asked as she drew him to the dining room.

"To make a good impression."

"I don't get it," Matt said sulkily. The absence of a greeting, let alone Faith's warm welcome, spoke volumes.

"It's an idiom," Joe told him, "a phrase people use that doesn't mean what the words say."

Faith frowned. "Why do people say it?"

Joe shrugged. "Usually it comes down through the ages." He surveyed the table and broke out into a big grin.

"I maked it all by myself," Faith announced proudly.

"Well, you're a regular five-star chef."

Set out were the most lopsided sandwiches he'd ever seen, piled high on plates. If he wasn't mistaken, they were peanut butter and jelly. Next to them was a cut-up banana, a quartered apple and a pitcher of milk.

"Mommy helped me with the cake."

"Cake?"

"Uh-huh. It's in the kitchen."

"This is baby food," Matt said.

Faith's face fell.

Without missing a beat, Joe dropped down to his knee. "It's been a long time since I've had PB and J." He grinned. "And chocolate is my favorite kind of cake."

That brought the sun back into her face. "How'd you know it's chocolate?"

"You got a little on your sleeve, honey." With a flourish he stood and pulled out a chair. "May I seat you, madam?"

Faith giggled but sat with dramatic flair. From the corner of his eye, he saw Matt scowl. "You know those idioms, Matt? They have some interesting origins."

He saw a glimmer of interest before the kid doused it. "So?"

"Why don't we sit and I'll tell you about some?"

Annie had been standing in the doorway watching the scene. Finally, she said, "I'll be upstairs."

Linc was next to her. "Since I've already eaten, I'll be in the living room. I think the Knicks are on."

And he could see them from where he'd watch TV. The fact that Joe needed a chaperone cut him to the quick. He'd discussed it with Pete yesterday, and his counselor had preached patience once again.

Faith talked away as the three of them choose food from the plates. After several minutes of her chatter, and Matt's incessant pout, Joe addressed his son. "So, Matt, you wanna know where *putting your best foot forward* came from?"

Matt shrugged.

"I do," Faith said, bless her soul.

"Well, in earlier centuries, wealthy people were overly concerned with a person's beauty. They wore ruffled sleeves and powdered wigs."

Faith's eyes were owl wide. "Even the boys?"

"Yep. Many rich men, who didn't have anything better to do, took pride in showing off a good pair of legs. Some went so far as to think one leg might be more attractive than the other."

"That's stupid." Matt donned a sneer, but Joe could see he was listening attentively.

"At parties and balls—dances—they'd find a place where they could stand with their best looking leg in front."

Faith giggled. "It's dumb, Daddy."

"I know. People do dumb things." Joe smiled. "Anyway, that's where we get *putting your best foot forward.*"

Matt was silent, munching on an apple, which he'd dipped in

some caramel sauce. Almost against his will he said, "There's lots of those sayings in sports. I read about them."

"Yeah? Tell me some." Joe helped himself to the fruit. It was tart and, cut by the sauce, tasted better to him today than Godiva chocolate.

Matt's natural enthusiasm kicked in and his blue eyes glimmered with interest. It took him a minute to quell it. "I don't remember any."

"Are there some for dance?" Faith asked ingenuously.

"Hmm, I'll have to think about that." Joe smiled. "Tell me about your dance."

"We're getting ready for our recital now."

"What's its theme?"

"Broadway Musicals." She studied him. "How do you know about recitals?"

"I went to every one of Mommy's when she was in high school."

"Mommy's a beautiful dancer."

"She was then, too. I remember one time when she was in *Swan Lake,* she looked so pretty it almost made me cry." Joe could still see her float across the stage, dressed in puffy white gossamer, her long hair in a knot at her neck. The fleeting image was tainted when he remembered what happened afterward. He hadn't been happy about the male partner who had touched her. His throat seized up at the loathsome image.

"Daddy, you okay?"

"Sure." He forced himself out of the past and struggled to keep the bad memories at bay. "Tell me what song you're dancing to."

"My class got three." Her tone was proud. "Aunt Suzie picked her favorites for us."

Faith told him all about her recital; she fawned over him as he ate the somewhat gooey cake she baked, and that Matt complained about. It didn't take Joe long to realize he was going to have to talk to Matt about his behavior. He got the opportunity when Faith fell asleep on the couch while watching Disney's *Sleeping Beauty.*

His son had gone to the dining room to do some homework, and Linc had trekked upstairs to see Annie. Joe heard noise—scraping and some pounding up there—and wondered what she was doing. Matt demanded his attention, though, and Joe left the couch and found his son with *Sports Illustrated* out over his math book. When he saw Joe, he promptly secreted the magazine away.

"Need any help here?" Joe asked, plopping down in a chair. Once he'd recovered, and gone back to school, he found that everything came easily to him.

"Nope." Matt pretended interest in his schoolwork.

"Thought of any of those sports idioms?"

The kid swallowed hard and glanced at the magazine. "No."

"Matt, I—"

"Do you mind? I got homework to do."

Drawing in a heavy breath, Joe shook his head. "Yes, I do mind. Especially your attitude."

Sulky blue eyes leveled on him. "I don't care what you think."

"Well, I care what you think. And I'm not going to give up on trying to forge a relationship with you."

Matt said nothing, but Joe saw the need in his eyes. To believe. To make peace with his father. He'd seen it a hundred times in the kids he worked with.

And remembered vividly having felt it himself.

"However, I won't allow you to hurt Faith because you're mad at me."

Little-boy innocence won out. "Hurt Faith?"

"You were nasty about the meal. You knew she was excited about it."

"I wasn't nasty."

"Yes, son, you were. Because you're mad at me."

"Don't call me that."

"What?"

"Son."

Joe hadn't even realized what he'd said. But he'd go with it. "You are my son."

"Yeah, some father you are." He threw back the chair. "I don't wanna be with you anymore."

Joe snagged a handful of his sweatshirt and held him back. "I'm sorry to hear that, Matt. Because I want very badly to be with you. I'll let you go now, but remember what I said about Faith. Don't take your anger at me out on her."

As soon as he released the shirt, Matt bolted away. Joe heard heavy footfalls on the steps, then a door slammed.

Sighing, he mentally repeated his mantra. *Remember why you're here. You can do this. You've changed.*

His gaze fell on the *Sports Illustrated* under Matt's book. Leaning over he slid it out and perused the cover. His spirits lifted when he saw it was an older edition, and in big black letters on the bottom of the cover, "Where did those sports terms come from?" He glanced after Matt. Maybe this wasn't such a disaster with his son as he thought.

NINE

———

LINC bolted awake, his body covered in sweat. He was breath-ing hard and didn't know where he was. Immediately, he reached for Margo, but his hand landed on a hard surface. Sucking in air, his eyes began to focus. He was in his church apartment. On the couch. He was thirty-eight, instead of seventeen.

And Margo was not here.

Laying back on lumpy cushions, he glanced at his watch, the lighted dial telling him it was almost midnight. Now he remem-bered. He'd come back to his apartment from an emergency hos-pital visit and found a message from Margo. It said she wasn't home and wouldn't be able to talk tonight.

But he could tell by the tone of her voice, she didn't want to talk to him. Pissed off at her distancing, he didn't bother calling her back.

Not a good idea, son. God's voice came to him in the dark-ness.

No?

You know it isn't. You can't help her if you don't talk to her.

Does she need my help?

What do you think?

Come on, God. Give me a break. Just answer the damn ques-tion.

God paused. *All right, call her.*

And?

Don't blow it. Be patient. Kind. Understanding.

Hey, that's me to a tee, he said, though sometimes, with Margo, he reverted back to Jesse James.

I liked Jesse, too, you know?

Oh, sure, he told God as he picked up the cordless and dialed her number.

After four rings, he heard a slurred, " 'Ello."

"Aw, geez, I woke you."

"Linc?"

"Yeah. I'm sorry. Listen, baby, go back to sleep."

"What time is it?"

"Midnight. You're a night owl, and you're usually still up."

"It's fine. Actually, I dozed off on the couch reading some specs." A rustle. A chuckle. "I was dreaming about you." Her defenses must be really down from sleep for her to tell him that.

"Funny, I was dreaming about you, too."

"Bet mine was better, Rev."

"Yeah?" God, she could be a tease. "Don't count on it."

"It was X-rated."

"Mine, too."

"Shit." She sighed. "This isn't doing us any good."

"Margo, can't we—"

"No!" Her voice lost its husky teasing. "Why'd you call?"

"It's Sunday night."

"Didn't you get my message?"

He could lie. But he caught a glimpse at the cross she'd given him, illuminated from the outside streetlamp, and decided not to. "Yeah. I was hoping you'd be back by now."

"Nothing's wrong, is it? With you or Beth or Annie?" She drew in a breath. "That goddamned Murphy didn't do something, did he?"

"Please, honey. Don't take God's name in vain." Usually she didn't, out of deference to him.

"I don't believe in God, Linc." Her tone told him she was exasperated.

"I know. And I can't tell you how sad that makes me."

A very long pause. Then, "Why would I, Linc?"

He stilled. She *never* wanted to talk about this. God was right in advising him to call her. "I know you suffered at the hands of the commune, in His name. But that wasn't God working there. It was evil."

"If He existed, He should have helped me."

"I think we're what we are today because of the troubles we had then."

"I think He abandoned us then. I'll never forgive him for that. I'll never trust him."

"God never abandoned any of us. He got us through it all."

"You got me through it."

"Then you owe me. Give God a chance."

"No."

"Think about it."

"No."

"Please."

"Either change the subject or I'm hanging up."

Change the subject, boy.

"All right, how's work?"

Her hesitation was just long enough to alert him. "Good. We're going hot and heavy on the new products."

"And Pretty Boy? Is he still going hot and heavy for you?"

I told you to be kind and understanding, Linc.

"I'm sorry," he said before she could answer. "I hope everything's okay with him. I know you were upset about his hitting on you."

"I think I overreacted, Linc."

"What?"

"I overreacted. He misread the signals."

Linc's whole body froze. The only thing he could feel was the rapid tattoo of his heart. "You mean, you . . ." He couldn't get the words out. "You . . . led him on?"

"No! Of course not. But we spend a lot of time together. And he's a toucher, you know. I realized I let him be affectionate, maybe more than I should."

A long pause on his end this time. Finally he asked, "Margo, what are you saying?"

"Nothing, this is coming out wrong."

"Exactly what signals did you give him?"

"Don't interrogate me."

Calm down, Linc. This isn't helping.

"I'm sorry," he said again. "Really. Please, talk to me."

"Linc, he and his wife are having problems."

Oh great. "Margo, that's the oldest line in the book."

"No, really, he's messed up because of it. We're friends. He turned to me . . . it was no big deal."

Use your degree in psychology, jerk. "You thought it was a big deal Friday night."

"I was just upset about Ronny. And Tucker Quaid showed up. And seeing Joe again. Fuck it, Linc, that was emotional for all of us."

"I know. But don't fall for Philip's lines, honey."

"They aren't lines." Her voice had gone cold.

"The hell they aren't."

"Linc, you're pushing. You can't run my life anymore."

"I don't want to run it. I want to be part of it." A big part. Bigger than she'd allow.

"You are. But we can't depend on each other like we used to."

"Why?"

"You know why!" Now she was pissed.

Well, so was he. And just like in the old days, her temper spiked his own. "If you'd try to get over your hang-up about religion and put some trust in God, maybe we'd have a chance."

"Hang-up? How dare you? Of all people, you should know . . ." She stopped abruptly. Then she said, "This conversation is over. Good night, Linc." And the phone went dead.

He stared at the receiver, feeling like he'd just gotten off a roller coaster. Disoriented. Displaced. How the *hell* had the conversation taken that turn?

You weren't kind and understanding, son.

No kidding.

You blew it.

Should I call her back?

No, you'll just make it worse. Go to sleep. Things will be clearer in the morning.

It took all of Linc's willpower to listen to God's advice. Slowly, he got up and headed toward the bedroom.

AFTER hanging up, Margo rose from the couch and strode into her bedroom. As she undressed, she thought about the phone conversation with Linc. She couldn't stand fighting with him. But he was so hardheaded sometimes, and she got so mad at him. For asking her to think about God.

For choosing God over her.

Ah, she thought as she slid into three-hundred-dollar silk pj's. *There's the rub.*

She went through her nightly routine. Brush her teeth. Clean her face. In the mirror, she caught sight of her eyes. They were troubled. She dropped the soap in the sink. Damn it, she hated hurting Linc. It made her sick to her stomach. And attacking him tonight would hurt him in a way nobody else could. She knew she had power over him, knew she could inflict a kind of pain that would stay with him for a long time.

"You're a bitch," she told herself. "A first-class bitch. He's the nicest man you know, and you jab him about religion, jab him about his life all the time."

Finishing in the bathroom, she padded to the bed and slipped underneath the Ralph Lauren sheets. It was dark in her room. Dark like . . .

Usually, she short-circuited the images. But tonight she didn't. Instead she let them come.

Because, if she was honest, she was tempted to think about God. Okay, so she'd think about Him. About what He'd let happen to her. In His name.

It was dark, then, like now.

Only she lay on dirt, instead of silk sheets, and she was cold, so cold, she was shivering. . . .

And crying. "Mama, please, let me out of here."

No answer.

Then she heard it. The scratching. Oh, no. She was in the basement of the commune. In a small room off to the side. It smelled like rank water and old potatoes. They kept food down here and it must have spoiled.

Something was after the food.

Rats.

"Mama, please!"

She didn't know why she was yelling. They wouldn't hear her. They'd left her here forever. She wasn't sure how long, because there was no light. But it had to be more than a day. She was starving, and cold, and dirty . . .

"Mama . . ."

Maybe she should just pray. Get it over with. If she did what they said, if she gave in, maybe it wouldn't be so bad. She could bide her time until Linc got her out of this godforsaken town.

God. Where was He?

More scratching, then something scurried past her. She screamed. Her whole body shook. Okay, she'd try it. The words fell clumsily from her mouth. "God, please, if you're there. Please, help me, I can't stand this. I'm so scared."

Nothing.

She waited.

Still nothing.

She tried three more times.

And nothing happened.

Except a rat ran across her foot making her yell out again. Except that she got sick to her stomach from the fear that it might bite her. Except that she had to wait hours and hours more until at last someone released her. . . .

She shook herself out of the past; she was cold and hungry and shivering again. It always happened when the images came. She sat up and switched on a light. She was no longer that vulnerable fifteen-year-old girl.

Who had indeed prayed. To a God, who could have helped her but hadn't.

If you'd try to get over your hang-up about religion and put some trust in God, maybe we'd have a chance.

Like hell, she thought, lying back down but leaving the light on.

Linc was wrong. There *was* no God.

"YOU look like you just lost your best friend, big brother."

Linc peered up at his sister from the turkey soup he'd been stirring, staring at, and occasionally sipping. "I think I have."

Beth wiped her hands on the towel around her waist and leaned over the counter of her diner. The bright lights were dimmed to a pleasant glow in deference to the late hour. "Margo?"

"Give the lady a cigar."

"Something happen?"

"Yeah, we had a whopper of a fight on the phone last night."

"A fight? You two? That's headline news."

He grunted. He'd been an ass. He'd tried to call her at work and apologize, but she'd been in a meeting and never called him back.

The meeting was probably with Pretty Boy. Was she with him right now?

He misread the signals.

Beth gave him a quick squeeze on the arm. "I'm sorry. I know this is hard for you." There were few secrets between sister and brother. There never had been.

With uncustomary vehemence, Linc slapped the countertop. "You know, just when I think I've accepted not being able to have her like I want, it starts again."

"You've seen a lot of her lately." Beth bit her lip. "Because of this thing with Ronny. Maybe that's why."

"Maybe." Proximity had never been good for them. Sometimes, when she was in touching distance, Linc remembered vividly what it was like to be inside her. They both knew it and limited their contact as much as they could. "You miss sex, Bethy?"

"Yeah, I do." She glanced toward the end of the counter. "Lately, especially."

"Me, too." He studied his sister. "Sorry you gave up on Roman Becker?"

"No." She grabbed a cup of coffee and circled around to sit next to him. Facing sideways, she hooked her feet on the rungs of his stool. He was reminded of the time they spent at their grandparents' home after their parents died. They were forced to share a room because of the tiny house. Sometimes, at night when she was scared, she'd crawl into his bed and they'd sleep back to back. "He isn't my type."

Linc glanced at the wall of pictures. "Just Danny, huh?"

Thoughtful, his sister shook her head. "I could love again, Linc. It's been a long time since Danny died. It's just that nobody in Glen Oaks has pushed any buttons for me." She nudged his boot with her toe. "What about you?"

"Me either. I wish . . ." He didn't finish. Verbalizing it made it worse.

"You need a good woman, Reverend. And kids."

"I do." He sighed and shook off the mood. "Until then, I'll have to be satisfied watching out for Ronny." He glanced at the clock. "Want me to go get him at the lake for you?"

"No, I'll do it."

"I'll ride with you."

"No, you won't. You're exhausted." She stood and began to

massage his shoulders. "You're trying to take care of too many
people, Linc. Annie, Margo, me, Ronny, the church women."

He sighed as she kneaded his sore muscles. "Margo calls it
my savior complex."

"She's right." Beth grinned. "Sometimes I miss Jesse
James—the preacher's son."

"Ironic, huh, what he was?" To break the pall, he swiveled off
his seat, stood, spread his legs and pretended to pull guns from
an imaginary holster. "Jesse's still around, ma'am. Best you remember that."

Rising too, Beth smiled. "Yeah, so is Bonnie." She looked
away. "Sometimes, I wish she'd surface more, though. That girl
who took chances, risked . . . things."

Her tone sobered him. "What would you risk, honey?"

"I'm not sure." She ripped off the towel around her waist and
tucked in her flannel shirt. "Do I look okay?"

"To go get Ronny?"

"Um, yeah. I mean, is my face clean? Do I have spinach in my
teeth?"

He wondered about her self-consciousness. "You hate
spinach."

She grasped his hand. "Come on, Jess, I'll walk you out."

TUCKER stood outside of the back room Doc had converted to
an office and watched the old man and Ron at the computer.
Backdropped by a wall of windows facing the lake, filled with a
scarred desk and a couple of chairs, with stacks of racing books
and magazines on the floor, the room was Doc's favorite.

"Now, watch, boy. You ain't gonna believe this one."

A pause. "Holy shit, Doc, how'd you do that?"

The old coot had finally found a playmate on that thing. For
years, Doc tried to interest Tucker in the design of race cars using
the newest computer programs to hit the market, and some that
he'd developed on his own. Tucker didn't give a hoot about car
design, computers, and especially not NASCAR websites.

Sipping his Corona, tanged up with just the right touch of
lime, he studied the two of them as they bent over the keyboard.
Ronny's face had lost its earlier starkness—because Doc had
asked him about jail. Tucker had stood in the shadows listening,
this time in the kitchen. The kid hadn't said much, just that he'd

been in his cell most of the time and he was bored to tears. But Tucker had heard the fear in his tone. Prison was prison.

He wondered how Beth had dealt with it. What had Ronny told her? If unspeakable things ever did happen there, would he tell his mother? Tucker hoped not. Ron should have a man to talk to about it. Beth didn't need to know.

"Can you show me how to get on that website again, Doc?" Ron's voice held a burgeoning affection for the old man. Tucker understood it, as he'd been about Ronny's age when he'd met up with Doc. And like Doc, and now Ronny, he'd loved the sport, too.

Tucker turned away and sauntered into the living room, surprised he felt left out. After all, he was the one who'd made it clear to Doc that he didn't want to be around Danny Donovan's son. But for some reason, the sight of the two of them at the computer, with Tucker looking in, resurrected the sight of his stepfather and Mac, the old man's *real* son, all those times when they'd excluded Tucker.

Christ, why was he going there? It had been a long time since he'd thought about Ralph Pearson, though he heard from Mac occasionally. Tucker dropped down on the couch in the early evening darkness, flicked on the TV with the remote, propped up his feet on the old chest that served as a coffee table and sipped his beer.

But instead of the candy-ass game-show host asking if you'd like to win a million bucks, Tucker pictured Pearson's face. He saw the man the night Tucker's mother died, and his expression which said, *Now I'm stuck with you.* He saw the man hug Mac, tell him how proud he was of his success in the baseball game, while Tucker lagged behind. He saw the man's wallet with only Mac's picture in it. And he saw the empty seat in an audience full of loving parents on graduation day.

An abrupt buzz startled him from his memories. At first he thought somebody had won the grand prize on TV. But when he heard it again, he realized it was the doorbell.

And knew it was Beth Donovan, coming to get Ron.

He should call the kid to answer the door. He should go upstairs and avoid her. Instead, he stood, tucked his black T-shirt into his jeans, slicked back his hair and went to the door.

From under the glow of the outside lamp, she smiled real soft at him. Her hair shone like sable. Her cheeks were rosy from the cold, and her chestnut eyes sparkled. "Hi."

"Hi." His gaze narrowed on her. He hadn't realized how thick her eyelashes were.

"Is, um, Ron ready?"

"Ron?" He stared at her blankly. "Oh, yeah. Come on in."

He stood aside and once she was in and headed to the living room, he closed the door and hit his head with his hand. *Idiot, what's got into you?*

Following her, he said, "Go on through. He's in the back office with Doc."

"He's working in the office?"

Tucker noticed she looked taller tonight. Must be those boots she wore. Just like an outlaw. He grinned. "Yeah, they're on the computer."

"That doesn't sound like punishment to me."

"Punishment?"

"This community service is supposed to be . . . unpleasant."

Tucker came close and squeezed her shoulder. "It was, up until about ten minutes ago. Doc had him cleanin' out the garage. Dirtier work than diggin' ditches; it had to be done for when the car's chassis is delivered."

"When is that?"

"I'm not sure."

She glanced to the back of the house. "Is that the room?"

"Uh-huh. Go on in." He forced himself to stay where he was.

Giving him a smile that reminded him of the ones shy girls had shot his way in high school, she headed back. He dropped down on the couch to watch the people in the audience cheer on the contestant. She was a pretty blonde—his type. Tucker had always liked his women tall and slender with breasts that could more than fill a man's hand and long legs that could wrap around . . .

"Aw, please Mom, five more minutes. I just got into this site and I wanna see . . ."

Tucker tuned out the rest. What the hell was the kid doing? Wanting to stay here?

In his peripheral vision, he saw Beth come up beside the couch. "He doesn't want to leave yet."

"So I heard."

Glancing around nervously, she shrugged. "I . . . I'll wait in the car."

He bolted off the couch. "The hell you will. My mama'd skin me alive if I let you do that."

She gave him a sideways glance. "I never noticed that drawl was so pronounced before."

Winking at her, he said, "Whenever necessary, ma'am. Let me have your coat." She unzipped the tan canvas jacket she wore, revealing a simple red-and-black plaid flannel shirt that she filled out real fine, tucked into jeans that were hug-me tight.

Clearing his throat, he took her jacket. "Want a beer?"

"Sure." She eyed his. "I like Corona."

"A woman after my own heart." He grinned and, feeling like he'd just qualified for a Winston Cup race, went to the fridge. When he returned with a beer, she was checking out his trophies.

He stayed across the room from her. "Here's your beer."

She pivoted and angled her head. "This is impressive."

Carelessly he shrugged, set the bottle on the table and sank onto the couch. She took the hint and joined him. "You don't like to talk about racing, do you?"

"Nope."

She sipped her beer and gave a satisfied sigh. "You aren't going to have a choice, though, are you? When the publicity for the exhibition starts."

Frowning, he shook his head. "I'm lookin' forward to that about as much as eatin' liver and onions."

"Ever since Danny's death, you've shied away from publicity."

He stared at the screen watching the slick host get in a few jokes. "You know, you can watch *this* show, *Jeopardy* and reruns of *The Price is Right* all at once with some careful channel surfin'."

"Hmm."

He could feel her eyes on him.

Finally, he met her gaze. "They were always wantin' to know about it. How I felt." He drew in a deep breath. "I agreed to publicity stuff for the exhibition race here *under duress,* as they say."

"It'll come up, about Danny, since the race is in Glen Oaks."

He watched her face for signs of resentment. Again he saw none. "Will it hurt you?"

She shook her head. The action dislodged a strand of hair

from behind her ear. His hand itched to replace it, but he gripped the bottle instead. "Not me." She glanced toward the back room. "I'm a little worried about him, though." Then she sighed. "So, what else is new?"

He hadn't planned on asking. "What'd he say about this weekend? I heard him tell Doc he was bored."

"Thank God for boredom." She sighed heavily. "I guess it went okay."

This time, he did reach out and squeeze her shoulder. "Let's hope it stays that way. Murphy said it should."

"You talked to Joe about this?"

"Um, yeah." For a long time. "I ran into him and it came up," he lied.

"It's so weird. Having Joe back, in charge of Ron's case." She studied Tucker's face. "Having you here, working with him. Working with the town."

"Life's a bitch." He heard the bitterness in his tone.

"No, I think it's good you're back. And Joe, too. He's got unresolved issues." She frowned. "I think he's suffered. A lot."

Tucker had had the same impression about the solemn man with the haunted eyes. Felt some kinship with him.

"You, too," she said softly, reading his mind.

"Nah. I don't have any unresolved issues." He glanced at the TV again. "Now don't that beat all. The guy's gonna win a million bucks tonight."

She said nothing, so he looked at her. "Don't feel sorry for me, Beth. I ruined your life."

"No, Tucker, you didn't."

"Yeah, he did," they heard from a few feet back.

Both turned.

Ron Donovan stood behind them, hands jammed in his jeans, the collar of his leather jacket turned up.

And pure venom in his young face.

LOOSE Anderson was a mean son-of-a-bitch. Having lived in the city most of his life, he said he needed to be mean to stay alive. Ron always thought he liked being tough.

"Scram, jerk," Loose barked at the freshman who followed him into the boys john. "I got business in my office."

The pimply kid clutched his clarinet case like it was a shield and did an about-face. Ron turned his back to wash his hands.

"How's my man?" Loose asked as he hiked himself up to sit on one of the sinks, shook out a cigarette and lit up. His brown hair was pulled back in a ponytail. It always looked dirty.

"Your man is in deep shit, Loose. Put that thing away, will ya? If I get in any more trouble, my ass is fried."

Loose took a long drag, then butted out on the small ledge near the mirror. His black eyes sparkled like they always did when he was excited. "Yeah, but you been to the pen. That's awesome."

"It's not the pen." Ron thought about the stark cell with its gray walls. And bars. He'd been scared shitless the first night there. The jail was minimum security, with no hardened criminals in sight, but he'd been hit with a mega-bad case of claustrophobia when the door had clanged shut. He wondered what Loose would say if he knew Ron had wished for his mother so bad it hurt. "It's a goddamned cell, is all. I get to stare at the walls for twenty-four hours."

Tell me about it, Ron, Murphy had said.

I don't wanna talk about it.

I can help.

I . . . was scared, being in there all alone.

What else are you scared of, son?

"Hey man, you spacin' out again. I swear, this Quaid thing's got you by the balls."

"Whose got Ronny by the balls?"

Ron turned to see Maze LaMont swagger into the bathroom. Dressed in pure black—a slinky shirt, worn jeans and boots—his bleached-blond hair had been spiked into several points. Beneath it, hostile blue eyes stared out at the world. Though he never let it show, Maze's eyes made Ron shudder sometimes. The three of them, along with Sammy Shecker—who was more of a gofer and on the outskirts most of the time—had formed their own group of sorts.

Ron, you've got to stay squeaky-clean now. Your mom's worried about the guys you hang out with. Was Murphy right?

"The Menace's got Ronny dangling." Loose laughed. His father had worked at the racetrack since they moved out from the city, and thought Quaid walked on water.

Quaid, who'd been having a cozy little chat with his mother last Monday night. Christ, Ron couldn't even think about that.

The bell rang, signaling the end of the day. "Sprung!" Loose exclaimed, jumped off the sink and high-fived it with Maze. "Come on, my man, we outta here."

Maze swore colorfully and they turned to Ron. "Sorry you can't come, Ronny boy. We got these chicks lined up at the cottage." His grin revealed yellowed teeth. "They squeezable as hell. And I'm tryin' to lure Lily White into coming out."

Lately, Ron had been relieved when he couldn't go with them, but he'd never let on. And he hoped Lily didn't go, though he wasn't sure why. "Breaks my heart, Maze."

"See ya." The boys bumped into somebody on the way out. "Watch your fuckin' step," Maze spat out.

"You watch your filthy mouth, LaMont."

"Oh, yeah, sorry Mr. Johnson." Loose grabbed Maze by the arm. A wild card, there was no telling who LaMont might pick a fight with, or what he might do. Rumor had it at his last school, he knifed the principal.

Johnson was shaking his head as he came inside. His brows lifted when he found Ron there. "Hi, Ron." The teacher scowled. Glanced behind him. "I know this is none of my business, but you shouldn't be hanging out with those guys. You or Sammy."

Ron picked up his books. "We're buddies."

"They're on the downslide. I don't think you are."

"Mr. Johnson, *I'm* the one who's going to jail. Not them."

"Yeah, I heard. Everything." He checked his watch. "Want to come and work on the computers? My department meeting was canceled."

Ron smiled before he remembered. "I gotta be at my community service by four."

"Hmm. Well, I'm heading out to the lake after school. I could drop you off. That way you could get a good half hour in on the CAD program."

It was too much to resist. And this way his mother didn't have to take him to Holt's. Didn't have to get near Quaid. Maybe Ron could call Uncle Linc to pick him up. "Yeah, sure, if my old lady says it's okay."

Johnson gave him a playful punch on the arm. "You can call

her from the math office. Come on kid, let's go see that machine."

Forgetting all about his mother, and Loose and Maze, Ron followed the teacher out of the lav.

TEN

"THIS was a great idea." Annie took a bite of her Caesar salad and munched on the lettuce. "And this place is terrific."

Margo sipped her minestrone. "I love it. I used to eat here all the time with Philip."

"Used to?" Annie asked. There was something about Margo's tone.

"Yeah, he's on my shit list."

"Why?"

"You don't want to know. It'll ruin all our appetites."

Annie surveyed her best friends. They were dressed in their usual attire, which always gave her a sense of security. She herself wore layers of black leggings, a black Spandex top and a light blue sweater over them. Beth had on a pretty angora sweater in deep pink, which she wore with dark slacks; it set off her coloring. Margo stayed typecast, too, in tight brown jeans, suede boots and an off-white sweater. The three of them were so different now, but it didn't matter. They were closer than most sisters.

Beth toyed with her quiche and said nothing. She wasn't even paying attention.

Annie and Margo exchanged glances.

"Bethy, you okay?" Margo asked.

Her head came up quickly. "Yeah, sure." She looked to Annie. "You?"

"I guess I just hope the kids'll be all right."

Beth asked, "Isn't Suzie with them?"

"Uh-huh. It's just that I don't like leaving them overnight." She took a taste of her iced tea.

"Hey, we agreed, time for a girls sleepover." Margo sighed. "I miss you guys."

Beth's look was shrewd. "I know this is really all for me, but I don't need baby-sitting. I'm okay."

"You cried when we dropped Ron off at Lancaster this morning," Annie said. "You need distraction." She studied the decor. Like so many of those in the city, the restaurant was long and narrow and paneled in deep mahogany. There were about twenty tables. The three of them sat in the front, facing Madison Avenue through a huge picture window.

Gently, Beth touched her hand. "You're spacing out, too."

Annie nodded. "I'm worried about Joe being around the kids."

"No need for that," Margo told her. "Joe's not in Glen Oaks this weekend."

"Oh." She scowled. "How do you know that?"

"I, um, met him for coffee right around the corner from here this morning." She pointed to a building across the street. "He's got some business over there today, he said."

The thought discomfited Annie. "What did he want with you?"

"To assure me that he's recovered. That he's not going to hurt you or the kids." She shrugged. "He thought it might ease your mind if he could convince me, since I'm such a tough nut to crack." She grinned on the last accurate description.

Beth sighed. "He's *not* going to hurt them, honey. I believe that in my heart, but in any case, Linc's always there; he'll watch out for them."

"Linc already has too much on his plate." Annie shook her head. "He doesn't need this."

"He thinks he's responsible for everything." Glancing away, Margo watched pedestrians cross the busy avenue. "He needs a woman in his life to give him balance. Damn, I hate even saying that."

Neither Annie nor Beth spoke.

"I'm just sorry it can't be me."

"I am, too." Beth's gaze was sympathetic. "I think he's really lonely."

As always, Margo grasped for any crumbs she could get about Linc's life. When she heard he had a date, or was serious about somebody, Annie knew it killed her, but she asked anyway. "Did he say that?"

"In so many words." Beth grasped Margo's hand. "After the fight you two had on the phone."

"He told you about that?"

"Not the details. Just that he hates to fight with you. He misses you, Margo."

"We haven't talked since then. It's why I didn't go to Glen Oaks this weekend."

"Instead, you stayed in the city, lured us to town, therefore avoiding Linc."

"Yeah."

Margo stared out the window at the building she said Joe worked in.

After a moment, Annie tracked her gaze. "I wonder what kind of building that is."

"I've been in there several times. It has offices and studios and stuff."

"Linc told me Joe has a part-time job." Beth watched out the window, too. "Maybe it's in there."

Annie bit her lip. "From the looks of his clothes and car, it must be lucrative." Her eyes closed briefly. "God, I hope he's not into anything illegal."

"Linc talked to him about that, too," Beth said. "Joe swears it's not."

"Joe puts up a good front, Beth."

Deliberately, Margo pushed her food away and leaned forward on her elbows. "Do you still think about it?"

"What, how he used to beat me up?"

Beth winced. "Oh, God. I hope you don't."

"I *do*. I make myself, so I won't forget what a puppet I was. And so I'll never let any man pull those strings again."

"You don't let any man near you," Margo said candidly.

"And that's not healthy either," Beth agreed.

Annie snagged Beth's gaze. "I'm not the only one. You avoid involvement like the plague."

"I date."

"Yeah, you never made it to the sack with Roman Becker, though, did you?"

"Nope." Beth giggled. "I was afraid I might mess up his hair." Beth got a faraway look in her eye and squirmed in her seat.

"What?" Margo asked.

"Huh?"

"What are you thinking? You look like you just got caught snitchin' cigarettes." She winked at Annie. "You got a guy on the side we don't know about?"

"Of course not." She sighed. "I wish I did, though. I'm lonely, too. Like Linc."

"How's Quaid doing with Ronny?" Margo asked.

"Um, good." Beth's face flushed, always an indicator that something was going on with her.

"Too bad you have to drive the kid out and back to the lake. Damn his hide for losing his license."

"I don't mind." The waitress cleared their plates and brought coffee.

Margo ordered a piece of mocha mud pie to share. "Linc says Quaid and his henchman, Holt, have been great to Ron."

"Ronny doesn't realize how much he talks about them." Beth shot a quick glance at Annie. "And about Joe. In just a couple of weeks, they've rivaled Mr. Johnson in his conversations."

"Linc says Quaid's quite a hit with the ladies in town, too," Annie put in.

"Why wouldn't he be? He's great-looking. He's got terrific shoulders . . ." Beth stopped when Annie and Margo cocked their heads. "What?"

Annie was surprised. "I've never heard you say anything like that about a man other than Danny."

"No big deal."

Dessert arrived, and they dug into it; they were unable to continue the conversation around mouthfuls of sweet hot fudge and frigid coffee ice cream. As they'd devoured the treat, Annie was bombarded by images of the past. Sometimes they came without warning, and she couldn't stop them. She tried to concentrate on eating, but her comment to Margo stuck in her mind.

She *had* let Joe pull the strings, treat her like a puppet. He'd demanded it. She remembered one time when she didn't want to go out . . .

The slap came quick, and out of the blue, like it always did. Annie reeled back.

Joe was shouting. "You'll do what I say, you hear? Any time I tell you."

"But why, Joey? I—"

Another slap. "Don't *ever* question me." Then, he fisted his hand and punched her side.

She staggered back into the chair, fell onto it. She could taste blood on her lip. But the pain in her heart was worse—he'd never used his fists on her.

He squatted in front of her. "Learn your lesson, little girl, and I won't have to do this."

Hurt, and afraid, she couldn't look at him. Couldn't look at the man she'd trusted more than anyone in the world. She just nodded.

He'd stepped back then. "Now, get up and get ready."

Annie struggled to her feet, feeling dizzy. He grabbed her arm . . . not to help her. "Remember what I said about obeying me . . ."

"Annie, what's wrong? You're not eating." This from Beth.

"Oh, um, I—"

Before she could make up an excuse, Margo nodded to the window. "Look, there's Joe again. He's with some woman."

Annie's head snapped around. Despite her desire to remain distanced, her heart lurched at the sight of him. For a minute, the past and present converged, and she was back in that kitchen, shrinking away from him. To counteract the feeling, she straightened and faced the street corner where he stood.

This was the present. She'd deal with it as it was.

He and a brunette were close, their heads bent almost touching each other. Joe wore a long khaki raincoat belted at the waist. They stopped for a light and Annie watched him throw back his head and laugh. The dark-haired woman grabbed his arm and said something that made him laugh harder. Then they crossed the street and entered the building.

"I wonder what he's up to." Annie hated the tremulousness in her voice

Standing, Margo threw some bills on the table and dragged on her suede blazer. "Let's go find out."

"What?" It was the last thing Annie wanted.

"Let's follow them. See what his second job is."

"Maybe it's a love tryst." Beth stood and donned her raincoat. "But I'm game."

Both her friends' eyes sparkled with challenge. Hell, Annie wasn't afraid of him. And maybe, just maybe, she would learn something about her ex-husband that she could use against him.

So the three of them hurried out of the restaurant into the mild March afternoon, made the green light and entered the building just enough behind Joe and his girlfriend to see them step into the elevator.

"Come on," Margo said, dragging them to the elevators. The lighted dial showed the car stopped at *ten*. Margo scanned the directory. "Hmm. There's studios up there."

"Studios?"

"Yeah, like for movies, commercials and catalogs."

The elevator opened and Margo pulled Annie and Beth in.

"Hey, maybe Joe's making movies," Beth said.

"Porno films," Margo suggested. "You could keep him away from the kids on that one."

Despite her earlier memories of the bad times, Annie thought about the way Faith hugged Joe before he left Sunday, and how she prayed for her daddy before she went to bed. "Maybe this isn't such a good idea."

"I was kidding. The man's smart, Annie. He wouldn't do something that stupid." Margo pushed number ten. As the car rose, they looked at each other. "Come on you guys, smile; this is fun."

Beth tossed back her hair. "Yeah, Ma Barker, y'all always did like gettin' us two innocents into trouble."

"Bonnie Parker's a wimp," Margo taunted.

"Nah, I'm the wimp." Annie fell into the play. "Belle Star was the lady bandit, remember? Quite dainty and fastidious about getting her velvet dress dirty."

"Over which she strapped on a gun belt," Margo said dryly.

They giggled again. But quieted when they reached the tenth floor. Cleaning fluid and the lemon scent of a newly waxed floor was strong. It was still and silent up here. Except for the lights at the end of the hall, it was dark. Margo's boots clicked on the wood, echoing in the emptiness, so she immediately went up on tiptoes. Annie and Beth crept down the corridor behind her.

The outer door to one of the studios was open. The three of

them slipped inside; noise came from an inner room. Annie could see flashes, like somebody was taking pictures.

"Nude photos?" Beth whispered.

Well, he still had the looks for it. Annie shrugged.

As they neared the door, a female voice purred, "Ah, Joey baby, that's great."

Annie halted. The voice sounded sexy, like a come-on.

Beth grabbed her hand to tug her along. When they reached the doorway, the three of them scrunched into it for a clear view.

The back part of the studio was dark; up front was brightly lit with tall, free-standing lamps. The drop-dead gorgeous brunette held a camera and cooed to the man in the center of the lights. "Ah, yes, that's it, baby. Make my mouth water."

Annie's ex-husband stared at the camera, a sexy look on his face. He reclined on a white leather couch, surrounded by sprays and vases of white roses. He held one red rose in his hand, and bent his head to sniff it.

His George Clooney hair was a bit mussed. His bare chest sported whorls of dark hair. He was naked except for bloodred briefs bisecting his body. Slowly, he peered up from the rose. And smiled invitingly at the camera.

"Oh, God, just looking at you makes me wet," the photographer purred. A big grin flashed across his face, which she caught on camera. "All right, Calvin Klein man. Let's get you into another pair of skivvies before I lose control of myself."

Margo gasped.

Beth gasped.

Annie gasped.

And the photographer looked their way.

"WHO the hell are you?" Taylor had turned to the door; Joe couldn't see who was there because of the lights, but he'd heard the gasps.

"Well, I'll be damned," someone said. "Billy the Kid's a model. For men's undies." The sassy voice was familiar.

Scowling, he raised his hand to shade his eyes. "Taylor?"

"We got company." She switched off the lights, plunging the room into darkness. Joe hated when the spots swam before him. It was disorienting and threatened his hard-won control. He sat up, waited a second for them to disappear, then stood as Taylor switched on a normal lamp. "Who is it?" he asked.

"I dunno." Taylor sounded disgusted. "Your fan club, maybe?"

"Hardly." That voice he recognized immediately. He heard it in his dreams—a few good ones, mostly nightmares.

"Annie?" He crossed the room until he was about ten feet from them. The triumvirate. Though they looked more like a posse, out for his hide, now. "What are you doing here?"

Margo was laughing. Beth hid a smile. Only Annie's face was sober. She stared at him with an expression he couldn't read.

"You know these babes?" Taylor asked.

"Yes." He smiled. "Taylor Cummings. Meet two of my friends from Glen Oaks." He introduced Margo and Beth. "And this is my ex-wife, Annie Lang."

Taylor whirled around, her long dark hair trailing down her back. "So this is the little lady who's got your jocks in a twist. Pardon the pun."

Joe winced. Meaningfully he glanced at the clock. "Can we take a break?"

"We just got started again."

"Please, Taylor."

"Okay. Not too long, though. We only got the studio until three." She faced the women and gave Annie a long, hard look, then walked to the back room.

Annie stood stone-statue still and stared at him.

He plopped his hands on his hips, only then realizing he was almost naked. "Jesus." He turned and strode to the table at the side of the room, where he reached for a robe. Its deep blue accented his eyes, Taylor had said. Right now he was more interested in covering up his body. He felt like a kid just caught in the bathroom with a *Playboy*. Shrugging into the robe, he nodded to the table. "Would you like some coffee?"

Beth said, "We just ate."

Margo shook her head.

Annie still didn't move.

"Annie, are you all right?" he asked.

She roused herself. "You model men's underwear?"

Again, he swore under his breath. Though he was grateful for the money this side job had provided him for the last five years, nobody other than Taylor and Pete knew about it. "Yeah, I do."

He cursed his voice for being hoarse. It was an honest living, damn it. "Sit down."

The three women crossed to the table and sat, Annie as far away from him as she could get. It dug like a knife into his heart. Sometimes, he actually forgot what a monster he was, but it only took a few minutes in her presence to remind him.

Then stay away from the bitch, Taylor had said.

Taylor, you don't know what I did to her.

He took in a deep breath. "I model for an exclusive men's underwear catalog. It goes mostly overseas." He shrugged. "It's good money." His eyes narrowed on Annie. "And it's completely legal and aboveboard. If you like, you can see my W-Two forms."

She remained maddeningly silent.

Crossing her legs and bobbing one foot up and down, Margo seemed to be enjoying this. "How'd you get into it?"

He wished he never had to think about those times. "As you know, when I first came to the city, I was in a Batterer's Recovery Program." Annie stiffened. "They recommended AA."

"You're an alcoholic, too?" Annie's words set off cruel emotional fireworks in his heart.

"I have a problem with drinking. Many batterers do, though it wasn't the cause of the . . . abuse."

Her eyes widened, accusing him more than if a jury had pronounced his guilt. *It's the booze, Annie. It makes me lose control.*

"I know, I said it was the liquor, but I was wrong. Anyway, it wasn't too hard kicking the habit, so I'm not sure I'm an alcoholic. But it doesn't matter. I don't drink, and I still go to meetings occasionally." Damn, he was always so defensive around her.

It's called paying for your sins.

"What does that have to do with the modeling, Joe?" Beth's tone was kind. She'd always been the most forgiving, and he knew she was grateful for his work with Ron.

"I, um, met Taylor at AA a year later."

Margo's brows arched. "The Andie McDowell lookalike is an alcoholic?"

"Yes. She openly admits it." Though he felt uncomfortable discussing his friend. "She's a professional photographer, and after a few meetings, told me I had good bone structure."

Margo laughed. "That's a new one."

"She meant my face, wiseguy." His mouth curved in a small smile. "My hair had started to turn gray by then, and it seems that was an advantage. I look older than I am, but my body . . ." Again he shrugged.

"We saw it," Margo quipped again, wiggling her brows. "We understand."

"It seems I'm a perfect model for the over-forty crowd." He turned to Annie and his smile died. "I make good money. It's how I was able to send you some back then."

She nodded. Stood. Stared down at him. His breath caught in his throat at the anger he saw in her pretty amber eyes. "Landed right on your feet, didn't you, Joe?"

Forcefully, he swallowed back an objection. For a minute he was bombarded by the black hell of self-discovery he'd gone through—*you hit a defenseless woman . . . only scum would do that . . . you're no better than a worm. . . .*

He said only, "Yes, I landed on my feet."

Annie threw back her chair, gave him one last contemptuous glance and stalked to the door.

ELEVEN

THE little silver Jag took the left turn onto Main Street with the ease of a Grand Prix qualifier. Doc said to Tucker, "Hungry?"

Shrugging, Tucker stared out the windshield. "Not really."

He'd been in a rotten mood since Friday when Ron Donovan had come out to the cottage to work. Nothing unusual had happened between them—Ronny had snarled once or twice at him and he mostly avoided the kid—so Tucker couldn't figure out why he was still feeling sour today.

"Well, I am." Doc glanced out the window. "Let's stop and eat lunch. It's past one-thirty."

Tucker grunted and parked at the curb in front of the drugstore. Doc got out of the car and, after a moment, Tucker followed.

"I ain't eatin' no drugstore food," Doc said as Tucker circled the Jag. "I'm too old to sit at a soda fountain."

That made Tucker smile. Turning up the collar of his navy blue fleece jacket against the March wind, he quipped, "Whatsamatter, old man, never shared sodas with your best girl?"

Doc cussed and headed down the sidewalk to The Downtown Diner. It took a minute before he realized he was alone. He pivoted. "Tuck?"

Tucker jogged up to him. Raking a hand through his hair, he

met Doc's gaze. "I, um, I don't feel real comfortable going to the Donovans' diner."

Thoughtful, Doc shook his head. "Gotta toughen up." When Tucker just stared at him, Doc shook his head. "Guilt's gonna eat you alive, boy."

Tucker stuck his hands in his jeans pockets. "I feel better about that."

Doc started to walk, forcing Tucker to keep pace. "Yeah? Why?"

"I guess because of Beth Donovan." He pictured her the time they were in the diner alone that night.

It wasn't your fault, Tucker. . . . You have to forgive yourself.

"She's just about the most forgivin' person I ever met. Even if her kid would like to see me strung up by the cahonies."

Doc didn't say anything.

"What?" Tucker asked at the scowl on Doc's face.

"Nothin'. Just wonderin' how the Donovan woman could make you feel better when I been bustin' my ass for years to get you to see clear on this thing and hit a stone wall."

"She's prettier than you are, old man." Though he joked, the way her hair curled at her shoulders and how her dark eyes sparkled when she laughed made him smile.

They reached the diner. "Well, then, there ain't no reason to stay away from this place." As he pulled open the door to the restaurant, he said, "Okay?"

"Fine." Tucker became The Menace as soon as they entered the diner and he had to face his ghosts.

They waited in the entryway. Beth stood at a table, talking with somebody. Tucker tried not to stare at her but she looked so good—she was medium height and well rounded, not rail thin like some of the models Tucker dated; she wore black slacks and a simple white cotton sweater. Her hair was pulled up in some kinda knot on her head, making her look young and innocent. When she turned around, her gaze landed on them.

Her smile was dazzling. Aimed at Tucker, it flew across the room like a well-aimed arrow. Tucker grinned when it hit its target.

She approached them. "Hi, Mr. Holt." She nodded. "Tucker."

"Make it, Doc," the old man said.

"Afternoon, Beth."

Again the smile. "Are you here to eat?"

"Uh-huh." Doc scanned the diner.

"Come on, I'll give you a booth; it's cleared out some."

They followed her down the spacious aisle; Tucker's eyes were glued on the sway of her hips.

"Hello, Doc, Tucker," they heard from a couple they passed.

Tucker gave Beth's brother a small wave. "Hi, Linc."

Doc nodded, then sat in a booth down from them.

"Want something to drink?" Beth seemed oblivious to the fact that he was eating her up with his eyes.

"Coffee," Doc said.

"Make his decaf," Tucker added. "I'll have high-test." She smiled at his order, reminding him of her comments that night in the diner.

"I can have *some* caffeine, boy. I'm not ready to keel over yet."

"The doctor just told you an hour ago to cut back. You're cuttin' back."

"The doctor said my heart was just fine."

"It's not fine. Your angina's under control is all."

To change the subject, Tucker knew, Doc looked over at Linc Grayson. "That guy don't look like no preacher I ever seen."

"Former gang leaders usually don't."

Doc chuckled. Tucker knew Doc got a kick out of the checkered past of the town's now-upstanding citizens. "Cute girl he's with."

"Is she?" Tucker perused the menu. "I didn't notice."

"Nope, you just got eyes for the owner."

Tucker's head came up fast. "I don't know what you're talkin' about."

"Like hell," Doc said, but didn't pursue it.

Tucker surveyed the diner. The smell of fresh bread filled the air, and there were some pretty flowers on the counter. The kitchen door opened and Gerty Stoffer stepped out.

"Oh, hell." This from Doc, who buried his face in the menu like some lovesick kid.

Gerty was dressed in a fringed dress and moccasins. Carrying coffee, she made a beeline for them. When she reached their table, she put down his coffee and Tucker's. "Hello, Mr. Quaid."

"Ma'am." Tucker picked up his cup and sipped.

She zeroed in on Doc. "Hello, Leonard."

Tucker's drink spattered all over his shirt. But he kept his mouth shut and just cleaned himself up.

Gerty told them the specials without blinking an eye. "There's a low-cholesterol, high-fiber lunch plate on the menu."

"Probably tastes like cardboard." At Doc's comment, Gerty's face fell. He said quickly, "Okay, I'll give it a try."

Smiling at the waitress, Tucker ordered the veggie chili and cornbread.

Gerty nodded. "Man after my own heart."

I like Corona.

A woman after my own heart.

Tucker sighed at the memory. He'd been thinking about Beth Donovan and wasn't happy about it. He'd even dreamed about her, not the nightmare kind this time where she called him a murderer. The X-rated kind, where she called out his name when she was under him. He'd been disappointed when Ron had gotten a ride from somebody else both ways on Friday. Shit.

"Jesus, boy, where are you? I asked you a question."

"Just gatherin' wool, *Leonard*." Tucker chuckled. "Thinkin' about what the doctor said," he lied, but it was something he wanted to discuss anyway.

"Hrrmph." Doc sipped his coffee. His cheeks were rosy, and his eyes clear. Tucker's heart went to his mouth and stayed there every time he took Doc in for a checkup. This visit he got a fairly good clean bill of health, though the doctor warned about too much physical exertion and stress, and about his patient's eating habits. Tucker worried like hell about the old man. Angina didn't mean a heart attack was going to happen, he assured himself, but the doctor did say a change in the pattern of the angina, or successive attacks, could mean future susceptibility.

"Got a delivery date for the chassis this morning." Doc was clearly after a detour.

"Yeah, when?"

"Next week sometime."

"Good. How long before she's put together?"

"Least a month till you can test drive her, if that's what you mean."

"It isn't what I mean." Tucker refused to let himself get excited about racing again. "I gotta do some publicity shots with the car, which pisses me off big-time."

"Won't be ready for shots till May. Probably before we go to the Indy, though."

"Damn it, Doc. I'm not goin' to Indianapolis. And you know it."

"Thought you'd change your mind this year."

"When snakes walk upright, old man."

"I got tickets."

"You always got tickets."

"Stubborn mule."

They made stilted conversation until Gerty brought their food. The cornbread smelled like homemade, and Tucker eyed it appreciatively.

"Enjoy," she said pleasantly. "Oh, and Leonard, I got a book out of the library on those new kinds of delphinia I was telling you about. Come to the office and see it when you're done."

Doc averted his eyes. "Maybe."

Tucker decided to bust Doc's chops about Gerty—and his new interest in gardening. "Delphinia?"

Before he could do it proper, Linc Grayson approached their table. "Sorry to interrupt your lunch, but I just wanted to tell you two how good it's been for Ronny to work with you. When I picked him up on Friday night, he couldn't stop talking about it."

"The kid sure is a blabberer." Despite his words, Doc's voice was laced with grudging affection. "Couldn't get him to shut up about anything. He pestered the hell outta me about puttin' the car together."

"Ronny loves the sport." Linc glanced over his shoulder, where Tucker saw Beth had come out of the kitchen and was wiping up the counter. "And he's good at art. I wouldn't mind seeing him get interested in the design end, as opposed to the driving side. For his mother's sake."

"He should stay outta racin' altogether." Tucker looked back to the pictures of Danny on the wall.

"Yeah, but that's not going to happen. I thought maybe you two might be able to redirect him."

"I hear ya," Doc said easily.

Linc smiled and left. Tucker watched him stop and kiss Beth's cheek before he headed out.

He and Doc ate the rest of their meal in silence, broken only by a few idle comments. As soon as they were done, Beth appeared, cleared their plates, then returned. "Can I interest you in some dessert? Nana's trying out a new recipe—yogurt granola parfait."

Tucker felt his stomach turn, and Doc looked a little green. "Not for me, ma'am."

She laughed. "We have the traditional stuff, too." She smiled at him. "Doc?"

"Ah, no thanks."

"If you're done, Gerty wants you to come to the office."

The old man feigned irritation, but he got up pretty spry for a guy his age. "Be right back."

"I think she's sweet on him," Beth said, when Doc was out of earshot.

Tucker smiled.

She stared at him.

He nodded to the seat. "Keep me company?"

She surveyed the almost-empty diner. "All right. I won't be busy again until the after-school crowd comes in."

"What time is that?"

"About three." She sat down across from him.

He took a sip of coffee. "How you doin'?"

"Fine." She twisted a stray napkin in her hands. Pushed up the sleeves of her sweater. It took him a minute to realize she was nervous. That *he* made her nervous. He settled back and studied her. Her hair looked cute as a button, up like that. And she seemed rested.

"Do I have something on my face?"

He grinned, liking her honesty. "Just a few more freckles."

"Oh, from walking around New York this weekend. It was sunny."

"You were in the city for the weekend?"

"Yes, Margo and Annie dragged me away for some R and R."

"It worked. You look good." She smiled, and his stomach contracted. "Did you do anything fun?"

"Hmm, nothing specific. Just walked around a lot. It was pretty mild for the middle of March."

"Who took care of the diner?"

"Gerty and Nana. I also have some part-time help. I don't usually go anywhere to need it."

"Something special this weekend?"

She shrugged. "Margo and Annie are worried about me. Because of Ronny. They thought I needed some time with them."

"It must be nice to have such good friends." He watched her. "How'd it go with Ron at Lancaster this time? Doc said he's okay with it."

"He is. We're settling into it." Her chestnut eyes darkened. "I still can't believe my kid's in jail."

"*Weekend* jail. It's a lot different, Beth."

Now her eyes clouded. Shit. Every time he was around her, he had the absurd urge to play knight in shining armor. He reached out and grasped her hand. At first she startled. Then she let him hold it. He squeezed tight, noting her silken skin and feeling the long bones of her fingers. "Take it one step at a time. Before you know it, it'll be Memorial Day."

Nodding, she raised her eyes to the ceiling. "I'm not usually this emotional. Every time I'm around you, it seems to come out."

"You don't have to play tough guy with me."

She sighed. "Good thing. I can't seem to." She visibly gathered herself together and he let go of her hand.

"Are your no-account in-laws still givin' you trouble?" He laid on the accent thick. "If so, I can slap them upside the head, you know."

She rolled her eyes. "Thanks, cowboy. But they're in Europe still. They call Ronny a couple of times a week, but have left me alone."

"Good. I'm glad, Beth."

She drew in a deep breath. "So, what's going on with you? I haven't talked to you since last Monday."

I know. "The car's comin' next week." He sighed heavily.

"Aren't you glad?"

"Nope."

"Don't you like working on it?"

"Nope. But even worse, that publicity stuff we talked about'll start as soon as it takes shape."

"It's a long haul to September, isn't it?"

"Yep."

This time she reached for his arm and curled her fingers on him. Her touch felt so good he leaned into it. "I'm sorry. Maybe it won't be so bad." She raised her delicately arched brows. "One step at a time for you, too, I guess."

Looking into eyes as deep as a backwoods gully almost made

him believe it. He was about to say something when the door to
the diner opened and a crowd of kids piled in.

Among them was Ron Donovan. He was laughing with a
beanpole of a boy with dark red hair and glasses. Ron scanned
the diner, and his gaze landed on his mother. She drew back her
hand and waved to him; her whole face lit up when she saw him.

Ron's didn't. He scowled at them, then headed straight over,
the tall lanky boy behind him. "What are you doing here?" he
asked Tucker.

"Ron, you're being rude," Beth said.

Tucker told him, "I came in for lunch."

"Why you sitting with him?"

"Ron!"

Obviously upset, Ron stared at them. The other boy shifted
uncomfortably.

Beth noticed. "Hello, Sammy."

"Mrs. Donovan." He looked at Tucker. "Hi. I'm Sammy
Shecker. Ron's buddy."

"Hi, I'm—"

"The Menace. Everybody knows."

"We're going to the lake, okay?" Ron's tone was surly. And
challenging.

The other boy frowned. "I thought you told Loose we weren't
coming. You told Lily that, too."

Ron threw daggers at Tucker with his eyes. "I changed my
mind."

"Well, I haven't changed mine." Beth slid out of the booth. "I
don't want you spending so much time with Loose and Maze.
Besides, you have no community service and you're not meeting
with Joe, so you can help out here for a while."

Adolescent anger burned in Ron's eyes. Tucker met them candidly, wondering what the boy was thinking.

*Liar. You know what. That the sight of you with his mother
makes him sick.*

Tucker looked away, just as Doc came to the table. "Hey, boy,
how ya doin'?"

Ron gave Doc a weak smile.

"This your buddy?" Doc asked.

Ron introduced Sammy to Doc.

Sammy's eyes just about popped out of his head. "I can't believe I'm getting to meet the legend."

Doc grinned. "Chassis's bein' delivered next week."

"Chassis?" Sammy asked.

Doc preened like a peacock. "Yeah. We gotta put the suspension on it—shocks, wheels, springs. When that's done, we hang the body." He winked at Ron. "That's the fun part, kid."

"It's all fun." Ron's tone softened in the wake of Doc's attention and talk of the car.

"Can I come out and see it?" Sammy asked.

"Sure, bring your buddy along any time," Doc told Ron. He glanced at Beth, who was scowling. " 'Course, you gotta do your dirty work first."

Ron shrugged.

Doc looked at Tucker. "Ready to go?"

"Yeah, I'm ready to go." He didn't even glance at Beth. He was ready to go all right. He'd been crazy as a loon to come here in the first place.

LATER that day, Beth had the hot chocolate ready when Ron came out of the kitchen. It sat steaming on the counter, warming her insides with its familiar cocoa smell.

"I'm done." He was going for sulky, but Beth knew he'd lost his attitude.

"Thanks. I appreciate the help."

He glanced at the drink, then up at her. A little-boy smile curved his lips.

"I know you're mad at me for keeping you from your friends." She nodded to the chocolate. "A peace offering?"

He slid onto a stool; she took the one next to him. It reminded her of the night she sat here with Tucker. Promptly she banished the image. It seemed sacrilegious in front of her son.

"I'm not mad."

"No?"

"I can't go to the lake with those guys. They get into trouble there. I'm on thin ice as it is."

"Yes, honey, you are." Beth waited. When no more was forthcoming, she asked, "Why'd you say you were going?"

He drew in a deep breath. He looked pained.

"Honey, you can tell me anything."

"It was because of him." Ronny angled his head to the booth where Tucker had sat hours before. Where she'd felt comforted by his presence. Where she'd enjoyed being with him more than she'd enjoyed anything in a long time.

"Seeing Mr. Quaid upsets you? Makes you want to act out?"

"Sometimes, but I talk about it with Joe. I'm getting better about that."

"Then what?"

Ron's look was very male, and very adult. "He's hitting on you, Mom."

Beth's heart stopped cold. When it started beating again, she said, "No, honey, of course he's not. We were just talking."

"Yeah he is. Like last Monday at Doc's place when you had a beer with him?"

"No, Ron."

"He looked at you like Linc looks at Margo."

"You know about . . ."

"I'm not a baby. Besides, I asked Linc. He told me about Margo's hangup with the religion and all the crap keeping them apart. I think it's stupid."

Beth had to smile. Though she knew Margo had suffered greatly at her mother's hands, sometimes, Beth wanted to wring both hers and Linc's necks. "It's complicated. Because of Margo's background."

Her son wouldn't be detoured. "I don't like seeing you around Quaid."

"Oh, Ron."

"No, Mom, it's not what you think. You're pretty and nice; any man'd be a fool not to see it. And I know you gotta be lonely. But this guy . . . he killed Dad, Mom."

"No, honey, he didn't."

"Okay, he didn't." Ron's frustration level was mounting. "Just tell me you're not interested in him. Tell me it goes one way."

"I'm not interested in him." She pictured sad green eyes that seemed to lighten when she was around. "What's more, I can't imagine somebody like him being interested in me." She smiled as best she could. "So there really isn't an issue here. But honey, you've got to put your father's death in perspective and stop blaming Tucker."

"Tucker?"

"I mean Mr. Quaid."

She sipped her cocoa and Ron sipped his.

"Will you promise to try, for me?" she finally asked.

His face got that little-boy look on it, like the day he cried all the way to kindergarten and she got him to go in by playing the same trump card. *Do it for me, buddy.*

"Okay, Mom. I'll try."

Well, that was close, she thought as they finished their cocoa. But she handled it pretty well.

Beth wondered why she felt so awful.

TWELVE

APRIL blew into Glen Oaks with shining glory. The trees had begun to bud, crocuses and daffodils peeked through the grass and sometimes, on his morning runs, a mild breeze made Joe feel that all was right with the world. Though some things in his little corner of the universe had gone right, others hadn't.

He sat on the enclosed back porch of Annie's house with Faith while he watched Matt through the open screened windows. His son perched on the swing in the yard and kicked at the dirt with his Nike high-tops. His Yankee baseball cap shaded his face as he listened to Linc, who leaned against the tree, talking to him. In the four weeks Joe had been allowed to see his children, he'd made almost no progress with Matt. And it just about broke his heart as he stared at the son he'd abandoned.

Faith, in her pink overalls and T-shirt with ballet slippers on it, snuggled in next to him on the old slipcovered couch Annie had put out here. She was a bit of sunshine in his dreary days— his little girl, who harbored no trace of the animosity that colored her brother's relationship with him. She tracked his gaze, said, "I think he got up on the wrong side of the bed, Daddy," and handed him the book, *The Things We Say,* that Joe had run across in a Barnes and Noble.

He laughed aloud. "I wonder where that saying came from."

One of her favorite things to do was to try to use the phrases he read to her every time he visited and, Annie begrudgingly told him, she wanted read to her at night.

Don't think about Annie. Because there was full-blown, Technicolor resentment if he'd ever seen it. Actually, contempt was more like it. *Do you blame her?*

"Read it to me again," Faith said. "I forgot."

"All right." He found the page with the idiom she'd quoted. "The majority of people are right-handed," he began.

"Not us, Daddy."

"Nope, we're both *southpaws,* princess." He'd read her the origin of that phrase, too. "Anyway, in the early days, being left-handed became associated with something evil. Almost like a curse. And people avoided doing things on the left side of their body. Innkeepers even used to push the beds to the wall so that people could only get up on the right side. Any lefty had trouble getting out of bed that way, and it often made him irritable—therefore, it was said that *he got up on the wrong side of the bed.*"

Faith giggled and hugged him.

"Want to go out and see what Matt's up to?" Joe asked after a few more choice readings.

"Will you push me on the swing?"

"Sure. Get a sweater."

When Faith darted into the house, Joe threw on the hooded blue sweatshirt he'd brought along, and retied his sneakers. He'd been hoping to get to play with the kids outside. But Matt had, indeed, *gotten up on the wrong side of the bed.* He was more hostile today than usual. Joe had to find some way to break through to him, or this estrangement was going to drive him crazy.

He'd talked to Linc about it, in one of the many discussions they had on Sundays when they left the kids. He'd been thrown together with his old buddy a lot—here, at the Council meetings, where afterward they often shared a cup of coffee. He was even using Linc as a sounding board for some of the programs he was setting up for the youth of the town. On the cusp of racing season, it was important to find ways to keep the kids busy.

He grinned, thinking how he'd been right about Linc's reaction to the modeling job. He'd razzed the hell out of Joe, calling him Boxer Joe. Joe still blushed when he thought of Annie, Margo and Beth catching him *in flagrante,* so to speak.

When Faith returned, they headed outside. He saw Matt stiffen as he came up to the swings. "Mind if we join you?"

Linc smiled. "'Course not."

Faith climbed on the swing and began to hum. Joe pushed her, while Matt wandered to the tree. He picked up his baseball and glove and began to toss it up in the air.

"I'm going to the sandbox," Faith said after several pushes. "Wanna come, Daddy?"

"You go on, honey. I'd like to talk to Matt." He bent down and hugged her. She gave him a big slobbery kiss and skipped off to the sandbox. Joe crossed to Matt. "Want to throw the ball around?"

Matt shrugged. Well, that was progress. Usually Joe just got the cold shoulder. He wondered idly where that phrase came from as he picked up a glove.

His son stared longingly at the bat on the ground. "Maybe I could hit some. You could pitch and Uncle Linc could play outfield."

"Sounds good to me." Joe struggled to keep his pleasure concealed. This was the first overture Matt had made to him. Joe glanced at Linc. "What about you, Uncle Linc?"

"I'm at your disposal." Linc took Joe's mitt and jogged to the "outfield."

At the "mound" Joe assumed a pitcher's stance. "Ready?"

Matt nodded. He watched the boy focus. Grip the bat. Zero in on the ball as it flew toward him. The bat connected solidly, and Linc had to stretch to catch the pop fly.

Four pitches later, Joe called out, "You're good, Matt. Very good."

Matt grumbled something, and play continued. After a half hour, Linc begged off to get a drink, and taking Faith with him, trekked into the house. Joe jogged up to his son. "You've got a lot of talent, Matt. What position do you play?"

"First base." He stared over Joe's shoulder. "I *did* anyway. Our team doesn't have a coach this season. Mr. Pike moved to the city, and there's not a lot of fathers who wanna get involved."

"What happens if you don't get a coach?"

"We're dropped from the league. Uncle Linc could do it. But Mom says he's busy and he'd be spreading himself too thin." Matt rolled his eyes. "You probably know where that phrase came from."

Joe laughed. "Not off the top of my head."

Matt bit back a grin. "Geez, you're full of 'em."

Joe thought for a minute. "What would you say to my coaching your team?"

Winning the lottery couldn't compare to what the look on Matt's face did to Joe's insides. It made him vow to get close to his son, no matter what he had to do.

"Could you?"

Joe understood the implication of the question. "I'll have to ask your mom. You're right, Uncle Linc is too busy to be there for the games and practices."

"I, um . . ." Matt kicked the dirt with his toe. "I still don't understand all this. Why he has to be with us."

"I know, Matt. It's hard." He glanced to the upstairs where Annie was working. Faith had told him she was renovating the house. She'd gotten to be one tough cookie. Geez, now he was *thinking* idioms. "I'll go ask her."

With Matt's pleased grin firmly in mind, he headed to the door, where Linc was just exiting. "I need to talk to Annie."

Linc said nonchalantly, "I'll come up."

Joe bit back his objection. Damn, it had been weeks since he'd been coming here, proving himself. He'd never once lost his temper with his kids. And he'd done wonders in his counseling sessions with Ronny. The boy had settled down and even started talking about what might be causing his misbehavior. Annie knew all this and, still, she wouldn't let him near the kids alone.

God give me strength, he prayed as he and his chaperone trudged into the house and upstairs.

DIPPING the paintbrush into the can on the ladder's shelf, Annie reached up to cut in from the ceiling. Instead of choosing a dull beige or off-white, she'd picked a pretty peach for the walls of her bedroom. Very feminine. She planned to buy that brass headboard she'd seen in a catalog as soon as she could afford it and refinish the pine dresser and nightstand next week.

"Annie."

The brush slipped and she swiped her sleeve with a streak of paint. Damn it, his voice still held power over her. She whirled around. "What are you doing here?"

Linc materialized behind him. Her heartbeat quieted as she set down the paintbrush and stepped off the ladder.

"I want to talk to you." Joe's voice was soft, like he was soothing a mare. She didn't particularly like the image.

Flicking off the radio, she faced him. "I don't want you up here."

"Why?"

"It's too . . ." Intimate. And she remembered one time in a bedroom they'd shared that he—oh, God, she had to block the nightmare. "Never mind. Just don't come here again."

"Fine." His lips thinned.

Too bad. She refused to succumb to his *hurt feelings.* Every time she made a negative comment, or criticized him, like about the underwear thing, he looked like a kicked dog. She didn't want to hurt him, but she was still very frightened of him.

"What do you want to talk about?"

"Matt's Little League team doesn't have a coach. He says they'll be dropped from the league if they don't find one."

"Somebody'll volunteer. They always do."

"I'd like to."

"What?"

"I'd like to be his coach."

"Matt wouldn't want that."

"He must be desperate." Joe shrugged, donned the little-boy look that she used to fall head over heels for. "He said I could ask you."

"You already discussed this with him?"

"Well, it just came up."

"Don't ever do that again."

"Annie, I . . ." He ran his hand through his hair, mussing it. Reminding her of the photo session. And what he looked like lazing on that couch. There were other times, in the bedroom, that were pleasant memories. She banished those, too. "I need some way to connect with Matt. His animosity's gone on too long."

"He has good reason to resent you. He saw a lot." Even if he'd never witnessed the worst.

Joe swallowed hard. "I know. And I have to regain his trust. If I could see him more, I'd work on that. If we could do fun things together, he'd get to know me and realize I've changed."

She angled her chin. "The verdict's still out on that one."

His eyes got bleak. "Please, give me a chance to replace his bad memories with good ones."

Annie sighed. She remembered seeing Matt study those stupid

idioms in the book. She'd also found him looking at an old picture of Joe in a photo album. Her son's face had been . . . yearning.

"You'll be alone with him. Linc can't go to games and practices."

"I know. Don't you think I'm trustworthy enough for that?"

"No." She stared past Joe at Linc, who gave her his disappointed minister look. They'd had a discussion about this already.

Linc came fully into the room. "Can we talk about this alone?"

Slowly, she nodded.

Joe turned and headed for the door. When he reached it, he pivoted around and dug his hands into his back pockets. "I know I hurt you in a way no man has a right to hurt a woman, but I don't know what else to do to show you how sorry I am—and that I've changed. Please, Annie." His voice cracked. "Give me a chance with Matt."

After he left, Annie sighed and dropped to the floor. She blew her bangs out of her hair and played with the tie on her sneakers. Contact with Joe put her through an emotional wringer every single time.

Linc sank down beside her. They stared at the half-painted walls, the furniture covered with drop cloths. Finally he took her hand and squeezed it. "It's time to let go a little, Annie."

"Of?"

"The anger. He did despicable things to you. But you have to let go of that rage inside you. For your sake and for Matt's."

"Matt's?"

"I've watched him. He's taking his cues from you. Part of his attitude toward Joe comes from how you act."

"Oh, God, I don't want that." She stared at her fish tank on the other side of the room, watching the angelfish cruise and dart. "I'm not happy with how I'm behaving, either, Linc. It's just that I'm scared of him."

"He's changed."

"How do you know?"

"God told me."

They both chuckled.

"I feel it in my gut. I've spent time with him in the last month. You've seen how brilliant he's been on the Council. He's starting some good programs for kids, and Beth thinks he walks on water because of how he's helped Ronny."

"Beth's a pussycat. So are you."

"Well, tiger, maybe it's time to sheath your claws. Give him this opportunity with Matt. I think it's the right thing to do."

Annie sighed. "I'll think about it. Maybe he can be alone with Matt for the game stuff. There'll be others around, anyway, most of the time. And Matt's old enough to tell me if anything happens." She looked at Linc. "I'm not ready to be alone with him in this house, though."

Linc cocked his head, his dark eyes sad. "Maybe you should go back to see your counselor. Talk about Joe being back in town."

"Maybe." If she could get rid of the fear, it would be worth it. "Maybe I will."

JOE dropped down on one of steps halfway downstairs, waiting for Linc to come out of Annie's room. He'd only made it this far when the sight of her on the ladder resurrected another time, years ago, when she'd been on a ladder painting. . . .

He'd been hoping for a promotion at work. Sensing he was on a downslide he might never recover from, he'd applied for a supervisor's position and been turned down. "No college," the boss had told him. "You're smart as a whip, Murphy, but the job calls for more education." As if he felt sorry for him, the boss added, "Why don't you take some courses at the local community college?"

Joe had walked out and gone to Zip's Bar and Grill. Could he really go to college? It was something he'd never dreamed of, even though Margo and Linc had gone and finished. He was nursing a beer when his father walked in. The old man was already drunk. He crossed right to Joe. "Heard you blew the promotion at the B plant."

Joe said nothing.

"I was right about you. You're goin' nowhere, son, just like me."

The *just like me* made Joe order a shot, then another, to go with his beer. He was drunk when he stumbled his way out of the bar, thoughts of college disappearing like mist off the lake with his father's taunting. When he'd walked into their apartment and found Annie up on a ladder, painting Matt's room, all his frustration focused on her. "What the hell are you doing?"

"Painting Matt's room. Since he's staying with your mother tonight, I thought . . ."

"I told you we couldn't afford the paint."

Her wide-eyed innocence had enraged him. "I used my dance money. The paint was on sale . . ."

Blindly he stalked to her. Irrational, he stuck out his foot and kicked the bottom of the ladder. Paint went flying . . . and so did she. Like a baby oak tree felled by an ax, she tumbled to the floor, right on her wrist. It was her sobs that cleared the haze of his anger. He'd been astounded by what he'd done, remorseful. He'd taken her to ER, but he remembered she didn't look at him, all the way there. Afterward, he tried to apologize, but she blanked her face and averted her gaze. During the night, she cried her eyes out.

He'd finished painting Matt's room the next morning, and proceeded to give the whole place a fresh coat. Eventually she'd forgiven him.

But it had taken her broken wrist six months to heal.

His own moan brought him out of the black hole of memory. No wonder she couldn't trust him. He was a bastard. He was scum.

Was *is the operative word here,* Pete would say.

He couldn't see that now. He guessed it was time for another session with his counselor.

SARA Fox had saved Annie's sanity six years before. At that time, the therapist had worked in Glen Oaks's social services office, but in the intervening years, she'd moved on to a private practice in the city. Now, she saw patients in a small town house on the Upper West Side near Lincoln Center. After two years of intensive counseling, Annie had never expected to need her again. They sat in her living room, with hardwood floors, teak furniture and beautiful artwork on the walls; Annie filled her in on the recent turn of events.

"Well!" Sara arched thick eyebrows into curly bangs. Her pretty blue eyes were full of surprise and sympathy. "This is unexpected."

Annie tucked her feet under her in the comfortable leather

chair. She'd come right from work and made the hour train ride in a sweater and long denim skirt thrown over her tights and leotard. "I was shocked when he walked into that room for the Council meeting. And angry at his surprising me."

"His reason for doing that is clear, Annie. And pretty good planning on his part. He's obviously got all his ducks in a row."

The familiar resentment when one of her friends sided with Joe burned like a low flame in her stomach. "It worked."

"I can tell you're angry."

"I'm furious."

"Tell me at what, specifically."

"For one, he's slowly converting everybody to thinking he's a great guy—Linc, Beth, Faith, of course, maybe even Matt."

"And you don't want that." When Annie started to speak, Sara held up a palm. "No, think about it for a minute. Do you want Joe to have changed?"

God, she'd never allowed herself to get this far in her thought process. She pictured Ronny and how things were going so much better for him since his meetings with Joe. She witnessed the attention and patience he showed Faith. She thought of her son studying *The Things We Say*.

"In the long run," Annie said, rubbing her ring finger where his wedding band had once rested, "I have to, don't I? He's my kids' father. If he's really changed and can be a part of their lives, I have to want it."

"Let's talk about what you're really feeling, besides anger."

She thought for a moment. "Fear."

"Of?"

Coldness invaded Annie's stomach, streaked through her limbs and settled in her heart. It happened every time she thought about Joe hitting her. "I still remember what it felt like when he hit me."

"And you think he's going to hit you again?"

She pictured Joe tying Faith's ballet slipper so she could show him a new dance she'd learned. She saw him hug his son, even when Matt stiffened up on him. "I don't know. He seems to be gentler now, calmer."

"Batterers Recovery Programs work, in the right circumstances. Did he get more therapy in the years after that ended and before he came home?"

"Yes."

"Good reasons to think he's changed." She smiled. "And Annie, you're not defenseless anymore. Physically or emotionally. You've got all those self-defense courses behind you, but more so, battered women allow the abuse for emotional reasons. You're not the girl who took it once."

"So what are you saying?"

"He won't hurt you again. Not just because he doesn't want to, but because you won't let him."

"What about the kids?"

"Did he ever hit Matt?"

"You know he didn't."

"Matt's almost twelve now. A big boy. And he's had karate training. I don't think your son's in danger."

"Are you saying I should let him see the kids alone?"

"No, I'm saying you have a lot less to fear than you think. If you could get rid of the fear, the anger might go away and you could see things more clearly."

Annie just stared at her.

"Unless there's something you're not telling me."

"Like?"

"I don't know. Are you having feelings for him?"

"No, of course not." Annie bolted out of the chair and began to pace. It wasn't until she caught the knowing look in Sara's eyes that she realized her reaction was a big tip-off to her true emotions. She stopped and stared at the counselor. "I can't have feelings for him after what he did."

"An abused wife's profile contradicts that. She really does love the man who abuses her. Mostly, she just wants him to change."

"I don't love Joe Murphy."

"You loved him since you were thirteen. It's not an easy thing to overcome." Sara cocked her head. "And you can still be attracted to him."

Annie remembered how he'd looked modeling the underwear. He was taut and firm and beautifully proportioned. As a dancer, she could appreciate the near perfection of his body. "Even if that's true, I can't imagine letting him near me."

"Because of the rape."

The word swamped her. She was back in that bedroom, totally helpless, totally at his mercy. She'd never told anybody but Sara about it, not even Beth or Margo. "Yes."

"I'm not recommending you have a relationship with your ex-husband, Annie. I'm just saying that Linc's right in some ways. You've got to let go of the anger, for your own sake as well as Matt's."

"And how do I do that?" Joe's handsome features, contorted in a mask of rage as he forced her to have sex that last time, made Sara's recommendation seem impossible.

"The first step is to decide you want to let go of it."

Annie's shoulders slumped. Did she want to let go of it? The anger took so much energy. The resentment ate away inside her at night, after Joe's visits. And in church, on Sundays, she felt estranged from God.

"I guess I'd like to let go of it. I just don't know how."

"Let's brainstorm some strategies, shall we?" Sara smiled. "And for the record, I think that's the right thing to do."

THIRTEEN

"BE careful what you wish for," Beth mumbled as she assembled the last of the order for the big powwow taking place in her diner. She'd anxiously awaited the opening of the track, even for qualifying and other preseason events, because it meant business would really pick up. Placing parsley sprigs on a western omelette, she *was* grateful for the added business, topped off by the official meeting Mayor Hunsinger had scheduled to have here over breakfast today.

She just hadn't known it was to discuss the publicity for Tucker's exhibition race in the fall. Tucker, who sat stone-faced, glaring at Doc who apparently—she overhead this—had not told him the meeting was at her diner. Tucker, who was obviously avoiding her, and whom she'd likewise avoided, the past two weeks.

Ever since Ronny's interrogation. *He's hitting on you, Mom . . . He looked at you like Linc looks at Margo . . .*

"Fritatta's ready." Gerty raised her eyes from the stove. "Lordy, girl, is it letting up out there at all?"

"A bit from the breakfast crowd." Beth glanced at the clock. "But lunch'll start soon. I'm sorry about this, Gerty."

"Not your fault Nana got sick. Then Milt and Nancy," her two part-timers, "got in that fender bender on the way to work."

"I'm just glad they're all right."

"Are you holding up?"

Knotting the towel tighter around her waist, she straightened her pink blouse and hefted the tray onto her shoulder. "I'm fine."

Only she wasn't. As she headed to the tables set up for ten, she prayed her hand didn't tremble like when she'd taken Tucker's order. He was dressed in a forest green sweater and tan Dockers that looked like a million bucks on him. When she'd bent over to take his order, the masculine smell of aftershave had zinged right through to her toes. She'd noticed a cut he'd gotten from shaving near his ear and she'd had the absurd urge to touch it. Chiding herself for her feelings, she reached the back of the diner.

At the table—Tucker sat facing Danny's picture and she'd caught him staring at it a few times—she set the heavy tray down on a serving stand. "It's here," she announced to the group. "I'm sorry it took so long."

"Not to worry, little lady." The mayor nodded to the group. "We've been making plans."

She gave them a weak smile. As she'd filled coffee mugs, she'd overheard those plans—and Tucker's stoic reaction to them. Publicity shots with him in the racing suit he'd worn when he'd won the Daytona 500 . . . pictures of him around Glen Oaks . . . shots showing the *sexy race car driver relaxing in the the Big Apple*.

The last had come from Tara Snow, the shapely blonde from an advertising agency in New York, who was in charge of the PR.

And who had her hands all over Tucker.

She'd touched his arm as she'd outlined her strategy. Her vampire-red fingernails had scraped down his shoulders as she'd made a point of how he looked in his racing suit. She'd giggled breathily as she'd leaned over to say something in his ear.

Beth tried not to react when she delivered the woman's order—an egg-white omelette that Gerty had had to fuss over. Just at that moment, Tara reached out and squeezed Tucker's big masculine hand. "Pass the salt please, Tuck."

Beth served his fritatta next.

"Looks good," he said, eyeing it appreciatively.

"I'm sorry service is so slow."

"You should hire more help, dear." Tara smiled at her sweetly. "This place will be hopping from now until the race."

Tucker threw Tara an annoyed look. "Beth told us she was short three people this morning." He gave Beth a grin full of warm Southern honey, and her heart turned over. "You're workin' miracles by yourself out here."

"Gerty doin' okay out in the kitchen?" Doc asked.

"She's keeping up."

Doc scowled. "I hope her back's okay." Gerty had thrown her back out the week before, but Beth wondered how Doc knew about it.

She smiled at him. "She went to some Chinese masseuse in the city and he cured her."

Doc rolled his eyes. "Damn fool woman."

"Beth, could you cash us out?" a customer called from the front.

"Excuse me." She placed the last plate in front of Doc and hurried away.

At the counter, she tried hard to keep her gaze away from Tucker. But business slowed enough for her to get a cup of coffee, and her eyes wandered to him as she sipped it.

She'd successfully stayed away from him. Because, Sunday morning in church, she'd admitted Ronny was right. She'd seen the spark of interest in Tucker's green eyes when he looked at her. And she was attracted to him. Of all the things that could have happened when he came back to town, this was the worst, and most unexpected.

She was attracted to a man who, along with many people in town, thought that he'd killed her husband. To a man who Ron thought had killed his father. How the *hell* had it happened? They hadn't been together that much. But they'd made connections when they *had* been in each other's company. She remembered talking to him at the police station, crying on his shoulder the night she took Ronny to jail, standing up to Julia and Carl with him. Or maybe it was just plain old chemistry. Who knew?

She told herself that at least Ronny had seemed happier in the last two weeks. And Doc had said he'd been nicer to Tucker. They were even working on the car together.

When Roman Becker came in and sat at the counter, she welcomed the distraction. "Hi, Roman."

"Morning, Beth." His thick black hair was slicked off his

face as if he'd just showered, accenting his chiseled features. He always reminded her of a young Laurence Olivier. He was only a few feet away from Tucker. Her gaze strayed past Roman to those linebacker shoulders that she'd read had given Tucker trouble getting out of race cars.

"Busy today?"

"Uh-huh." She explained her situation.

"You work too hard." He reached out to squeeze her hand. Just as Tucker drew back his seat, stood and turned.

His gaze fell on their clasped hands. His eyes darkened. He nodded to Roman, didn't look at her and headed to the bathrooms.

"What's the matter with The Menace?" Roman asked.

She drew her hand away and indicated the back tables. "That's a meeting with the brass. He hates the publicity part."

"Are you kidding? The babes hang all over him."

Beth had seen some pictures of Tucker and the racing groupies. Though the married race car drivers often brought their wives on the circuit, and many had RV's they stayed in, the single drivers were pursued like rock stars. She couldn't think about it. She was almost grateful when the lunch crowd started to file in.

Tired though she was, she'd preferred working herself to exhaustion to watching Tara Snow fall all over Tucker.

TUCKER couldn't keep his eyes off of Beth. She was a rare and precious cameo next to the glare of costume jewelry like Tara Snow. As they all stood to leave, Beth circled the counter to grab a big gray tub. Scanning the diner, he saw people waiting by the door and several tables in need of clearing.

"Where's Doc?" the mayor asked.

"He went to the kitchen. He's friends with the cook." Tucker suspected Doc was out there helping Gerty get the food out.

Tara Snow shook back her mane of streaked blond hair with supermodel style. "We don't need him anyway." She batted heavily made-up eyelashes at Tucker. "We're done now, Tucker. Want to show me around town?"

"Sorry," Tucker lied. "Doc and I have an appointment."

She pouted her rouged lips. "You have to spend all of next

Monday with me, remember? I'm coming back for the photo shoot of you and the town."

"Sure."

Tara scanned the diner, noted Beth working like a demon to clear the tables, and took in the crowd impatiently standing at the door. "I do hope they get their act together here before the onslaught descends on them for the race."

Tucker said nothing, though he took her criticism personally. For Beth. Who he'd avoided for two weeks. He'd managed to be upstairs or out in the garage most of the time when she dropped off Ron or came to pick him up. And when he *had* seen her, he was remote. Once, though, he'd literally bumped into her coming out of the office as he headed to the kitchen, and had grabbed her arms to steady her. She'd felt strong and solid under his hands and he experienced a longing so deep it made his knees weak. She'd been as skittish as a newborn colt that night, and he knew why.

Ron. Tucker had guessed, after her son's open animosity that afternoon at the diner, that the kid had said something to her. Not that there was much to say. He and Beth had only been together a few times. And it wasn't until Ron had been outright rude, that Tucker had admitted to himself he *was* attracted to Beth.

Which only added to his list of sins. How could he want the widow of the man he killed?

You're not responsible for Danny's death. She'd told him a hundred times.

And the problem was, when he was with Beth Donovan, he believed it. Which probably accounted for the heat he felt every time he was near her. Not her dry sense of humor. Not her devotion to her son. Not her hard work ethic. And certainly not that body that he'd dreamed about in 3-D living color.

A rattle, then a crash, drew him from the X-rated thoughts. He heard, "Oh, no!" Beth had dropped the tub of dishes. Several had bounced out and broken on the floor.

Tara shook her head. "Let's get out of here."

Tucker scowled. "Go on, I'm waitin' for Doc."

The others filed out as Tucker crossed to Beth. She was bent over the mess, picking up the pieces. He tossed his jacket on a stool and squatted down next to her. "Can I help?"

She raised worried eyes to him. "No. I'm such a klutz. I was watching—" She stopped and blushed. "I wasn't watching where I was going." She swiped a strand of chestnut hair out of her eyes.

He smiled. "Hey, Bonnie Parker's no klutz. She was a great waitress. Just like you."

"How do you know she was a waitress?" They talked as they picked up the dishes.

"I read about it."

"You did?" Distracted by a customer calling her, she scanned the diner. Her pretty brow creased.

"Why don't I finish up here? You go seat those customers."

"I couldn't ask you to do that."

"You didn't ask." He raised his thumb and pointed. "Scoot."

He could tell she was torn. But when two people turned to walk out, she stood. "Okay. Just until I get this under control."

Tucker smiled like he hadn't smiled in a couple of weeks as he gathered up the last of the shards and disposed of them. He whistled as he found the mop inside a closet and swabbed the floor. In minutes, the mess was gone, and the customers seated.

By the time he stowed the mop, three more booths had emptied. Beth was in the kitchen.

Aw, hell, he couldn't just leave them. Snagging a big white towel from behind the counter, he tied it around his waist, picked up an empty tub and had the booths cleaned and three more parties seated by the time she returned.

Her pretty mouth fell open when she saw what he'd done. She headed right toward him, like a female vigilante; he was behind the counter where he was pouring soft drinks.

"What are you doing?" she asked.

"Helpin' out. My mama taught me the way around a kitchen when I was knee high."

"Tucker, you can't do this."

"Why?" He placed four cokes on a tray and lifted it up.

"I . . . you're a . . . I . . ."

He chucked her under the chin. "You're stammerin', dollface. Why don't you just take the orders and we'll discuss why I can't do this later."

She had no choice. As she left him to tend to her customers, she was shaking her head.

By two o'clock the diner had finally cleared out. Tucker had bussed tables, served drinks and hummed along with the jukebox to some Tammy Wynette and Garth Brooks. Beth plopped down on a stool and blew a stray strand of hair out of her eyes. She looked tired and a little sad.

He turned, got her coffee and put it in front of her.

"Tucker, please, you've done enough."

"Hell, I hardly exerted myself." He grinned down at her. "It was fun."

Shaking her head again, she smiled. "The customers loved it. I think they stayed longer just to watch you."

"Hey, I wield a mean towel."

"And Doc's a great cook."

"Yeah, I know." He leaned over and braced his arms on the counter. "Now tell me, pretty lady, if he can help out, why can't I?"

"You're a superstar."

"Shucks, ma'am, I'm just a country boy."

"You've been listening to too much Western music."

He grinned again.

"How can I thank you?"

Swallowing hard, he straightened. He tried looking at the wall—at her husband's picture—but the reminder didn't work this time. An image of her *thanking him,* wrapped up in white satin sheets like his own personal birthday present superimposed itself over the photos. His body hardened. "No thanks necessary." He tried to joke, letting his accent thicken. "I'm happy to oblige, ma'am."

When he faced her again, she'd cocked her head. "You're a nice guy, you know that?"

"Don't tell Tara Snow. I think she's after a different image."

"I think she's after a lot more than that."

He rolled his eyes. "God forbid."

"Why? She's beautiful."

"She's plastic and painted." It used to be his type. "I prefer my women natural and wholesome." At least now he did.

Her eyes, fringed with naked thick lashes, widened. And her unpainted lips parted.

It was just like that night he'd come here after Ron's first jail weekend. He was lured in. Drawn to her, like a sexual magnet. He stepped to the counter, leaned over and reached out his hand. Slow and easy, he ran the pad of his thumb over her lips.

She swallowed hard.

So did he.

Locking his gaze on her lips, he said, "Real natural." Tracing his finger over the few freckles on her nose, he whispered hoarsely, "And real wholesome."

He continued to stare at her.

Only when Doc and Gerty came out of the kitchen did he draw back.

FOURTEEN

———

"Did you get what you needed, Linc?" Jane Meachum peered up at him from her desk in the reception area of the new Social Services wing of the town hall. Her deep blue eyes held warmth and concern.

"Yes, I did. Thanks for typing this." He held up the schedule for the next Council meeting.

"You're welcome. It took all of ten minutes."

"Ah, Super Secretary."

Her smile was wholesome. Like her outfit—a maroon sweater and turtleneck and a black pleated skirt with tights. Very preppie. Margo wouldn't be caught dead in those clothes.

Jane glanced at the clock. "I'm, um, due for a break. Want to get some coffee with me?"

"I'd love to, but I have a women's group meeting in fifteen minutes at the church."

"Oh, well, I know how that is."

"That's right. Your dad's the minister over at Glen Presbyterian."

"That's me, a Preacher's Kid."

"Lucky you." He grinned. "Maybe next time?"

"Sure." He turned to go. "Linc?"

He pivoted.

"I'd really like to have coffee with you. Or lunch sometime."

It had been so long he didn't recognize the come-on, demure and ingenuous as it was. Margo's face appeared before him. She'd always been his type—sassy, stylish and sexy. But his conversation with Beth rang in his ears. *You need a woman by your side . . . you should have kids.* And he hadn't heard from Margo since their disastrous phone conversation. He'd called and left messages twice. Then he stopped.

Linc gave Jane a huge grin. "How about lunch today?"

She blushed. It was cute. "Sure. I'm free."

"Wanna meet at Beth's diner or shall I pick you up?"

"I'll walk over and meet you. About one?"

"Great. See you then." And he strutted out whistling.

Hmm, he said to God as he walked back to the church. *Now, that's interesting.*

I provide, my son, I provide.

Are you my personal date consultant now?

He heard God snort.

And started whistling again.

He was no longer whistling when he arrived at church, entered the fellowship hall and found a stream of water seeping out from under a closet door. *Oh God, give me patience,* he prayed as he headed to the janitor's closet. In a hurry, he slipped and fell right on his ass. "Damn it to hell!" Standing in now wet jeans, he picked his way to the closet. Inside, he found the utility sink overflowing onto the floor, out of the closet all the way to kingdom come. Again, carefully—his back was already starting to ache—he waded in and shut off the faucet. Where the hell had Henry gone? He heard the women for his Tuesday group arriving as he walked out of the storage area. "Be careful ladies, we've had a slight leak here."

Barbara Mandarino smiled. "What a mess."

Linc shook his head. "Go on and sit down. I'll mop this up in a sec. I just want to check on Henry and see if he's okay."

He took the stairs gingerly, his loafers squeaking on the vinyl floor. "Henry?" he called out when he reached the narthex. "Are you here?" He checked the sanctuary. Dark, no Henry. Linc's heartbeat skittered. The guy was old. Injured. Linc prayed nothing had happened to him. He headed down to the Sunday school classrooms. A door to one was ajar. Inside he found Henry.

It was a ludicrous sight. The big man was stuffed into one of the little kids' chairs reading a book. His knees hit the top of the table, and his arms dangled at this sides. Linc pushed open the door and said softly, "Henry, are you all right?"

The janitor looked up. Nodded. Linc glanced at the book. "Did you find something that interests you there?"

Nodding again. Linc crossed to him and stared down at the children's Bible which was open to an illustration of Noah's Ark. Now that was irony. The corners of Linc's lips turned up. "Don't you know the story of the flood, Henry?"

He nodded.

"Was the Bible just open to that page?"

"Uh-huh." Well, that was progress.

"Did something interest you?"

Henry lifted the Bible to Linc. Linc focused in closer. Cartoon drawings of Biblical characters were sketched in full color. On this particular page was the Ark. Right in the center Noah stared up at the sky. Linc smiled. "He looks just like you, doesn't he, Henry?"

Vigorously, Henry nodded.

Linc laughed aloud. "Why don't you stay here a minute and bask in your fame, old buddy." He squeezed the man's shoulder and headed back to the fellowship hall, rolling up his sleeves.

When he got there, not a drop of water was on the floor. Everything was dry, and clean. Rags were stacked in a bucket, and two wet mops propped against the wall.

Of course. The women. Light-footed, he walked to the back room. They were in a circle, chatting quietly. Anita noticed him first. "Hi, Rev." Her sass reminded him of Margo.

"You didn't have to clean up after me, ladies."

They shrugged it off. They were used to cleaning up after men. The automaticity of their actions saddened him.

"But I appreciate it." He wondered how often they heard that. "Very much." Taking a chair, he read the board, where he'd written the topics they'd brainstormed a few weeks ago. "Okay. Which of these shall we start out with?"

Anita spoke again. "Loneliness."

Something Linc was on intimate terms with. "All right. Take the pads and pencils I left on the chairs." He'd set up the room himself this time. "Let's all write about what makes us feel lonely. Then we'll share our experiences."

To a person, every woman's face blanked. He drew in a deep breath. "Um, don't put your names on them. I'll collect them and read them aloud; they'll be anonymous and we'll talk about them in general terms." Then he planned to elicit ways to curb loneliness. He was no divine magician, though, and he wasn't sure he could pull that rabbit out of the hat for them—or for himself.

He thought of Jane Meachum as he wrote, *lack of companionship*. He didn't mean sex, although that was an issue, too. He wrote it down.

It immediately conjured up images of Margo. Damn! He would not do this today. She'd made it clear she was staying away from him. It was for the best.

Isn't it? he asked God as the others wrote.

You tell me.

Come on, I need a little guidance, here.

Okay, go to lunch with Jane. See what happens.

Is Margo all right?

All I can tell you is that I'm watching over her.

The thought comforted Linc and he turned back to his list.

STARING out her window at the hustle and bustle of New York, Margo tapped the memo she held against the pane of glass. The missive had been on her desk that morning when she'd arrived at work. She'd been lulled into thinking things were back on track with Philip. The last two weeks had been business as usual. Which was why she'd been ambushed by this information.

At the end of the week, he'd taken her to lunch; they'd had a relaxed meal at Izzy's in Times Square. Even if he did have bad news. He'd ordered a martini, which was unusual, as he rarely drank during the day. Then he'd stared somberly out at the square.

"What's wrong, Philip?"

He shook his head. He looked tired, and lines of wear creased his forehead and mouth. He'd been impeccably dressed in a navy pin-striped suit, but his usual calm demeanor was agitated. "Things aren't good at home."

"No?"

"Sally and I are talking seriously about separating."

"Oh, no, I'm sorry."

"Me, too. I'm worried about the girls." He studied her. "I know I've been acting strange lately. That's why."

She'd squeezed his hand. "Have you thought of counseling?"

"Sally won't go."

"I'm sorry," she repeated.

"Me, too," he said again. He shrugged. "Let's not discuss this anymore. It's too depressing. How's everything with you?"

"Good, why wouldn't it be?"

"I got the impression things were rough for your *friends* back home."

The emphasis on the word alerted her. "Things are rough for Beth. You know, I've talked about her. Her son's in trouble again. It's been hard on her." She frowned as she nibbled on her quiche. "And Annie, my other friend?"

He nodded, leaving his food untouched.

"Her ex is back in town, claiming he's a changed man. They're both struggling."

"Did you go home again this weekend?"

"No, I haven't been home for several."

"I see. So you haven't seen the minister?"

"His name is Linc, but why would you ask that, anyway?"

Philip shrugged. "Margo, you talk about him all the time. If I didn't know you so well, I'd think you had a thing for him."

"Know me so well?"

"Yeah. Religion's your hot button. You grew up tormented by it." He regarded her gray suit and light pink silk T-shirt. "Besides, you're not exactly minister's wife material."

She wasn't sure why his remark offended her. It was certainly true.

Philip gave her a very male grin. "I'm really more your type, sweetheart."

She rolled her eyes.

Serious now, he tilted her chin and looked deeply into her eyes. "You know Margo, I could be a free man soon."

The statement stunned her. "Philip, please, I thought we put this behind us."

Taking her cue, he dropped his hand. "We did, I'm sorry. I'm just raw today . . ."

She'd felt uncomfortable about the comment and had avoided him all week until she'd talked to him about her impending vacation.

And now this.

She read the memo again. "The Laufler's factory automation program will be out-sourced to Spencer and Co." An independent contractor. "Please meet with their reps on April 4, at 2 P.M., before your vacation. P."

Out-sourced. That usually happened when there was too much work for in-house engineers, so independent contractors were brought in to take up the slack. But Margo wasn't overworked. She'd finished the designs on the Jamison account and planned to start Laufler's when she returned from her week's vacation.

The vacation she'd offered not to take if there was a problem with the schedule. . . .

"No, go," Philip had said. "You've been planning this trip to Cancun for ages."

She was about to tell him she'd canceled that trip to go to Glen Oaks and spend some time with Annie and to help Beth out with the diner now that some early racing events had started at the track. She'd halted, though, remembering his tone of voice when he'd asked about Linc. "It can be postponed," she'd said evasively.

He'd been distracted, and had simply said, "No, go. . . ."

So she'd planned, against her better judgment, to go back to Glen Oaks Sunday after church was over. For the week.

Not a good idea, Mary Margaret. All that time in proximity to Linc was playing with fire. But she did want to help Beth out, and Annie was a wreck over Joe's presence in town.

And . . . Linc was dating someone. Bethy told her.

No, that had nothing to do with it. It was good that he was dating. She was even a PK. God, how ironic. The love of her life was dating a preacher's kid. She probably played the organ, sang in the church choir and wore lace collars and pearl earrings.

Forget about it. Go see Philip.

Margo circled her desk and strode out of the office to the elevator, up three floors, then into his outer office. "Hi, Geraldine, is he in?"

Geraldine's kind blue eyes smiled at her from where she sat behind a computer. At fifty-five, she'd been with Philip since he'd come to CompuQuest. "Ah, no, he has a few days off."

"Really? I didn't know he was taking vacation."

"He's not. This was an emergency. It came up suddenly."

Margo held out the memo. "Do you know anything about this?"

Geraldine read the paper. "Why, no. I didn't even type that."

Hmm. What to do? "Do you know when he'll be in the of-fice?"

"He said maybe Tuesday or Wednesday. He called in this morning, but didn't give me any details." The woman scowled and Margo thought about how she doted on Philip, like a son. And how Philip had held her hand all during her husband's funeral. "He was fine last night when I left."

Fine enough to send Margo this memo. She couldn't help wondering at the coincidence of the timing. Margo was going on vacation. He'd taken a product away from her. He wasn't here to ask about it.

And she'd refused his sexual come-on. Were they connected?

"Margo, do you want me to call him?"

"No, thanks, Gerry. I'll deal with this when I get back."

"Have a great time in Cancun."

"Cancun?"

"Your vacation."

"Oh, sure. Thanks."

Timing continued to plague her as she made her way back to the office. The all-male weekend. The confusion over the Jami-son account. Philip's separation from his wife. Was she just being overly suspicious?

Damn, she wished she could talk to Linc about this.

MARGO arrived late Sunday night in Glen Oaks without telling anyone she was coming and headed right to Beth's house. Her friend hugged her tightly, and after Margo spent a couple of hours with Ronny, she and Beth stayed up late talking. Beth seemed edgy and preoccupied, but didn't want to share any of what was on her mind. Since the same was true for Margo her-self, they did what they always did—respected each other's pri-vacy and vegged out. They made popcorn and watched *The Thomas Crown Affair* again and drooled over Pierce Brosnan. They slept in Beth's big bed, reminding Margo of the sleepovers they'd had as kids. No bad dreams assailed her that night. But Beth had a beauty. She woke up shivering, and sweating, but wouldn't discuss the nightmare. She had trouble sleeping after that, so the next morning, Margo insisted Beth stay in bed and catch a few more z's; Margo got up bright and early and went to the diner to cover for her friend. She was behind the counter serving an omelette to Jim Tacone, the weary but kind probation officer, when Linc came in.

And he wasn't alone.

The sight of him with another woman poleaxed Margo. She froze right in the middle of a sentence. Linc stopped, too, and stared disbelievingly at her. Then his eyes flickered with something she rarely saw these days. Hated to see. Anger. Because she hadn't returned his phone calls all week, and because she hadn't let him know she'd be in town, she guessed.

To dilute it, she waved. "Hi, Rev. Make yourself at home."

His face flaming, Linc nodded and steered the woman he was with to a booth. He helped her off with her prim beige raincoat and shrugged out of his denim jacket, revealing a plaid sports shirt Margo had bought him for his birthday.

She focused on the date. So this must be the preacher's kid. Just as Margo had thought, the woman was angelic looking. Innocent in a way Margo had never been. She was a head shorter than Linc, with soft brown hair; she looked at the Reverend like he was the second coming.

Be glad for him.

I am.

Liar.

Jim Tacone tugged on her sleeve. "Hey, Margo, what were you saying?"

Through the sheer force of will, the kind that had made her strong enough to leave this hellhole of a town, and to leave Linc twice—once when he went into the seminary and once when he told her he was coming back to Glen Oaks—she smiled at Jim and made some quip. Hoping Gerty would materialize to wait on the two new customers, Margo talked with Jim, then was forced to go to Linc.

The Ma Barker in her surfaced as she approached their table. "Hi, Linc," she said easily.

Right away she noticed his first-thing-in-the-morning smell of soap, shaving cream and shampoo. The scent made her shudder. His deep brown eyes were almost black with emotion that he was clearly holding back. Jesse James could be a hellion when he got his dander up. She'd seen it many times. It used to excite her.

It still did.

So she faced Mother Teresa. Damned if the woman didn't

have pearls and lace on today. "I'm Margo Morelli. An old friend of Linc's."

"Jane Meachum." She smiled shyly at Linc. "A *new* friend of his."

Margo gripped the pencil in her hand hard. "Nice to meet you." She smiled again, a real Oscar-winning performance. "Are you ready to order?"

"I'll have decaf coffee." She shrugged. "We've been chatting. I haven't had a chance to look at the menu."

Linc's look was fierce. "I want regular coffee." He'd been trying to give up caffeine.

"Tough night, Rev?" she asked.

"An even tougher morning," he said tightly. With his own death grip on the menu, he asked, "Where's Bethy?"

"I made her stay in bed this morning. I'm covering for her."

"What are you doing in Glen Oaks? I thought you were going to Cancun for the week."

"Changed my mind." God, this was hard. "I decided to take my vacation to be with Beth and Annie. I'm baby-sitting for Matt and Faith later today."

Hurt flashed across his face. "I see." She hadn't said she'd come to town to see him. "So that's why I couldn't reach you last night."

"I was at Beth's."

He nodded and looked at the menu. "We'll order in a minute." His voice was cut-glass cold. She knew then she'd made a huge mistake in not telling him about her plans to come home.

It got even more obvious as she surreptitiously watched him for the next forty-five minutes. He flirted like hell with Miss Pure and Simple. He laughed at everything she said, teased her about her shyness—Margo heard that little tidbit when she delivered their meals—and was a regular courtly knight in escorting her out of the diner with his hand resting cozily at the small of her back. The fist crunching Margo's heart twisted tighter when he said a curt goodbye. He was really, really mad.

Which was why, ten minutes later, she was shocked when he burst through the kitchen doors like a gunslinger looking for his quarry, grabbed her by the arm, said to Gerty, "Don't disturb us!" and dragged Margo to the small office.

Slamming the door, he let go of her arm and whirled around to face her.

*   *   *

LINC was so furious he wanted to wring somebody's neck.
Hers, specifically. He'd been pissed at her anyway for not returning his calls, but he started seeing red when he walked into
Beth's diner and found Margo flirting with the probation officer.
He'd been stunned to see her, all bright and chipper in a sexy V-
necked black sweater with nothing underneath it, those damned
black jeans that made his mouth water and the belt he'd given her
for Christmas—a handmade leather one that wrapped around her
waist like a man's hands.

"Is there some *reason* you didn't tell me about this little
visit?" he shouted.

"Don't yell at me." She plopped her hands on her hips.

"You deserve to be yelled at."

She stuck out her chin. "I didn't know I had to run my schedule by you, Rev."

"Damn it Margo, you know what I mean."

"Uh-uh-uh!" she said saucily. "Your God won't like to hear
you swear."

Spots swam before his eyes. He grabbed her arms and was assaulted by her sexy perfume. "Well, God will like it even less if
I strangle your pretty neck, which is what I *want* to do right
now."

"Such a thought for a man of the cloth."

Desire curled inside him, shocking him with its lightning
quickness, its summer-storm potency. In the past, their fights had
ended in bed. Even as teenagers, it had been their best sex. He
swore again.

Shrugging out of his grasp, she crossed to Beth's desk and
inched her sexy little hips onto the edge of it. "What are you so
mad about?"

He turned his back on her. Rubbed his neck wearily. Took in
a deep, hopefully cleansing breath. "I guess if you don't know
the answer to that, we really are on different wavelengths these
days."

The problem was, they'd always been in tune. She was his
soul mate, even when she'd married somebody else. If they were
growing apart now . . .

It's for the best, he told himself. *When are you going to get it
through your thick skull you can't have this woman?*

Still, he didn't dare face her. "Never mind, Margo. You're right. You're a free agent. You don't owe me anything. Not even a little consideration." He flung back the door so hard it hit the wall and strode out of the kitchen.

His heart felt like she'd stomped on it with those damn boots she wore, picked it up with her beringed hands and thrown it out into the cold.

FIFTEEN

———

WITH a lonely Saturday night looming ahead of him, Linc had to get out of here. Every once in a while, the walls of the church and his garage apartment started to close in on him; he imagined it was what hell would be like. The same thing had happened in his small bedroom at his grandparents' house when he was young. It was why he'd gotten into trouble—in part, to alleviate the boredom, and in part to rage against God for his parents' death and his grandparents' ineptitude. Because of it, Linc understood Ronny's angst. God's divine plan in the works, he thought wryly.

Switching off the last of the lights, he grabbed his battered bomber jacket, threw it on over his long-sleeved red T-shirt and jeans and was just locking up the door when a truck swerved into the lot. *Please don't let it be a parishioner in need of help.* He wasn't sure he had the strength right now to deal with anyone's crisis.

A bulk of a man bolted out of the car and stormed toward Linc. If he hadn't had God on his side, Linc would have been scared. That, and the knowledge that he never forgot the street smarts that had saved him in sticky situations before.

"I wanna talk to you, *Reverend* Grayson." Sam DeMartino's face was flushed and he smelled like gin. From the looks of him, Rosa's husband was ready to go a few rounds in the ring.

Linc's instincts went on red alert, telling him not to under-estimate the man. "Fine. Shoot," Linc said without a trace of fear in his voice. Jesse James could bluff better than the best of them.

"I don't want Rosa coming to that group no more."

"Why?"

"You filling her head with this self-esteem shit." To under-score his attitude, he spit off to the side.

"Rosa's a wonderful person. She should think more of her-self."

"She's got a family to take care of. She shouldn't be off with all those wacky women who don't have nothing better to do."

"I don't agree."

"Yeah, well, I'm her husband. What I say goes in my house."

"Sam, she isn't a possession. She has rights." He angled his head to the door. "Look, why don't you come in, we'll talk about this and maybe—"

"I ain't coming in. And maybe Rosa ain't coming back to church, neither."

"I really hope that won't happen."

DeMartino stepped close. He was a bruiser of a man who towered over Linc by a good head. His shoulders were as wide as a coke machine. "It will. If you don't stay outta her head. This is between a man and his wife."

"It's also between a woman and her God."

Sam's fists curled. Linc felt his whole body tense. He raised his chin and stared up at the man, just as he had the street thugs in New York all those years before.

And just like them, Sam backed up a step. "Go to hell, Grayson."

Linc blew out a heavy breath as he watched Sam stalk away, get in his car, and burn rubber wheeling out of the parking lot.

Leaning against the church door, Linc closed his eyes. Damn it. First Margo, then this. Defenses down, he allowed himself to think about her. She'd been in town all week and had avoided him. It was a matter of pride that he'd left her alone, too.

Ah, Linc, pride is the work of the devil.

I don't wanna talk to you right now.

You don't get to pick and choose when we talk.

Why the hell not?

Because I'm God, that's why.

Linc snarled at God as he strode to his motorcycle. Though it was still too cold to be riding it, he'd dragged it out of the garage anyway, hoping to work off his pique with a long ride. He thought the wind and noise would drown out his Maker's advice as he got on, kick-started the bike and spun toward town. Since he was staying away from Bethy's diner, he decided to escape to the drugstore soda fountain and eat.

God followed him right inside.

Tell me why you're angry.

You're God, Linc sacrilegiously told the voice in his head. *You figure it out.*

JOE stared over to where his mother perched primly on the couch. He'd stopped at his old house on a whim to see Grace Murphy, mostly because he was so lonely he couldn't stand working in his office any longer on a Saturday. He'd sat with her for a half hour, chatting companionably. She looked older than when he'd left six years before, now sporting totally white hair and more lines on her face. She still wore those flowered housedresses with a sweater no matter what time of year it was.

Just then Suzie walked in with Faith after dance class; he felt like God had given him a gift.

Suzie called hello and headed upstairs. His daughter made a running leap for him. "Dad-dy!" she said throwing herself into his arms.

Standing to catch her, he savored her solid little body. As he hugged her, he listened to her chatter about her plans; she was spending the night with her grandma while Matt had a sleepover with a buddy. Joe wondered what Annie was doing. Did she date? Was some other man kneading her sore muscles, putting her to . . .

Don't go there. It's dangerous territory.

Trouble was, since he'd been back in town, his mind had been *going there* without his consent. He thought about Annie a lot, sometimes in sexual ways. He had to admit, though, that it was good to feel alive again. For years he'd had no interest in sex; his therapist had told him guilt and depression did that to a person's libido. He'd had a few casual relationships since he'd come out of the funk, but nothing serious.

Face it, buddy, Annie's a tough act to follow.

"Joey? What are you thinking about?" his mother asked.

"I was thinking about Annie."

A spark of anger lit Grace's eyes and her thin frame tensed. "Faith honey, go see if Aunt Suzie's almost ready."

Faith bounded away and Joe stared at the faded flowered couch where his father used to drink his Molsons. When he'd had enough, he'd start with his fists.

Just like you.

Oh, God.

Grace straightened a doily on the worn wood table. "I think it's a sin. Annie not letting you see the kids more. She's a hard woman."

Annie's pale face whenever she was in his presence appeared before him. "Annie's got reason. We need to talk about that, Ma." For weeks he'd tried to get Grace to address the issue of his abuse, and his father's. But she had always circumvented the discussion and, coward that he was, he'd let her.

"No reason's good enough to abandon your husband."

"Is that why you stayed with Pa?"

Grace's eyes narrowed on him. "Don't be playing the psychologist with me, Joey Murphy. I don't need a shrink. I need a son."

He heard Faith and Suzie upstairs, and knew he couldn't get into this now.

"Well, you got him." Joe stood. "How about if he comes over Tuesday and takes his ma to lunch." Maybe they could talk then.

"She'd love that." Grace eyed him carefully. "Maybe you'll tell her how you afford those highfalutin' clothes."

Joe looked down at his black chinos, silver Polo sweater and hand-tooled boots. Underneath which he wore scandalous underwear. He saw Annie's face again—the look in her eyes when he stood before her almost nude. It hadn't been totally unpleasant. He grinned. "Maybe I will."

"You sure you don't want to come with us to the movie?" Grace and Suzie were taking Faith to see a remake of *The King and I.*

"I'd love to come, but Annie wouldn't like it."

"Shouldn't need permission to see your own daughter."

"I deserve it, Ma. It's what I want to discuss with you."

Clatter sounded on the stairs. Suzie appeared in the doorway

carrying Faith piggyback style. Joe had a sudden image of
Suzie, at Faith's age, and how he'd carried the little pigtailed
girl around just like that. Suzie's pretty eyes flickered, and he
wondered if she had the same thought.

Faith slid to the floor. "Can Daddy come with us?" she
asked.

Even Suzie looked torn.

"Nope, sweetheart." He bent down for a hug. "It's your night
to spend with Grandma and Aunt Suz. I'll see you tomorrow."
With a chaperone. And only for the afternoon. It wasn't nearly
enough. "I love you," he whispered in her ear. "Keep a stiff
upper lip."

She smiled. "It means be brave. It comes from . . ." She
scrunched her face up, again looking like Suzie used to look.

"We'll check tomorrow." He stood and hugged his mother.
He wanted badly to hug Suzie. But he didn't chance it.

With one last wave, he grabbed his leather coat and strode to
the kitchen, feeling like a leper in his old house, an outcast from
his own family. The depth of the emotion blindsided him. He'd
just opened the door when he felt a hand on his arm. Turning,
he found his sister standing before him. Her eyes had lost some
of their animosity over the last four weeks, but there was still a
wariness embedded in their cornflower depths.

After a brief hesitation, she reached up and hugged him. He
felt his eyes sting. She whispered only, "I remember all those
piggybacks, Joey."

"Good." His voice was raw. He held on to her tight, drew
back and gave her a weak smile.

Then he went out into the night.

Alone.

TUCKER was gonna lose his everloving mind if he didn't get
out of the house. Which was why he was driving Doc to town.
Doc, who had a freakin' date. With Gerty Stoffer.

"It ain't a date," Doc grumbled, tugging at the collar of the
starched blue dress shirt he'd put on.

"Yeah? Then what's got you smellin' like a field of daisies?"

Doc swore colorfully. "I told ya. Gerty's at the diner alone
with Nana. I'm gonna help out."

He tried not to ask. "Oh, um, where's Beth?" Please don't

say she has a date. With Roman Becker. Whose hand she'd held in the diner the week before.

"She's out with her girlfriends tonight. Seems that pistol Margo arranged somethin' for the three of 'em before she goes back to the city tomorrow." In the headlights of oncoming cars, Doc smiled. "She sure is a handful. Needs a good man to tame her."

"You must be losin' it, old man. She's . . ." The kindest woman I've ever known. The sweetest. The sexiest . . . "She's an angel."

"Who the hell you talkin' about, boy?"

"Beth."

Doc shook his head. "I was describin' Margo. You got a one-track mind these days, Tuck."

A little too fast, Tucker pulled up to the diner. "Don't know what you're talkin' about."

Doc didn't get out right away. He seemed to think for once before he spoke. His tone was grave when he finally said, "It'd be a mistake, son. The boy . . . the town . . . the past."

Tucker wilted into the Jag's seat, laid his head wearily on the leather, and closed his eyes. "I know."

"Wanna come in and eat with us?"

"Nah, I'll get somethin' in town." He shot Doc a wiseass grin. "Wouldn't want to cramp your style."

"Bullshit." Doc opened the car door, but before he got out he squeezed Tucker's arm. "Take care, boy."

"Hey, The Menace is fine."

After Doc was inside, Tucker stared out into the semi-darkness. The town was deserted for a Saturday night at six. Hell, there wasn't much to do in this hick place, where they rolled up the sidewalks at dusk.

He should go to New York. Jamming his fists in his pockets, his hand connected with a card there. From Tara Snow. All day Monday she'd purred like a kitten wanting petting. *Call me,* she'd said when he'd dropped her off on Main Street after spending a boring several hours taking pictures around town. Like his mama had taught him, he'd escorted her to her car; once there she'd reached up and kissed him, a big openmouthed kiss that had him grabbing onto her for balance.

She'd slid into her car and he'd headed toward his Jag only

to stop like a man struck blind to see Beth staring out the diner window. Damn, she'd seen the kiss. He just knew it.

For long seconds, he'd simply watched her. Then he'd gotten in his car. It was best she think he was the worst kind of playboy . . .

A tap on the side of his car jarred him. He looked out to see Joe Murphy at the door. Tucker lowered the window.

"Hi, Tucker. Something wrong? You been sitting here awhile."

"Nope. Nothin's wrong. I just dropped Doc off and was tryin' to decide how to fill up my night."

"Me, too. I was thinking about getting something to eat."

Tucker glanced at the diner. "In there?"

"Nope. They're closing early tonight."

He looked after Doc. The liar.

"I just saw Linc go into the drugstore," Joe told him. "Wanna check out the food there with me?"

Hell, he didn't have anything to lose. Tucker exited the car and accompanied Joe down the street.

Sure enough, they found Linc at the soda fountain, staring at a menu. He looked like a lost little boy. Come to think of it, so did Murphy. When Tucker caught a glance of himself in the mirror, he chuckled. They were Peter Pan and his friends to a tee.

Joe and Tucker slid onto stools flanking Linc. The Reverend looked up at them. Tucker recognized the loneliness in his face, the need for company. "You eatin'?" Tucker asked.

"I was thinking about it."

Joe scanned the menu. "Some Saturday night dinner, huh?"

"I could go for southern ribs and cornbread right now," Tucker mused.

Joe looked at Linc. Linc smiled at Joe. "The Crocodile still open?" Joe asked.

"Yep. Dinner's till eight, then some down and dirty dancing."

"What's The Crocodile?" Tucker felt perked up all of a sudden.

Joe didn't look so sad either. "Just about the best rib place outside of New York City."

"Yeah? Far as I can tell, you Yankees don't know beans about ribs."

It became an issue of pride. Their hometown reputation had

been challenged. The two other men stood. Puffed out their chests.

"You think so, Rebel?" Linc asked.

Tucker laughed. "I'd downright bet on it."

They each grabbed him by an arm. "You're on. We Yankees gonna show you how wrong you are." Linc's voice took on a Western accent. Tucker was reminded of the Outlaws.

"And you're gonna pay, Reb, if we're right." Joe fell into the byplay.

Tucker let himself be dragged out. "Ain't gonna have to shell out a dime!"

Suddenly, for all three, the night ahead seemed brighter.

"NO way in hell am I going to wear that." Annie stared at the shirt Margo held out as if it were see-through with cutout boobs. "Where'd you get it, anyway?"

"At Hot Spots." She glanced at Beth who sat on her bed sipping a glass of wine. "It's where Ronny gets all his T-shirts."

"Oh, well that convinces *me*." Annie's tone was dry.

"Damn it, you guys. You've turned into regular lily-livered matrons."

Before she could stop herself, Annie wondered where that phrase came from. Joe would know. It'd be in his book.

Beth's eyes narrowed on Margo. "Not after you got done with our hair." She fingered the curls Margo had put in her usually straight locks. It was wild, bouncing all over the place, but it looked great on her. Sexy.

"Your hair looks terrific that way, Bon. It frames your face; you could model for a shampoo commercial." Annie turned back the mirror. "Now mine, on the other hand . . ."

Margo came up to stand in back of her. "It looks mag." Margo had straightened Annie's curls just until they fell in soft waves to her shoulder; then she'd pulled a few strands back off her face with a clip. Her bangs feathered across her forehead. "You're ever the lady, Belle Star." She held up the Western shirt. "Which is why you need this fringed thing. With your denim skirt and boots, you'll be all set for some fancy two-steppin'." She arched a brow. "You ain't afraid, are ya, girl?"

Sucked in by Margo's charm, Annie grinned and stood. She

whipped off her cotton blouse, snatched the shirt out of her friend's hand and donned it. "Oh God, I can barely button this."

Margo giggled. "That's the point. Besides, Crocodile's is out of the way. You won't see anybody you know there."

It did look sort of sexy. And the silk felt good against her skin. And it had been so long since she'd cared about her appearance. . . .

Margo grasped her shoulders. "It's time you looked like a woman again, Annie. You've got a great build from dancing. Show it off a little."

"Maybe just this once." She angled her head to the bed. "If she does."

"Me?" Beth glanced down at her jeans and shirt. "I look fine."

"Fine won't cut it." Margo strode to the closet where she'd hung her clothes for the week. She dragged out a pair of leather pants. "Here." She tossed them to Beth. "We're the same size. Put these on."

"Over my dead body." Beth fingered the black leather. "God they're soft." A vest joined the pants.

"Come on. It might just spruce up that plain white blouse you got on." She winked at Annie. "If you don't wear a bra."

Beth's eyes narrowed on Margo. "You don't think I'll do it, do you?"

"Nope. You're a chicken. Even wimp Annie's braver than you are." Margo proceeded to select her own duds from the closet. She chose an oversize suede shirt and a short matching skirt.

"That's not so daring," Beth said as she watched Margo.

With flair, Margo pulled out a suede halter top. "It is with the top unbuttoned and this underneath."

"Oh, God, if Ma Barker dares wear that . . ." Standing, Beth put down her wine, whipped off her shirt, then unclasped her bra and threw it at Margo.

They all giggled like kids.

Ten minutes later, they stood in front of the mirror.

Annie said, "Who are those women?"

"The girls we used to be." Margo's smile was a little sad.

Beth cocked her head. "It feels good, doesn't it?"

"Real good." They linked arms. "Watch out, Crocodile's. The female Outlaws are a-comin'."

*   *   *

"OH my God, look at that blouse."

"I haven't seen leather like that since Doc took me to my first . . . Never mind!"

"What the *hell* does she have on under that suede shirt?"

Like twelve-year-old boys discovering girls, Joe, Tucker and Linc stared at the door where Annie, Beth and Margo had just appeared; the girls hadn't noticed them and pranced through it.

Linc started to stand but Joe restrained him. "Not a good move," Joe said. "They look like they're out for blood."

"They look like they're out to get laid."

Tucker moaned and turned aside, shifting his position.

Joe rubbed his eyes with this thumb and forefinger and moaned, too.

Feeling his own body harden at the sight of Margo dressed like . . . like the star of *Debbie Does Dallas,* Linc recognized the reaction of the other two males at his table. And since camaraderie had been established early on as they'd shared ribs and cornbread, and he and Tucker downed a few beers, Linc smiled. "We're pathetic."

Joe grunted. He angled his head toward Tucker. "Hey, it's your sister he's ogling."

Tucker reddened.

"Yeah, well, she deserves to be ogled in that outfit." Linc stared at Tucker. "But I can't believe I missed the signs."

Still speechless, Tucker scrubbed a hand over his face. The Menace was a private man. Finally he was able to look Linc in the eye. "It's complicated."

"It's always complicated." Joe continued to stare at Annie.

Tucker checked him out. "Still got the hots for your ex, Murphy?"

"Not until about five minutes ago." He shrugged. "Or at least I wouldn't let myself admit it."

"Join the club." Tucker watched Linc. "What's with you and Margo?"

"Irreconcilable differences."

The women finally took a booth. It was then that they noticed the guys. Margo's brows arched in arrogant acknowledgment as she shimmied into the seat. Linc swallowed hard.

Beth's head snapped up, catching Tucker devouring her outfit. She gave him a soft smile full of promise.

Annie peeked around Beth and scowled.

"Maybe if we turn our backs, it won't be so bad." This from
Tucker.

"Maybe." Joe said.

The three men continued to stare.

A half hour after they arrived, and after they'd blisteringly
cursed the occupants of a certain table on the far side of the bar,
a hulk of a guy asked Margo to dance. She got up with as much
sass as she could muster. "All right, big guy."

On the floor they did a mean two-step. Hulk's eyes lingered
on her shirt and she rolled her eyes. Damn, this wasn't turning
out as she'd planned. She'd just wanted a fun night out with the
girls. She never expected to see the good Reverend here, looking sexy as hell in plain jeans and a red shirt. When the song
ended and the bruiser tugged her toward him for dance to *Midnight Train to Georgia,* Margo drew back. "Ah, I . . ."

She felt a hand on her shoulder. "Sorry, this dance is mine."

Hulk puffed out his pecs. "Yeah, who says?"

"I do."

"Who're you?"

"Her brother."

"Oh." He scanned Margo's top and skirt. "You let your sister come out lookin' like this? What are you, nuts?"

"Yeah, I'm nuts." He tugged Margo to him. They were equal
height when she wore four-inch boots.

Margo didn't even think about resisting. It felt so good to be
close to him, smell him, feel his hands on her. As the song
began, she melted into him. His hand clenched hers, and his
arm banded around her waist.

She remembered seeing him with Jane at the diner, then at
the movies, then in the PK's car. She nestled in closer. Two
slow songs later, she whispered, "I'm sorry."

"Me, too."

"I should have told you I was coming home."

"Why didn't you?"

"Just because of this." Her body had been aligned too close
to his for her not to notice. She bumped his middle with hers.

He laughed, low and sexy. "I'm in pain, baby."

"So am I." She grinned against his chest. "We could always go out and screw in the backseat of your car, like we used to."

Lifting his hand to her hair, he caressed it tenderly. "If only it were that easy."

She sighed. "It hurts, Linc. To be with you."

"It hurts me, too." He kissed her forehead. "But it hurts more when you don't return my calls and when you won't see me."

"I'm sorry."

"Why'd you come home?"

"To be with Beth and Annie. To help out at the diner, and with Annie's kids." She found his ear, and admitted, "To see you."

"Beth said you were going to Cancun."

"It lost its appeal."

He drew lazy circles on her back. "What are we gonna do, honey?"

"Nothing. Let's just not fight."

"I've been miserable."

"Me, too. And jealous."

"I'm not sure we can keep going on like this."

"We've done it for years." She hated the pleading tone in her voice.

"It's getting too hard."

She rubbed against him. "It is."

"I'm serious."

"I know."

"I love you, Mary Margaret."

She drew back, looked into his face. "I love you, too, Rev."

BETH detoured to the jukebox when Tucker rose and headed to the men's room. He'd gotten up as she did, so she went to play some music instead of going to the ladies' room. In a few minutes, she felt him come up behind her.

"Hi," he said as she pressed *Black Magic Woman*.

Slowly lifting her eyes from the song listings, she smiled. "Hi."

She wanted to jump his bones, he looked so good in tight jeans and a long-sleeved green shirt with a racing logo on it.

The song began to play. He raked her outfit with a hundred-watt gaze. "Appropriate tune," he said.

She blushed.

Shaking his head, he took her hand. "It's beyond me how any woman can blush wearin' something like that." Without her consent he drew her to the dance floor. For a minute she stood a little away from him, but then stepped right into his arms.

His touch was electric. The feel of his arms around her made her nerve endings tingle. Beth sank into him; her skin heated at his nearness. He smelled of the same cologne as at the diner—woodsy and very male. "Hmm."

She felt him smile against her hair. "Do you have any idea how good you feel?"

Inching closer, she shut her eyes. "As good as you do?"

He chuckled.

They swayed to the music. His hand came up and snared a few strands of her hair. He drew back. "What'd you do to it?"

"It's Margo's handiwork." She shrugged. "So's the outfit."

He let his hand wander lower. Caress the leather. Flirt with her hips. "It'll haunt my dreams, Mary Elizabeth, but I'm damned grateful to your friend." His green eyes sparkled with appreciation. His body hummed with arousal.

So did hers. "I thought you liked your women natural."

"I like *you*," he said honestly. "Much more than I should."

A lump formed in her throat. "Oh, Tucker, I . . ."

He abandoned her hand and placed his fingers on her mouth. "Hush. I know."

She stared up at him.

"Don't say anything more. For tonight, just let me hold you." He kissed her hair and brought her face back to his chest.

She burrowed into him. Shutting out the world, she let him hold her.

IT wasn't because she was suddenly alone that Annie stood and made her way to Joe's table. Several men had asked her to dance. It wasn't that Joe sat by himself, sipping a coke, angling his body to the wall so he didn't look at her. It was because, all week she'd been making some decisions. When she reached him, she said simply, "Joe?"

He whirled around. And the look of surprise on his face, combined with the pleasure there, gave her courage.

"Can I sit down?"

"Sure." He cleared his throat. "You want something to drink?"

"No, thanks. I've had my limit."

His eyes smiled. "Still two glasses?"

He'd always coaxed her not to drink much because she got sick if she had more than a couple of glasses of wine. In some ways, he'd taken good care of her. She tried to summon those memories.

"Yeah. I wanted to talk to you." She scanned the bar. "I guess this isn't the best place." She tugged self-consciously on the front of her shirt.

He grinned. "Not your usual style."

She rolled her eyes. "It's Margo's. I'm bigger than she is, and . . ."

He gave her a wry grin. "Yes, I remember. You still look good, Mary Ann."

For a moment she startled. But she'd worn the damn shirt of her own free will. She couldn't condemn him for noticing. "I've been thinking, Joe."

His gray eyes lit up, matching the silvery cotton sweater he wore. "About?"

She bit her lip. "I think you're right about Matt. I've decided you can coach his team. Be alone with him."

Swallowing hard, he closed his eyes. "Thank you."

Her heart turned over in her chest at his honest reaction. "Let's see how it goes for a while. Then maybe you can start coming over to the house to see them alone, too." She glanced out at the dance floor where Margo and Linc were locked in a deep embrace. No surprise there. But seeing Tucker and Beth wrapped up in each other was a shock. Bonnie was in for some explaining tonight. "Linc already has too much to do. He shouldn't have to take care of us."

Joe said, "I won't hurt them, Annie. I give you my word."

"I want to believe that."

"I won't hurt you, either."

She angled her chin. "No, you won't, Joe. I'm not the girl you left here six years ago. I wouldn't allow it, even if you wanted to."

"I'd cut off my right arm before I touched you in anger again." His voice was heated, passionate.

She noticed the phrasing. He didn't say *before I touched you again.*

Are you attracted to him, Annie? Sara had asked.

Against her will, she studied his face. He had such sculpted features, perfect, really; and his hair only made him handsomer, especially with his gray eyes. No wonder they'd chosen him for modeling. To lighten the atmosphere, she said, "You'd lose your second job if you cut off your arm, *Joey baby.*"

He actually blushed. "Please, don't remind me."

"I'm sorry for what I said about the modeling a few weeks ago. I've given it some thought. I want you to have changed. And if you have, you must've gone through hell to get where you are."

He started to say something; she held up her palm. "I'm not there yet. But I'll give you the space to prove it. For the kids' sake."

"I will, Annie. I promise. You can trust me."

Suddenly she felt drawn into the silver heat of his eyes, which shone like liquid mercury. And it scared her, because that feeling had once made her do whatever he asked, made her allow unspeakable things. She stood abruptly. "We can discuss this more tomorrow." Nodding, she started across the dance floor. As she passed by Linc and Margo holding each other, and Tucker and Beth cuddling like kids hiding out from the world, she felt a wave of loneliness and regret so great she was physically shaken by it.

She refused to wonder if Joe was feeling the same thing.

NEITHER Linc, Tucker or Joe, nor Annie, Margo or Beth saw the two boys behind the pillar at the bar.

"Fuckin' A," the one with the spiked blond hair said. "That fox in the black leather is Ronny boy's mother."

The ponytailed guy with him chugged the last of his beer and focused hazy eyes on the dance floor. "The one draped all over the racing dude?"

Maze began to laugh. It was an evil sound. "The racing dude who killed his father, Loose, my man."

"Holy shit. I wonder if Ronny knows."

Maze hooted, looking like he was about to pull the wings off a fly. "He will, buddy. He will. As soon as he gets back from the pen." Maze shrugged into his jacket. "Man I wish I could be around for the fireworks."

"I dunno, Maze. He's in a shit load a trouble already."

"Hey, I'm just bein' a good buddy. Wouldn't you wanna know if your old lady was screwin' your worst enemy?"

Loose smiled. "You're such a Good Samaritan, Maze. Sometimes you just make me wanna cry."

SIXTEEN

———

YOU need to trust the adults in your life, Ron. They care about you. A lot more than any adults cared about them.

Remembering the counselor's words from the day before at the jail made Ron feel good as he headed to the bathroom before Mr. Johnson's class. Finally, something had sunk in.

He saw his Mom's face in the diner that night. *There's nothing going on with us, Ronny.*

He felt Margo hug him hard, tell him she loved him.

He heard Uncle Linc say, *We know you can do this, buddy.*

And, last, he heard Doc Holt grumble, *Quit callin' me Mr. Holt, boy. You make me feel like an old man.*

Tucker had grinned. Tucker, who'd been so nice to him, it made Ronny feel bad that he'd been so rotten in return. *Yeah, I guess I'd prefer Tucker to "that bastard."*

Maybe he'd jumped the gun about Quaid and his mother, maybe this jail thing was going to help him to—

Suddenly, he was attacked from behind, almost knocked off balance and dragged into an alcove. Fear rose in his throat and he tried to think about the self-defense classes he'd taken with his mother and Annie and Matt.

"Hey, man, we been lookin' for ya all day."

Ron's whole body sagged. After a second, he yanked away

and whirled around. "Christ, Maze, you scared the shit outta me."

"Just jivin', buddy."

Loose stood behind Maze. Both were grimy in dirty jeans and wrinkled hooded sweatshirts.

"Don't do it again," Ron warned. He studied their faces and saw signs of booze and pot. "You guys have a rough weekend?"

The trio headed down the hall as they talked. "Nah," Maze said shooting a sharp glance at Loose.

Loose smiled. "We had our usual weekend pussy."

Maze mumbled under his breath, "And we ain't the only ones." Louder, he said, "Along with a pile a pills. Man, sex, speed and Scotch are a great combo."

Ronny didn't comment.

"And we spent Saturday at Crocodile's."

"How you get in there?" Ron noticed, for the first time, that he started talking like them when they were around.

"Fake ID. And the new chick bartender's on my list."

"What list?"

"Jesus, buddy, you blind? My supplier list."

They reached the lav and went inside.

"You dealin'?" Ron asked.

Maze's face darkened. "Shut the fuck up." He went to the stalls and checked for occupants. Satisfied there weren't any, he took a seat on the sink while Loose leaned against the wall.

"You young as hell, Ronny boy. I been dealin' since I was twelve."

Ronny scowled. "I'm not young. But *you're* pretty stupid to be doin' that. You gonna end up in the real pen, not just some weekend jail like me."

Maze's skinny body stiffened. His eyes bulged. But his voice was calm when he said, "They gonna have to kill me before I'd let 'em lock me up."

Ron shrugged. Maze was acting even more crazy than usual.

"And you ain't just stupid. You an innocent, man."

"Whatdaya mean?"

"We got an eyeful Saturday night."

"Of?"

"Your Mama."

Ron's throat clogged. "My mother?"

"Yeah, at Crocodile's. She was cozyin' up to your arch enemy."

"You don't know what you're talking about."

Maze came off the sink fast. He grabbed the front of the sweatshirt Ron wore and fisted it in his hands. "I know, sissy boy. I saw them bumpin' and grindin' on the dance floor with my own eyes."

Maze let him go and Ron sagged against the sink.

"Your old lady's fuckin' the dude who killed your father. It ain't my fault."

Ron went numb. He grasped the sink for balance.

Loose said, "Hey, Ronny boy. We your buddies. We wouldn't lie to ya." The bell sounded. Loose chucked him playfully on the arm. "Remember that, man."

As they left, Ron heard Maze say, "He's an asshole. We gotta reassess our connection with him. We don't wanna ruin . . ."

The last words trailed off. But it didn't matter. Ron had heard the ones that counted.

Your old lady's fuckin' the dude who killed your father.

SIPPING his coffee, Tucker stared at the partially assembled car in Doc's garage. He could feel the mild mid-April breeze off the lake and languished in the smell of the grass and earth as it sneaked in through the half-open door. Although all wasn't right with the world, things sure felt a might better.

He could still summon the feel of Beth in his arms as they'd danced at Crocodile's. She'd fit into every nook and cranny of his body and had felt like heaven against him. Lately he'd begun to think he'd deserved a piece of that paradise.

I want to kiss you, she'd whispered out by his car in the parking lot of Crocodile's. He could still smell the leather she wore and the sexy perfume that also belonged to Margo.

I want that, too, Tucker had told her, wrapping a hand around her neck. He'd settled for a hug, because of where they were. No telling what would've happened if they'd been alone.

"Even the kid likes me a little," Tucker told the car. "You can see that, can't you, when we work on you?"

Feeling like a fool, he shook his head at his whimsy. He always used to talk to his cars. Rising from the stool, he crossed to it. Slowly he rubbed his palm across the unpainted panel he'd showed Ron how to solder the week before. "It's because of you, sweetheart. The damn kid's even makin' me like you again."

The words were out before he could stop them. For years, since Danny Donovan's death, Tucker had denied himself the joy of racing, of loving the car, the track, the smells and the downright fun of his career. When he quit, he'd forsaken everything, like a monk who'd given up the pleasures of life to suffer for his sins.

Maybe, just maybe, he didn't have to live that way anymore.

The door to the garage burst open. It slammed angrily against the wall, rattling its glass windowpane.

Tucker spun around to see Ron in the doorway. He was about to ask what the kid was doing here at noon—he wasn't due till four—when he recognized the look on the boy's face.

"Ron, what—"

Quicker than braking for the pit, Ron was on him. Surprised, Tucker stumbled backward, dropping his coffee mug. The ceramic shattered on the cement floor.

"You lying son of a bitch."

They hit the car with a thud and Tucker heard the thin sheet metal crunch. His eyes clouded as his head connected with the frame underneath.

Still he didn't react.

Ron raised his fist and slammed it into Tucker's jaw.

Primal instinct took over. Bigger than Ron, he pushed against Ron's chest. The kid was forced back and Tucker rolled away.

"What the hell—" Tucker shouted.

Ron bent over, lunged forward and tackled him.

Together they careened backward, like a car out of control, bounced off the wall, smashed against the shelves and hit a stepladder. Tucker's back took the brunt of the contact. The sound of aluminum cans tumbling off the shelves echoed in the garage.

He saw the fist coming again and grabbed for Ron, stilling his arm, if not his curse.

"You cocksucking—"

Suddenly Ron was pulled off him. Doc was behind the kid, grabbing him in a headlock.

Tucker panicked. "No, Doc, stay outta this. Your heart—"

Again his words were cut off. Wild-eyed, and adrenaline

pumped, Ronny tried to throw off Doc. It didn't work. Ronny tried twice more, then finally he succeeded.

It happened in slow motion. Doc stumbled backward. Into the car. His head banged it hard.

Then his face contorted.

He grasped his chest.

And slid to the floor.

"Oh, my God." Tucker rushed to him.

Doc was out cold.

Don't move him. Call for help.

He looked up at the boy, who stood white-faced and frozen in mid-stride. "Ron, grab that phone over there and dial 911. Tell them we need an ambulance right away." Blindly he clutched Doc's arm. *"Ron,"* he barked when the kid didn't move. *"Call!"*

Ron came out of the trance and dived for the phone.

Tucker held onto Doc and prayed for the first time in ten years.

"YOU all right, kid?"

They'd sat across from each other in the ER without speaking, like strangers at a bus stop, just as they'd driven to Glen Oaks Hospital in silence. The tension in the car had reached the nervous pitch Tucker felt before a Daytona 500. He'd barely looked at Ron, who sat sullenly in the passenger seat. Now, concealing his own concern, he watched the boy on the sly; Ron had gone from shocked to scared to resigned. But the hollow sadness in his eyes finally prompted Tucker to ask how he was doing.

"I'm fine." At least the white rage that had possessed the kid when he'd burst into the garage and attacked like a wild dog without warning was gone. Tucker still had no clue what had brought on this new round of fury.

The ice broken, Ron glanced at the treatment rooms, then back to Tucker. "How much longer, you think?"

"No tellin'. You heard the doctor say she'd come out when they had a diagnosis."

Though the conversation was stilted, it seemed to ease Ron's mind. Tucker started to ask if he wanted to talk about why Ron had tried to beat the crap out of him, but the door to the ER waiting area opened, halting his question.

"Ronny?" Beth hurried into the room looking harried and

upset. She still had a white apron tied around her waist over which she'd thrown her tan canvas jacket.

Slowly, Ron rose and just stared at Beth; then he flew across the room and flung himself into her arms. Deep in his gut, Tucker wished he could do the same.

"Oh, honey." Her fine-boned hand smoothed down Ron's hair, as she might've when he was a little tyke. "What happened?"

Silence. The boy held on tight. Tucker's gaze connected with hers. The last time she'd looked at him, there'd been passion in those eyes.

Now, her face was filled with questions and concern. She squeezed her son's shoulders. "Ronny?"

Finally, the kid drew back. Swiped at his cheeks. "It's my fault, Mom."

"What is? What happened? All you said on the phone was you were down at the hospital, but you weren't hurt."

"I did something terrible. The worst thing I ever . . ." His grown-man's shoulders started to shake again. "Doc had a heart attack and it's my fault."

Each stiff movement of Ron's body and the raw suffering in his voice was familiar to Tucker. All those years of blame, of guilt, were ahead of the boy. Unless . . .

Without second-guessing his gut reaction, Tucker stood abruptly and strode to Ron. Grasping his arm, he spun the kid around. "No! This isn't your fault."

Ron's mouth gaped like a hooked fish. "How can you say that? If I didn't come out there, gone after you . . ." He swallowed hard. "It *is* my fault."

Gripping Ron's shoulders, Tucker shook him hard. "You aren't responsible for accidents. Sure, you did something stupid, but you didn't cause Doc's collapse. He's got a history of angina and they've been trying to get it under control."

"What's angina?" The hope in Ron's voice gentled Tucker's tone.

"Severe chest pains caused by not enough blood gettin' to the heart. At his last checkup, the doctor talked about doing some angioplasty, but Doc didn't want it."

"Angioplasty?"

"Where they insert a small tube into the artery. There's a balloon on the end that gets inflated, to open up the arteries." He glanced at the doors where Doc had gone. "The old coot wouldn't go for it."

"But I—"

"No!" Tucker shouted. He'd be damned if this kid would do to himself what Tucker'd done when he'd killed Danny Donovan.

Suddenly Beth's words sounded in his head . . .

You're here to pay a debt you don't owe, Mr. Quaid. . . . Auto racing is a dangerous sport. . . . Everyone out there is at risk.

Oh, God, was the same true for him? Had he been wrong to blame himself, too?

Beth interrupted his thoughts. "Will somebody please tell me what happened?"

Tucker stared at her. The worry grooves on her face had deepened. His fists curled with the need to touch her, to soothe her. But he only said, "Doc had a heart attack. At least we think that's what happened. He passed out clutchin' his chest."

"How could Ron have caused that?" Her eyes narrowed on Tucker's mouth, which he knew was swollen and had bled. "What did he mean, he went after you?"

"That's not important now."

"How can you say that?" Ron's tone was disbelieving.

"Because I know what guilt . . ." Tucker's voice trailed off when the double doors to the treatment area opened and the doctor who'd taken Doc's case came through them.

She headed right for him. "Mr. Quaid?"

Tucker's whole body stiffened. Images flashed before his eyes: the first time he'd met Doc and the old man's sneer, *What makes you think you got it, boy?* Tucker's first win—and watching Doc beam like a proud father. That time he was hurt and Doc spent the night in his hospital room on a sad excuse for a cot.

"Is he . . ." Tucker's voice cracked. He jammed his fists into his jeans pockets. "How is he?"

The doctor's smile eased the severe pain in Tucker's own chest. "Mr. Holt is stable. He suffered a concussion and is in some pain."

"Concussion? I thought he had a heart attack."

"No, he passed out because he hit his head on the car." Her tired blue eyes flickered with exasperation. "He told us he was in some . . . scuffle. He *did* have a severe angina attack, though, which leads us to think his condition is unstable now."

"Unstable?"

"Yes. His previous angina attacks were less severe than the last two. At the onset of the first one, he took some nitroglycerin, but it didn't work. Then he had another attack during the scuffle." She glanced from him to Ron with an admonishing frown.

Tucker's shoulders sagged. "What does all this mean?"

"The occurrence of two attacks so closely together, as well as the severity, may indicate he needs more advanced treatment."

"Bypass surgery's been mentioned, but his arteriosclerosis wasn't bad enough."

"We're still not sure if that kind of radical treatment is called for. We need to do tests first."

"What tests?"

"An ECG. Then an arteriogram." She explained the heart-monitoring exam and the dye injection which would show how clogged Doc's arteries were. "We'll know more after we run these tests." She glanced at the clock. "We're going to do them now. Then, we'll determine what procedure to do." She smiled again. "If it *is* surgery he needs, or angioplasty, we'll probably just keep him in the hospital and schedule it for tomorrow morning."

Tucker nodded.

"Will you be here, or should we contact you at home?"

"No, I'll wait here. Can I see him?"

"Not now. He's being prepped for the tests." She gave him another smile. "I'll be back out when we have more information."

Watching the doctor's retreating back, he felt Beth come up behind him. "Tucker?"

He pivoted. "You hear?"

"Uh-huh."

"Now we just wait, I guess."

Ron turned his back to them, stuck his hands in the pockets of his jeans and stared out the window.

Tucker addressed the boy. "Ron? Did you take in what the doctor said?"

Not facing him, Ron nodded.

He and Beth exchanged looks.

"What happened between you two?" she asked.

Backing away, Tucker averted his gaze. "I think he should

tell you. I don't know the whole story." He touched his jaw and winced. "I don't know why he did this."

Ron said nothing. Wouldn't face them.

Beth crossed to her son. "Ronny, tell me why you attacked Tucker."

Ron's shoulders went rigid. Beth felt as if that famous sword of somebody was hanging over her head, about to fall. Still, she had to know. Placing a hand on his shoulder, she whispered, "Honey, I'm not letting this go. I have to know what happened."

Slowly, Ronny pivoted. His face was full of regret. He glanced at Tucker, then back to her. "I heard something."

"About?"

He nodded to Tucker. "You two."

"Me and Tucker?"

"Uh-huh."

"What?"

"That you were together Saturday night at Crocodile's."

Dear Lord, how could he have found out? Beth felt the raw edges of guilt flutter in her stomach.

"You lied, Mom. Two weeks ago you told me there was nothing going on between you."

Beth opened her mouth to tell him there wasn't anything going on, but she couldn't get the words out. Saturday night might have been a mistake, but she wasn't able to deny its significance. "I meant it when I said it."

"Maze and Loose said you were . . . on the dance floor . . . you looked like you were gonna . . ." His face reddened.

So did Beth's.

When she glanced at Tucker, his complexion had flushed, too.

"What were Maze and Loose doing in a bar? They're underage."

"It doesn't matter what they were doing there, Mom."

"Not for the purposes of this discussion, maybe. But it underscores why I don't want you to see them."

Ronny faced her like the man he'd become. He seemed bigger, more streetwise than ever before. "Tell me what's really going on, Mom. Did you lie to me?"

"No, I told you Tucker and I were friends. Nothing more. But

Margo, Annie and I bumped into him and Linc and Joe at Croc-odile's." She shot Tucker an apologetic glance.

He stood there grimly, in a denim shirt, jeans and navy Nike windbreaker, just watching her.

"We were all dancing." Now, of course, she *had* lied. The feel of Tucker's body next to hers was still vivid. More, much more, was shared than a few dances.

"I . . ." Ron raked a hand through his hair. "They made it sound like more."

It was. Carefully, she avoided comment. "In any case, you had no right to attack Tucker. This is between you and me." When Ron said nothing, she added, "Did you hear me, young man?"

Ron nodded.

Pivoting to speak to Tucker, her attention was diverted to the doorway; Joe Murphy strode into the ER and crossed to them. "Hi, guys."

"What are you doing here, Joe?" Beth asked.

"I stopped by the diner looking for Ron. They told me you were here." His gaze narrowed on her son. "Mr. Johnson called me. He said you skipped his class. He didn't report you because your friend Sammy said something bad happened between you and Maze and you left school mad."

Ron closed his eyes and sighed. "It's a long story."

For a minute, Joe watched him, then surveyed the scene— Beth's tight expression, Tucker's swollen mouth, Ron's stiff body. "Why are you all here?" He motioned to the ER.

"Doc had a couple of bad angina attacks." Tucker's voice was grave. "We're waiting for some tests."

Like a man who cared about his friend, Joe zeroed in on Tucker. "Are you all right?"

Tucker nodded.

Turning back to Ron, Joe said, "I need some answers here, son. I'm in charge of your case, and skipping school isn't part of the deal." He nodded to Tucker. "Nor is whatever else went on here."

Ron closed his eyes wearily.

Again Joe scanned the room. "Look, let's go get something to drink in the cafeteria. I'd like to talk to you alone."

"What about Doc?" Ron asked, but his tone was agreeable.

"They're doing tests, right?" Tucker nodded. "If there's word, your mother will come and get us." He looked to Beth.

"Of course."

Ron turned to leave, and Joe squeezed Beth's arm. His expression said, *I'll help,* and she couldn't have been more grateful. She'd been on an emotional roller coaster since Saturday night, and Ron's call had caused her heart to leap to her throat and lodge there permanently.

As the door closed behind them, she turned to face Tucker.

They were alone once again.

"YOU should go." Even to his own ears Tucker's voice was shaky. He was pretty near to losing it with worry over Doc. And torn up with feelings for this woman who stood before him with so much damn understanding in her eyes he wanted to bawl like a baby.

"No." *Her* voice was strong and sure.

"I'm not in a good place, Beth. I been keepin' it together for Ron, but . . ." His words trailed off. Noticing an anteroom adjacent to the main waiting area, he nodded to it. "I'll talk to you later. It's best you go tend to your son."

Unsteadily, he stood and made his way to the smaller room. Though he didn't believe in prayer, he asked God with every step he took to make Beth leave. He didn't want her to see him like this. He reckoned he didn't trust himself near her now, either.

The room was small and private, with a big window facing the parking lot; he crossed to it and stared out. Spring was coming to Glen Oaks real pretty. Would Doc get to see those flowers he'd planted in the cottage's side yard last fall? Would he get to take out the new boat he'd ordered? That he might *not* hammerlocked Tucker's heart.

When he heard the door close behind him, he shuddered.

After a long silence she spoke. "It was more than a few dances to me, Tucker."

"I know." He tried to swallow back the words, but couldn't. "To me, too." Again he waited. "I can't talk about that, now."

"I understand. I just wanted you to know." She came up close behind him. He could smell the scent she wore—something light and flowery. "Tell me about Doc."

"You heard the facts."

"No, I mean about Doc and you."

With worry about to swallow him up whole, he couldn't resist the lure. He pictured a younger, broad-shouldered Doc barking orders at his pit crew like a five-star general. His blue eyes had challenged Tucker every step of the way of his career. Tucker had to smile, remembering their first meeting.

At his side now, Beth caught the brief curve of his lips. "What? Tell me."

The words tumbled out like an overflow of gasoline to a car's tank. "I was near about Ron's age when I met him. At Darlington, in South Carolina."

"That's where you're from, right?"

"About thirty minutes from the track. Some backwater hellhole. Doc was workin' in the pit for Dale Earnhardt in his early days. I waylaid him on his way to the trailer after a big race that Earnhardt lost. I told him I had a real bad hankerin' to make it in the circuit. And I had it in me to be the best."

"What did he say?"

"He told me to scram." Actually he'd said, *Fuck off, kid.*

"But you didn't?"

"Nope, I followed the Southern circuit that year, whenever I could. Doc got his own crew and driver. After each race, I pestered him like a gadfly. Finally he let me be a gofer on his team—but only after I graduated high school. More than a year later, he let me drive."

Tucker's fist curled, remembering the power of a ton of metal under his hands. His heartbeat quickened just as it had when he'd taken that first slick turn. He could hear the motor roar, smell the grease and gas and sweat. But the biggest high was being in control. For a boy who'd had such little say over life after his mother died, it was a rush greater than having his first sex.

"Had you ever driven before?" Beth asked.

"Circuits and sprints is all. But Doc said I was a natural for stock cars."

"So did all the papers."

He grinned then, recalling how much he'd loved to race. "It got better. I did some test drives, then I started racin' on another team the sponsor ran. Eventually, I took the pole in a big event and got to be Doc's main driver."

"And the rest, they say, is history." She mimicked what announcers quipped about the legend of Holt and Quaid for years.

Tucker smiled. He raked a hand through his hair, soothed enough by the memories to face her. She'd removed her coat and the apron, and stood there in tan Dockers and a navy blue cotton sweater. Her hair was pulled back in a ponytail again. She looked so different than she had Saturday night in the leather, but just as beautiful. "It was more than the racin', Beth."

She dropped down on a couch. "Tell me," she repeated.

"I . . ." He began to pace. God, he'd never done this before. Never spilled his guts, not even to Doc who'd had to put two and two together over the years. "I had a bad situation at home. My mama died when I was five."

"I'm sorry."

"She was a wonderful woman. Warm. Loving." He smiled sadly. "A lot like you are with Ron."

Though her face glowed with the compliment, Beth just cocked her head, silently urging him to go on. For some reason, he trusted her enough to dig out his wallet. From the inner recesses, he pulled an old photograph. It was faded with age and crinkled around the edges. But his mother was there with her blond hair and smiling green eyes. Holding him, as an infant.

"Oh, Tucker." Reverently Beth fingered the rim of the photo.

"I got used to the hugs, the . . . tenderness, I guess. When it stopped, I was shocked. Sad. But I caught on fast." He put the picture back in his wallet and returned it to his pants pocket.

"What do you mean?"

"My father died just after I was born. My mother got hitched to a coal miner, Ralph Pearson, when I was three. He had a son who was thirteen." Tucker smiled, remembering MacKenzie, the tall lanky boy with the big heart. "If it hadn't been for Mac, his real son, I might not've survived until I met up with Doc."

"Why? What did Pearson do?"

"Nothing."

"I don't understand."

"He never paid a lick of attention to me. It was like I didn't exist. After my mama died, I took care of myself, and what I couldn't do, Mac did for me."

"When you were *five*?"

He nodded, remembering the painful craving for attention. For affection. "I vowed in those long days and near endless nights that I'd die before I'd seek out that kind of attention, or affection, from anybody again. Particularly from anybody unwilling or unable to give it to me."

Saying it aloud made him realize that was why he needed to stay away from *this* woman—she could never give him what he needed because her love and obligations belonged elsewhere. He glanced at the door, out to the ER. It was bad enough needing Doc. If something happened to him . . .

Once again, he turned his back on Beth. Felt the emotion crawl up his throat. Through sheer force of will he back-stopped it.

She came up behind him.

Oh, God, please don't let her see me like this, he prayed a second time.

"Doc's the only real family you've had, then, since your mother died?"

Swallowing hard, he nodded. And felt a hand on his arm. Control slipped, inch by icy inch.

"I'm so sorry, Tucker. I've had a rough life, but I've always had Linc, Margo and Annie. I can't imagine . . ."

He drew in a deep breath. He wanted to tell her to go, but he couldn't get the words past the emotion in his throat. He bit the inside of his mouth and clenched his hands.

And then she was in front of him, insinuating herself between him and the window. The understanding, the sympathy and the naked caring in her face did it. Released the tears that he'd held back since those black and lonely days after his mother died.

She froze for a minute, then reached up and cradled his face in her hands, scrubbed the wetness from his cheeks with her fingers. He closed his eyes, leaned into her caress. Banding his arms around her, he pulled her up to him.

And came apart.

All the years of loneliness, of subtle rejection, of not being good enough, erupted out of him like an emotional volcano too long suppressed. Embarrassed though he was, terrified though he was, he couldn't stop it. He buried his face in her hair, her shoulder, and wept like a newborn babe.

She held him. Whispered nonsense words to him. Stroked him with warm and loving fingers. Thankfully the outburst didn't last long. After a minute or so he quieted.

But he still held on to her. He became aware of the strength in her embrace, the sturdiness of her frame. This was a woman who could relate to his pain. Understand it. Take on some of it and help him deal with emotions he couldn't handle alone. It took him a minute to remember she was also a woman he couldn't have. He swallowed hard, let himself wallow in the feel and scent of her for a few seconds, then drew back.

Her face was wet. Tiny tracks of tears—for him—marred her pretty cheeks. At that moment, he realized the depth of his feelings for her. In a few short weeks, he'd come to care for Beth Donovan, Danny Donovan's wife, in much more than a physical way.

And standing haloed in the bright afternoon sunshine filtering through the window, he realized that it was about the worst thing that could have happened between them.

SEVENTEEN

JOE rang Annie's bell only once before the front door flew open. Matt stood there in a Yankees cap and shirt, and with a hopeful look on his face. It was how his son used to look at him when he came home at night from the electronics plant all those years ago.

"Hi, Matt." Joe shifted from one sneakered foot to the other. Geez, he was nervous at the prospect of being alone with his kid.

"I thought you weren't coming."

Quickly, Joe glanced at his watch. He was ten minutes late, but he'd given them a half-hour leeway to get to practice. "Sorry. I was at the hospital."

Matt frowned. "You okay?"

"Yeah. I had some business there."

Thankfully, it had turned out all right. Doc Holt was scheduled for angioplasty in the morning, and Joe had spent a productive hour with Ron. The guilt eating away at the kid was the same haunting feeling that flickered constantly on the edge of Joe's consciousness and was brought into sharp focus whenever he came to this house.

He glanced over Matt's shoulder. "Is your mother here?"

"Uh-huh. She's outside on the deck." He rolled his eyes. "She's sanding some furniture."

"Where's Faith?"

"Doing costume stuff for the recital with Aunt Suz." Matt angled his head to the back of the house. "Mom said not to leave without saying goodbye."

"You'd better do it, then."

Watching Matt go, Joe wanted to follow him in the worst way, to see Annie for the first time after Saturday night. He'd thought about her all weekend. Not a good thing, he admitted, as he wandered around the living room, looking at pictures and picking up various knickknacks; he'd been letting his mind drift into X-rated territory, having seen her in that damn shirt of Margo's. Though he knew that he couldn't ever have her again, sometimes his libido outdistanced his common sense and ran away with his thoughts. He jammed his hands into his pockets, telling himself to concentrate on his kids.

"Dad, come quick." Matt appeared in the archway, his face flushed, his eyes flashing worry.

Joe bolted through the house behind Matt, barely registering that it was the first time his son had called him *Dad*. Something was wrong.

When they reached the deck, Annie was sprawled out on her butt, as if she'd fallen back; she was covered with a fine layer of dust, gripping a cloth around her hand. An electric sander lay on the deck next to her. He closed the distance between them and knelt down. "Are you all right?"

She looked up at him. Her mouth was tight with pain. "The sander slipped. I cut my hand."

Reaching out, he went to grasp it.

She drew back as if she'd been scorched.

He froze. But understanding came quickly. He sat on his haunches, his sneakers digging into his backside. Slowly, he rested his palms on his jeans where she could see them. It was a few seconds before he could speak. "Part of the Social Services program includes first aid training. If you'd open the cloth, I can probably tell if you need stitches."

Her amber eyes scrutinized his face. He wondered if she saw the new him, the man he'd become, or the beast that he feared still lived inside him. Who was he kidding? It was the beast.

Warily, she shifted her gaze to her hand and unwrapped it. Careful not to touch her, he bent over and looked at the wound. "It should be cleaned. Then I can tell better."

"All right. You can get the stuff from the kitchen."

Rotely, he stood; Matt plopped down next to her. Joe heard

her reassure the boy as he went inside, filled a pan with some water, grabbed paper towels, and hurried back out to the deck. He kept his mind blank and tried not to let the hurt show in his face. *She's got reason,* he told himself, though it didn't help the pin-pricks of pain her automatic reaction had caused.

Back on the deck, he found her sitting at the umbrella table, Matt adjacent to her. When he placed the pan before her, she dipped her hand in the water. And drew in a breath.

"Hurt?" he asked.

"I've had worse."

He closed his eyes. Swallowed hard. *Worse from you, Mur-phy.* When he opened his eyes, she was watching him. She said to Matt, "Honey, would you go get me a glass of water?" When Matt left, she faced Joe. "I'm sorry. I meant what I said the other night; that was a knee-jerk reaction."

"But deserved. How does it look?"

Hesitating a minute, she lifted her hand out of the water. He studied it.

"I think it's okay," she said.

"So do I. You should clean it with antiseptic, then use Neo-sporin on it." He surveyed the deck as Matt returned with the water she didn't really want. "We can clean this up, so you don't get the cut dirty."

"I can do it."

Every instinct in him warred to take control of the situation. *Part of the problem,* his therapist Pete had said, caused mostly by a childhood with an abusive father who always had to be in con-trol.

Joe stood. "Fine." He faced Matt. "Ready, son?"

Matt looked torn. "Should we leave Mom?"

Ah, here was Joe's first chance to right some of the harm he might have caused Matt. To *not* bequeath to his son the legacy that Joe Murphy, Sr. had left him. Joe looked Matt in the eye, man-to-man. "Your mother's a capable person. She says she's fine, and wants to do it herself. It's not our place to decide for her."

Still Joe didn't look at Annie. He'd come to believe what he told Matt, but old habits died hard. He heard Matt say goodbye, kiss her, then he and his son left together.

Matt was silent in the Bronco. Joe dragged his mind away from Annie and concentrated on why he'd come back to Glen

Oaks. He tried to take joy in his first moments alone with his son. "You excited about practice?"

"Yeah." Matt dug the ball into his glove. "Thanks for coaching."

"Nothing could please me more." Well, except for Annie to stop looking at him as if he were Jack the Ripper.

A silence. They drove through streets lined with sturdy maple trees. April buds had begun to fill out the branches, and Joe breathed in the smell of the new foliage through the open car windows.

"How come?" Matt asked.

"How come what?"

"How come you're so happy about this?" He held up his mitt.

Joe braked at a stop sign and glanced over at his son. "Don't you realize that I came back to Glen Oaks because of you?"

The boy shook his head.

"I told you that."

"You meant it?"

"I swear to God."

A long pause. "Why'd you leave us?"

In the back of his mind, Joe had known this would come, had practiced his answer. Still the words stuck in his throat like an emotional cotton ball. "I wasn't a good man when I left. I had to get better before I could be around you."

"You told Faith that the first day." Joe nodded. "I don't remember much from when you were here before."

Thank God. "You were just a little older than Faith when I left."

"I remember playing catch. And riding on your shoulders. But I don't remember bad stuff like Jimmy says happened when his parents got divorced."

"I'm glad."

Matt's face closed down. "I don't wanna talk about it now."

Joe knew the coping mechanism, had worked with kids enough to understand they had saturation points where they could remember, or admit, only so much.

"Okay, why don't you tell me about the guys on your team, slugger."

A smile curved his son's lips. "Most of 'em are pretty wet behind the ears."

Joe smiled, too. "You been reading my sayings book?"

Matt shrugged. "To Faith. She pesters the heck outta me to read it to her."

"I see." And he did.

And, just like when Matt had taken that first baby step toward him babbling, *Da Da Da,* Joe felt the pleasure of his son's first emotional step toward him after so long.

ANNIE and Faith sat on the front porch swing reading the sayings book together. She was explaining where prima donna came from when Joe's green Bronco pulled into the driveway. Two things happened simultaneously: her son bounded out of the car and raced toward her yelling, "Mom, you should've seen Dad. He was awesome."

On his way to the porch, Matt passed Faith, who'd leaped out of the swing and also ran, at warp speed, in the opposite direction toward Joe, her pink-ribboned pigtails flying behind her. In the instant the two kids passed on the sidewalk, Annie had an epiphany. Somehow, she had to help make their father's return work for them.

Scooping up Faith, Joe carried her in his arms and came toward the porch.

" . . . hit hundreds of pop flies without getting tired . . . taught Billy Cameron how to field better . . . and took us all out for ice cream." Matt hadn't been so enthusiastic in months.

Hugging Joe's neck, Faith frowned. "Ice cream? No fair."

Just as they reached the steps, Joe whispered something in her ear. She scrambled down and rushed to her brother who was carrying a white bag along with his mitt. Snatching it out of his hand, Faith dragged out two clear-topped, plastic cups. *Two.* Annie's initial reaction was to refuse the one Faith handed to her. "Mommy, it's your favorite. Pistachio."

For a moment, Annie's eyes met Joe's. Once, with pistachio ice cream, they'd spent an interesting afternoon in bed. The memory made her shiver, and not from fear. Pulling the navy hooded sweatshirt closer around her, she managed a quiet thank you. Faith ran to get spoons.

"I'm glad you had a good practice," she told Matt.

Matt tugged on his baseball cap. "All the guys thought Dad was way cool. He never yelled once. Even when Jimmy pitched a ball heading right for his . . ." Matt's face reddened.

Joe chuckled and gave him a playful sock on the shoulders. A natural gesture. "I managed a quick sidestep, thank God."

Annie smiled weakly, overcome by the evidence before her. Matt needed a man in his life. To share the joys of baseball and guy stuff that, at this age, he couldn't share with her. Though Linc spent a lot of time with Matt, it wasn't the same as having his own father.

As Matt recounted the practice play by play, Faith returned and climbed on her father's lap to eat her ice cream. Annie nibbled on hers, unable to keep from noticing how good Joe looked in his own baseball cap, sweaty gray jersey and low-slung beltless jeans. Worthy material for an underwear commercial.

The phone rang in the living room. Matt jumped up to get it. "It's probably one of the guys," he said and ducked inside.

Wiping her face with the back of her hand, Faith looked at Joe. "Wanna see my costume for the recital, Daddy?"

"I'd love to. Try it on for me?"

Annie's heart began to race in her chest. She swallowed back her initial reaction as the kids left, remembering Sara's words, *You're making progress, Annie. Overcoming your fear of him and losing the bitterness are good goals that you've set.* Determined, Annie bit back her protest at being left alone with Joe.

He knew. It was reflected in his sad silvery gaze. "I can go inside and wait for Faith," he said gruffly.

"You don't have to." She angled her chin. "I'm not afraid of you."

"You don't know how much I want that to be true."

"It is."

"On the deck earlier . . ."

"I apologized."

"I don't want an apology."

Deliberately, she set the empty cup on the railing, tucked her feet under her and crossed her arms over her chest. "What do you want from me, Joe?"

His answer was automatic. "Forgiveness."

She rubbed her shoulder. "I see."

"I'm willing to earn it." His brows arched like a little boy's.

She angled her head to the path the kids had taken into the house. "You're making a good start."

"Thanks."

"I'm willing to give it a shot."

He cleared his throat. "I appreciate that." A tense silence hung between them. "I'll earn back your trust, Annie. I promise."

Demons surfaced, from the deep recesses of her unconscious. *I'll never hit you again, Annie, I promise.* She fought them back, but couldn't erase them completely. *Shouldn't* erase them completely. "Let's just concentrate on your relationship with the kids." Her voice was stronger than she felt. *Forgiveness* was a tall order, and she wasn't sure she was up to filling it.

"How's your hand?" he asked.

She held it up, revealing a small bandage. "Not much damage."

Then Faith floated back out in her red spangles and chiffon, and danced around Joe, who was suitably awed, and Matt returned to give the official verdict that the guys were *way impressed.* As she watched them, Annie vowed silently to strive for forgiveness. If it enriched her kids lives like this, it was worth it.

EIGHTEEN

"PHILIP? I'd like to talk to you." Margo strode into her boss's office bright and early Tuesday morning, ready to do battle if necessary. Her week at home had made her face some hard truths. The hopelessness of her situation with Linc, which they'd confessed Saturday night, had renewed her dedication to her job—which was, and should be, the focus of her life.

From staring out the window, Philip turned to face her. "Sure. But I have to tell you, my emotional equilibrium is zilch right now."

Margo's eyes narrowed. Though he was dressed impeccably as always, in a gray suit with a pinstripe shirt and navy tie, his eyes were bloodshot, and the skin on his face taut with strain. "Are you all right?"

He angled his head to his big leather couch. "I slept there last night."

"Things aren't going well with you and Sally?"

Shaking his head, he gave her a grim smile. "We've been battling for over a week. I didn't see you before you left for Cancun because she got on my case that week, and I took a few days off to see if I could calm her down. Finally, after *this* week, I gave up. We went to see lawyers yesterday, which is why I wasn't at work. The whole thing's a nightmare."

"I'm sorry."

He shrugged. "You wouldn't be free for dinner tonight, would you? I'd really like some company."

Linc would tell her not to go. "I don't think so, Philip."

His eyes turned bleak and she felt bad. She also didn't want to add to his distress. "Maybe it's not such a good time to talk about this right now."

"No, I can't let everything slide. What's on your mind?"

"I'd like to know why you out-sourced the Laufler's factory automation program."

With a puzzled frown, he dropped down behind his desk and raked a hand through his hair. "Hell, when was that?"

"It probably seems like a lifetime ago. But it was the Friday before I took my vacation."

His eyes scanned her in a purely male way. She'd seen the same kind of perusal from Linc often enough to recognize it. "How *was* Cancun? You don't look tanned like you usually do when you come back from the Caribbean." His grin was long and slow. "Did I ever tell you how sexy I thought that was?"

Had he? "I, um, don't remember." She sat down in a plush burgundy leather chair facing him. "The out-sourcing."

With an unreadable look on his face, he picked up the phone. "Geraldine, could you bring in the files on the Laufler account." He hung up and leaned back in his chair. "So, what about Cancun?"

"I didn't go."

"Why?"

"Good question." She'd had a wonderful time with *the girls,* and they'd shared secrets and intimacies like the old days—especially after running into the guys Saturday night. Both she and Annie had been startled afterward when Beth admitted she was having feelings for Tucker Quaid. It was as hopeless a situation as Margo and Linc.

"Margo? Where'd you drift off to?" Philip asked.

The door opened and Geraldine entered. "Hi, Margo." She handed Philip the files and smiled. "Would you like some coffee, Philip? You look a little worn."

"I'd love some. Margo?"

"No thanks."

Taking the folder, he opened it and read the contents as Geraldine left. "Come over here and look at this."

Uneasy, Margo stood and circled his desk. She leaned over his shoulder, near enough to smell his citrusy aftershave; he pushed back on his chair a bit. They were uncomfortably close. "This is a fax from Jamison's marketing department. It came the night before I left for a few days to take care of this stuff with Sally. They asked for a rush job and I knew you were going away so I out-sourced it."

Geraldine returned before Margo could reply. The secretary frowned slightly at them. Automatically Margo stepped back.

Philip grinned at Geraldine and accepted the steaming mug. He sipped. "Hmm, just like I like it. You're an angel, Ger. Where were you when I was looking to get married?"

The older woman beamed as she left.

Margo circled back around the desk and sat. "Philip, I don't understand the out-sourcing. I asked you if you wanted me to cancel my vacation to work on this product."

"Why should you? There was no need. We've out-sourced before." Again he smiled. "Truthfully, I thought you could use some time off. You've been tense. Several of the guys commented on it."

"When? And who?"

Philip leaned back in his chair, staring at her over the rim of his coffee. "It's not important, who. When? Well, since . . . Boston."

Her heartbeat quickened. Before she could quiz him further, he glanced at his watch. "Look, I've got a meeting at nine. Let's finish this conversation over dinner."

"I said I didn't think dinner was a good idea."

"Fine, then this will have to wait. I'm at our plant all afternoon, then I'm attending a seminar the rest of the week." He glanced at his calendar. "We could meet next Monday."

Damn. "All right, I'll have dinner with you."

His brows arched in surprise. "Oh, well, good. Let's go to Adrian's over by your place."

"Fine by me." She stood, feeling manipulated.

Oh, hell, she told herself as she left Philip's office. It was only a dinner.

MARGO was mellow as she left Adrian's at ten that night. It was partly the wine, partly the mild end-of-April evening and partly that Philip had quelled her fears about the out-sourced product. He explained again the need to get the design done quickly, minimized his remarks about her being tense—actually he'd been right about that—and promised never again to out-source a product of hers without checking with her. He also implied none of this would be an issue once the new VP of Engineering was appointed next month.

Which he was strongly recommending to be her.

They reached her apartment building in a slow ten-minute walk. The trees were budding in the courtyard and the street-lamps cast eerie shadows on them as they stood at the front entrance. "This was nice tonight."

"Better than nice. I haven't felt this relaxed in weeks." He gave her a half grin. "We're good for each other, Ms. Morelli."

Margo smiled, forcing herself not to overreact. "Thanks for dinner. My treat next time."

"You're on." The breeze picked up and ruffled his wheat-colored hair. He stuck his hands in his pockets and donned a boyish expression. "I could be talked into coffee."

"That's not a good idea."

Stepping closer, he placed his hands on her shoulders. "You know, I'm a free man now."

"Hardly. You're not even legally separated."

"If I was, would you invite me up?"

"Philip, you know as well as I do, it's not a good idea to mix business and personal lives."

He rubbed his palms up and down her arms, from shoulder to elbow. "It could be very good for you."

"What does that mean?"

He shook his head. "Nothing, it's the wine and lack of sleep talking." Before she could resist, he pulled her to him and hugged her. Kissing her hair, he whispered, "Sleep well," turned and headed back toward a main drag to catch a cab.

Dismayed, Margo watched him go. Shit, what had happened here? She was frowning when she pivoted and caught sight of a figure emerging from the shadows on her left. Her breath hitched in her throat and her hand went to the door to the entrance before she recognized the size and shape of the man.

It was Linc.

*   *   *

"WHAT the hell was that all about?" Linc's tone was furious, but the anger was a good masquerade for his hurt. She'd been hugging the guy, letting him touch her, and Linc was ready to explode at the evidence before him.

"What are you doing here?" Tossing back hair that Philip Hathaway had kissed, for God's sake, she sidestepped the question.

Linc's hands curled into fists. "Margo, have you been *lying* to me?"

That got her back up. Her slender shoulders squared in the short velvet jacket she wore over a purple silk pantsuit. Looking him dead in the eye, she said, "First of all, I don't have to answer to you. Second"—she motioned to the street—"I refuse to discuss this out here. Come on up."

The hell she didn't have to answer to him. There was no one in the world she owed more. But he couldn't go up to her place. He didn't trust himself. "I don't think so." Jamming his hands in his black jean pockets, he gave her his back and headed down the street.

"Damn you," she called after him. "Damn your holier-than-thou attitude." He kept walking. "Go ahead, go," she yelled to his retreating back.

Let me get out of here, God.

I'll do what's best for you, son.

Linc hurried along, like a repentant sinner trying to outrun temptation; but in minutes, he heard heels clattering on the pavement. She caught up to him and, grabbing his arm, tried to stop him. "Linc, wait."

Damn it, God.

No answer.

He kept walking, dragging Margo along with him.

"Linc." Her heels continued to click on the sidewalk. "Damn you." She stopped abruptly. "I don't deserve this."

He whirled around. "You deserve to be turned over my knee and paddled. That's what you deserve."

Falling into femme fatale mode, she batted her thick eyelashes. Though it was dim, with just a few lights from the windows around them, he could see every movement. "Now, who would have thought the good Reverend had a kinky streak."

The humor missed its target. He swallowed hard and his

whole body tightened. The sounds of the city echoed around
him—taxi horns, faint music from a restaurant—but his total
focus was her. He grabbed her so quickly she stumbled in the
heels. Roughly he yanked her to him. Her hazel eyes glittered
with fury—and something else. She'd kept that something else at
bay for a long time—as had he. They were eye level, eye-locked
and simmering with suppressed emotion. He had a brief flash of
sanity, enough to glance around, spot the deserted parking area
next to one of the buildings, and, none-too-gently, drag her off
the sidewalk into the dark.

Then he shoved her up against the building.

And took her mouth. In a way he hadn't taken her mouth in
years. His lips met hers with savage force, Adam branding Eve,
Samson claiming Delilah, David at last having Bathsheba. He
was no longer the good Reverend as he devoured her. He thrust
his lower body forward, and she arched into him. Moaned. Dug
her fingers into his back—he could feel it through his jacket. His
hands slid down to her bottom and hiked her up.

As always, she matched his ardor and wrapped silk-covered
legs around him with no more urging. They ground against each
other with pure, carnal pleasure.

It was a long time before he released her. When he did, she
eased her hammerlock around his neck, but started to slide to the
ground. He held her up. Breathing like a sprint runner, he managed to say, "Easy, babe."

She melted into him, aligned her whole body with his. But it
was tenderness, this time, not passion which weakened him. He
held her close, could hear her heart thundering in her chest, feel
her tremble against him.

"Linc. Make love to me." Her words were slurred like a
drunk's; she was intoxicated by desire.

"Let's go back to your place," he said.

Leaning heavily on him, she let him lead her down the
street.

LINC would have made love to her in a heartbeat. But sanity returned with the subtlety of an emotional sledgehammer, hitting
him over the head with the reality of their lives: if he took her
again, as he had so many times in the past, he feared she could

make him give up his God. And because of that, he refused the temptation.

Once, she'd confessed, too, that she was afraid if they made love ever again, she'd do anything he asked, even go back to Glen Oaks and become a minister's wife.

Which would kill her wonderful spirit, as surely as it had once been killed by the cruel vigilance of Virginia Morelli. Margo's bitterness over what religion had done to her seemed insurmountable.

So it was with that quiet understanding and that awful fear of what they could do to each other, that they ended up at her kitchen table instead of in her bed, drinking hot chocolate.

"Your lips are swollen," he said, carefully brushing the bottom one with the pad of his thumb.

She lowered her eyes.

"Did I do it, or did Hathaway?"

"You're trying to make me mad."

"No, I want the truth."

"He didn't kiss me tonight." She looked up at him, her eyes almost green now, full of mixed emotions. "On the mouth."

It was the hardest thing he'd ever had to ask. "Has he, again, after Boston?"

She shook her head. He shouldn't be so relieved. But against his will, the vise around his heart loosened for the first time since he'd seen Margo in Pretty Boy's arms.

Sipping the cocoa in front of her, she averted her gaze again. "He and his wife are splitting up."

"How convenient." The words were out before he could stop them. He wouldn't have stopped them anyway. Because in his heart, he knew if any man could take her away from him, and keep her away from him, unlike her ex-husband, it was Philip Hathaway.

"Linc." She whispered it quietly, sexily.

He grasped her hand and laced their fingers. "I don't trust him."

God please let that be true. Don't let me be manipulating her to keep her tied to me.

Follow your instincts, boy.

A look flashed across her face. He'd seen it before, when she first admitted to sleeping with someone other than him.

"What?" he asked.

"Nothing."

"Tell me."

Margo bit her lip. "I . . . he . . . said some things that were disturbing."

Linc called on every minister tactic he possessed to get her to tell him. Silence, an encouraging squeeze of her hand, sincere eye contact.

Finally she said, "He wanted to come up, because he was a free man."

"He isn't." *Yet.* But he would be.

"I told him that. And also that it wasn't a good idea to mix business and personal lives."

"Smart girl."

"Linc, he said it could be good for me."

"What?"

"I know. I didn't like the sound of it either."

"The *sound* of it? Margo, it reeks of sexual harassment."

"Not necessarily. For Christ's sake, Philip initiated the sexual harassment policy for our company, oversaw its drafting. I need to think about this. Dissect it. Not overreact." She narrowed wary eyes on him. "And don't use this to get me to do what you want. I won't tolerate it. What's more I won't tell you anything more."

"What more is there?"

"Promise me you'll be objective."

Briefly he closed his eyes.

"Linc, I need you to pull through for me now."

"I promise."

"Swear by your God."

She knew him so well. "I swear by God."

"Strange things have been happening." She told him about the all boys' weekend and how Philip had out-sourced a product.

"Honey, it doesn't sound good."

"I know. I'm not stupid. But I can't jump to any conclusions, either. He's the fair-haired boy of CompuQuest. I can't go off half-cocked. I need time to sort this through."

Please God, let me give it to her.

You can do anything you have to, Linc.

"All right." He stood. And glanced at his watch. "I've got to catch the midnight train back."

"Why are you in town, anyway?"

"There was a seminar at Union Divinity I wanted to take. It was on women's self-esteem groups."

"You've been here all day? Why didn't you tell me you were coming?"

"Why didn't you tell me you were home for the week?"

Silent understanding passed between them.

He held out his hand. "Walk me to the door."

As always, she took it, and he felt the current leap from her body to his. Desire still hummed between them.

They faced each other at the front of her fancy condo like best friends and worst adversaries. His eyes dropped to her mouth. "Oh, hell," he muttered and lowered his head. Their lips melded. But instead of the savage passion of earlier, the contact was so sweet it made Linc ache worse, in a completely different way.

"Stay," she whispered against his lips.

"I can't. You know what we'll do."

Her eyes shone with understanding. "I hate this."

"Me, too." He brushed back a wild lock of hair, kissed her nose and left before temptation won out and she made him forsake all that was important to him.

NINETEEN

───

IN the lunchroom on Wednesday, Ron watched as Lily Hanson shook her long brown hair back; it fell down past her shoulders, instead of over her boobs. The guys said she did it on purpose, to show her stuff, but Ron didn't think so. There was something about the tough-as-nails image she projected that didn't ring true. Maybe it was because she had an innocence in her that was buried in him, too.

When she leaned over the math book, grazing his arm with her breast, his body responded with a great big boner. "So, how does knowing what they have in common help you figure out the circumference?" Lily asked.

Ron forced the Venn diagram into focus. His pencil skittered across the paper, keeping time with his pulse. "See, if you figure out this common section . . ." He made his brain function by concentrating on the math problem instead of the scooped neck of the little white T-shirt she wore.

Ten minutes later, she was gazing up at him like he was Euclid himself. "You're so smart, Ronny."

Ron shrugged. "I like math." He nodded to the entrance to the cafeteria where his teacher stood guard and shot the breeze with Sammy. "Johnson's pretty cool."

Lily agreed. "I'm in the low-level class, you know?" Her eyes had flecks of green in them, though they were mostly brown. "He never makes us feel stupid."

"You're not—"

A cloud came over them, blocking the light from the window. "Hey, Ronny baby. Whatcha doin'?" Loose slapped his tray down, his lunch consisting of two ice-cream sandwiches and a can of soda.

"Helping with math," Ron grumbled.

"Hey, Lily White, you need help with anything else, I'm willin'.'"

Lily stiffened. Before she could respond, Maze dropped a brown paper bag on the table and straddled the bench. "Hi, guys." He scanned the area. "I sure could use a cigarette to perk me up." His bloodshot gaze dropped to Lily's tight shirt. "Or somethin' else." He and Loose laughed crudely. "What ya doin' after school, Lily White?"

Ron opened his mouth to say something, but Lily stood and gave Maze a cold stare. "I'm busy, little boy. But if I wasn't, it would *so* not be you I'd get it on with." She stalked away.

"That isn't how you felt up at the lake last week," he yelled after her.

Her back to him, she threw him the finger over her shoulder.

"She loves me," he hooted, digging into his bag and stuffing Jellie Bellies in his mouth.

Ron watched Maze, faintly disgusted by his appearance, sick, big-time of his crudeness. "Why don't you just leave her alone?"

"What, and miss some of the greatest head I ever got in my life?"

The image of pretty Lily on her knees before Maze made Ron's stomach turn.

"What's a matter, Ronny boy, you got the hots for Lily White?"

"Don't call her that."

"Ow-ee." Maze slapped the table with his hand. "You do. Hey man, it's okay, I don't mind sharin'."

"I didn't know she was yours to share."

"You got that. If doin' me means she's mine, then she belongs to half the football team, too."

Though Ron had heard the rumors, and witnessed with his own eyes how Lily dressed and acted, he saw red at the comment. "Shut your fuckin' mouth, Maze."

Maze started to rise. "Who the—"

Loose vised Maze's arm and pulled him back down. "Hey, Ronny boy, why you gettin' humped about a chick? They all cunts, man!"

Nobody spoke. The air crackled with adolescent challenge.

Then in a silky smooth voice, Loose asked, "You ever ask your old lady 'bout that night at Crocodile's?"

"Why you son of a—" He was halfway out of his seat and over the table when a hand gripped his shoulder. He turned to see Sammy behind him, along with Mr. Johnson.

"Everything okay here, guys?" Mr. Johnson asked easily. But his gaze was steely and had narrowed in on Loose and Maze.

"None of your fuckin' business," Maze said loudly enough for the next table to *ooh* and *ahh* at the curse.

Mr. Johnson shook his head. "Get your stuff, LaMont. You're coming with me."

Maze picked up his brown bag and the leather jacket he'd dropped on the bench. "No, thanks, dickhead. I'm outta here." He turned and, kicking a book bag out of his way, swaggered out of the cafeteria.

Mr. Johnson looked at Ron. "I'm going to write up this referral now, but I'd like to talk to you before the end of lunch, Ron."

Ron said nothing. Instead he was snared by the look on Loose's face. He expected venom directed at the teacher. But when it was focused on him, Ron felt a chill crawl up his spine.

TWENTY

———

ON her way home from an evening dance class, Annie swung by the church. It was ten at night, and too late to be visiting anybody, but if Linc's light was on, maybe she'd stop. Suzie was with the kids and had decided to sleep over with Faith. Belle Star was entitled to seek out Jesse James when she wanted a friend, wasn't she?

The garage was dark when Annie pulled into the parking lot. Either Linc wasn't home, or . . . then she saw him at the door to the church. He was with a big man she recognized as the janitor.

Exiting the car, she headed for them.

"Henry, it's all right. No real harm done."

The man frowned; his face and clothes were grimy with some kind of soot. When he saw Annie, he ducked his head, nodded to her and loped down the sidewalk.

"Hi, kiddo." Even Linc's voice was tired.

She surveyed him—he looked like he'd done a stint as a chimney sweep. The black film on the janitor covered Linc, too, and his clothes were hopelessly soiled. "What happened to you?"

Weary, Linc sank against the door. It was cool out this late on an April night and he shivered a bit in his faded navy sweatshirt and jeans. "I had a little run-in with a couple of open bags of charcoal on an overhead shelf in a storage closet."

Annie looked after Henry. "What'd he do now?"

Linc snorted. "He knocked them over when we were looking for some cleaning supplies. They must have been old. When they hit me, and the floor, they practically disintegrated. You wouldn't believe the mess." He grinned. "Henry gives new meaning to the word *irony.*"

"Are you gonna fire him?"

He straightened. "Now, why would I do that?"

"You're a nice guy, you know that?"

"You wouldn't say that if you could have heard me swearing at the charcoal."

"God won't care."

"No, I don't think He would." Linc took her hand. "Come on in." They made the short trek to his office. "Did you come right from the studio?"

"Uh-huh." She followed him into the room. "I wanted to tell you something, but I can come back when you're not so tired."

"As my grandfather used to say, you'll have to wait for the cows to come home for that to happen."

"Joe would know where that saying comes from."

Linc sank onto the couch and patted the seat next to him. "Sit."

She sat, smoothing down the oversize multicolored sweater she wore with leggings.

"Is that what this is all about? Joe?"

"Yeah."

"Tell me."

Glancing around the room, she remembered Joe's first meeting here with them all, and how stilted it had been. How afraid she'd been. "Things have been going well with the kids and Joe."

"And what about you?"

"I've seen Sara a few times." She sighed. "I let Joe coach Matt's Little League team."

"I know. I think it's good for them both. Joe loves it."

"You see him a lot, don't you?"

"He was a good friend all those years ago." Linc scowled. "Which was why it killed me when I found out what he'd been doing to you. I didn't have a clue."

"It wasn't your fault. I got good at hiding it." She rubbed her arms. "Bruises and all."

"He's changed, Annie."

She nodded. "That's why I'm here. I've decided you don't need to chaperone his visits anymore."

"What brought this on?"

"Mostly how he's been with Matt, alone." She stared off into space picturing Joe braiding Faith's hair. She wondered where he'd learned to do that, then thought of Taylor Cummings's long dark mane. "But he's gentle with Faith, too. He treats her like spun glass."

"Funny, that's how I always thought he treated you."

"He did. Before he got abusive. Even then, he was so tender in between . . . bouts. So nice. It's crazy."

"That's common, isn't it, in abusive relationships?"

"Yeah. At least it's common for there to be long periods of repentance and peace. The gentleness, I'm not sure. I always thought that side was Joe's true nature. The periods of violence were the aberration." She shivered.

"Maybe they were. I know he worked on a Jekyll and Hyde theory with his counselors."

"Does he talk about it?"

"Yes. He says it keeps him healthy."

"Well, in any case, I think he's healthy enough to see the kids alone."

"What about you?"

"Me?"

"You'll have to be alone with him sometimes then."

"I know. But I'm not afraid. He won't hurt me, like you and Sara say, if I don't let him." She watched Linc closely. "Thanks for helping with this. I don't know how I would have gotten through his coming back to town without you."

"I should have done more. Before."

"Oh, Linc. You take on too much. With me, Margo, Beth." She indicated the office. "And the church."

He shrugged.

"How's it going with Margo?"

"Shitty."

She smiled at his curse. "Want to talk about it? I missed dinner. We could get a pizza, have a few beers . . ."

"I'd love to," he said grinning at her. "I need—"

A knock on the door stopped his response. Since he'd left it ajar, both he and Annie could see a figure standing there. He shot her a questioning look, got up and crossed to the entrance.

"Rosa?" Linc said, blocking Annie's view. "What are you—oh, Lord, Rosa, what happened?"

Annie heard mumbling.

Linc stepped aside. "Come in and sit."

The hunched-over figure crept into the office. Slender shoulders were covered in a faded black raincoat. A kerchief shielded Rosa DeMartino's head. Annie knew her from church activities and had always liked the demure woman. But she sensed something in her . . . something familiar.

When Rosa raised her head, Annie realized what it was. In an instant, she recognized the damage a man's fist could do to a woman's cheekbone. She'd seen it many times in her own mirror.

"OH, my, I didn't know you had company." Rosa's voice was warbled, and Linc noticed a small cut on her lip, too.

"I—" He looked at Annie. "This is my friend, Annie Lang." Whose face had gone stark white with the evidence before her. Lord knew what ghosts Rosa's appearance conjured. "You know Annie from church, Rosa."

Rosa turned her head away, hiding the evidence of her husband's abuse.

Frozen, Annie just stared at Rosa's back. Linc wasn't sure what to do.

Rosa shook her head. "Sorry to interrupt. I'll be leaving."

Linc said, "You'll do no such thing."

Finally Annie spoke. "Of course not."

Still Rosa wouldn't face them. Linc watched Annie carefully, he didn't want to set off any emotional land mines, but he had to help Rosa. Annie stared over at him. Her eyes went from shock, to understanding to anger.

Linc went to Rosa. "Let me have your coat and scarf."

Rosa waited, deciding. Linc stood close but didn't touch her. He'd learned that from Annie. At last, Rosa shrugged out of her coat, but she wouldn't remove her scarf. Scant cover for the condition of her face. Then she sat down, keeping her head averted.

Again, Linc looked at Annie, silently asking for understanding. Annie gave him a weak smile, then with a reassuring nod, she headed to the door. But she stopped when she got there and turned around. "Rosa, I'll leave if it's what you want me to do. But you know what? I think I should stay."

Rosa's head came up slowly. "Why?" she asked Annie.

Annie's chin angled. She swallowed hard. "Because I've been through what's happening to you. I understand where you're coming from."

"You?" the woman asked incredulously.

Linc had to smile. Joe's abuse was not common knowledge around town. Annie had made sure of it to protect her children. But he knew that Rosa's shock came from the fact that Annie Lang was no cream puff. Everybody respected her for running her own business, raising two wonderful kids by herself, being on the Community Youth Council and other committees.

Annie understood Rosa's comment, too. Coming back into the room, Annie sat down beside her. "Yes, Rosa, *me*. My husband hit me for years before I kicked him out." She reached over to grasp Rosa's trembling hands. "Linc can help you, Rosa." She raised strong, sure eyes to him. "And maybe I can, too."

LIKE a tender lover, May came to Glen Oaks gently. At the first Little League baseball game of the season, Annie sat in the bleachers and let the still-warm six o'clock breeze stroke her cheek. The newly mowed grass wove its rich scent around her and a chorus of yellow daffodils peeked out from behind the dugout, where her son's team sat listening to their coach give them last-minute instructions.

"There's Lisa, Mommy. Can I go play with her on the swings?" Faith was already scrambling down the bleachers.

Annie's first response was to tell her daughter that she wasn't allowed to go unsupervised.

"Let her go," Suzie coaxed from behind. As a close friend as well as a sister-in-law, she knew Annie's tendency to be over-protective of the kids. Suzie and Grace had turned out for this big family event, too, though to be fair, they regularly attended Matt's games. Annie and Grace had a tentative truce, effective if they didn't talk about Joe.

"Okay," Annie called out to Faith. "But stay in the play area where I can see you."

Lisa, who'd appeared at the fence with her mother, was a new friend of Faith's, and new to Annie's dance studio. She'd joined because of her mother, Rosa DeMartino, who'd quickly become a part of Annie's life in the last two weeks. As Rosa waved to Annie, and threaded her way up the bleachers to sit with her, Annie gave her a warm, if somewhat forced smile. She was very worried about the woman.

It's the first time he hit me. He won't do it again.

I thought that too, Rosa.

Then, of course, a week later Annie spotted the bruise on Rosa's waist when she'd lifted Lisa up and her shirt had pulled past her slacks.

They hit where it can't be seen. It happened to me more times than I can count. You need help, Rosa.

Bleak eyes had agreed, and Rosa had made an appointment at Social Services for the following afternoon.

"Any action yet?" Rosa asked, glancing toward the field. Unbeknownst to them both, their sons had been assigned to the same Little League team this year.

"None. The coach is talking to the guys."

"Tommy hasn't stopped talking about Coach Murphy. He loves him." Though Rosa was a plain woman, wearing basic tan pants and a plaid blouse, she had beautiful blue eyes which stared wistfully out at the diamond. "I wish his fath . . ." She let the thought trail off, but Annie knew she was wishing Sam was more like Joe. The irony was striking. Annie had only found out today that Tommy was on Joe's team. She hadn't the wits or the time necessary to tell Rosa who Joe was, necessary because once she realized Joe was Matt's father, Rosa would make her own connection between the beloved coach and the abusive ex-husband.

"Annie, you okay?"

"Sure."

Rosa ducked her head. "I shouldn't speak out of turn like that."

"Oh, Rosa, you've got to say what's on your mind."

Glancing around like a gunrunner making a drop, Rosa nodded. "But we shouldn't talk about it here."

"You're right. Want to come over to my house after the game?"

"Maybe. Sam's working tonight."

Annie squeezed Rosa's hand gently and turned her eyes to the diamond. She'd avoided looking at her ex-husband all night. Watching him now, standing off to the side of the boys, Annie admitted that the sight of him in the Good Father role often disconcerted her. She also admitted he physically attracted her, too, especially when he looked so wholesome and healthy. His green T-shirt stretched across his chest and tucked into navy shorts that accented the corded muscles of his legs. She'd seen him running in town and guessed it was part of his rehab program to stay fit and sober.

Play began.

"Matt's lead-off batter," Grace announced from behind.

Joe had told them that Matt was the best on the team. Annie watched her son stride to the plate, dig in his cleats, hit the base with his bat and glance over to the dugout. Joe cupped his hands and yelled something to the boy that made him smile.

Matt connected on the first pitch. Annie watched it soar—over the pitcher's head, past the second baseman, way out into center field. Then she bolted up with the rest of the crowd.

"Oh, my God, it went over the fence!" Suzie screamed.

Bouncing up and down, Annie watched Matt's graceful trek around the bases. She didn't think she'd ever seen a wider grin on his young face.

Dad's really helped with our hitting. He changed my stance, and I can get a lot more power behind it.

When her son reached home plate, his team converged on him. A little taller than most, he looked over their heads for his father, who stood off to the side, beaming. As Matt came toward the dugout, Joe approached him. Without censoring his response, Joe grasped his son in a heartfelt bear hug. Matt returned it.

Amid the comments like, "Hey, Annie did you see that?" and "Wow, another Mark McGwire," from other parents, Annie battled back tears. Nothing had happened as she'd planned since Joe had come back to town two months before. It was hard keeping up with the emotional whirlwind he'd brought with him. First, the horror. Then doubt. Then he seemed to be . . . good for the kids. Her conflicting feelings warred heatedly inside her.

Stop it, and just enjoy the game.

Which only got better from there. Donovan's Sluggers—they were sponsored by Beth's diner—were leading four to two at the end of the fifth inning when Beth waved to her from the grass. She was with Ronny, Linc and the woman he was dating, Jane Meachum.

"Hey, is there room up there?" Beth called out.

"Yep, come on up."

Annie watched Beth say something to Ronny, who pointed across the field. Beth nodded, and followed by Linc and Jane, climbed over people to get to Annie. Ron loped to the other side of the diamond.

"Sorry we're late," Beth said when they reached Annie, greeted the Murphys and sat down. "I got held up."

"Nothing's wrong, is it?" Annie asked, scooting over.

"No, just business. It's picked up since the races started." Beth looked drained. Her usually serene eyes were sad, and for once the red color of her sweatshirt didn't complement her dark looks. She was pale.

Annie had tried to talk to her about Tucker Quaid after she'd confessed her attraction to him that night at Crocodile's. But Beth had told her that, because of Ronny's attitude toward Tucker, their relationship was a dead end and nothing could be done to change things.

"How's Matt doing?" Linc settled in next to Jane, who sat beside Suzie.

"He got a homer first time at bat and a single and a double after that." Grace's voice was filled with grandmotherly pride.

"He should be up again soon," Annie told him.

Linc smiled pleasantly enough, but he too seemed unhappy. However, the big-eyed woman next to him appeared to have found paradise. She stared at Linc adoringly.

Rosa gave Linc a smile and he winked at her. "What about your boy, Rosa?"

"Tommy got on base twice," she said proudly.

"Super."

"He's younger than Matt. This is his first time for Little League," Annie put in. "He's doing great."

Linc watched Rosa for a minute. He was worried as hell about her. Which was only one of a whole swimming pool full of concerns he had right now. If he wasn't careful, he was gonna drown in them.

We found somebody to help Rosa, didn't we, buddy?

Frowning, Linc shook his head. He didn't want to talk to God now. He was *not* a happy camper.

You think I don't know that? God asked.

Linc pretended to watch the game.

So, how's Jane?

Fine.

I sent her to you, you know.

My, haven't we been busy lately.

Anger's good Linc. It'll spur you on to decide what to do.

No decisions to be made, he told God as the other team got on base.

There are always decisions to be made.

Hey, lay off tonight, will you? I'm trying to enjoy the game.

Are you going to call Margo when you get back home?

Yeah.

Good, she needs to talk to you. It wasn't nice of you to miss the last two Sunday phone calls.

I have to stay away from her.

Why?

You were there a couple of weeks ago. You know what almost happened.

Do you really believe she can take you away from me that easily?

Can't she?

Mmm. Let's watch the game, now.

Oh, sure, as soon as we get into something interesting, you clam up. You got a mean streak in you, God, you know that?

He thought he heard God chuckle.

"Linc?" Jane asked. "Are you all right?"

He glanced over at Jane and his mood lightened. She looked so innocent in her prim little white blouse under the navy jacket and matching slacks. *Please, don't let me hurt her.* "I'm fine. Hey, thanks for coming with me tonight. When we made the date, I forgot about Matt's game."

"I love baseball."

And everything else Linc enjoyed—and needed in his life. Like God. Like going to Bible study—she'd attended two of the sessions he'd held these last weeks, even though her daddy's church offered them, too. She also liked watching reruns of *Emergency* on TV, Italian food and walking in the rain.

And, he suspected, she liked *him* a whole lot. More than once she'd indicated that a real kiss, a warmer-than-chaste hug would be welcome. For some reason, he'd never initiated either.

"Who's Ronny with?" Linc asked Beth as the side was called out and he tried to distract himself from his introspection.

Beth stared across the field. "He saw a girl he knew. I think her name's Lily. I wondered why he was so interested in Matt's game tonight."

Annie chuckled. "Is she nice?"

"I haven't met her, but he's talked about her some." Beth scowled. "She dresses like we used to."

"We turned out okay, Bonnie."

Beth forced a smile. "Oh, look, our team's up." She pretended to concentrate on Matt but she was watching her own son. He seemed less sulky with Lily Hanson than he'd been for the last few weeks.

"Oh, God, look!" Suzie's comment, and how she shot out of her seat, had Beth's mind back at the field; she stood, too.

Matt had hit a line drive to first. The baseman fumbled it. The pitcher, coming to the baseline, picked it up and tried to tag Matt, but missed. The umpire, however, called the runner out.

Everybody was on their feet from the Sluggers' side of the stands, including Linc, who was yelling like an Outlaw, not a town minister. "What's the matter, ref? You need glasses?" he shouted.

Matt's startled look turned to adolescent outrage when he realized he'd been called out. He yelled something to the ump.

Immediately Joe jogged out to first base.

"Oh, no, I hope he doesn't get mad." Beth saw Annie's fists clench at her sides.

Reaching out, Beth grasped her friend's hand. So many bad memories faced Annie every day since Joe's return. Though her faith in Joe was a lot stronger than Annie's, Beth also held her breath.

Joe headed right for his son; when he reached him, he put his arm around Matt and drew him off to the side. Matt said something, and Joe leaned over and spoke in his ear. Matt shook his head hard. Again Joe spoke to him and Matt nodded; more advice from Joe and Matt shrugged and headed to the dugout.

Then Joe faced the umpire.

He made a comment.

The umpire said something back.

Joe gestured to first and to the baseline.

The umpire answered, then shrugged.

Finally, Joe nodded. Turned. And jogged back to the dugout.

The breath escaped Annie in a whoosh.

Beth patted Annie's arm. "Seems okay, kid."

The game began again, but a few plays later, Beth's gaze drifted back to Ron. He and Lily had gone to the playground and were pushing Faith and some of her friends on the swings. Beth smiled at them. Ronny was going to be all right. Just a few more weeks of weekend jail. Now if she could just stay away from Tucker like she promised.

"Beth, you okay?" Linc had grasped her arm and gave her a questioning look. "We won, honey. And you're frowning."

"No, I'm fine." *Or least I will be,* she thought. Her eyes straying to Ronny again, she vowed she would be. Fine. Without Tucker Quaid. Someday she'd even be able think that thought, make that promise, without feeling the prick of tears behind her eyelids.

"Okay, Bonnie, if you say so. How about coming to get ice cream with me and Jane?" He scanned Annie and Rosa, and included the Murphys in the invitation. "You guys, too. My treat."

"You're on, Jess," she said to her brother.

AN hour after the game, Linc eased open the door to his apartment and stood back so Jane could go inside before him. He followed her in, and reached for the light switch.

A soft, lithe hand stopped him. "Don't." Jane's voice was sweet. But husky.

Though he was a man of God, he was still a descendent of Adam; he leaned back against the door in the darkness. Only the sliver of moon peeking in through the sheer curtains illuminated them. He reached for her waist and brought her to stand before him. "You're pretty tempting, do you know that, Jane Meachum?"

"Am I?" She stepped closer. Her trim navy pants fit her hips loosely.

His hands flexed on her sides. "Hmm."

"It's taken you a long time to get this close," she whispered. "And then you needed urging."

He slid his arms further around her and he shoved back the memory of the feel of Margo, supple and muscular beneath his fingers. "I don't want to push you into anything too soon."

A heartbeat later she said, simply, "Push."

Linc drew in a breath and drew her closer. She smelled like peaches. He was only five-nine, but he had to bend down to reach her mouth. It was soft against his. He pulled her closer and kissed her gently. When she cradled his neck in her hand, and moved against him, his body responded.

But it was her moaned words that doused his ardor. Her *Linc,* against his mouth flashed Margo, like a brilliant billboard advertising hot sex, before his closed eyes. *Linc,* she'd told him, *take me home. Make love to me.*

It was blasphemous to think of one woman while you were kissing another. An insult to both of them. He wound down the contact as diplomatically as he could.

Getting the message, Jane stepped back from him and he groped the wall for the switch. When he flicked on the light, he could see questions in her eyes. Her pretty brown hair had fallen into her eyes and he brushed it back. "Let's take this slow," he said.

Not angry, just confused, she cocked her head. "Because of my father?"

He chuckled. "Your daddy's the furthest thing from my mind right now, sugar."

Jane sighed. "You have a Gatsby quality about you, you know that? Like you've lost the great love of your life."

Looking her in the eye, he said honestly, "I have." He rubbed her shoulders. "But contrary to good old Jay, I don't want to pine my life away for her."

"What do you want, Linc?"

"A wife and family and a normal life." *Like I never had.*

Her smile was sunshine bright; he didn't understand why it caused him pinpricks of pain. "All right, let's take it slow."

Smiling falsely—he wondered if dissembling was a sin—he asked, "How about some pizza and . . . some music?"

"You're on, good Reverend."

Hmmm, who would have thought the good Reverend had a kinky streak?

Damn it, Margo, he thought, heading for the phone to call the pizza place. *Get out of my mind.*

Miraculously, she did. By ten o'clock, he and Jane had devoured a Pizza Supreme with everything on it, two beers each and he was showing her how to do *The Stroll* from the sixties.

She'd taken off her jacket and shoes and leaned against the back of the couch. "Really. Linc, that's so . . . dumb."

"Come here, woman, and try it." He was having fun.

She pushed off from the sofa just as the phone rang. He groaned. She angled her head. "Shall I screen it? I got pretty good doing that for my dad."

Hell, he was only human. Winking at her, he shrugged. "Give it a try."

"Hello," she said sweetly when she picked up the receiver. Linc saw her frown. "Um, yes, Reverend Grayson's here. Who's calling?" Another hesitation. Then she chuckled. Covering the mouthpiece, she said, "The woman says she's Ma Barker. That's a new one."

All the air and good humor and sexual interest in Jane drained out of him. He took the phone. "Turn that down, will you?" he said to her and then into the receiver, "Hello, Margo."

"Well, it sounds like Jesse James is having himself a grand old time." Her words were meant to tease, but her tone was raw.

After lowering the music, Jane sat demurely on the couch, and crossed her pretty legs.

"Um, I am. How are you?"

"Just peachy."

"Hold on a sec." He covered the mouthpiece, said to Jane, "Sorry, be right back," and headed for the bedroom. Once there he closed the door and flopped on the bed. "Margo."

"What?" She sounded sulky.

"What's going on?"

Silence.

"You're upset."

And even longer silence.

"Margo? Talk to me."

"Have you screwed her?"

"Oh, honey, that's beneath you."

A very long pause. "I'm sorry. It kills me to think of you touching her."

"This isn't helping anything, love."

A longer silence. "Is she why you haven't called?"

"No."

"Is what happened two weeks ago why?"

"Yes."

"I shouldn't have pushed you to that."

"Margo—"

"Listen, never mind. Go back to your girlfriend. She's good

for you. Forget I called." Before she hung up she whispered, "Forget about *me*."

The phone went dead. The annoying *beep beep beep* drummed in his head. Finally, he said into the mouthpiece, "I wish I could."

ANNIE and Rosa settled in the living room alone, sipping some tea. They'd gone to Porky's Ice Cream Shoppe with Linc, Jane, the Donovans and the Murphys, and then had come back here. Their daughters had just retreated to Faith's room. It was getting late, and Matt and Tommy, who had gotten ice cream with the team, would be home momentarily. This was Annie's first opportunity to talk to Rosa alone.

Not that Annie was anxious to explain about Joe. What could she say without sounding trite, or worse, betraying? *Yeah, he beat me up, but he's better now. It's not like you and Sam.* Lord, would Annie's situation with Joe cause Rosa to not seek help?

"Rosa, I need to tell you something."

The woman's kind blue eyes held a question. "Something's been wrong all night, hasn't it?"

"Not wrong exactly."

"You acted funny about the boys' coach."

Silently Annie thanked God for the opening. "I know. I was afraid he was going to fight with the umpire about the bad call against Matt."

"Why? He seems like a nice man."

"I know he does. And maybe he is. Now."

"Now?"

"Rosa, do you know Coach's last name?"

"Yes, it's Murphy. I read all the information on the sheet."

"He's Matt's father."

Her eyebrows arched in surprise. "Matt's name isn't Lang, like yours?"

"No, Lang is my maiden name."

"Are you saying Joe Murphy is . . . he's your . . ." Reflexively the woman grasped her waist. "Oh, no, Annie, he's the one that . . ."

Annie grappled for courage. Rosa might not be able to say the words aloud, but Annie could. "He's the one that beat me up."

"But he's so nice. I've talked to him a couple of times."

"I know. And maybe it's real. Joe claims he's a recovered batterer."

"What's that?"

Taking in a deep breath, Annie explained the term and also Joe's long years of therapy. Though she might be betraying confidences, she wouldn't let all Linc's work with Rosa, and how far the woman had come in two weeks, go to waste. More important, she couldn't let Rosa's plan to seek help go by the wayside.

"I don't know what to say," Rosa told her after Annie finished the story.

Annie leaned over the coffee table separating them. "I told you this story so that you don't think Sam's going to miraculously change. If Joe *has* changed, he managed it with a lot of counseling and hard work. And it took years."

Rosa stared at her mutely.

"Do you understand, Rosa? Sam won't change unless he gets a lot of help."

Before Rosa could answer, there was a commotion in the kitchen. Joe and Matt and Tommy trundled into the living room.

" . . . really good, Tom." Joe's low voice was a pleasant rumble.

"My dad helped me with hitting, Tommy. And see what I did?"

"Will you work on the catching with me, Coach?"

"Hello, everybody." Though Annie was disturbed by the bad timing, her greeting was pleasant.

"Hi, Mom."

"Hi, Ma."

"Hi, Annie." Joe's face held the flush of victory and a deep sense of contentment. He looked younger, less weary. He smiled at Rosa. "Mrs. DeMartino."

Rosa froze. Stared at Joe. Christian woman though she was, she couldn't keep the look of contempt from her face. Then, automatically, she sidled back in her chair.

At her expression, and silence, Joe also stilled. His face drained of color. He studied Rosa, then he shot a look at Annie. She was stunned by the pain in his eyes, the bleakness.

For the very first time since he'd walked out of her life, five years and ten months ago, she felt sorry for him.

*   *   *

HE had to escape. Before his face cracked. Before his shoulders, brittle and unyielding, slumped with the weight of his guilt. He was bruised from the inside out and wasn't sure how to deal with it.

But he couldn't flee. As he went through the motions of saying good night to his kids, and ended up reading a short passage from the sayings book to Faith, he forced himself to deal with reality.

"Read me what *face the music* means, Daddy."

Ah, irony.

Joe cleared his throat. "When old-time soldiers were dismissed from the army for bad behavior, they were often made to march slowly between the ranks of former comrades. Drums and other instruments marked their time. Meeting the unpleasant head-on came to be known as *facing the music.*"

So, Murphy, he told himself as he stared at the book, *face the music*. Annie had obviously told Rosa DeMartino about him. And he didn't have to stretch far to guess why. He'd processed Rosa's forms for counseling himself, and though no specifics were given, she'd asked for Carol Lopez, who was a domestic violence counselor. It didn't take Einstein to figure out the rest.

Rosa was an abused spouse.

And Joe was the enemy. That Annie had told her about him was no more than he deserved, but it knifed him inside.

"You okay, Daddy?" Faith asked as she cuddled into him on her canopied bed.

"Just fine, princess."

"You look sad. Like Mommy used to all the time."

One more nail in the coffin. "No, I'm not sad. Daddy's just . . . *pooped.*"

Faith giggled. "Oh, Daddy."

That had been one of the first phrases she'd wanted to know the origin of. She'd been gravely disappointed to learn it had to deal with the winds at sea battering a boat's poop deck on long voyages, not the bathroom habits of humans or animals.

Closing the book, he stood and bent over the bed. He kissed her on the cheek and pulled up the covers. "Sleep tight."

"I love you, Daddy."

"I love you too, sweetheart."

Robotically, he left her room. Matt's door was ajar. Joe stifled his need to escape, to lick his wounds somewhere, and crossed the hall to knock on his son's door.

"Come in."

Matt sprawled on his bed, tossing up a baseball and catching it in his glove. His whole posture was relaxed. His welcoming smile warmed Joe. "You leaving?"

"Uh-huh."

Matt grinned broadly. "It was a great game."

Joe gave a good attempt at returning the smile. Though it wasn't a thousand-watt, it seemed to pass. "Yeah, it was." He scanned the room. "Ready for bed?"

"I have to do my math first."

"Okay, then. I'll see you for practice tomorrow." Joe turned to leave.

"Dad?"

Pivoting back around, Joe faced him. "Hmm?"

"I was real proud of you, tonight."

Joe swallowed back the lump in his throat. He'd never, ever thought to hear this from Matt's mouth. "I was proud of you, too, son. See you tomorrow."

Outside the door, Joe leaned against it wearily and drew in a deep breath.

Three steps forward, two back. Pete had said it often enough. *Concentrate on the forward motion.*

With that in mind, Joe headed for the stairs. The light was on under Annie's door. Well, he thought as he jogged down the steps, at least he wouldn't have to deal with her. His feelings were a jumbled mass of contradictions, and he couldn't afford to be vulnerable in front of her. He'd just made it to the front door when he heard from the semi-dark living room, "Joe?"

His hand on the doorknob, he stilled. "I thought you went to bed."

"I wanted to talk to you." Her voice, for once, held no re-crimination. Its softness, its . . . kindness was almost worse because it accented what he'd once had and stupidly thrown away.

"Now's not a good time, Annie."

She hesitated. "You're hurt, aren't you?"

"I have no right to be hurt." He had no rights at all.

Don't start feeling sorry for yourself, Pete had told him a thousand times. *It's counterproductive.*

"Still, you are."

Joe shook his head. God, he just wanted to leave. To be alone to figure out how to handle his feelings. But whereas the old Joe might have run and hid, the new Joe didn't. He'd deal with this up front, then get out of here. Circling around, he stuck his hands in his shorts pockets and looked at his wife.

She'd left a small light on in the corner of the room. It cast her in a surreal glow. She was so petite, yet tonight she seemed strong and sure of herself. Her jeans made her legs look longer, and he knew the power of the muscle underneath the denim. Her slender shoulders were squared in the navy sweatshirt she wore. Her face was calm. "I didn't go broadcasting . . . it."

The memory of *it* made him sick, but he forced himself to say, "You didn't?"

"No. I can't go into detail about Rosa, but—"

He interrupted her. "You don't have to."

She cocked her head.

"I see all the client applications at work. I put two and two together." He scanned the living room, focusing on the pictures of his kids. "I just didn't know you had any connection with her."

"It's complicated why. We've become friends." She bit her lip. "I told her about my past to help her."

"Well, that's good."

"She didn't make the connection with her son's coach because of the last name thing."

"Until tonight."

Annie nodded.

He struggled not to sound whiny. "It's nothing I don't deserve. I'm surprised the whole town didn't find out years ago."

"I kept it quiet for the kids."

"Yes, Suzie told me that."

"I'm sorry if Rosa finding out hurt you."

He shook his head. "No, you have nothing to be sorry about. I'm the one . . ." More images, dark and dirty, filled his mind. The man he used to be rose up out of the scum and roared full-blast in his head. "Look, I need to go. I'm feeling raw. None of this is your fault. It's all mine." He circled around and grabbed for the door handle. It turned, but wouldn't open. He blinked hard. Fumbled with the lock. He'd just released the catch when he felt a hand on his arm. It was the first time she'd touched him since he'd come back to Glen Oaks.

That did it. He slumped forward. Lay his forehead against the glass pane.

Annie spoke. "I know you say you've changed. It looks like it's true." She hesitated. "I want it to be true."

Still he said nothing. He dug his fingernails into his palms to keep back the emotion battling to get out.

"I don't want to hurt you, Joe."

Oh God, after how he'd hurt her . . . Hunching his shoulders, he scrubbed his hands over his face, trying to wipe away the wetness there. Then he drew in a deep breath, squared his shoulders and nodded. Reaching for the door, he opened it.

She let go.

Without turning around, he stepped out into the now-dark night. The air was brisk on his bare legs, and a slight breeze cooled his cheeks.

Quickly he descended the steps.

TWENTY-ONE

JOE Murphy's office at Social Services overlooked the playground area of the town hall. The swings, teeter-totter and jungle gym were adjacent to an outdoor basketball court whose nets had recently been set up. Spring was definitely here!

As he stared out the window, Tucker tried his damnedest to enjoy the new season, tried to bask in the warm weather, which made today a just-jeans-and-T-shirt day, but it was hard when he was waiting for Beth and Ron to arrive. Digging his hands into the tan sportcoat he'd donned to appear a bit more dressed up, he sighed. "Where the hell is everybody, do you think?"

Doc sprawled on a chair like a lizard in the sun. "Keep your britches on, boy. We're early."

Tucker studied Doc. He looked good for a guy who'd been rushed to emergency three weeks before and had angioplasty the next day. He'd dressed up again today in neat tan pants and another pressed shirt; Tucker sniffed. "Got that sissy cologne on again, old man? Where you fixin' to go after this meeting?"

Raising his chin, Doc locked a steely gaze on him. "Just 'cuz you got a sorry social life don't mean you gotta pick on mine."

Tucker could feel the sadness creep up into his throat. Apparently it was visible on his face.

"Aw, shit," Doc said. "I didn't mean to make it worse."

"Don't know what you're blabberin' about." Tucker crossed

the room to study the books that lined one whole wall of the office. "Think Murphy's read all these?"

"Tuck?" Damn, the old man wasn't gonna let it go.

"What?" He tried to sound ornery and didn't turn around.

"I, um, reckon that was outta line. 'Bout your social life."

Tucker pivoted and ducked his head. "No, Doc, it's how I'm feelin' these days that's outta line."

Doc started to say something when Murphy came through the doorway. "Sorry, I got held up." He scanned the room and arched his brows. "Beth and Ronny aren't here yet?"

"Nope. We're early." Doc smiled easily at the counselor.

Joe took a seat at the big oak desk. It was neatly organized, unlike Doc's office, where you could conduct a regular scavenger hunt. Tucker studied Murphy. His face was drawn and bore the lines of sleeplessness. Buttoned up real tight in a khaki jacket over a blue shirt and striped tie, Joe was keeping some kind of demons at bay with his organization and neat-as-a-pin dress. There was never any word around town about the reason for the breakup of the Murphys' marriage. Tucker remembered vividly the way the man had looked at his ex-wife that night at Crocodile's.

Don't think about Crocodile's.

Or Beth.

And how she looked

And felt.

His hands clenched.

Like a summoned genie, she appeared at the doorway.

Shit. She'd dressed up for today. His hands itched to touch that pretty pink blouse she wore with a short black skirt, dark stockings and heels that made her legs look Rockette-long. She'd folded a gray blazer over her arm and had swung the handle of her purse over her shoulder.

She also didn't spare him so much as a glance.

"I hope we're not late." She spoke to everyone in general. "It was so nice outside, Ronny and I decided to walk over."

"You're not late." Murphy nodded to a table adjacent to the door. "Let's all sit there."

Tucker waited while Beth chose a seat, Joe sat next to her and Ron took the other side, flanking her like bodyguards. Doc took an end chair and Tucker settled in as far away from Beth as he could get. Still, he watched her. She wore a little rum-colored lipstick and for the thousandth time he wondered what she'd taste like.

He'd never even kissed her!

Joe smiled warmly at everybody. "The purpose of this meeting is to review Ron's community service. I've already met with the Lancaster County Correctional Facility, and I'll be meeting with the school. We'll have our three-month accounting of Ron's progress right before Memorial Day. I'll give my findings to the Council, and if we're on target, we'll go ahead as planned." Joe zeroed in on Ron. "Let's start with you, Ron. How has the community service been going?"

Ron squirmed in his chair, a little boy in the hot seat. He glanced at his mother, who gave him an encouraging nod, and at Doc, who smiled at him. Last, he looked at Tucker. Though the boy was far from accepting him, he'd lost the rage and accusing glares that used to be there in his face. Not giving him anything else to be upset about was important. Tucker nodded at him to talk.

"'Cept for the, um, the time I went out to the garage, you know, when Doc had . . . when I hit . . . except for that, it's been okay."

"Let's leave that incident alone for a minute." Joe's expression was stern. "The service has been just okay?"

Clearing his throat, Ron's eyes lightened a bit. "Better than okay. I been working on the car."

His mother frowned.

"But I did all the shi—the dirty work, too. Cleaning out, cleaning up. Lifting heavy stuff. Right, Doc?"

"Far as I'm concerned, he done his share." Doc glanced at Tucker. "You?"

"Yeah, sure, the kid's worked his behind off most of the time. Just because he likes it don't mean it's not hard work."

Ron smiled and Tucker returned it.

"What's the status of the car?" Joe wanted to know.

"It'll be ready to go to the track garage in a week." Doc gave the information. "We need the experts from here on out."

Joe scowled. "Will there be work to do, then, for Ronny? He's got till September for this service."

Tucker and Doc exchanged grins. Doc angled his head to Joe. "Talkin' like a real Yank, ain't he?"

At Joe's questioning look Tucker explained Doc's comment.

"You can tell you never been in a garage. Ronny's gonna do all the grunt jobs there. We're also thinkin' about puttin' him in the pit for the test drives and the race itself."

"I'm gonna be in the *pit*?" Ronny's voice held the awe of a fan meeting Richard Petty.

"You got it, boy."

Tucker's gaze skittered to Beth. She'd gone pale.

Her eyes finally met his. He gave her a sympathetic look and tried to curb the need that revved up inside him like an engine she had no problem starting with just a glance.

"Beth?" Joe asked. "You okay with that?"

"It's no secret I don't want Ronny involved in racing."

"Aw, Mom."

"Normal reaction, son," Doc said. "After what happened to your daddy."

After what I did to your daddy. Geez, just when Tucker started to forget it, it was right there, staring him in the ever-lovin' face.

Beth said, "Accidents happen in racing all the time." She gave Tucker a pointed look. "It's no one's fault. But it's why I don't want him racing." She threaded her hair off her face. "None of this is really the issue, though, is it? All we need is to make sure Ronny's community service gets done. I'll deal with this racing thing later." Her voice cracked and Tucker wanted to wrap her up in his arms so bad he hurt.

Joe scanned the group. "All right. For my report, I'll just say I'm satisfied with the community service projections and his behavior up till now." Joe focused in on Ron like a strict parent. "However, the attack on Tucker has to be dealt with."

"What happened 'bout school?" Doc asked Joe.

"Nothing. Mr. Johnson never reported his skipping class. I don't approve of letting bad behavior go like that, but the teacher was adamant. As for what happened with you, Tucker . . ."

Straightening, Tucker blocked out the vision of Beth sitting there about as pretty as a Carolina sunset. "Look," he said summoning The Menace. "We all know what the kid was thinkin' and who got him into thinkin' that way. I'm not blaming his actions on those kids, but there was a misunderstanding, is all." He faced down Joe. "I been cooperative about everything your Council's asked me to do, even if I didn't want to. Now I'm makin' a demand of my own. Drop this, Joe. It wasn't the kid's fault this time."

Ronny's mouth had gone slack. He stared at Tucker like a thief who'd gotten pardoned by the person he stole from.

Joe leaned back in his chair and stared at Tucker, too. He rolled his pencil between his palms. "All right, but on one condition. Ronny takes the anger-control class I'm teaching over at the high school."

"When will he have time for that?" Beth asked.

"It doesn't start until after Memorial Day. It's every Saturday morning in June."

Beth looked to Ron. Ron shrugged. Tucker could see he knew he'd gotten off light.

"Then it's done." Joe focused hard on the boy. "Other than that incident, Ron, I'm proud of your performance with community service and weekend jail. And I think you're learning a great deal in counseling." He squeezed Ron's arm. "All that will be in my report."

Ron's look was grateful. "Thanks, Joe. You helped a lot."

Joe nodded. Everybody rose. Doc turned to the Donovans. "You guys walkin' back to the diner?"

"Yes we are." Beth's voice was breathless with relief.

"Mind if I go with you? I wanna talk to Ronny about that computer program I been workin' on before I pick up Gerty."

Shoulders relaxed, Ron said, "Great." He shook hands with Joe. "Thanks again."

"It's not over yet. But you're gonna make it, I think."

Beth had circled around the opposite side of the table from Tucker. She gave Murphy a big hug. "Thanks, Joe. You've been a lifesaver."

He patted her back and whispered something in her ear that made her smile.

Finally she looked at Tucker. "You, too, Tucker. Thanks."

He said only, "You're welcome."

Beth and Doc headed for the door. Doc called over his shoulder, "I got a ride with Gerty, Tuck, so don't worry 'bout me."

Tucker nodded absently, watching Ron. The boy watched back for a minute, then came up to him. Ron swallowed hard. He averted his eyes, looked back at Tucker. Then he held out his hand. "Thanks, Tucker. For everything."

Battling back emotion—thank God he'd had so much practice—Tucker shook his hand. "You're welcome, Ron."

* * *

JOE studied Tucker as the others filed out of the office. He was a hurting guy, if Joe ever saw one. And part of what was eating away at him was something Joe was all too familiar with. When everybody else was gone, he said, "Your feelings are on your sleeve, Quaid."

Tucker watched him for a minute, then apparently decided to be honest. "I'm tryin' to be clear-headed here, but it isn't easy."

"I know." He glanced out the window. "Reason can only go so far."

Tucker's eyes narrowed. "You look whipped."

"Bad night last night."

"Yeah?"

"Yeah." Joe glanced at his watch. "I got Little League practice at six." That was two hours away. He stared at the gym bag he'd brought to the office. "I gotta work some of this off before I go crazy."

"What're you gonna do?"

"Shoot some hoops." He nodded out the window. "If that isn't enough, I'll run."

Tucker eyed the basketball court. "Mmm. Shot some hoops in my day, with my step-brother."

"Yeah?" Joe liked the idea. "Wanna play some one-on-one?"

Shrugging like a tot finally asked to play with the big guys, Tucker nodded eagerly. "Got my sneaks in the car."

"Get 'em while I change and meet me outside on the court."

"You're on, Yank."

Ten minutes later, they briefly outlined the rules—playing on half the court, Tucker would take the ball to the top of the court and go in for a basket. If he scored, Joe would take it out of bounds and go for a shot. If Tucker missed, the ball was up for grabs. They'd play to twenty-one.

Tucker dribbled in slowly and Joe was all over him. In seconds, Joe stole the ball away and made a two-pointer.

Glowering at him, Tucker took it to the top of the key, and this time, he was ready. He dodged to the right. Joe tried to block and Tucker practically mowed him down. With a grunt, Joe jumped out of the way. Tucker missed. Joe went for the rebound and elbowed Tucker in the ribs to grab it.

Tucker cursed, muscled in front of him and got the rebound. He scored. Joe took it out and faked to the left, circled right, and went for a shot—that Tucker blocked. His hand came down hard on Joe's chest.

"Sorry," he said, not meaning it.

Joe grabbed the ball saying, "Like hell," and scored.

It got worse from there.

Dimly, Joe was aware of the demons he was fighting, pushing him to be physical and aggressive. But mostly it felt good to play hard, loose and rough. Tucker matched him move for move, body slam for body slam, and grunt for grunt. He didn't seem to mind the force, either.

In thirty minutes, they were tied at twenty-one.

Sucking in air like a rookie runner, Joe hugged the ball to his stomach; Tucker bent over his knees gasping for breath. His black T-shirt was soaked through. His right cheek looked bruised. Feeling his own ribs, Joe hoped he hadn't cracked one on that last collision. "You think we'll live through a tie breaker?"

"No way. My side's killin' me."

"From running?"

"No, hotshot, from where you rammed into me."

Joe chuckled. Tucker smiled. They were suddenly two little boys on the playground. It felt good.

Finally managing to stand upright, Tucker said, "I reckon I needed it." He eyed Joe. "You look better."

"You, too."

"Got some water in there." Joe indicated the duffel bag that he'd brought out. "Want some?"

Tucker nodded.

Gingerly shuffling to the side of the court, Joe fished out two bottles of Poland Spring. Still breathing hard, he headed back to Tucker, who'd taken a seat on the surface of a picnic table. Ten feet away, Joe tossed him a bottle. He joined Tucker on the table, feet braced on the bench seat.

Joe took a long swig and Tucker an even bigger gulp. "You're a hell of an athlete," Joe said.

Tucker nodded. "Race car drivers have to be in top shape." He grinned.

"What?"

"I was just thinkin' of the story Richard Petty always told."

"What was it about?"

"One time a guy was raggin' on him about race car drivers not

bein' real athletes. Petty patiently explained the stamina and en-
durance necessary to drive a car at two hundred miles an hour.
When the guy still didn't buy it, Petty told him to put on a woolen
sweat suit, shoes, gloves and a helmet, then get in his family car
at noon one day in the middle of July. He should roll up all the
windows except for the left front, turn the heater wide-open, and
crank the radio as loud as it'd go. He said to drive around in rush-
hour traffic for four hours, without stopping except for twenty
seconds every half hour for gas and tires. And try not to hit anybody or get hit while he was at it."

Joe laughed aloud. After a pause, he said, "Richard Petty was
always Danny's idol."

For a moment, Tucker stilled. "What was he like?"

"Danny?"

"Uh-huh."

"Nice guy. Friendly as hell, even though his parents had a ton
of money."

Tucker picked at the label on the bottle. "He loved her a lot,
didn't he?"

"Yep. And Ron."

Sighing, Tucker stared out at the grass and trees in the field.
"I took it all away from them."

"It was an accident, Tucker. Not your fault."

"So she says." He hesitated. "This newest thing? It *is* my
fault."

"Ronny's trouble?"

"Yeah. First I come to town. Then he gets in a huff about
my . . . feelings for . . . oh, hell, Joe, you know how it is."

"Ronny's trouble isn't your fault. You gotta let go of the guilt,
Tucker."

"You can't imagine what it's like not be able to change something terrible you've done."

"Don't bet on it."

Joe could feel Tucker's eyes on him. "What monkey's on your
back?"

Joe waited a long time to answer. "I've hurt people worse than
you."

"Can't have."

"Yep. Mine was intentional. Vicious. Unforgivable."

"Talk about lettin' go of your guilt, buddy . . ."

Joe said nothing, just welcomed the light breeze that cooled his skin, the smell of honest, hard-earned sweat. And he was grateful for the camaraderie that he missed from his Outlaw days.

"What'd ya do?" Tucker asked after a long silence.

Immediately, Joe's heart beat quicker than when he was tearing around the court. His hands sweated more than at the end of the game. He shook his head.

"Sorry, didn't mean to pry."

As a trained counselor, Joe knew it was best to get this out. It was why he'd called both Pete and Taylor the night before, but they weren't home. He would have gone to New York after work tonight if it hadn't been for the Little League game.

Take help wherever you can get it, Pete had told him.

"I beat up my wife."

Tucker dropped the bottle. *"What?"*

Joe watched the plastic bounce off the bench, turn upside down and spill onto Tucker's sneaker.

"I'm a recovered wife beater."

There was a very long silence. "I never would have guessed."

Joe forced himself to continue. "Next to child molesting, it's the worst crime, don't you think?"

Tucker waited a minute before answering. "I dunno. Killin' somebody's husband and father ranks right up there."

A little stunned, Joe stared over at Tucker.

Tucker said, "Look, all I'm sayin' is I'm in no position to cast the first stone." He averted his gaze, shrugged in the uncomfortable way men often do when they discuss something personal. "You wanna talk about it, I'm not passin' judgment."

Without giving himself a chance to decline, Joe nodded. "Maybe over a quick burger at Mickey D's before practice?"

"You're on."

As Joe rose along with Tucker, he realized he already felt better.

Pete was on to something.

". . . SOFTWARE'S a hobby of mine, is all." On the way back to the diner, Doc had discussed his newest configurations with Ron, and as they'd walked through the door, Beth had asked about it.

"Some hobby." Ron headed behind the counter to get a soft drink. "You should see the graphics. Better than the racing video games I got, Mom. Margo's gonna flip when she gets a look at them."

Ducking his head, Doc flushed. "Just for fun, boy."

"Want me to get Gerty for you, Doc?" Beth asked. She was sad, but trying not to show it. She and Tucker had struggled to keep their eyes off each other, but Tucker's whole body language spoke volumes, and Beth guessed hers did, too.

"No, it's okay," Doc said. "I'll just wait here. I'm early."

"Do I have to hang around, Mom? The diner isn't busy."

"Not yet. We just missed the after-school crowd, and we have about an hour's reprieve before supper." She studied Ron's face. "Why, honey, you got plans?"

"Somebody asked me to help with their homework, is all."

Beth glanced at Doc and caught the twinkle in his eye. "This somebody doesn't happen to be a girl, does it?"

"Aw, Mom, come on."

"All right. You can have a couple of hours off. Milt and Nancy are coming in to work at dinner. I'd appreciate it if you were back to help me close up."

The boy sprouted wings on his feet. Leaving the soda abandoned, he flew past Doc with a quick goodbye, stopping for a peck on Beth's cheek, and was out the door.

"Young love," she said with a sigh.

Doc cocked his head. "He's got alotta good traits, that one. Kinda reminds me of Tucker as a boy."

Oh! She hadn't expected that. Beth circled around the counter. "Really?" She plopped down on the stool next to Doc. "Tell me what he was like at seventeen."

"A lot like Ronny there. Restless, with all the Johnny Reb in him you could imagine."

"He told me about his stepfather."

Doc's grizzled eyebrows knitted. "I'm shocked. He never talks about it."

"We've become friends of a sort." Hell of a lie. They'd become a lot more than friends. You didn't dream about your buddy, crave his touch whenever he was within ten feet, wish like hell he was inside you.

"Then you know what a tough life he had." Doc waited for her nod. "He don't need no more heartache, Beth."

At first, she didn't answer, just held Doc's gaze. "I don't want to hurt him, Doc. He's a good man."

Doc reached out and covered her hand. Hers was trembling. "It ain't that I don't like you, girl. It's just that you could hurt him. You been the first one, in a long time, that could do that."

Beth swallowed hard. "I don't want to hurt him. I'm trying to stay away."

"I know you are. I 'preciate that." He hesitated before he went on. "If things were different with Ronny—the boy's startin' to warm up to Tuck, but all it'd take is for him to think you two was lyin' to him, that maybe Tucker was likin' him 'cause of you . . ."

"I know." Shaking back her hair, she smiled. "I appreciate your concern and all you're doing for Ronny. You've helped him so much, Doc."

"Even if it does deal with racin'?"

Glancing back to her husband's pictures on the wall, she smiled wistfully. "I'm just afraid for him."

"Racin's in the blood. You gotta know that."

"I know. I just wish he'd get into some other part of it." She turned her soft gaze back on Doc. "Like you."

"Maybe he will."

"Maybe."

"I gotta ask you somethin'. Don't say no right away."

"All right."

"I got tickets to the Indy over Memorial Day."

She smiled. "That's nice."

"I wanna take the boy."

Beth stopped smiling. "Oh, Doc."

"Now, hush. Listen. I'm gonna find a way to drag Tucker along, too."

Beth cocked her head. "He doesn't go to races anymore."

"Nope, not since . . ." He glanced back at the wall, too. "I wanna get 'em both to go. Throw them together for a period of time. It'd do 'em a world a good."

"How?"

"They need to keep buildin' this relationship. Far as I can see, it has good footing in the ground, but needs some . . . cement. The Indy might give it to them." He added, "Especially with you out of the picture."

"I don't want to encourage Ronny's interest in racing."

"It's too late. The most you can do is redirect it."

"That's what Linc said."

"He's right."

"Have you told Ron?"

" 'Course not. Not before askin' you."

She stood as she saw Gerty coming out of the kitchen. "You're a good man, Doc." Leaning over, she kissed him on the cheek. "I'll think about it."

TWENTY-TWO

"MARGO, Jack wants to see you." Philip stood in the doorway of her office, smiling. He looked happier than he had in weeks. His movie-star good looks were accented by his animated face. "I think it's good news."

"Good news?" Man, she could use some. She thought about Linc, and his relationship with a preacher's kid.

If you'd at least try to get over this hangup you have about religion, maybe we could . . .

Standing, smoothing down the beige silk skirt she wore with a cocoa-colored blouse, she banished the thought. It would never work. He was better off with the PK. She grabbed her matching jacket and asked, "What kind of good news?"

"I'm not sure, but I'm invited, too." He waited for her by the door and when she reached him, he placed his hand on the small of her back and escorted her to the elevator.

Inside, she leaned against the railing. "What's going on, do you think?"

"Maybe something to do with the VP of Engineering." He tucked a strand of hair behind her ear. "This could be the announcement."

She was too stunned to object to the personal gesture. "Really?"

The elevator stopped at the executive level, and Margo and

Philip exited. Again he guided her, his hand at her back. Like a husband might. Or a lover. When Geraldine looked up from the desk outside his and the CEO's office, though, he quickly stepped back.

"Hi, gorgeous," Philip said. "Is he ready to see us?"

"Hush your flattery." She smiled. "Go on in."

Jack Sheer's office was nothing like the man himself. Whereas the CEO was an average-height, pleasant-looking man with thinning gray hair and a sincere friendliness in his brown eyes, it seemed he might be more at home coaching Little League baseball than running a multimillion-dollar firm. In contrast, his office was large and impressive. Facing Sixth Avenue, it commanded a breathtaking view of the city.

From behind his oak desk, Jack waved them in as he spoke into the phone. "No, it's fine, Brad. I'll be home for that. I promise. Sure, son, call any time." He smiled self-effacingly at them when he hung up. "I'm too old to have teenagers."

Jack was sixty. He'd had kids late in life; everybody in the company knew both of his children wrapped him around their little fingers. And Margo had always considered Jack and his wife Catherine as the ideal couple.

"What's the boy up to now?" Philip asked easily.

"Oh, he's in a *psychic* phase. He wants me to take him to this store in the Village tomorrow when he's off from school." Brad attended the famous School of the Arts in New York and was a budding actor.

Not losing his easy manner, Jack zeroed in on Margo. "Thanks for coming up, Margo. I wanted to talk to you about a couple of things. Have a seat."

She and Philip faced Jack across his desk, seated in two taupe leather chairs.

"A couple of things?"

"Hmm." Jack's warm brown gaze focused on her. Family man though he was, he changed from Clark Kent to Superman when business was involved. "It's no secret you're being seriously considered for the new VP of Engineering. I'd just about made up my mind when something happened this week."

"Made up your mind?"

"Yes. I'd like you as the next VP, if I can get this straightened out in my head."

Margo felt warmth spread through her. This was exactly what

she wanted, worked for all these years, what she'd given up a man and a family for. She took a quick moment to relish the feeling of success. "What needs to be straightened out?"

"We've had some odd complaints in the last few days."

"About me?"

"About your work. I have to admit, they don't fit in with your usual MO."

"What's the problem? Who are they from?"

He held up two memos. "One is from Brubeck's. It says the last product you finished up for them was late."

"Late? I had that in weeks ahead of time."

Scowling, he handed her the memo across the desk.

She scanned it. "I don't understand." She looked up at Philip. "Do you know anything about this?"

"Nope."

She transferred her gaze to Jack. "I'll check with manufacturing and distribution. But this doesn't make sense. The product was ready to go into production weeks ahead of schedule." She frowned. "Who else complained?"

"Laufler. Their contract is important to us, because of their diversity. They own a number of companies that could give us business."

"I know it is. What did they say?"

"They're unhappy about being out-sourced. They were very impressed with you when you went to visit them in Boston; they thought they were getting your personal attention on the product."

Margo's gaze shot to Philip. He watched her; a flicker of emotion in his eyes caught her attention. She waited for him to say something. After an uncomfortable silence, he straightened. "I'm afraid that was my fault, Jack. I made the decision to out-source because Margo's schedule has been hectic and I didn't realize the contract was so dependent on her." He shrugged boyishly. "I kind of thought it was me that snared them in Boston."

Jack smiled. "Sounds like you, buddy. Must be a miscommunication. In any case, call and soothe their feathers. Tell them there was a glitch." He faced Margo. "Is everything going well with you, Margo? Any problems I should be aware of?"

Margo lifted her chin. How could she say she was concerned about Philip's behavior when he'd just bailed her out? "No, nothing out of the ordinary."

"Fine. Consider this finished."

She faced the president squarely. "How will these two issues affect your decision about the vice presidency, Jack?"

"They probably won't. You have a perfect deadline record for the eight years you've been here. Philip has assumed responsibility for the Laufler thing. This Brubeck deal—check it out, see why delivery was late. Get in touch with Brubeck himself. And let me know."

"All right."

They stood just as the door opened. It was Geraldine. "Jack, Amy's on the line. From college."

"Ah, my little girl." He shook his head. "I told you I was too old for these kids. They call me like I'm one of their friends any time of day." Again, it was common knowledge that Jack's children were free to phone whenever they needed him and he was gotten out of all but the most important meetings.

"I admire that about you," Margo said.

He rolled his eyes. "Easy for you to say." He picked up the phone. "Get back to me as soon as you can." As Margo exited the office she heard, "Hi, sweetheart, what can I do for you?"

Philip chuckled as he closed the door behind them. "He's such a good guy. I don't know how he ever rose in the ranks of business."

Flying high from the news about the VP, Margo drew in a deep breath. "Maybe because he *is* such a good guy. Rumor has it he's never stood for any unethical behavior."

Philip didn't respond as he followed her to the elevator. "Want me to check out the date thing for the Brubeck product?"

"No, Philip, you've done enough."

"Is something wrong?"

"No, of course not."

"Aren't you happy you're the first choice for the VP?"

"Yes."

"Hey, look, I'm sorry about the Laufler thing. I had no idea the out-sourcing would be a problem."

"So you said." The elevator dinged. "I'll let you know what happens with Brubeck's."

Margo stepped into the elevator. *Don't jump to conclusions. Take this slow. Figure it out. Maybe it's just as it appears.*

And pigs fly, Linc would tell her.

But she needed to think. To piece it together. Not, as she'd told Linc, to go off half-cocked.

This is new evidence, kiddo. You can't ignore it.

I won't, Margo thought, heading for her office. *Oh, I won't.*

LINC smiled as he scanned the five women in his Thursday group. "Morning, ladies."

Each uttered a good morning. Anita Camp's feisty, "You look tired, Rev," brought Margo to mind. He pushed her out of his thoughts. He was done feeling bad about her. After the wrenching phone call Sunday night, and all the other problems they'd had lately, he vowed he was going to get on with his life. And, damn it, he needed rest. Everybody was commenting on his fatigue lately, and he'd looked like Frankenstein even to himself in the mirror that morning.

"Been burning the candle at both ends," he told the women and smiled. "But I'm going to change my ways, ladies." He looked at the blackboard. "So the topic today is growing old."

Anita moaned. "And just when I noticed another wrinkle on my forehead."

"You're still beautiful," Rosa told her. "I like the way you dress, too."

Rosa—who always chose plain, nondescript clothing—had had two visits with the Social Services counselor, and several talks with Annie; already Linc could see she was gaining some self-insight. He was worried about her remaining in the home with Sam, but you couldn't forcibly drag a woman out of an abusive situation. Still, he wished he could do more.

"Linc." Barb Mandarino nodded to the door.

Henry stood there, big and bulky and with a question in his eyes. Today, he was a little hunched over. Linc wondered if the rain was bothering his back injury.

"I didn't know you were coming in this morning, Henry." Linc smiled pleasantly. "Can I help you?"

Henry shook his head. His face seemed more lined than usual.

"Just wanted to let me know you were here?"

The older man nodded.

"Good. Maybe you could mop the kitchen floor, then." Though Linc knew it wasn't safe to let the man near water, he was afraid Henry would try to clean his office while he worked with the women, and Linc wouldn't be able to find anything afterward. The last time Henry had *straightened up,* the room had looked like a battle ground during a jungle counterattack.

Henry shuffled away.

"Now, where were we?"

"We're growing old," Mary O'Brien quipped, touching her graying hair. "Fast."

Linc laughed. "All right. Let's brainstorm some of the worst and best things about being older. We can do it on the paper, first, if you like." The leader of the seminar Linc had attended in New York had suggested that anonymity was useful initially, but he should try to lead the women toward more openness. "However, we've been conductin' this little shindig for several weeks now, and I was hoping we could think about brainstorming out loud."

"I think we should do it." This from Barb Mandarino. "Let's live a little and actually *say* what we think."

The others smiled at her dry humor and agreed. Linc stood. "All right, I'll write on the board." As he picked up the chalk, he heard a door slam and hoped Henry hadn't gone to the office after all. But Linc wouldn't go check. He just put it in God's hands. "I'll go first. I think not fulfilling your life's goals is one of the worst things about growing old."

"What are *your* goals, Reverend Linc?" Joanie Jorgensen asked.

He pivoted. Dimly he was aware of some stomping out in the fellowship hall. Bravely he ignored Henry's antics. "I'd like a wife and kids." He watched the women. Workshop presenters called this a teachable moment—where you went off the track, but the new discussion was better than the original and you should pursue it. "Anybody else want to share their goals?"

"I'd like to be more independent." This was the same point Ona James had made when she'd suggested her topic for discussion.

"Ona, what's standing in your way?"

"I—"

"So this is where you go when you sneak out on Thursdays," a gruff voice barked from behind Linc. He whipped around to find Sam DeMartino looming in the doorway. Rosa's gasp came on the heels of her husband's comment. Dressed in baggy pants and a sloppy flannel shirt that was tight around his middle, Sam's face was a contorted mask of anger. A heavy growth of beard completed the sinister picture.

"Sam." Linc set down the chalk. "Can I help you?"

"I told you to leave my wife alone, Grayson." He faced Rosa, whose eyes were full of fear. "Come on, Rosa, we're leavin' here. And you ain't never comin' back. He's caused us enough problems."

Shakily, Rosa stood.

Linc drew up to his full height, which was considerably less than Sam's. *Okay, God, I need you on this one. Be with me.*

I'm right here, son.

"Rosa's having a good talk with us, Sam. She's not doing anything wrong."

"Hell she ain't. All this talk is ruinin' my life."

Rosa shrunk back. "Don't swear in church, Sam. I'll come with you."

Jesse James surfaced. Physically Linc placed himself between husband and wife. "Rosa, I don't think that's a good idea."

The frightened woman's gaze shot from him to Sam. She seemed to get the message. If she left with Sam, he'd hurt her. Slowly, she sat back down. Anita Camp, bless her soul, crossed to stand behind Rosa and put her hands on the trembling woman's shoulder. One by one, Ona, Barb, Mary and Joanie formed a half-circle around the frightened woman.

Linc faced Sam. "How about if you and I go into my office, Sam? We can talk."

Sam shifted unsteadily. It was then that Linc caught a whiff of the booze emanating from him. And his eyes were bloodshot.

You can handle this, Linc. Stand your ground.

"Don't wanna hear what you have to say." Sam's eyes lit with fire. "You started this."

"If you won't talk to me, I'm going to have to ask you to leave."

Sam laughed, a gritty, unpleasant sound. "Yeah, and who's gonna make me?"

"I am."

Sam rolled his eyes. "Come on, Rosa, we're goin'."

"Not right now, Sam." Though soft, Rosa's words were determined.

It all happened fast. An ugly flush ran up Sam's neck to his face. His hands fisted. He took a step toward Rosa. Linc blocked his way. Thwarted, Sam waited only a split second then bent at the waist and lunged for Linc.

DeMartino's huge shoulder rammed into Linc's stomach, knocking the wind out of him. Linc fell backward into the black-board. He went down, his arm twisting behind him. His head banged on the metal chairs and his vision blurred. Sam was on top of him then, grabbing his shirt collar; with one jerk, he smashed Linc's head into the cold vinyl floor.

Suddenly, Sam was dragged off of him—had God done that?—and then the world went dark.

"THAT'S it, Gerty. Good." Doc smiled. "Ain't it almost as pretty as a West Virginia mountain?"

Beth stared at the flower arrangement Gerty and Doc had made for the entry. They'd joined a garden club, and Beth had been the first recipient of their handiwork. A huge spray of del-phinia, along with other exotic flowers, graced the front of the diner.

"I think it's those special lilies you got from New York that do it, Leonard." Gerty smiled at Doc, and the older man blushed. Beth hid a grin. Ronny. Gerty. Even Linc and Jane. Everybody around her was in love.

Don't think about it. "Flowers are so—"

The door burst open, cutting off her remark.

Annie rushed inside, her face flushed, her eyes wide. She wore a leotard and tights, over which she'd thrown a tan raincoat. Beth's brain registered that it was odd her friend didn't have street clothes on just before she realized something was wrong.

"Annie, what is it?" Beth hoped nothing had happened with Joe. She was really coming to like the guy again.

"It's Linc," Annie said simply. "He's been taken to Glen Oaks Hospital by ambulance."

In one split second, Beth's entire world shifted. Sounds, smells, everything was blocked out but Annie's words. *Linc. Hospital.* Just like Danny. Beth grasped onto the table. "W-what happened?"

"Something at church. One of the women from his group called me. All I know is that Linc was knocked unconscious. Rosa was pretty upset, and I couldn't get much more out of her. Come on, I'll drive you to the hospital."

Beth stayed frozen to the spot. Linc. Hurt? It couldn't be. He was too good to be hurt, too kind . . .

Annie was in front of her. "Bethy, honey, are you okay?"

Beth swallowed hard. Shook herself out of the trance.

"Look, I know this is a shock. Let's get to the hospital and see what's going on." Annie looked to Gerty. "Can you hold down the fort?"

"Of course. Go ahead, Beth."

Numbly, Beth took her coat from Annie and followed her out the door. Beth was aware that it was raining; she let Annie usher her into the car, strap on her seat belt and start the engine. Annie took her hand as they started to drive. Heavy drops of rain pattered on the roof.

Over the quiet hush-hush of the windshield wipers, Beth managed to ask, "He's alive, right?"

"Yes, of course."

"How bad is he hurt?"

"I really don't know. Rosa just said he was unconscious."

They didn't talk further on the ten-minute drive, but Annie held her hand all the way.

Once there, they bounded out of the car and raced into ER. Glen Oaks had a high-tech, top-notch hospital, due to frequent injuries on the race track. That was good, Beth told herself. Having a state-of-the-art hospital was good.

When she entered the waiting area, Beth remembered being here only a few short weeks ago with Doc and Tucker.

Then she remembered that Danny had been taken here.

Oh, God. Danny had died *here.*

Annie found the nurse, spoke to her, then came back and dragged Beth to the waiting area. "No news yet. He's still being examined."

Determined not to fall apart, Beth nodded and tried to internalize what she'd been told. "What happened? Who called you?"

"I told you honey, it was—"

There was movement from the other side of the waiting area. Beth's gaze was drawn to five women huddled together in a row of chairs. She recognized them as Linc's women's group. Slowly one stood and came toward them. "Beth, I'm so sorry."

Who was she? "Oh, Rosa. What . . . what are you sorry about?"

Rosa's bleak gaze flew to Annie then back to Beth. "Linc got hurt during our women's group meeting."

"Did he fall down? Henry . . . he's always leaving stuff around . . . water spills all the time. . . ." Beth's voice drifted off.

"No, it wasn't a fall." Rosa gripped her hands together. Somebody came in and attacked Linc."

"Who would attack *Linc*? Everybody loves him."

Rosa faced her squarely. "It was my husband, Beth. He was mad about me being in the group. And he was drunk."

"Oh, no." This from Annie.

"I don't understand." Beth stared at Rosa.

Suddenly Annie straightened and slipped her arm around Beth. "Sam was mad and his anger was misplaced. It's how abusive men are."

"I just want my brother to be all right." Beth felt her stomach pitch. "Is he still unconscious?"

"We . . . we don't know." Rosa's voice was raw.

Beth buried her face in her hands. *Pray,* Linc would tell her. *Pray to God for strength to get through this.* Swallowing back the tears, Beth prayed.

It was an endless amount of time before the doctor came out. Beth recognized Doctor Jacobs, a neurologist, from the diner. "Beth?"

She stood. So did Annie—who wrapped an arm around Beth's shoulders again.

"Your brother's condition is stabilized, but he has some injuries. He's still unconscious. And his arm is broken."

"Unconscious? After all this time?"

"Yes, we're surprised about that. We're taking him down for a CAT scan now. There's a large bump on the back of his head, but we're not sure what's wrong." He glanced at the clock. "We should know in a few hours. I'm sorry I can't tell you more. I'll bring you news as soon as I can." He looked to Annie. "I suggest you wait down the hall, in the family emergency area. It's private and more comfortable. You'll be here awhile."

Stunned, Beth stared after him as he left, then looked at Annie. "That's all? We just wait?"

"I think so. But we, um, should call Margo."

"Margo?" Linc was that bad? Oh, God. *Get a grip Beth,* she told herself. "All right."

"What about Ronny?"

"He's on a field trip to the Math Museum in New York. He won't be back until four. Linc was going to pick him up at school and take him to the lake for his community service." Beth's voice broke on the last word. Still, she held back the emotion.

"Then for now, we'll go where the doctor said and call Margo from there." Annie glanced over to the women. "We're heading back to the family waiting area. You're welcome to come."

Each shook their heads. "We'll wait here," Anita Camp said for the group.

Slowly Annie led Beth to the waiting area; it was new and hadn't been here when Danny had died. A pleasant room, it sported soft blue-striped wallpaper, three stuffed couches and several chairs. Beth could smell the coffee brewing in the corner, see the rain hit the three huge windows off to the side. How many times had Linc waited here, counseled families here? How many fears had he quelled with his soft assurances, how many souls had he soothed, gently assuring them God was with them? Annie sat her down, then crossed to a small desk and picked up the phone.

Shaking her head, Beth lay back against the couch and closed her eyes. Oh, God, how could this be happening?

"HOW could this happen, Tom? I don't understand." Margo tapped a pencil on the desk as she spoke to the product distribution manager. She'd been unable to get an answer to this problem the day before and she was not happy.

"I don't know, Margo. All I know is the date of delivery on my order form is different from yours."

"I've got my paperwork in front of me." The button on the phone, signifying another call, lit up. Margo ignored it. "We need to meet on this."

Philip came to the doorway. She waved him in.

"I can do it after lunch," Tom told her. "Shall I come up there?"

"That would be fine. Bring your forms."

As she hung up, she sighed. "That was Tom Newman. Seems the paperwork is screwed up on the Brubeck order."

Philip loosened the striped tie he wore with a pristine white shirt and soft wool sportcoat. "How'd that happen?"

"I don't know. I'll find out after lunch." She shrugged into her gray jacket and fixed the scarf she'd worn over the pink silk T-shirt. "I'm going to go . . ."

Margo's group assistant appeared at the doorway. "Margo, there's a call for you on line two."

"Can you take a message, Joanie?"

Joanie's pretty face scowled. "When you didn't pick up, I tried to. The woman said she's from Glen Oaks and it's an emergency."

Margo's fingers gripped the edge of the desk; one of her rings bit into her hand. Beth. Or Annie. She whipped up the phone and pressed the button. "Yes?"

"Margo, it's Annie. I'm at Glen Oaks Hospital. Linc's been hurt."

Margo's breath stopped in her throat. "Linc? Hurt?" She clutched the phone with an icy palm. "How bad?"

"We're not sure. Seems some irate husband of a woman in his self-esteem group came to church and plowed into him. He's unconscious, and they're doing a CAT scan."

"*Unconscious?* How long has he been unconscious?"

"Rosa, the guy's wife, called me at ten."

Margo glanced at her watch. It was almost noon. "Two hours. That's not good, is it, Annie?"

"No, honey, it's not good. I think you should come home."

"I'll catch the next train."

"Are you all right?"

"I'm fine. I'll be there as soon as possible."

Margo hung up and smoothed down her skirt. Adjusted her belt. Woodenly, she reached into the drawer and got her purse.

Philip asked, "What's happened?"

"I've got to go."

When she circled the desk, he stopped her with a firm grip on her shoulder. "Tell me what happened."

"That was my friend Annie. Apparently Linc's been hurt. I've got to go to Glen Oaks right away."

"How badly?"

Margo never cried. Absolutely never. She drew in a deep breath and willed back the emotion threatening to swallow her up. "I don't know. He's unconscious."

"Oh, honey, I'm sorry." He stepped aside. "I'll come with you to the station, get you on a train."

"No, Philip. You don't have to do that."

"I won't take no for an answer."

She glanced around the office. "I've, um, got work. A meeting with Tom this afternoon."

Taking charge, he opened her closet and got her raincoat. "We'll have Joanie reschedule things, or I'll deal with it."

Draping her hooded coat around her shoulders, he escorted her out of the office, holding her arm tightly.

She was too shaken to protest. Even her legs were wobbly.

In a daze, she found herself at her assistant's desk, then in the elevator, then out the door. It was pouring rain as Philip hailed a cab and eased her inside. She barely noticed his arm go around her, or how he grasped her hand. All she could think about was Linc, in the hospital, unconscious.

Finally Grand Central Station came into view. She bolted out of the car with Philip right behind her. Once inside, the loudspeaker and buzz of people jolted her; Philip purchased her ticket for the next train, which was due in five minutes.

Thank God, she caught herself saying.

Yeah, some God. Where the hell was he when his most devoted follower in the whole world needed him?

But the accusation rang false, for some reason.

She bade Philip goodbye and boarded the train to Glen Oaks.

Seated by a window, she stared out sightlessly as the city scrolled by. Suddenly, she was seized by a panic, a fear she had never known before, not even in her worst times as a child.

Think about God, please . . . Linc had asked.

So, for only the second time in her entire life, she whispered the words, *Please, God* . . .

TWENTY-THREE

ANNIE was running on automatic pilot, just as she had when Joe left town and she was forced to deal with the reality of her life. Now, reality was that Linc was still unconscious and the ramifications of that could be brutal.

She stared out the window as the rain came down in sheets, preparing herself. Danny had died. It *did* happen. Linc *could* die. She glanced across the room at Beth, who sat curled up on the couch like a little girl, her legs under her, her head resting on her hands. Her plain white sweater accented her pallor, and Annie ludicrously noted her jeans were still damp. Annie had retrieved jeans and a flannel shirt for herself from her car when she'd gone to park it in a long-term lot.

Her friend had been so strong through Danny's death, through Ronny's legal problems. But Annie knew this would push her over the edge. Linc was her rock, her lifeline. He was that to all of them. How would any of them survive without him? Oh, God, when Margo got here, it would be worse. She loved Linc so much . . .

"Beth? Annie?"

Pivoting, Annie saw her ex-husband standing in the doorway. His head beaded with water, his belted raincoat wet, he was frowning, and his shoulders were stiff.

For some reason, her eyes misted at seeing him. "Hi."

"I just heard." He crossed to Beth. Kneeling down in front of her, he grasped her hands. "How you holding up, honey?"

Beth nodded. Her expression was so bleak Annie's stomach clenched. "Okay."

As Annie stared at them, Joe leaned over and, in a totally natural gesture like he might bestow on his sister, kissed her head. He stood, gave her shoulder a squeeze and crossed to Annie. "You all right?"

Wrapping her arms around her waist, she swallowed hard. "Yes."

"What happened? All I heard was Linc was here and he was seriously hurt."

Annie asked, "How did you hear?"

"Rosa canceled an appointment with Carol Lopez. She told Carol she was at the hospital and why."

"Rosa's not out in the waiting area?"

"No, no one was out there except for that janitor that works at the church. He looks a little lost."

"The women must have gone for coffee."

"Annie, what happened?"

Shaking away her distraction, she said, "Apparently Sam De-Martino attacked Linc at the church during one of the women's group's meetings."

"Sam?" Joe's healthy complexion turned ashen. "Oh, God." He got the meaning loud and clear. And he'd be affected by it in a different way than anyone else here. "What are Linc's injuries?"

"Sam's a big guy . . ." Annie straightened. "He hit his head and went unconscious. They're doing tests now. And his arm's broken."

Taking in a heavy breath, Joe scowled. "Poor Linc."

Again, Annie felt her eyes tear. Joe must have seen it. Reaching out as easily as he had to Beth, he squeezed her hand. She froze, and when he realized what he'd done—that he'd touched her for the first time since his return—he went to draw back his hand. But she held on. Squeezed tightly. "I'm so scared, Joe."

"Me, too."

"I don't know what everybody'll do if . . ." She shook her head, then drew back and wrapped both of her arms around her waist again. "It's amazing how important people become to us. How we take them for granted." Joe just nodded. She glanced at

Beth and whispered, so her friend couldn't hear, "Remember when we were here for Danny?"

Joe swallowed hard. "It was a horrible night."

"He died in this hospital."

Her ex-husband's gaze was stark. She remembered how he had cried like a baby when his friend had died. They all had. And for months afterward, the bleakness had not left Joe's gray eyes. She studied him, now. "Do you pray?"

"Yes, I pray."

"Good. Linc would want us to."

"Yes, he . . ." Joe's words trailed off as someone came to the doorway.

It was Margo. Always so tall, so strong, so full of sass, today she looked slight and brittle, her hair and raincoat wet and her face chalk white. "Bethy? Annie?"

Unfolding from the chair, Beth stood up. Both Annie and Joe faced Margo.

She said, "How is . . . you look so . . . did he . . ."

"No, Margo," Annie put in quickly. "There's no more word on him. He's still down for tests."

Bonelessly, Margo gripped the doorjamb, leaned into it. Annie rushed to her, as did Beth. The three women hugged. No one spoke. Not one of them cried. They just stood there locked in an awful embrace.

IT was stupid to go. Tucker knew he couldn't help her, shouldn't help her, might even make things worse. But he couldn't stay away. As he entered the ER, he glanced at the clock over the nurse's station. One P.M. He'd just stay a minute, find out how Linc was, and leave before Ronny got back from his field trip. Tucker wouldn't steal too much of Beth's time or attention.

Doc had called Tucker at eleven o'clock, but he'd been working out and hadn't gotten the message until after he'd showered. The Menace had made the half-hour ride to Glen Oaks Hospital in seventeen minutes. By the time he'd gotten here, he was near-about crazy with worry.

He found them in the family waiting area. For a minute he was frozen by the scenario—Margo and Annie holding hands on a couch, talking softly. Joe sat near Beth, his arm loosely draped around her. Neither of them spoke, but their closeness was that of a family. And Tucker was an interloper.

Joe noticed him first. "Tucker?"

Beth's head snapped up.

"I . . . um . . . Doc called me." He shrugged. "I just wanted to . . . is there any news?"

Standing, Joe crossed to him and filled him in on the vigil they'd been keeping. Tucker listened, but his eyes kept straying to Beth, who stared at him during the recitation.

When Joe was finished, Tucker focused on him. "Thanks for the information. I don't want to intrude on y'all. I reckon I'll just wait out here with the others." With a toss of his head, he indicated the large area where the nurse had told him several people from church were also gathered.

He'd stepped out the door when he heard, "Tucker?" Beth's voice was as rough as sandpaper.

Swallowing hard, he pivoted back around.

She'd stood. She looked so small and fragile he ached real bad with the need to take her to him, protect her, shield her. She said, "Stay. Here. With me."

Oh, God. He crossed to her, came close. She peered up at him, her arms wrapped around her waist as if she could keep the emotion inside, the fear from clawing out. He reached over and circled his hand around her neck. She leaned toward him, put her forehead on his chest. And then she was in his arms. Burying her face in his sweatshirt. Clutching at the fleece. Burrowing into him like a hurt child shutting out the world.

He held her tight, kissed her hair, oblivious to anything but the driving need to comfort her. She began to cry and he was reminded of their private joke. . . . *We both turn into blubberin' babies around each other.*

With gentle care, he drew small circles on her back, kissed her hair again, whispered nonsense words. All the while, he thought only, *Please, God, don't let her lose Linc, too. Please.*

It took Tucker a minute to remember he didn't believe in prayer. But right at the moment, he didn't care. He prayed his heart out just in case.

AT two o'clock Doctor Jacobs finally returned to the family waiting room. Behind him, the five women from the group had come from the outer area and huddled in the doorway to hear his news.

From where they sat in the corner, Beth let go of her death grip on Tucker's hand and stood. Annie put down her coffee cup and rose from the chair, and Margo uncurled from the couch where she'd sat with Joe and stood, too. The three women converged in the center of the room, Margo and Annie flanking Beth. They grasped hands, as if that was the only way they could face the doctor. Joe was reminded of their childhood, and how they'd endured the trials of growing up with only each other, and the guys, there for them. The Outlaws against the world.

"Good news," Jacobs said right away. "He's going to be all right."

Beth's knees buckled and Margo and Annie held her up. "All right?"

"Yes." The doctor drew off wire-rimmed glasses and rubbed the bridge of his nose. "He regained consciousness during the CAT scan, which, by the way, revealed no damage to his brain."

"Why did he pass out?" Beth asked.

"He must have hit his head just right. What we were concerned about was the length of the unconsciousness, but he's lucid, and talking."

"How is he?" This from Annie.

The corners of the doctor's mouth curved up. "Worried about everybody else. Started barking orders that he wanted to see all of you"—Jacobs scanned the room—"and someone named Rosa."

In the doorway, Rosa gasped and put her hand to her mouth.

"He's trying to take care of us." Annie shook her head.

"Yes, well, he's going to have a hard time doing that. He's run down to begin with, and with his broken arm, people are going to need to take care of *him* for a while."

Joe could see that Beth was shaking. But, true to form, good old Bonnie surfaced and she tossed back her hair. "I'll take care of him for as long as he needs. Can I see him?"

"Yes. He's been brought up to a room. I want to keep him here for a few days, but he can have visitors." Jacobs smiled. "I can't tell you how glad I am it turned out this way. Linc helped my youngest daughter through that Community Council of his. Really turned her life around."

"He's a wonderful man." Annie was smiling now. That was

good to see. Though she'd pulled through for Beth in the crisis, Joe could tell the toll it took on her. Foolishly he wished he could help her in the aftermath, when she'd probably break down. As the doctor turned to leave, she and Beth started for the door.

Beth glanced over at Tucker, who stood by the window. He winked at her. "Go see your brother, babe."

The smile she gave back was full of gratitude—and love. Joe shook his head and wondered briefly what would happen to them.

Beth's gaze swung to Joe. "Come with us?"

"No, you three go on ahead. I want to talk to Tucker a minute. I'll be up later."

Annie started to say something to him, but her attention was diverted to Margo, who'd broken away from the trio; she crossed to the couch and picked up her coat and purse.

"What are you doing?" Annie asked.

"I'm not coming up to see Linc." Margo's words were stark. Her body was as rigid as a mannequin's.

"*What?*" Beth's look was incredulous.

"You heard me. I'm not going up."

"Why?"

"I have my reasons."

Beth strode to her and grabbed her hand. "Oh, Margo, don't do this. Don't cut yourself off."

Joe remembered something from long ago. When Margo was thirteen, her father left town. He was married to someone else, not Margo's mother, and the man had taken his other daughter, and wife, away from Glen Oaks. Margo had disappeared for three days, and Linc had been crazy with worry until he found her.

Brusquely, Margo shook off Beth's hands. "I'm fine. You guys go up. I'll call you later."

Before anyone could react, she swept through the door.

"I'll go after her," Joe said, rising.

"Don't." Annie's voice was firm. "Let her handle this in her own way."

Though it went against every instinct he had, Joe nodded. The women left to go see Linc.

From by the window, Tucker stared after them. "Nothin's easy, is it?"

"You can say that again." Joe sighed and sank onto a chair. "It sure as hell isn't."

MARGO had prayed during the interminable vigil they'd kept, waiting for news of Linc. It had felt foreign and stupid, but she did it, just in case. For Linc. She'd even tried to make a deal with his God. She'd leave Linc alone, not try to corrupt him anymore, if God would just let him be okay. She'd follow through on that, even though she didn't really believe God had listened to her. And she wouldn't tell Linc about her lapse. He'd be too glad, too encouraging. She didn't feel right about what she'd done, about talking to God after so long.

The only thing that mattered was that Linc was going to be fine.

The streets of Glen Oaks were gray and foggy, as the rain had dwindled to a fine mist. Her hood up, her hands in her pockets, she sidestepped a giant puddle in front of Zip's Bar and Grill and let her shoulders relax. How stupid to pray. It would have been more in keeping with her outlook to have made her deal with the Devil.

You don't really think there's a Devil, do you?

Margo halted in the middle of the sidewalk. Then she laughed at herself, but the sound was hollow and mirthless. Now she was hearing voices. She was really losing it. She had to get out of this town.

You've gotten pretty good at running away, Mary Margaret.

Again, she halted. "Jesus Christ," she whispered.

Yes?

Oh, great, the crushing fear, the undiluted terror was making her delusional. Making her hear voices.

Margo, Margo, Margo, you're not delusional. I've decided it's time we had a little talk.

Okay, she could play this game with her mind. *Yeah, and you are . . . ?*

You know who I am. You just prayed to me.

Stop it!

I'm Linc's God, Margo.

Fine, go keep Linc company.

I just did.

Like hell. If you really existed you would have kept him from getting hurt in the first place.

I work in mysterious ways.

So I've heard.

You prayed to me.

Did I? I don't remember.

You said if Linc would be all right, you'd leave him alone.

Ah, so that was it. He was calling in her marker. *I will leave him alone. Now go away.*

I'm not going anywhere. And neither are you, this time. You're my child, too.

Margo stopped. Stamped her foot. *Don't tell me that.*

All right. Listen to this one. I want you and Linc together.

She started walking again. *Give me a break.*

I'll give you more than that.

No, thanks. I don't want anything from you.

It doesn't work that way, Margo.

What? Gifts from God aren't declinable?

Something like that.

Leave me alone.

Never. Go to Linc. It's your way back to me.

No.

Trust me, Margo.

On a cold day in hell.

Hmm. That can be arranged.

SERENE, and just a little woozy from the drugs they were pumping into him, Linc smiled up at his sister. "Don't hover, Bethy, I'm all right."

Beth nodded, drew on that inner strength she'd honed for years, and then stepped back from his hospital bed where she'd gripped his hand like a lifeline. She sank onto a straight chair.

Annie came up and kissed his cheek. "Hey, buddy."

He squeezed her shoulder with his good hand and she took a seat on the other side of his bed.

Oh, Lord, how *was* he going to function with this cast for six weeks? He didn't even know how he'd broken his arm. "I got a question."

Beth nodded.

"What happened to Sam? One minute he was on top of me,

then he was gone." Linc remembered the sickening blast of pain when DeMartino had slammed his head into the floor, then the man was miraculously off him.

"I talked to Rosa when we were waiting." A pretty smile flirted with Annie's lips. "Henry Portman dragged Sam off you and literally threw him out of the church."

"Henry?"

Beth smiled. "Who would have guessed?"

Linc laughed out loud then clutched his ribs. "Ohh." At their worried looks, he waved away the concern. "Henry was in Vietnam. Of course, he never told me much about it . . ."

"Anita said he was a regular commando." Annie smiled. "Guess God knew what he was doing when He had you keep Henry on at church. By the way, Henry's here at the hospital, too."

"Really? Still?"

"I think so. With all the women in your group."

"You should let them come up."

"We will." Beth and Annie exchanged worried glances.

"What is it?"

"Nothing."

" 'Fess up. Belle and Bonnie still can't lie to their fearless leader." He scowled. "I'm not sicker than the doc said, am I?"

"No, of course not." Beth smiled. "I remember our pact, Jesse." Long ago, when they realized they had only each other to depend on, they'd promised never to withhold any truth from one another. At least they could count on that.

"Then what?"

"Margo's here. Or at least she was."

At first he was surprised. "Was I that critical?"

"We didn't know. You were unconscious a long time. So we called her."

"Well, that was the right thing to do." He eyed them knowingly. "Ah, I get it. She took off, didn't she, when she found out I was all right?"

Beth nodded. "We didn't go after her."

"You shouldn't. She'll come back."

"I don't know, Linc. She was pretty shaken."

"God will take care of her." He'd better. "Now go get the others." Linc scowled. "I'm kinda surprised Joe isn't here."

Annie said, "He is. He stayed downstairs with Tucker."

Linc's eyes met Beth's. She shrugged.

"He can come up, too."

"We'll start with the women. And Henry. Then go from there."

"Um, somebody should call Jane." Linc's voice was rusty.

"All right," Annie said. "I will."

Beth stood. "I've got to go get Ronny at school."

"I can do that," Annie offered.

"No, I want to tell him myself."

Linc studied her. "You'd better lighten up, Bethy, or you'll scare the crap outta the kid."

Beth gave him a wobbly smile. "I will." She touched his face. "I'm just glad you're all right."

He kissed her hand. "Scoot, both of you."

When they left, Linc fell back into the pillow. He hurt all over, though he wouldn't tell anybody that, except maybe Margo if she were there. *You'd better look out for her, God. I'm counting on you.*

No answer.

Hmm. As his eyes drifted shut, Linc wondered where God was.

BETH found Tucker alone where she'd left him, staring through the window at the dark streets. The drizzle outside accented his solitary figure. "Tucker?"

He pivoted around. Right now, he reminded her so much of the little boy that Ralph Pearson had abandoned, it broke her heart. "How's Linc?"

"I think he's in pain, but he's worried about everybody else. We have instructions to bring up all visitors. He asked for you."

"I don't . . . it's not my place, Beth."

"Linc said so."

"Linc takes in strays, honey."

Her heart somersaulted at the endearment. "You're not a stray."

He glanced at the clock. "Doc said Ronny needs to be picked up at four."

"Yes, that's where I'm going."

Tucker swallowed hard. "Your son needs you."

"I need *you*." She didn't mean to say the words aloud. But

once they were uttered she didn't regret them. Wouldn't take them back even if she could.

His eyes flared at her comment. "Beth, don't."

She crossed the room and stood in front of him. "All right. I'll go. But hold me first."

His shoulders stiffened. She thought for a minute he might refuse. Then he opened his arms and she stepped in.

It was like coming home. His warmth enveloped her. His size made her feel safe in an afternoon full of nightmares. And the familiar scent of woodsy aftershave and the smell that was uniquely Tucker calmed her. She whispered against his chest, "I'm not sure I can do this. Leave you alone . . ."

He stilled. Then he gripped her tighter; one hand went to her hair, another to her back. "You've got to. Ronny's state of mind is at stake here."

"I know." She drew in a deep breath. "I've got to go."

With a soft sweep of his lips on her forehead, he released her but didn't say anything more.

She stepped back. "I don't want to."

"Your son needs you." He brushed her cheeks with his knuckles. "Don't worry about me."

But she *was* worried about him.

I vowed in those long days and near endless nights that I'd die before I'd seek out that kind of attention, or affection, from anybody again. But particularly from anybody unwilling or unable to give it to me.

"Tucker, I—"

His fingers came to her lips. "No, honey, don't say it. I won't be able to let you go if you say any more."

She bit off the words and turned her back to him.

It was the only way she could stop herself from saying it.

AFTER she called Jane, Annie talked to Henry and four of the women's group members and told them they could go visit Linc. They needed to see that their beloved minister was all right.

Then she went in search of Rosa. No one knew where the woman had disappeared to, but Anita thought she might be crying. Annie was on her way to the family waiting area when she passed a small anteroom and heard voices.

The deep, male baritone was familiar. Drawn by an irresistible force, she approached the doorway. And froze.

Rosa was seated on a couch, her head down, a handkerchief in her hand, sniffling and wiping her eyes.

Joe was across from her, hunched over. His shoulders looked massive next to the woman's small frame. "Rosa, please, if nothing else listen to that."

"I can't help it," Rosa said. She must be upset because she was normally a quiet woman who had to be prodded to talk about anything. "If it wasn't for me, for disobeying Sam, Reverend Grayson wouldn't be hurt."

"Abusive men are responsible for their own actions, just like everybody else. It's part of the syndrome to blame it on others, especially the women they're involved with."

"He warned me. He told me not to go to church."

A memory came to Annie out of nowhere. *Where do you think you're going?* Joe's hand had slammed the door shut. *I didn't say you could leave.*

"He has no right to keep you from doing what you want to do," Joe told Rosa. "It's a control issue. He wants to control you."

Big frightened eyes stared up at Joe. All too well, Annie recognized the confusion and pain in them. "Why? What did I do?"

Please don't, Joey. What did I do? Annie herself had once gasped out as she'd shielded her face with her arms. *What did I do?*

"You did nothing, Rosa. Nothing." Joe's voice was vehement. "It's inside *him*."

"What is?"

"Unhealthy needs. Insecurity."

"Sam's not insecure."

"Of course he is. If he wasn't, he wouldn't have to make you bend to his will."

You'll do it because I say so.

Rosa stared at the floor for a long time. Finally she said, "I know about you."

"I figured that out from your reaction the other night."

"It's hard to believe you're like Sam."

Annie saw Joe stiffen. "I'm not, Rosa. Not anymore. I'm a different man, now."

Your mother's an adult, Matt. She can make her own decisions.

He hesitated. "But the reason I'm so sure of what I'm telling you is that I *was* like him, once. I know where he's coming from."

"You think my Sam can change?"

"Only if he wants to. Only if he gets help. And only through a lot of hard work." Joe hesitated, then added, "It's crucial that you realize he won't change overnight. It will take a lot of time and outside help."

I spent fifty-two weeks in a Batterers Recovery Program. And I've had three years of therapy.

"I want him to change."

"Most abused women want that from their partners. They don't want out of the relationship, they just want the man to change."

Rosa wrung her hands in the handkerchief. "I don't know if I can do this alone."

Careful not to touch her, Joe smiled. "You're not alone. There are the counselors at the office, there's Linc. I know of some support groups. And Annie can be a real help to you."

"Annie's stronger than I am."

"She didn't used to be. But she is now. You can be stronger, too, Rosa, just like her. I know it."

Annie stepped away from the doorway. The past and the present juxtaposed starkly, causing conflicting feelings inside her. She was surprised to discover that anger wasn't one of them.

And shocked to find that respect for Joe was.

LINC smiled and kept his eyes closed. He loved to dream about her like this—tonight she was there with him, her lips brushing over his forehead. Her face luminous with love and acceptance. "Mmm." He was almost able to smell the rain mixed with her sexy perfume. Silly though it was, he reached out for her.

And connected with solid, supple flesh.

His eyes flew open.

In the dim light of the hospital room—it had to be midnight at least—she was there, leaning over him, kissing his forehead, brushing his hair back. Her face was ravaged, her eyes so hollow it made his heart hurt more than his arm.

He smiled at her. Tucked a strand of her damp hair behind her ear. Slid his hand to her neck. She cleared her throat, and he brought her head to his chest. Slowly he soothed down her hair.

She didn't cry, she never cried, but she held on so tightly his ribs ached. After a moment, she drew back and stood.

He watched her take off her coat. Kick off her shoes. Her pretty suit was wrinkled; she unzipped the skirt, shrugged out of the jacket, and whipped off the stockings she wore. Linc remembered teasing her about how panty hose were the ugliest garment he'd ever seen.

Slowly, he managed to ease to the edge of the bed without groaning, and draw down the sheet. Clothed only in her pink shirt and lacy black undies, she crawled into his bed, cuddled up beside him, and buried her face in his chest.

He drew the covers up, secured her with his good arm and closed his eyes. He said silently, *Thank You for bringing her back to me.* Then he smiled. *I knew You would.*

TWENTY-FOUR

———

"YOU okay kid?" Margo asked Ron in his mother's car the morning after Uncle Linc's attack.

"Yeah, I'm okay. I'm worried about Mom, though. And Uncle Linc."

Margo's face shadowed. "Me, too."

"I wish you could stay." He sounded like a whiny little boy, but he couldn't help himself.

"Stay?"

"In Glen Oaks. Linc needs you. So does Mom." Ron swallowed hard. Hell. He might as well admit it. "Me, too."

"Aw buddy." She grasped his hand. He held on tight. "Me and Glen Oaks don't mix." There was something about her tone, though. Something different from all the times before when she'd bad-mouthed where they lived.

"Couldn't you try? For Linc?"

Her face got bleak.

"God ain't so bad, Margo."

"So He says."

"What?"

"Nothing. Look, I'll come back more, I promise, but live here?" She rolled her eyes. "It's my worst nightmare." She nodded to the school. "Better get going, kid."

"Okay." He leaned over and kissed her on the cheek. She

grasped his shoulders to hug him. Man, she seemed vulnerable today, something he never, ever associated with his tough aunt Margo. She acted like she wasn't sure of things all of a sudden.

Hell, he thought, getting out of the car, *who was*? Not him. Everything was getting fuzzy. How Linc had gotten hurt. Things between him and Tucker Quaid. Nothing seemed black and white anymore.

As he entered school and headed for his locker, he saw Lily standing there waiting for him. Ron went up to her and, in need of human contact, slid his arm around her. "Hi, Lil."

He wanted to kiss her so bad he couldn't stand it. Hell, it was eight in the morning and the mere sight of her gave him a hard-on like granite. Shifting uncomfortably in his Levis, he leaned toward her, but she squirmed away. "Don't, Ronny, please."

He inched back. Dressed in a long shirt that covered the top of her jeans, she'd pulled her hair off her face with some kind of clips. It made her seem younger than eighteen.

"I'm sorry," she said softly from lips tinted a dark pink, "but I don't wanna be looked at like that anymore. You know, I told you that the day we walked in the park."

"You let me kiss you last night."

She smiled, and it lit up her big brown eyes. "We were in private then." She touched his face, her fingernails scraping along his jaw. "Besides, I wanted to comfort you."

"You did, baby." He gave her a quick peck on the cheek and backed off.

"Is your uncle gonna be all right?"

"Yeah." He *was*. Every time Ron thought about something happening to Linc, a black hole of fear formed in his heart; he could hardly deal with it. Like he told Margo earlier, if something had happened to Linc, his mother would die inside. Ron knew that from watching her in the hospital the night before, as sure as he knew she was hurting big-time about something else these last couple of weeks.

"What you scowling at?" she asked.

Bravado won out. "Just wishin' we were alone again."

"My ma said you can come over tonight."

"I got community service." He grinned. "Maybe you can pick me up afterward."

"Okay."

Sammy Shecker skidded to a halt in front of Ron's locker. His red hair was wild, and his face nearly matched its color. His outfit of brown jeans and a white shirt looked like he slept in them. "Ron, did you hear?"

Ron stepped away from Lily. He didn't think Sammy'd talk about them, and Sammy had been on the outs with Maze and Loose, too, but he wanted to make sure Lily got what she wanted. "Hear what?"

" 'Bout Mr. Johnson."

"No. What happened?"

"His car went off the road this morning and plunged into Coleman Street Crater."

Omigod. "Coleman's Crater?" It was an area of town that had been fixed a hundred times. But there was something about the drainage path that kept washing away the dirt. And it had rained for five days. The town was planning to fill the hole in with concrete this summer. "Is he hurt?"

"Yeah, pretty bad. The firemen couldn't get him outta the car and when they finally did, they rushed him to the hospital."

"That's awful," Lily said. "He's so nice."

Ron's insides clenched. This was the third person in his life who'd been taken to the hospital in a few short weeks. And Ron knew better than anybody what could happen in that hospital. Still whipped from his uncle's ordeal the night before, he had little reserve to draw on.

"Ronny, you okay?"

"Yeah. I wonder who we can find out more from."

"Mrs. Matthews is a good friend of his. Maybe she'd know something."

"I got her first period for English." Lily's frown marred her pretty brow. "Let's go down to her room now."

Ron just looked at her, concerned.

Lily grasped his hand. "It'll be okay, Ronny. I promise."

Though Ronny clung to the offered comfort, he was beginning to think nothing was going to be okay again.

What the *hell* was going on in this town?

ARMED with toiletries and sneakers, Margo climbed the steps to Linc's apartment around noon and pulled out the little-used key Linc had once given her. She was running on empty and scared shitless. Never in her wildest dreams had she ever thought about something happening to Linc.

Or that she'd pray to God for him.

I'm not going anywhere. And neither are you, this time. You're my child, too. . . . Trust me. . . .

She moaned aloud. This couldn't be happening to her, not Margo Morelli, confirmed atheist. *Think of something else.* She remembered how she and Linc slept together in the hospital bed last night with only one embarrassing moment when a nurse came in at four. But the woman had gone to high school with them, and had remained friends with Linc, so she'd merely warned Margo to be out of bed by six when the shift changed. This morning, when she'd awakened with Linc, she'd almost told him the whole story of what was happening to her. Only fear that he could draw her deeper into God's web kept her from saying anything.

Reaching the top of the steps, she went to put the key in its lock, but the door was already ajar. Pushing it open, she found sweet Jane Meachum inside cleaning.

The PK. Someone God surely would love.

Stop it! she told herself.

Jane jumped when she turned from the refrigerator and saw Margo there. She looked like a regular Donna Reed in her nice pants and shirt and kerchief around her brown hair. "You startled me."

"I'm sorry," Margo said. "I didn't know anyone was here."

"No, it's my fault." Even her smile was innocent. It made Margo's heart hurt. Jane continued, "I went to see Linc this morning and then came over here, thinking I could clean up a bit for him."

"Yeah?" Margo had dropped her shopping bag and purse on a chair and scanned the room. "He can be a real slob."

"Oh, well, he's so busy. He should have someone clean for him."

Margo knew that Jane Meachum would relish the job. She should just leave, go back to New York, and let the other woman take care of Linc's house, take care of Linc. She should let her *have* Linc.

As if reading Margo's thoughts, Jane threw back her shoulders and faced her squarely. "You're the one, aren't you?"

"The one?"

"Linc told me once he'd lost the love of his life."

Stunned, Margo swallowed hard and just stared at Jane. Suddenly, the woman didn't look so young anymore. Or so naive. She looked . . . wise.

"But he also told me he didn't want to pine away for you for the rest of his life."

"I don't want that for him, either." The hoarsely uttered words were difficult to get out, but true.

"Don't you? Then why do you keep stringing him along?"

"I'm not."

"Contact with you slingshots him back at warp speed."

Margo circled her waist with her arms. Deep in her heart she knew Jane's assessment was true. Because of that, she chose to be angry. "Look, this isn't any of your business."

"Yes, it is. I want Linc." The other woman's tone wasn't bitchy, just determined.

Surprised, Margo opened her mouth to tell Jane she could have him. But, again, she couldn't get the words out. Something stopped her.

"However, until you're out of the picture, I won't have a place in his life. Either let him go, Margo, or claim him. You're not being fair." Silent, Margo watched Jane turn back to the fridge. "I'll finish up here, and then be out of your way."

Like a child who'd been dismissed, Margo just stood there watching Jane's back. For a moment, she didn't know what to do. Then, she turned and headed for Linc's bedroom, closing the door tightly once she was inside.

She went to the bed and tugged up the covers he must have left mussed the last time he was here. Plumping his pillows, she threw herself on the bed, but that was a mistake. His musky, unique scent was on the linen. So she sat up and scanned the room. There was a cross on the wall. Pictures of Bethy, Ron, Annie and her kids occupied space on the top of an old and scarred dresser.

None of Margo. The notion hurt her heart.

On the nightstand was an empty beer can, a phone and a book. She picked it up. It was called *The Reluctant Atheist*. Hrrmph.

Casually she opened the nightstand drawer. Inside was a Bible. A beautiful leather-bound one that had obviously been given to him by someone. Without thinking, she fished it out. Opened it. And caught her breath. Tucked inside was a five-by-seven picture of her. She had no idea when it had been taken, but her face shone with love and need for the cameraman. It must have been taken by Linc.

She stared at the photo nestled comfortably inside the book of God. Linc the psychologist was just full of symbolism. She closed her eyes and sighed heavily. Well, it was all wishful thinking. No way in hell was she ever going to change her mind about religion and its role in her life. Not for Ronny. Not for Linc. Not for God himself.

Clutching the bible and picture to her chest, she started to doze when she thought she heard, *Don't bet on it, Margo baby.* But she fell into a deep sleep before she could analyze it.

DRESSED in a pair of Linc's sweatpants and one of his flannel shirts, wearing the canvas sneakers she'd bought at Killian's, Margo let herself into her co-op late Sunday night. The weekend had been unbelievable. Her shoulders ached with fatigue, worry and the tension of Linc's accident.

Dropping her raincoat and bag of clothes she'd worn to Glen Oaks Thursday on the chair in the foyer—God, was it just a few days ago that she'd left work?—she longed for a bath and bed. She particularly didn't want to deal with her feelings, which were galloping through her like an emotional posse looking for its prey.

The phone on the stand in the living room distracted her. Its red message light was blinking. She could ignore it, but there might be news about Linc, so she pressed the button.

"Margo, it's Philip." His deep voice was cold. "It's Saturday. I'm worried about you. I guess you stayed in Glen Oaks with the minister." A pause. "You know, I can't fathom what he's got that attracts you so much." Philip's tone softened. "I have to admit, I don't like it. But I hope he's all right. Call me at this number when you get back. I've got news on the Brubeck order."

Disturbed by his comments, she said to the phone, "It can wait until tomorrow at work."

A beep. "Hi, babe. It's me." Linc. Just the sound of his voice warmed her. She pictured him as she'd left him at his apartment, tucked into bed, eyes slumberous from the pain medication, his hand clasping hers as if he'd never let her go. "Call and tell me that you got home safely. Oh, and I thought you'd like to know,

Ronny's teacher's gonna be all right. He'll be in the hospital a while, and out of school until the end of the year, but they swear he's gonna walk again." He waited. "Thanks for hanging around here. I know it's not your style, but it meant a lot to me." Another pause. "We're gonna make it, honey, I promise."

"Yeah, sure," she said aloud again.

Ignoring the rest of the messages, Margo headed for her bedroom, thinking of the weekend. On Friday, there had been an emotional scene with Ron, who'd begged her to stay in Glen Oaks.

God's not so bad, Margo.

Then, she'd gone back to the hospital. Linc had had visitors and more tests, so she hadn't gotten to talk to him much. Her emotions had been a jumbled mass, and she wasn't even sure why she'd stayed, after planning to leave Glen Oaks right after she found out he was going to be all right. Something had driven her to stay, though.

In her own familiar surroundings, while she drew bathwater, poured in sinfully expensive bath oil and shed her clothes, she thought about the little surprise waiting for her when she'd gone to Linc's garage apartment.

Jane Meachum's words, *Let him go or claim him,* haunted her. Was there even a choice? she wondered as she climbed into the tub. She closed her eyes and leaned back on the terry-cloth pillow. The hot water soothed her.

You have a choice, Margo, I told you that.

Margo sat up straight, sloshing soapsuds and water over the side.

Oh no you don't. Don't talk to me again. You got me so screwed up Thursday I stayed in Glen Oaks all weekend. And it didn't help. It just makes me miss him more.

It's good to miss the people we love. It makes us appreciate them.

She slid down into the water. *Please, go away.*

Never.

Why are you doing this to me?

Because it's time to push you. I've waited years for you to do this on your own and you haven't. So now I'm helping.

You can help me by leaving me alone.

She thought she heard an exasperated sigh, like a parent trying to be patient with his child.

Margo, what your mother did was wrong. All atrocities committed in my name are wrong.

Before she could stop, she found herself asking, *Then why do you allow it?*

It's called free will. People have to have it or life is meaningless.

It hurt so much.

I know it did. I tried to help you through it.

How? How did you try?

By giving you Linc.

She felt her eyes tear. *You took him away. When you made him become a minister, he left me.*

No, I didn't do that either.

Well, I didn't make him leave me. She waited a minute. *Did I? What do you think?*

Oh, no . . .

The phone ringing in the bedroom brought Margo back to reality. Geez, she *was* losing it. This was nuts. She couldn't be talking to God. That was Linc's thing. To ward off the notion, she stood and stepped out of the tub. "No more. Just don't do it anymore," she told herself. "You'll be fine."

Dressing hurriedly in red silk lounging pajamas, she was on her way to listen to the rest of her messages when the front-door buzzer rang. She snagged a matching robe and hurried to the foyer.

She was utterly dismayed to hear Philip ask to come in over the intercom. Just what she needed. Could she say no? That was cowardly. So she rang him in and opened her door a few moments later. "Hello, Philip."

He stuck his hands in the pockets of his expensive, pressed jeans and whistled softly. "Wow."

She angled her head, then realized he meant how she was dressed. Ignoring the reaction, she tightened the belt of her robe. "What are you doing here?"

"I was worried about you. Why didn't you call me when you got in?"

"I just got back."

With practiced ease, he edged inside. She had no choice but to close the door. "Is everything all right in Glen Oaks?" he asked.

"Yes."

"Is the minister going to recover?" His tone was odd—little-boyish, almost whiny like Ronny had seemed that weekend.

"His name is Linc, and yes, he's fine. He has a broken arm, though, and it's going to be tough for a few weeks."

Uninvited, Philip wandered into the living room. Margo followed him, assaulted by the distinct smell of alcohol in his wake. "I hope this doesn't mean you'll be running back there every weekend to . . . help him dress, and things like that." Without even asking, he headed for her bar and poured himself a few fingers of scotch. Facing her, he finished, "I hear it's tough to zip up your pants when you have a broken arm."

Margo crossed her arms over her chest. "What's going on, Philip?"

"Can't you tell?"

She shook her head.

"I'm jealous." He sipped his drink. "Did you sleep with him this weekend? I know you can still do that with a broken arm."

"You've no right to ask that question."

Philip slammed the drink down on the glass table, splashing its contents onto the surface. A primitive man emerged from his civilized exterior. "I have every right to ask that. And you know I do. Or at least you would if you'd give me half a chance to convince you."

"I think you'd better go."

"No."

"Philip, I have no intention of getting personally involved with you. I've made that clear."

He fisted his hands on his hips, his shirt stylishly rumpled, the sleeves pushed up to reveal bare forearms. Even angry, he looked like an ad from GQ. "There's *no,* Margo, and then there's *no.*"

Outraged, she asked, "What does *that* mean?"

"Let's just say your actions speak louder than your words."

"You'd better go," she repeated, her tone icy.

"I'd think twice about rejecting my offer if I were you."

"Why?"

He picked up his drink and downed it. "It's not in your best interest, sweetheart."

Her pulse beat fast. "Personally, Philip, or professionally?"

His eyebrows shot up. "Why, both, of course." He set down the drink. "The gloves are off, Margo." With that comment, he crossed the room, grabbed her arms in a painful vise and gave her a bruising kiss. Letting her go, he said only, "Think about it," and left Margo staring after him.

"Oh my God," she said as the door slammed.

THE group assistant, Joanie, popped into Margo's office the following Thursday and smiled warmly at her. "Margo, Jack called down when you were on the phone. He'd like to see you."

"When?"

"As soon as you're available."

"I'm free now."

"He said if you were, to give him fifteen minutes to make a phone call and come on up. I'll confirm it."

"Thanks, Joanie. Close the door, would you?"

Fifteen minutes.

To decide what to do.

Unlocking her bottom drawer, Margo pulled out a manila folder and opened it. Paltry proof of what Philip had been up to. But the lawyer specializing in sexual harassment, whom she'd called bright and early Monday morning, had told her to start compiling any paper trail, recording any discussions or events, though the woman's schedule precluded meeting until the following Tuesday.

As Margo stared at the memos from Brubeck and Laufler, she shook her head. Had she really been such a fool? On the Monday after Philip's visit and his ominous words, she'd found the second memo on her desk. *I called Brubeck to discuss the product delivery. Tom Newman said we had different dates recorded. I planned to straighten this out over the phone, but Brubeck was out of town. Will call back in a couple of days. P.*

A few other meager memos were included, but the file was primarily composed of a record of her suspicions, and a listing of the events that led to them. She'd feel better when she got to talk to the lawyer. She was thankful that Philip was out of the office on business the rest of the week. With any luck she could avoid him, as she'd done since Sunday, until her meeting with the lawyer.

A wave of sadness enveloped Margo as she stood to meet with Jack; she remembered when she'd first come to work here, how excited she'd been, how sure she'd been that CompuQuest was a liberal place, with their aggressive recruitment of women and their extensive promotion policy. Philip's warm smile, his easy-going manner and his generosity with his time had made her feel right at home. And over the years, she'd thought he'd become her friend. It was hard to believe he was the enemy now.

Smoothing down her navy jacket, she thought about how everything was a mess. Work. Personal life.

What personal life? You have none.

Refusing to think about that, she made her way to Jack's office. In the elevator, she caught sight of herself in the aluminum reflection—looking back at her was a sleek, sophisticated executive and a grim-faced, lonely woman. Margo turned her back to the image, and gathered her thoughts until she reached the executive floor.

Outside Jack's office, Geraldine greeted her. "Hello, Margo. You can go right in."

No smile. No usual pleasantries.

"Is everything all right with you, Gerry?" Margo asked.

Geraldine raised her chin; her face was tight, reminding Margo of the women at the commune when she'd done something to displease them. "Of course everything's all right. Jack's expecting you."

Margo nodded and knocked on Jack's door. "Come in."

She entered the office. Jack was seated behind his desk, his glasses perched on his nose, reading a file. Ever the gentleman, he stood when she came closer. "Sit down, Margo."

Like the last time she'd been there with Philip, she took a leather chair across from the CEO. The May sunlight filtered through open blinds, creating little beams of sunlight that danced on the desk's surface.

Jack held her gaze. "I'll cut right to the quick. I received this fax a few hours ago." He handed her a paper.

As Margo scanned it, she could feel her heartbeat speed up. Through sheer force of will she kept her hands from shaking. "I don't understand. Philip told me this was taken care of."

Jack eyed her carefully. "I recall asking you to deal with it."

"I did. Or at least I tried to. I called Tom Newman and set up a meeting with him for Thursday afternoon."

"Which you didn't keep."

"No, I had a family emergency." She shifted uneasily in her seat. "I had to go to Glen Oaks right away. Philip met with Tom, then tried to reach Brubeck, but he was out of town. Philip was going to speak with Brubeck as soon as he got back."

"Were you out of the office all week?"

"No, I was back Monday. I was gone Thursday and Friday of last week."

Jack tapped a gold pen on his desk. "Well, once again, with Brubeck, there was some miscommunication. As you can see from the terse but clear memo, he's not happy with us, and we may not be getting any more business from them."

"I don't know what to say. I'm sorry I was gone last week."

"You can't help being out for emergencies. But I'm not sure why you didn't deal with this when you got back."

"Philip said he would."

"Did you follow up on that with him?"

"No."

A long pause from Jack, then a scowl. "Why?"

Because I was avoiding him. "He went out of town before I thought of it again."

"Margo, Philip didn't leave town until Wednesday."

"I don't know what to say."

Sitting back, Jack steepled his hands. He stared at her with kind brown eyes. "Ordinarily, I wouldn't jump on this because you have an impeccable eight-year record. But with the Laufler out-sourcing, this Brubeck thing, and then a new development, I'm forced to."

"A new development?" Margo threaded back her hair. "What?"

"Another firm called Philip before he left. They complained about your . . . inattention to them, too."

"Who?"

"Compton's."

Margo stilled. In that second, everything clicked. It was like finding the piece of a jigsaw puzzle that allowed you to put the rest together quickly. Eric Compton, owner of Compton Electronics, was Philip's old frat buddy and good friend. Margo gulped back the smothering feeling that came over her. "I see."

"Do you? Then tell *me*, because I'm in the dark, here. Up until recently, your work has been stellar. Suddenly, it's filled with missed deadlines and unhappy customers."

Thinking fast, Margo smoothed down her skirt. She watched her foot bob up and down as she mentally reviewed her choices.

It became crystal clear to her that she was in trouble. She should have said something before.

"Margo?" Jack's voice softened. "Is it personal problems? I know they can affect your work."

Swallowing hard, she made a split-second decision. One she should have made before. Oh, God, Linc had been right.

"No, Jack, it's not personal problems. Not like you mean. I'm afraid it's worse than that."

"How so?"

"I think something's going on here that you should know about. Something I've kept from you for several weeks because I didn't want to recognize that it was really happening." Holding up the memos, she said, "I have no choice, now."

All CEO, Jack straightened. "Then tell me, Margo."

Carefully, and logically, which was her forte, she outlined the events of the previous months: Philip's come-on in Boston, his apologies, his pushing to remain friends. The all-male weekend, the out-sourcing of Laufler's product, the dinners and coffee to discuss his marital problems, the innuendo that mixing personal and professional was a good idea for her, and finally his visit Sunday and what he'd said.

As she told him her suspicions, Jack's face reddened and his eyes became troubled. When she finished, he said, "Give me a minute, will you?" Pushing back his chair, he rose and crossed to stare out the window. She'd always appreciated his thoughtfulness, how he never said or did anything capriciously. Finally he faced her and drew in a deep breath. "I'm sure you realize the seriousness of this . . . charge."

"Yes, I do. I didn't make it lightly."

"Needless to say I'm shocked."

"I know you and Philip are friends."

"It's more than that."

"I'm sure it is."

Jack sat back down at the desk and clasped his hands in front of him. "First off, I asked you last week if everything was all right. Why didn't you tell me this then?"

"I was still debating if there *was* a problem, and what I should do about it. I wanted to give Philip the benefit of the doubt." She frowned. "Truthfully, I think I didn't want to admit the reality of it all to myself, Jack."

"All right, that's feasible. It's just that making the accusation after several things have gone wrong for you is highly suspicious."

Margo bristled, but kept her cool, like she had in her street days when the Outlaws ran into trouble. "Yes, I suppose it would be."

"Is there proof, Margo? Any witnesses? Any notes Philip wrote you? Anything like that?"

"No." She'd naively thrown away notes he'd left her and erased voice mail messages.

He sighed. "Then, of course, there's the fact that Philip initiated and supervised the development of our Sexual Harassment Policy."

"I know that. It complicates matters."

"He's also gotten many awards from city women's groups for his recruitment of women."

She swallowed hard. "I know."

Jack shook his head. "Ironic, huh?"

"I'm sorry, Jack. I wish this hadn't happened."

He nodded. "Me, too. All right, here's what we'll do. I'll meet with Philip as soon as he gets back"—he glanced at his calendar —"on Monday. Then I'd like to meet with you together, and the company's lawyer if that's comfortable for you."

"Of course. A person has a right to face his accuser."

"Fine." He stood indicating the meeting was over. "I promise you I'll investigate this to the fullest, and I'll be fair."

"I trust you will be. And in all fairness to you, I want you to know I've contacted an attorney. I wanted some legal advice before I brought this to your attention." She held out the memos. "However, I had no choice but to tell you today."

He nodded.

"Thank you for listening. I'll wait to hear from you."

She rose and headed to the door. When she reached it, he called to her. "Oh, and one more thing Margo."

She pivoted around. "What?"

"My wife and I had dinner with Sally and Philip this weekend. There didn't seem to be any marital problems between them then."

TWENTY-FIVE

———

TAYLOR Cummings was probably the prettiest woman Annie had ever seen. Even dressed in khaki cargo shorts, a loose navy T-shirt and a New York Mets baseball cap, she was as stunning as a runway model. Her dark curly hair hung in waves down her back, and every part of her was long, lean and toned. Right now, she was screaming her head off as Joe's Little League team went ahead five to four. Joe coached from the sidelines in jeans and the green team shirt.

"Who is she?" Suzie asked from next to Annie in the stands. Joe's mother Grace was home with Faith, who had the sniffles, and Annie didn't want her out in the just-stopped rain. The bleachers were still damp, and Annie felt the cold through her jeans.

"She's a friend of Joe's." Annie wasn't sure if Suzie knew about the underwear modeling, so she didn't want to talk out of turn.

"Oh, is she the photographer?"

So much for Joe's privacy. "Uh-huh."

Suzie laughed. Her eyes sparkled like Joe's did when he was amused. "You should have seen Ma's face when she first saw the catalog. I thought she was going to bust a gut."

"You've seen it?"

"Yeah. Real classy. I can't believe it's my brother." Suzie continued to watch the play. "I'll bring you a copy."

"No, thanks. I wouldn't want the kids to see it."

"It's honest money, Annie."

Annie's head snapped to the side. When had Suzie started to defend her brother? "I never said it wasn't. I just think it might be embarrassing for them. Especially Matt."

"These days, Matt thinks Joe walks on water."

"Obviously, he's not the only one."

Suzie's complexion flushed. She fiddled with the tie on her fleece jacket and moved her shoulders with an uncharacteristic lack of grace. "Does it bother you? He's my big brother, Annie. I missed him. I like having him back."

So do I. Oh, God, how could she even think such a thing? *Because he's changed.*

"Annie?"

"No, Suz, I'm not mad. I'm glad you have him back, and that the kids have him, too."

Suzie eyed the field, then looked to the stands. "I just hope he's here to stay." She nodded to Taylor, who was on her lovely feet, protesting a bad call. "And that *she* doesn't drag him back to New York to live."

"You could still see him. So could the kids."

"It wouldn't be the same."

No, it wouldn't.

Annie shrugged. "I'm going to get a drink. You want one?"

"No, thanks."

Annie climbed down the stands, which were sparsely populated, wrapping her long-sleeved tattered denim shirt closer around her. She hadn't realized how she'd dressed tonight—a regular Little Orphan Annie. And her hair was curling wildly from the rain. Oh, hell, why was she worried how she looked?

She wished Margo or Beth were with her. But Beth was at Linc's, probably driving him crazy, hovering like a mother hen, and Margo had gone back to New York the day before. Rosa hadn't come to the game either. Sam had not shown himself in Glen Oaks since he'd attacked Linc, and Rosa had had to take Lisa to her soccer game tonight. So Annie was alone, left to deal with her conflicting feelings by herself.

Ever since Linc's injury and the conversation she'd overheard between Joe and Rosa, Annie had been uneasy about her feelings

for Joe. They'd changed somewhere along the line, and in all
fairness, in good Christian fairness, she couldn't keep from ad-
mitting he was not the man who'd left Glen Oaks five years before.

The problem was that along with that admission came a fear.
A big fear. That she might begin to feel other things for him
again. And, given what he'd done to her, how could she?

Taylor Cummings seemed to bring it all to the forefront.
She'd arrived in Glen Oaks the day before, after Joe had canceled
a photo shoot on Saturday. Annie knew this because Joe had told
Linc, who told Beth, who told Annie. Not that Annie wanted to
know, not that she cared where the pretty photographer had
stayed the night before, or where she'd stay that night.

Joe was a big boy. An attractive man. A good lover.

Annie swallowed hard. How could she even think about that
after what he'd done to her? Not only the abuse . . . but the rape.
She didn't let herself dwell on it, but that didn't make it any less
real, any less an irrevocable chasm between them that could
never, ever be breached.

After purchasing a soda from the concession, she went to return to the stands and instead detoured to the playground. It was
deserted tonight, given the fact that the equipment was wet from
the earlier rain. Alone, Annie sat on a swing, kicked at the mud
with the toe of her sneaker and tried to deal with the feelings that
were swamping her.

SOMETHING was wrong with Annie. Something more than
just Joe being back in town. When he dropped Matt off, she was
in the basement. He followed his son downstairs.

"Mom, you down here?" Matt called out.

"Uh-huh."

"Geez, Mom, it's late. What are you doing?"

"Staining a dresser for Faith's room."

"Why you working so late?"

"It's not that late." She wouldn't look at Joe. Her slender
shoulders were tense beneath the white T-shirt. She'd taken off
the denim shirt she'd worn over it to the game. "Did you have fun
with the guys?"

"Yeah, Taylor treated us all to pizza. Her father was a Triple-
A baseball player in Rochester for years. Isn't that neat?"

Annie nodded.

"She played softball in college, too."

"How nice for her."

"And she knew all the sports sayings from Dad's book—where *bullpen, pinch hitter* and *Eagle* originated. I knew those, too. I found out where *throw in the towel* came from." Matt chatted with the animation of a child totally oblivious to the adult tension around him. "In boxing, when a guy decided he couldn't fight anymore, he tossed an article of clothing used to soak up blood into the ring to show he was giving up. Isn't that cool?"

She said dryly, "Wonderful."

"Mom, you okay?"

"I'm fine."

"Well, I'm gonna go call Tommy." He headed for the staircase, where Joe leaned against the wall watching the byplay. "Thanks, Dad. See you tomorrow."

His arms crossed over his team T-shirt, Joe smiled at his son. "Uh, maybe not. I have to go into the city with Taylor in the morning. If I'm not back, I've made arrangements with Tucker to coach practice."

"Oh, well, okay. See ya Wednesday."

Joe watched Matt take the stairs two at a time. Then he turned back to his wife. "Annie, is something wrong?"

"No." She applied a strip of stain on the dresser with the concentration of a heart surgeon.

"Did something happen? Faith isn't sicker, is she?"

"No." She still didn't look at him.

"Linc?"

"No. I said nothing's wrong. Now leave me alone."

Hrrmph. He thought they'd made headway when they'd pulled together over Linc's accident. "All right."

She turned to him just as he started upstairs. "You know," she began, her words stopping his ascent. "This is a small town. And Matt's an adolescent boy. Having women stay over at your place, and following them back to the city, isn't necessarily a good role model."

Joe's jaw dropped and he edged back downstairs. "What are you saying?"

"If you're sleeping with Taylor Cummings, you shouldn't flaunt it."

A smile curved his lips.

"Do you think this is funny?" Annie's face showed shock. He was entranced by the color that rose up from the neck of her shirt to her cheeks.

"A little."

"Why?"

He shrugged. "Maybe because Taylor and I are just friends."

"Oh, sure."

"And because she's gay."

Annie dropped the paintbrush onto the papers covering the cement floor. He watched a brown stain fan outward. "What?"

"Taylor's gay. She makes a point of not hiding it." He narrowed his gaze on Annie. "But if and when I decide to sleep with somebody in Glen Oaks, I'll be sure to be discreet." He waited a moment. "Is that what's got you in a snit?"

"I'm not in a snit."

"Whatever you say." He glanced up the steps. "I'm going to say good night to Faith and drop my mother off."

"Fine. Good night." Her little-girl surly tone was so unlike her, it, too, made him smile.

It wasn't until he was almost home that it hit him that Annie's behavior had smacked of jealousy.

Fat chance, he told himself. *You might gain her respect back, her trust with the kids. But she'll never let you near her body again.*

Rightfully so. After what he'd done.

He couldn't bear to think about that night. Even the counselors had recommended that he put it out of his mind.

Go find Taylor and talk about something else.

That worked until he tried to fall asleep. And then, for the first time ever, his mind insisted on replaying every obscene detail. . . .

He'd been enraged because she'd been late from work. With a can of beer in his hand, he'd met her at the door. "Where the hell have you been?"

Recognizing his belligerent stance, she'd said, in carefully modulated tones, "I told you, Suzie and I were staying late to plan the recital with Linda." Linda was the former owner of DanceWorks, who Annie had eventually bought it from.

"Suzie's home. I called."

Annie crossed into the foyer, took off her coat and hung it up.

"She left a little early. Look, Joe, I'm tired. I'm going to take a bath."

His hand had crumpled the beer can.

She'd escaped to the bedroom before he could object, and locked the door. Matt was staying at Joe's mother's, and they were alone. Joe had splintered the locked door with his booted foot and barged in like a caveman who'd lost his mate. "Don't you ever lock a door to me again. I'm your husband."

Clutching her open blouse, she swallowed hard, backed up. "I'm sorry. I . . . didn't realize I locked it."

"My, don't we have a lot of lies to tell tonight." He grabbed her roughly by the arm. "Who were you with?"

"No one."

"Who touched you?"

"No one, Joe, I swear."

He ripped off the shirt she wore over a half leotard. Then tore off the bra. He studied her, making her shiver. "You're black and blue below your breast. Who did it?"

"You did. Last time you hit me."

"I don't believe you." He pushed her to the bed. Came down on top of her. It was then that she realized his intent. "Don't Joey, please."

"*Don't?* To your husband? You're mine." He'd shoved his hand into her underpants. "This is mine. Whenever I want."

"Please, you've never done this before. Please don't do it now."

He slapped her then. Hard. She began to cry.

He did it anyway. Roughly. Callously. Like some Neanderthal . . .

Joe bolted out of bed, but the images accompanied him, so he let himself think hard about it. Psychologists were right. Rape was not a sexual act. It was an act of power. He'd never touched her intimately again after that. He'd known he'd stepped over a line. A month later, just after he'd hit her again, she'd told him she was pregnant, and he'd left town.

After returning to Glen Oaks in March, and finding out he had a daughter, Joe had a whole new demon to face—he didn't know if that was the night Faith was conceived. He couldn't tell from her birthday. So Joe had convinced himself Annie was already pregnant the night of the rape. If she wasn't, their sunny child . . . It made him ill, even now, to think about it. It just couldn't be true.

ANNIE went up on her toes, lifted her leg in a perfect arabesque and held it for two counts. Muscles pulsing, she breathed deeply and came down into a *demi-plié*, did two *ronde de jambe*'s on the floor and bent at the waist. She was ready to leap into the finale when she caught sight of Suzie entering the large mirrored practice room.

"Sorry. I didn't mean to interrupt. Go ahead and finish."

Crossing to the barre, Annie picked up a towel. She swabbed her face and plucked at the sweaty sheer maroon blouse she wore over pink tights and a matching leotard. "No, that's all right, I still have to work on the ending."

"You only got a couple of weeks, kiddo." Suzie's outfit mirrored hers, only she wore a DanceWorks sweatshirt over it.

"Don't remind me."

DanceWorks' annual recital was in three weeks; the details of putting it on were endless, and the month preceding it was always crazy at the studio. Annie swore this would be the last recital she danced in. Every year, Suzie talked her into it, and every year Annie vowed it was her swan song.

"You want to practice your jazz piece? I'll critique it." Annie smiled at her pretty sister-in-law. Fair was fair. Suzie performed, too.

"Nah. I just came in to get away from Ma. She's driving me nuts."

Grace Murphy pitched in at the end of the dance season for the recital. Right now, she was in working on the costumes with Rosa DeMartino. Annie had hired Rosa to help take care of last-minute details, then found she was a whiz at sewing. She and Grace were putting the finishing touches—feathers, beads and sashes—on the costumes. Rosa had also proved to be competent office help.

Grace had been unusually cold these last few weeks, since Linc's accident. "What's going on with your mother, Suz?"

Suzie shrugged. "Same old same old."

Annie picked up the water bottle she'd brought in, took a swig and sank onto the floor. "Sit."

Wearily, Suzie approached her. Gracefully, she settled down

next to Annie. They faced each other, cross-legged. It was time
for a girl-to-girl powwow.

"Come on, Suz. You can tell me."

"It has to do with you."

"I figured that out."

"She's bitchin' about Rosa. 'That the woman can't do anything right. She should just stay home and let her husband take
care of her.'" Suzie shook her brown curls. "I swear Ma's stuck
in the last century."

Annie sighed. Sam's attack on Linc had spread through Glen
Oaks like wildfire in a drought. The whole town knew about it.
Unfortunately, Grace's attitude was clearly unsympathetic to
Rosa. "Think she knows?"

"About Rosa or you?"

"I meant Rosa."

"I think she senses both. Sort of like a kindred spirit. The
point is, it doesn't matter. Somehow, Ma will always believe it's
the woman's fault."

"Joe should talk to her."

Annie saw Suzie tense. She drew a finger along the groove in
the wood flooring. "He's tried, Annie. She won't listen." When
Annie didn't answer, Suzie looked up. "You think that's an excuse, don't you?"

"Not exactly. It doesn't matter anyway. What matters is that
your mother doesn't treat Rosa badly."

A grin split Suzie's face. "The woman's a find, isn't she?"

"Yes. I was going to ask you about hiring her permanently."

"Can we afford it?"

"I think so. Having her work here would cut back on our
hours considerably, which is what we both want."

"Well, if you . . ."

"Annie?" Joe was at the door. Dressed in black nylon shorts
and a T-shirt, his hair was windblown, and his face red. Though
it was nine at night, he'd obviously been running. She hadn't
seen much of him since the week before, when they'd squared off
in the basement.

"Joe? What are you doing here?"

"I'm looking for Rosa." He smiled at his sister. "Hi, kiddo."

Suzie smiled. "Hi. Rosa's in the other room with Ma."

"Why?" Annie asked. Something about Joe's demeanor made
her tense.

"Sam's back in town. I saw him going into Zip's when I ran by."

Annie's heart rate speeded up. "Oh, no."

Wiping the sweat off his face with the black sweatshirt he'd tied around his neck, Joe scanned the room. "I need to see her."

"Come on, I'll show you where she is." Annie rose and headed toward the door. Surrounded by ghosts from the past—ghosts that the man behind her conjured—Annie remembered the fear she'd felt that Joe might return at any time. Poor Rosa.

Her gaze darted over her shoulder to her husband; his expression told her he knew exactly what she was thinking.

Three steps forward, two back, Joe repeated to himself as he caught Annie's look and followed her to the back room. The fear on her face, actually the *remembered* fear, cut like glass slivers into the skin. How, *how* could he have been like Sam DeMartino? Joe asked himself for the hundredth time. How could he ever have hit her?

Just asking that question means you've changed, buddy, Pete had told him in the counseling session he'd requested when he'd accompanied Taylor to New York the week before.

They entered the back room, filled with crinoline, taffeta and lace. Rosa sat at a sewing machine, while his mother did some needlework by hand on a couch. Neither spoke to the other.

"Hi, Ma."

"Joey." Grace smiled broadly at her son.

"Rosa," Joe said.

Rosa looked up from her costume. In the weeks since Sam had left, Rosa had gone from scared to resigned to, surprisingly, somewhat hopeful. The counseling sessions with Carol Lopez had helped, along with finding out she could take care of herself and her family, though money was a problem. "Hi, Joe." She smiled pleasantly. At least she didn't look at him like he was Bluebeard anymore.

"I need to talk to you."

Rosa glanced at Grace. "All right."

"You can use the office," Annie said.

"No, stay right here." Grace stood. "I want to ask Suzie something." With a brief squeeze of Joe's arm, she scurried out the door.

Annie stepped toward the door. "I'll leave, too."

"Wait." Rosa threw back her shoulders. "This is about Sam, isn't it?"

Joe nodded.

"Then I want Annie to stay."

Joe came further into the room. "Sam's back in town."

Rosa's mouth fell open.

"I saw him going into Zip's Bar and Grill."

Swallowing hard, Rosa stared over Joe's shoulder. "I thought he'd be arrested if he came back. Linc pressed charges . . ."

Linc had pressed charges in order to have Sam picked up if he returned to town. The ever-optimistic reverend intended to use the threat of legal repercussions to bargain with Sam about getting help. Joe didn't feel very confident about the plan, though.

Crossing to the sewing machine, Joe knelt down beside Rosa. "Did you get the locks changed on the house, like I suggested, Rosa?"

Slowly she shook her head.

"Does that mean you didn't get the restraining order, either?"

"No. I didn't." She glanced guiltily at Annie. "But since Linc pressed charges, won't the police take care of this?"

"I called the police. By the time they got to Zip's, Sam was gone."

"Oh, no."

Joe stood up. "All right. Let's deal with one thing at a time. If Sam comes home, you and the kids are in danger."

"Oh, Lord."

"Is there anyplace you can go tonight?"

Slowly she shook her head. Joe's heart clenched. Had Annie been through this alone? He knew she hadn't told Linc or Beth or Margo about the abuse. His insides knotted.

"Won't the police keep watch?" Rosa asked.

"They'll patrol the area, but I doubt someone will stay there with you."

"She can come to my house." Annie's voice was a little shaky.

Joe pivoted. "I don't think that's a good idea. You and the kids could be in danger if Sam figures out where his family is."

"That's highly unlikely, isn't it?"

"I'm not taking chances with your safety, Annie." Torn, he glanced at Rosa. "But I can come back to the house with you . . . stay until the morning, when we can change the locks on

Rosa's place and get an RO. In the meantime, the police might pick him up."

Rosa shook her head. "I don't want to be any trouble to you two."

Annie crossed to her and took her hands. "Rosa, we're not leaving you alone in this. Joe's plan is good. We'll go back to your house, get the kids and you'll stay with me tonight."

"What will we tell them all?"

"We'll think of something." She glanced at Joe. "How should we go about this?"

"Let's lock up here. Suz and Ma can go home. You and Rosa and I can go get her kids. We'll stop by my place so I can pick up some clothes, then we'll head on over to your house."

"Sounds like a plan," she said lightly.

Rosa's face was glum. "I'm sorry."

Joe circled around swiftly. "No, Rosa. This isn't your fault!"

"Yes, it is." Everybody faced the doorway. Grace stood with her hands clasped in front of her. "You shouldn't interfere between a man and his wife."

"Oh, Ma." Joe shook his head. "Somebody should always interfere."

"It isn't right."

"It's not only right, it's necessary." Joe took in a deep breath. "Somebody should have interfered with you and Pa."

"Hush." Grace clapped her hand over her mouth.

Joe glanced at Annie. Then Rosa. Guilt, and disgust, welled within him. He turned back to his mother. "And somebody should have interfered with me and Annie."

"I don't believe it." Though her words were a denial, her eyes indicated otherwise.

"Believe it, Ma. It's true."

Grace froze in the doorway. Joe made a quick decision. He turned apologetic eyes on Annie and Rosa. "Could you excuse us for a moment? There's something I have to do. I've put it off long enough."

Wide-eyed, Annie said, "Of course, we'll be in the office," and ushered Rosa out of the room.

Stepping aside, Grace crossed to a machine, sat down and began running some shiny red material through the needles. Her brow was knit with concentration.

He spoke gently. "Ma?"

"This fabric is so slippery," she said, not looking at him. "It isn't taking the thread well."

Slowly, he went to her. "Ma, we need to talk."

"Annie always picks the prettiest things. But sometimes she isn't real practical."

Determined not to take the coward's way out, Joe crouched down next to his mother. "Ma, I can't let this go any longer. We have to talk about Pa. And me."

She kept staring down, threading the fabric through, frowning.

Gently, he touched her arm. "Please stop for a minute. We have to do this."

At first she didn't seem to have heard him. Then, slowly, she eased up on the sewing-machine pedal. Folding her hands in her lap, she kept her eyes downcast. Joe took her hands in his. Her skin was papery thin, lined with blue veins. It was ice cold, too.

"What Pa did to you," Joe began hoarsely, "was unconscionable. No man has a right to do that to a woman."

Still nothing.

"Pa was wrong, Ma; nothing was your fault."

Finally she looked at him. Her face was ravaged. "He . . . he said it was."

"Abusers always blame the abused. It's part of the cycle."

Grace bit her lip. "You . . . you really didn't do those things to Annie, did you, son?"

Foolishly, he'd thought the big hurdles were behind him. He had no idea how much it would hurt to confess his sins to his mother. Still, if he could change her thinking . . . "Yes, Ma, I did unspeakable things to her. Things I'm so ashamed of I cry about them."

"Men don't cry, Joey."

"Yeah, Ma, we do. Especially when we have such despicable actions to regret."

She looked away again. "Why'd you do it? Why did your Pa?"

He sighed. "Aw, Ma, I don't know why Pa did it. Maybe he was as frustrated as I was." He clasped her hands tighter. "I always felt suffocated in this town."

"You were smart."

"Yeah, I was. But I blew my life, and when I couldn't take care of Annie like I wanted to, I turned violent."

"Your father was smart, too. Nobody knew that."

Joe shook his head. So many parallels. He just held his mother's hands, saying nothing, trying to keep his emotions in check. Abusers sought out sympathy, to take the attention away from the ones they hurt. Joe struggled for composure, though he wanted to bawl like a baby in his mother's arms.

Finally, Grace said, "I shouldn't have blamed Annie."

"No, Ma, you shouldn't have. Not Rosa either."

A beleaguered sigh.

"Maybe you did because if you admitted they aren't to blame, you'd have to admit you weren't either."

Again, she looked at him, clearly puzzled. "Why wouldn't I want to know that?"

"Because then you'd have to deal with why you let it go on."

"I shouldn't have." Her voice was tinged with anger.

"No, Ma, you shouldn't have. No woman should. Ever. Under any circumstances."

She reached out and brushed her hand down his hair. "You're different."

"Oh, yeah. I am. I'm better. I'd never hurt Annie, or any woman, ever again."

"I'm glad." She picked up the material. "Now, scoot. I've got to finish this costume."

He stood, then, and stared down at her as the machine began to hum and buzz. Leaning over, he kissed her hair, said, "I love you, Ma," and left Grace alone to deal with her memories.

THE clock chimed three times in Annie's living room. Joe thought about getting up to turn it off, but quiet wouldn't make any difference. He was beyond sleep. Sprawled out on her comfortable nubby couch, the smell of clean sheets and freshly laundered pillowcases surrounding him, Joe felt anything but clean and fresh. The drama with Sam DeMartino had soiled *him* again.

And then, confessing to his mother—God, he was wiped out.

Throwing off the covers, he got up and headed for the kitchen. He'd make some hot chocolate, or even coffee now. Inside the big remodeled room—Annie had done a great job with the house—he fished out a pan, found milk in the fridge and poured it to heat on the gas stove. He knew microwaving was easier, but

Annie had always made it this way, and he needed the comfort of ritual.

No one had spoken much on the drive to Rosa's, where they'd easily convinced the kids that there was some kind of gas leak in the house and wouldn't it be fun to sleep over with Faith and Matt. The four kids had been ecstatic to have overnight company on a school night, and no one seemed to be the wiser.

Joe knew that, eventually, a frank talk with the DeMartino children was in order, but not during a crisis like this.

When the milk bubbled and its sweet scent permeated the air, he poured it into real cocoa, added sugar and stirred. Picking up the mug, he crossed to the window to gaze out over the yard. Suddenly he was assaulted by a memory. . . . Annie, fixing him hot chocolate, sexy and cute in a little lace nightgown, after they'd made sweet and tender love. Once again, he was blown away by what he'd had and lost. All that love and trust . . .

"Can't sleep?"

He whirled around, sloshing the drink on his hand. He licked it off. She was standing in the doorway, dressed in a long plaid flannel robe. He wondered what she wore under it these days. He ducked his head. "Yeah, I can't sleep. Did I wake you?"

"No, I can't sleep either." She eyed him. "Aren't you cold?"

"Cold?"

She indicated what he wore—only low-slung blue sweatpants and a sheepish expression. "No, but I'll put on a shirt if it bothers you."

"It doesn't bother me." She crossed to the stove. "Can I have some?"

"Uh-huh." He watched her graceful movements. She was every inch the dancer even as she went about routine tasks. Had he ever appreciated how delicate she was, how fluid?

"What are you thinking about?" she asked as she turned around.

He lied. "That maybe I jumped the gun. Sam didn't show here."

Annie glanced at the clock. "The night isn't over. But you're probably right. Still, we don't know if he went to their house."

"I was going to call the police station when it got light."

"Hmm." She sank into a chair at the table. He hesitated, then joined her.

How many times had he sat across from her like this, in the

early hours of the morning when one of them couldn't sleep? They'd trade jokes, tell stories about the kids and keep the loneliness at bay. Did she remember any of the good times?

"You okay?" she asked softly.

He shrugged. "Yeah, sure."

Annie shook her head. "How did it go with your mother?"

"All right, I guess. I hope I did the right thing by forcing the issue."

She smiled. "You're a good counselor. Everybody says so. And I've seen you in action on the Council. I'm sure your instincts were right to set things straight with her."

He stared at her bleakly.

"What?" she asked.

"Am I ever going to set things straight with you?"

"I believe you've changed, Joe. That's enough, isn't it?"

"I wish."

"What do you mean?"

"I wish it were that simple."

She cocked her head. God, he couldn't do this. He thought he could. Pete and Taylor both advised him to ask her. To face this last truth—to slay this last dragon. But he didn't think he was capable of accepting the utter horror—and result—of his actions. Abandoning his cocoa, he stood and went back to the window.

"Joe, what is it?"

His hands clenched at his sides. "Nothing."

"You're lying."

He remained silent.

She came up behind him. He was surprised she got so close. "What is it?" she repeated.

Still, he couldn't ask. Until he felt a hand on his shoulder. Some of the pain blurred, some of the guilt abated. And some of his hard-won courage surfaced. "There's . . . there's something . . . I need . . . to know. About Faith."

"Faith?"

Oh, God. It would be easier to ask her with his back to her. But he was done hiding from self-truths. So he turned around. To face it, and her, head-on. "Annie, I know . . . I've never forgotten what I did that night."

She stilled. He didn't have to say which night.

Her eyes were wide and liquid. They sparkled like aged brandy in this light. "I remember, too."

"Was it . . . was Faith . . ." He bit his lip, unsure if he could continue. "Was that the night we made Faith?"

"Oh, Joe." Her face shone with something he couldn't name. "Is that what you've been thinking since you came back and found out about her?"

He could only nod his head.

"No, no it wasn't. I was pregnant that night. I already knew."

The stark words erased one guilt but unearthed another. "Oh, God, you were pregnant and I . . ."

She looked away. He swallowed hard. Relief overwhelmed him, but so did the shame at what he'd done to this woman. His knees weakened, and he grabbed onto the chair at his side.

"Joe, I . . ."

He lifted his fingers to her mouth. "Shh. Don't say anything. I'm . . . I'm glad." He searched her face. "Don't try to comfort me. I wasn't the one abused. I don't deserve to feel better about it."

She raised her hand to his wrist. He was shocked when she didn't fling him off; instead she caressed it tenderly. "I think you do deserve to feel better. I think you've changed. It's time to let go of all this, on both our parts."

He could feel the tears prickle beneath his lids. He willed them back. He would not solicit sympathy. He would not put that burden on her like before, when he'd been the one in the wrong. "Do you mean that?"

"Yes." She looked around. "We're both different people now. Let's put it all behind us."

Struggling for control, he averted his gaze. He heard the clock strike again four times. The refrigerator turned on. A branch beat against the window outside. Finally he could meet her gaze. "All right. I want to do that. For all our sakes. Let me just say one more thing."

She nodded.

He moved his hand to grasp hers—to link their fingers. "I'm sorry, Annie." He brought their clasped hands to his mouth and kissed hers gently. "I'm so, so sorry."

TWENTY-SIX

FOR the very last time, Beth pulled into Doc's driveway to drop Ronny off. It was the middle of May, and next week the car would go to the track garage where, under Doc's supervision, the remainder of the work would be done. Ronny could get to the track by foot or bus, so she wouldn't have contact with Tucker anymore. As had been the case most of the week before, she wouldn't even have to see him. The notion weighed like a concrete block in her heart.

"Mom? I said goodbye."

"Oh, I'm coming inside a minute. I want to talk to Doc."

Ronny shrugged. He was preoccupied.

"Is anything wrong?" she asked, before he opened the door.

"No."

"Is Mr. Johnson doing all right?"

"Yeah, Lily and I went to see him yesterday. Poor guy, though, he can hardly get around. And his wife's got this new baby. I feel bad for him."

"Maybe you could go help him on the days you don't have community service."

"I gotta work at the diner."

"You can go to your teacher's. I'll figure something out." She smiled. "It would be good for you and for Mr. Johnson." She stared at the house. "Let's go."

Exiting the car, Ron headed down the sidewalk to the back of the cottage that faced the lake; Beth followed his long strides, thinking again of how grown-up he was. Her own steps were slow, and she told herself to buck up. Things in her life were fine. Linc was on the mend, though with this injury a grumpy side of him had surfaced that Beth had never seen before. She smiled, thinking of her sainted brother acting like a cranky baby. Jane Meachum had been around a lot to soothe him.

And Ron seemed good, though worried about Mr. Johnson a little. The rest of his life was going smoothly, though.

Margo and Annie were both unusually quiet these days, but they said nothing was wrong. Oh, hell, maybe it was just *her* depression . . . over Tucker.

The day was warm, so the bay to the garage was open. Beth stopped when she saw the men inside. Tucker was bent over the engine, his long lean form clothed in denim shorts, Docksiders and a ragged gray T-shirt with an oil logo on it.

Doc was standing by Tucker, directing his actions like a crew chief over his pit. "Gall darn it, Tucker, you ain't got it right yet."

Tucker let go with a few colorful curses.

"Hi, Doc." Ron smiled at the old man.

Tucker's head came up fast. "Geez, I didn't know you'd be comin' in with the boy, Beth. Sorry." There was a grease mark across his cheek, which was turning red. But his green eyes drank her in with pure male thirst.

"It's okay." Beth smiled. "I wanted to talk to Doc."

All three men looked at her quizzically.

"In private?" Doc asked.

"No. Here's good." She smoothed down the hem of the light-blue blouse she wore over tan chinos. "Remember what you asked me a few weeks ago? About Ron?"

"Uh-huh." Doc ran a hand over his gray brush cut. "I thought you decided no. I didn't tell him 'bout it, Beth."

"I realize that. He can go, Doc. If it's not too late. I thought you'd like to be the one to tell him."

Doc's grin was megawatt, making Beth realize he'd probably been quite a lady killer in his youth. "You just made me 'bout the happiest man in the world, girl. Bless your heart."

Beth shrugged. "There's one condition."

"What?"

"That Tucker goes, too. Not that I don't trust you, Doc. But I worry about your health. I don't want Ron alone with you if something happened. For both your sakes, there should be another adult along."

Doc's eyes twinkled. Not much got past him. "Uh, yeah, that'd be real awful for the kid if we was alone and somethin' happened."

"Mom, what're you talking about?" Ron's mouth turned down in an impatient scowl.

Tucker eyed her, then Doc. "What you cookin' up, old man?"

Ambling over to the bench, Doc plopped down, stretched his legs out in front of him and linked his hands behind his neck. "I asked Beth here if Ronny could come to the Indy with us."

Beth watched her son. His face blanked, then his eyes widened like they used to on Christmas morning. The vision of him in red footed pajamas in front of the tree was juxtaposed to his six feet of denim and jersey poised before the race car. "You gotta be kiddin' me." He faced her, his hopeful look piercing her mother's heart. "Mom?"

"No, I'm not kidding. Doc asked a while ago. I needed to think about it."

"You hate racing. Why would you let me go to the biggest race of the year?"

"I realized I can't keep you away from the sport, Ronny. I'm hoping, though, that Doc can lure you into the technical end. He said there were some designers and mechanics going to the Indy that he wanted to introduce you to."

Tucker tapped the wrench he held into his palm. He didn't look angry. Just suspicious. When all eyes focused on him, he said, "I'm not goin' to the Indy, Beth."

"Oh, well then, I guess the deal's off."

Ron whirled around to Tucker. "Man, Tucker. I gotta go. I wanted to do this all my life. Please."

Grass-green eyes narrowed on her over the boy's shoulder, then landed on Doc; Tucker said, "This isn't exactly fair, you guys."

"Life ain't fair, boy. You know that better'n anybody." Doc stood. "Come on, Ron. Let's go into the house and let your mama talk to the boss man, here. I'll boot up the Indy site and show you some of the designin' gatherings we could go to." He turned to Beth. "How many days can he be gone?"

"He's got a four-day weekend. Maybe he could miss one day of school."

Doc and Ron did high fives, and Doc clapped Ron on the back as they headed into the house. Beth heard them mumble something about chassis specialists and engineering wonders.

Hiding a smile, she faced Tucker. Still he didn't look mad. "Hmm, I do believe Bonnie Parker's plum full of surprises these days."

"Is she?"

"Yep. I think I've just been flimflammed." His face softened. "How are you?"

"I'm okay."

He shot a guilty glance to the door, but said anyway, "I miss seein' you."

"I miss you, too."

He angled his head to the house. "Why'd you do this, honey?"

Once again, her throat clogged at the endearment. "I've been thinking about a lot of things since Linc got hurt. Life's so short, Tucker. Some things can't be changed, like you and me, but some can. Ronny should have this experience with Doc and you."

"I can't go, Beth."

"Why?"

"I never go any more."

"That's not an answer."

He shook his head.

"Listen, you and Ronny are starting to get closer. This would be good for both of you. Ronny might finally get over his resentment of you about his father's death if you had some quality time together." She smiled lovingly. "And maybe you'd lose the rest of that guilt you're still carrying around."

"You've already helped me get rid of most of it."

"I'm glad. So Ronny can finish the job." She looked at him beseechingly. "Go, Tucker, for both your sakes."

Tucker couldn't help it. He crossed to her and lifted his hand to cradle her cheek. His fingertips and palm were rough with calluses. "I reckon I can't deny you anything, you know that."

"Unfortunately, I do." For a moment she leaned into his touch, then stepped back. "But it's yours and Ron's relationship that's important here. Concentrate on that." She turned. "Tell Ron I said goodbye."

"Will you be pickin' him up?" *Will I see you again?*

She shook her head, facing away from him. Her hair was down around her shoulders, kissing her neck and back. He wanted to go to her, hold her, put his mouth on her, more than he wanted to take his next breath.

"No, I won't be picking him up. I'm . . . busy. Lily's coming to get him."

The *I'm busy* set off some primal male alarm. "You're busy?"

"Yes." Still, she was turned away.

"Doin' what?"

"Tucker, don't—"

His voice raised of its own accord. He didn't like the feel of this. "What, Beth?"

Sighing, she circled around. "I've got a date with Roman Becker."

He swallowed hard and just stared at her.

"And if you know what's good for you, for us, you'll start dating, too. Tara Snow, maybe. We both know she's interested."

He wanted to beg her to say she didn't mean this. At the very least to promise him she wouldn't let Becker touch her. The thought of the lawyer's slick hands on his woman made him tighten his grip on the wrench. He felt all riled up and depressed at the same time. But he'd learned from his past that you couldn't make relationships something they weren't just by wantin' it.

"I've got to go." With one last look, she pivoted, stepped into the pretty May day, and left him.

For a minute he stood there frozen, staring out at the lake, listening to the water lap onto the shore. Then he turned and hurled the wrench to the side of the garage. It hit paint cans with enough velocity to tumble several to the ground. Their tinny sound reverberated through the bay.

"What's going on?" he heard behind him. Ron's voice was concerned.

"Nothin'."

A very long pause. "Look, if you're mad about the Indy . . ." Ron's tone was so little-boyish it drained some of Tucker's anger.

"No, I'm not mad about the Indy."

"You gonna go?"

Was he? He stared after Beth. A ludicrous thought came to him. If he couldn't have a relationship with her, maybe he'd settle for one with her son. "Yeah, kid, I'm gonna go."

Another long silence. "Thanks, Tucker."

"You're welcome." Still facing away, he stared at the jumbled paint cans, absently noting the black drips down the side of one. "Go ask Doc what he wants you to do today, okay?"

"Okay." He thought Ron left, then heard the kid say, "You sure you're all right?"

"Uh-huh. Just go."

When he was alone, Tucker crossed to the bench. Dropping down, he buried his face in his hands. How in hell would he make it through tonight with the images of her and Becker torturing his brain?

Just like you did all those years when Ralph Pearson rejected you. Ignored you. Blank your mind, Quaid.

Taking in a deep breath, he summoned The Menace. If he ever needed his alter ego's stoicism, it was right now.

RON couldn't believe he was at the Indy! Over the past few days, he'd had to pinch himself to be sure this was real. From their VIP seats, he stared out at the two-and-a-half-mile track of the famous Indianapolis Speedway known as the Brickyard. It felt like Christmas, his birthday and the first day of summer rolled into one.

"Havin' a good time, kid?" Doc asked above the din of the thirty-some-thousand crowd. Both he and Tucker were dressed like bums in jeans and T-shirts, with Indy 500 racing caps and dark glasses. When Ron had asked why, Doc had rolled his eyes and said they wanted to be *incognito*.

"You kiddin'? This is the best day of my life." Ron breathed in the May air, heavy with the smell of gasoline, burning rubber, popcorn and hot dogs. He glanced down at the T-shirt he wore which read, *#52 Quaid/Holt Daytona 500 1990*. Doc had made him change his shirt when Ron came out wearing one that said, *Some days it's not worth chewing through the leather strap in the morning.* Ron didn't mind changing; he was getting sick of his nasty sayings.

From down below, two pretty young women spotted them. One called out, "Oh, there he is. Mr. Quaid, will you sign this?"

Ron saw Tucker's face redden. With a phony smile, he bent over the railing, took the pen and paper offered and signed his name. Geez, Ron didn't get the guy. Once word spread that The

Menace was here, he'd been pestered for autographs. But it was clear that Tucker shied away from the attention.

He liked the races, though. Ron could tell by how he smiled when they'd watched the qualifying rounds and pre-Indy events. Pure joy was painted all over The Menace's face. It made Ron feel a little sorry for him—like he'd lost a big part of his life when he'd given up the sport.

As he stared out at the warm-ups on the track, Ron remembered Doc's candid words two nights before, when they'd talked in their palace of a hotel suite after Tucker had gone to bed. One of the things Ron liked most about this weekend was the guy-time he had with Tucker and Doc and the guy-things they did— drinking orange juice right out of the carton, not watching their language and staying up late to shoot the shit.

That night, Ron talked to Doc about Tucker. "Why's he so . . . I dunno . . . modest about his success, Doc? Next to Richard Petty, he's the biggest legend in NASCAR racing."

Slouched in a chair, Doc was eating peanut butter almond ice cream from a round carton, now that Tucker had gone to bed and he couldn't bitch about the cholesterol. "Not sure you wanna go there, boy."

"Whadaya mean?"

Doc stared at him as he munched on the nuts. "Can I talk to you, man-to-man?"

"Yeah, sure."

Straightening, Doc had set the container on the table in front of him. He leaned over and faced Ron. "It's 'cause of your daddy, Ron. Tucker ain't never been the same since then. . . ."

Ron hadn't ever thought about the accident from Tucker's point of view. It hit him today as he watched the Indy that driving was a dangerous sport. Crashes happened for a zillion reasons. And for the very first time, Ron had begun to feel guilty for blaming Tucker for his father's death.

"Ronny, look." Tucker leaned over and slid his arm around Ron's shoulder—like a father might—as he pointed to a driver who'd just come onto the track and was waving to a gone-wild crowd. "Know who that is?"

"Oh, geez. Scott Goodyear. Sammy'll freak out." Ron grinned. "Think I can get his autograph?"

Tucker and Doc grinned at each other. They'd been doing that a lot this weekend. "I think Doc can manage it."

"Why?"

Tucker laughed. "Racin's a tight sport, kid. Goodyear's crew chief's an old buddy of Doc's."

"Man, you guys are gods in this sport, aren't you?"

That got a chuckle out of both men. It felt good, to be with them, and not just because they were famous. Not just because they were men on an all-guy weekend.

Ron was beginning to see they liked him.

And he liked them, too.

TUCKER leaned back in the bar and watched the boy. They'd let him come in this place because Doc wanted him to talk to some technical guys, but Tucker had told Ron he'd wallop him but good if he so much as touched a beer.

Ronny had rolled his eyes, made some smart-ass comment about not being a baby, but Tucker noticed he stayed away from the hooch. Right now he was talking to Eddie Cheever's crew chief and Buddy Lazier's designer.

"He's havin' a good time." Tucker took a long sip of his Budweiser and watched the boy like a proud papa.

"Yeah." Doc eyed Tucker. "He ain't the only one."

Tucker ducked his head. "All right, old man. You made your point. I had a good time."

Leaning over, Doc braced his arms on the table. "Seein' the big race ain't eatin' you up, is it? Like you thought it would?"

Tucker shook his head.

"How come?"

"I reckon maybe because of him." He nodded to Ron.

"He don't hate you no more, Tuck."

"I know." Tucker's grin was little-boyish. "Feels good."

Doc watched him. "You should have kids."

"I'm forty-three. I figure it's a little late for that." Tucker's gaze hooked on Ron again. "Sometimes I wish..." Tucker caught himself before he finished.

"... he was yours?"

Tucker shook off the thought. "Nah. What'd I do with a bratty teenager?"

"Seems you been doin' okay." Doc scowled. "But Tuck... it ain't that simple."

"I know."

Doc sipped his beer. "How is she?"

Tucker gave him his Menace look.

"Don't pull that shit on me."

Angling his head away, Tucker thought of the calls he'd made to Beth. He didn't know Doc had overheard them. "I was just checkin' to see if she was okay. All alone for five days."

She'd been okay, except for those in-laws she'd had to deal with. Seems when they got back from Europe and came to see Ron, the Donovans had thrown a conniption fit when Beth had told them she'd let Ron go to the Indy, with him and Doc. Geez . . .

"Ya gotta let her go, boy." Doc glanced at Ron. "Especially since you made so much headway with the kid. No tellin' what he'd be thinkin' if you hooked up with his mama now, after all your denials, after gettin' tight with him. He might get the notion that you bein' nice to him to get to her."

Tucker stood. "I know. I already thought of that." He downed the last of his beer. "I'm goin' back to the hotel. See ya later."

He left the bar without saying goodbye to Ron. This was all nuts. He and Ronny had gotten close, but where the hell had the idea about being the kid's daddy come from? For Christ's sake, *that* was a crazy thought.

"WHERE'S Doc?" Ron shuffled barefoot into the living room of their Marriott suite sipping a soda. The boy was still revved from all the excitement, but his face showed no lines of strain, or rebelliousness, anymore. Tucker was pleased as all get-out.

"He turned in. The pace finally caught up with the old buzzard." Tucker was leafing through some of the crew chief/designer material the guys, at Doc's request, had deluged Ron with. And it seemed to be working. Ron had taken a keen interest in that end of the business.

Sinking onto the couch, the kid plopped his feet up on the coffee table. "I can't believe I got to meet A. J. Foyt and Mario Andretti today after the race."

Tucker smiled. "Didn't know Doc had so many ins in this business, did ya?"

"You, too."

"Nah, the real pros are the designers and crew chiefs."

Like a typical teenager, Ron snorted. "I *got* the message already." He took a bead on Tucker. "It's called overkill."

"You're right." Tucker picked up the Indy program. "Your mama's just worried, is all. You gotta make your own choices." Tucker shrugged. They'd done all they could.

Silence. Rustling. Over the top of the program, he could see Ron thumbing through the magazine. After several minutes, Ron said, "Tucker?"

"Hmm." He didn't look up.

"I gotta tell you something."

"Shoot." Still, he concentrated on the magazine.

"Since you came to Glen Oaks, I been treating you like shit."

That drew Tucker's gaze. He stared at the boy for a long time. "Way I see it, I deserved some of it."

"Mom says that's not true."

"Your mama's too forgivin'."

"No, she's not."

"Huh?"

"I watched those cars today. I saw them jockeying for place. The crashes. I didn't understand it then, you know, when my dad died, but now, I see it's the way the game is played. Crashes are nobody's fault."

"I guess you could look at it like that."

"What I'm sayin' is, I don't hold you responsible for my father's death anymore."

Tucker felt like somebody stuck a sock in his throat. "No?"

"And Mom's right, you shouldn't feel you are either."

"Maybe. Your mama's pretty convincing." A vision came to Tucker. Beth, standing before him, so sure that first night at the police station. *For the record, I don't blame you for Danny's death, and if it makes a difference, I wish you wouldn't blame yourself.*

Ron stood and stretched. "So, we square on this?"

"Yeah, kid, we're square."

"I'm gonna hit the sack, then."

"Okay."

"Oh, and . . . thanks for takin' me here."

"You're welcome."

The kid crossed to his bedroom. At the door he turned. " 'Night, Tucker."

" 'Night, kid." As the door closed, Tucker lazed back on the couch and closed his eyes. He felt a mite like he'd taken the checkered flag himself that day.

"So they're due back any time, Bethy?" Linc sat in a booth with Beth, looking more rested but still out-of-sorts. Wearing a dark blue shirt and khaki jeans, he adjusted his arm, which, despite the lighter, more mobile cast, was still aggravating. And his inability to be Superman minister was making him antsy.

"Uh-huh." She glanced at the door. "I really missed him."

"Him?"

Beth's face colored. "Ronny."

"Hmm."

She fidgeted with the light-pink scoop-necked shirt she wore over jeans. She had *not* fussed with her appearance that day just because she might see Tucker. "It's over between us, Linc. Not that anything was really going on. Just feelings."

"Feelings are pretty powerful."

"Speaking of which . . . have you talked to Margo?"

"Nope. She won't return my calls. I'm worried." He waited. "You called her lately?"

"Yeah, yesterday. You know how she is when she doesn't want to talk. She babbled on a mile a minute about nothing."

"By the very fact that she won't talk to me, we know something's going on with her. Damn it, she always did have that stubborn Ma Barker streak in her."

"I'm sorry, Linc."

He shook his head as the diner door flew open.

Beth didn't know exactly what she expected from Ronny's weekend at the Indy with Doc and Tucker, but it wasn't that they would return to Glen Oaks like conquering heroes back from war. All three of them swaggered into the diner, jostling each other, and making guy remarks. When they came close, she drawled, "Well, I hope they at least showered in the last five days."

Ron rubbed his scratchy beard. "Looks good, doesn't it, Mom?" He leaned over and kissed her.

"Ouch." She soothed her jaw. But she kissed him back. She *had* missed him.

"Hi, Linc." Ron's color was high and his eyes danced. "How's the arm?"

"It itches." Linc smiled at Ron. "You forget to pack your razor?"

Doc had drawn up to the booth. "We had a pact. No shavin'. But we did bathe, ma'am." He glanced at Tucker. "Didn't we?"

"Yeah, sure." Tucker winked at Ron. "I think we did, anyway."

Rolling her eyes, Beth matched their grins. "I saw the race on TV. It was exciting. Especially at the end." She was trying very hard to keep her eyes off Tucker. With a few days growth of beard, in his racing cap and jeans and a T-shirt, he looked so good her body tingled at his nearness. Instead she focused on the obvious closeness among the three men.

"I can't believe I was there, Mom. You shoulda seen how these guys were treated. Like royalty."

Doc said, "That's a stretch." He glanced around the diner. "Gerty here?"

"No. She went home."

"Just as well," he said, scrubbing his hand over his beard.

"Come on, old man, I'll get you cleaned up before you see your girl." He smiled at Beth. "Thanks for lettin' us take Ronny."

Beth nodded. She longed to touch him. Just for a second.

Doc turned to Ron. He held out his hand and Ron gave him one of those handclasps that was more of a gesture of affection than a shake. "Good to have you along, boy."

"Thanks, Doc. I'll never forget it."

Doc gave him a sideways glance. "Be careful what you tell your mama about."

Ron looked at him quizzically.

"You know, 'bout those naked dancin' girls."

Ron laughed.

Tucker had stood back. When Doc eased away, he approached Ron and held out his hand, too. "Take care, kid."

It was like a freeze-frame in a movie. Ron looked at Tucker for a long moment, then glanced at his outstretched hand. And as Beth watched, her son bypassed the hand and enveloped Tucker in bear hug usually reserved for her, Margo, Annie or maybe Linc.

Tucker's face showed surprise as he clasped Ronny back. Then his eyes closed as if he was savoring the moment. Finally he drew back, and without a word, left the diner.

Ron watched him go. Hands stuck in the pockets of his jeans,

his back to Linc and Beth, he stared after Tucker. Then he turned
to his mother. "I gotta tell you something."

Willing back the emotion, she said, "What, honey?"

"I know it wasn't his fault."

Nobody needed to ask *what*.

Finally Linc spoke. "Good. It's important to know that."

"There's something else."

"What?" Beth asked.

"I jumped the gun accusing you and him of . . . that something was going on. I hated him at first, that's why I didn't want
it to happen."

"Okay, honey."

"But later, I was afraid he was being nice to me, just to get to
you. Just to make you like him."

"Tucker likes you for yourself, Ronny. So does Doc."

"I guess. I mean, it was pretty clear this weekend. I'm just trying to apologize for believing it was something else. Something
to do with you."

Bravely, like she'd had to face everything in her life, she said,
"It wasn't me, honey. It was you."

"I know." He leaned over and kissed her again. "Thanks for
being honest. And patient."

She gripped her coffee cup. "You're welcome."

"Can I go over to Lily's?" he asked, all teenage boy now.

"If you shave first."

"Naw. I want her to see this." He rubbed his jaw.

"Okay. I'll drive you."

"No, I'll call her from the office. She can come and get me."

Beth nodded, grateful when he disappeared into the kitchen.
She let down her guard with a big sigh. "So, I guess that's
that." She stared after her son. "I can't risk anything with Tucker
because Ron seems to need him now, more than me."

Linc reached over and took her hand. "I'm sorry, Bonnie."

"It's okay. I knew it before, anyway. This just confirms it."

"Reality sucks, though, doesn't it?"

"Yeah, it sucks. Big-time."

TWENTY-SEVEN

———

JOE slowed to a stop on the sidewalk in front of Annie's house and absorbed the sight of her in the front swing, wearing a light gray DanceWorks fleece shirt and shorts, reading a book. A cup of coffee lay within reach on the small table. The birds chirped around him, and the smell of newly mowed grass and summer flowers filled the air. "Well, if that isn't *the life of Riley*, I don't know what is."

Smiling, Annie looked up. "Please. Stop with the sayings. I can't bear any more." She straightened and motioned for him to come up to the porch. Every morning, regardless of how many had passed, he waited for the invitation. He'd run like the dickens around town, then cool down and mosey on by here. He was sweaty and grimy, but she didn't seem to care. He jogged up the few steps.

"Coffee, or water first?"

"Both. I can get them."

"Nope, sit." She stood and, setting her book down, darted into the house.

While she was inside, he did a few leg stretches, and reveled in the beautiful June morning. *Take your pleasure where you can, Joe. It's important.* Thankfully, he'd learned to heed Pete's words and was grateful for the day, as well as Annie's kindness.

"Here you are." She handed him a huge tumblerful of ice

water and set his coffee on the table beside hers. The mugs knocked against each other; there was something about them nestled together that made his heart catch.

"Thanks." He sipped the water, staring out over the grass. "Lawn looks good."

"Thanks for planting those bushes. You and Matt did a good job."

Joe gave her a long-suffering look. "How *is* the Grinch who stole Christmas today?"

Annie smiled, despite the fact that she too was worried about their suddenly moody son who didn't want to talk much these days and seemed reluctant to spend time with his father. She settled back onto the swing. "Still asleep. Faith's up, though."

Joe dropped down onto a comfortable wicker chair. "Oh, good. Maybe we can cook breakfast together." Since that morning with Rosa, Joe had stopped by every day after his run to see the kids. About a week before, he'd started cooking breakfast when Annie admitted she didn't relish preparing that meal.

Unfortunately, it was also three weeks ago that Matt had clammed up. He wasn't overtly hostile, just reserved and unhappy.

"Sorry. Faith's already eaten. Rosa's picking her up any minute for the end-of-the-year picnic at the playground today."

"Ah." He glanced up at his son's window. "So, I probably won't have any takers for my mystery omelette, will I?"

She wasn't fooled by his light humor. "You're on the rack about him, aren't you?"

Joe nodded. "I just can't figure it out. Ever since the episode with Sam DeMartino. . . . You sure Matt isn't upset that I spent the night here?"

"Joe, you were gone by the time he got up. But even if he did know you stayed over, why would that be a big enough thing to make him pout all these weeks?"

"I don't know." He swallowed hard.

Annie shrugged. "Maybe it's just typical adolescent angst." Again the mischievous little grin. "You need to *roll with the punches,* Dad."

His eyes narrowed on her, then he reached out for the book she'd been reading. Its title was *Behind the Words.* "No, fair," he said, unconsciously parroting Faith. "You guys got a new book."

"I—"

"Dad-dy." A cyclone in pink and white whirled out the door and into his arms. He hugged Faith ardently, tweaked her nose and tugged at the straps on her overalls. "Aren't you the *Eager Beaver* this morning." Joe and his daughter vied for who could get a saying in first. Mostly he let her win. Today, he felt the urge to tease her.

"No fair." She scanned him. "You don't exactly *smell like a rose,* Daddy."

"Hey, quick thinking, sweetheart."

A car pulled into the driveway. "Here's Lisa." Climbing off his lap, Faith pulled on a pink Barbie backpack and added purple sunglasses to her bright outfit. "I got a picnic today."

He yanked on her pigtails, grateful for her constant love. And ever since Annie had told him the truth about her conception, he thanked God every day for that gift. "I know. I hope you have fun."

"Will you pick me up?"

As always, he glanced at Annie for approval. She nodded. "Sure. What time?"

Telling him one o'clock, Faith scrambled to the steps and bumped into Rosa. "I'm ready, Mrs. DeMartino."

"Okay, honey, get in the car. I want to say hi to your mom and dad."

Joe noted Rosa looked tired today. But at least the haunted expression was gone from her eyes. "Good morning."

Annie and Joe exchanged greetings with her. "You all right, Rosa?" Joe asked.

"Yeah." She glanced at the car and lowered her voice. "We heard from Sam last night."

Alert, Joe straightened. "Is he in town?" The police had not arrested Sam that night three weeks before; Rosa had changed the locks and gotten a restraining order, but he hadn't been heard from since.

"No, he's upstate with his brother. There's a racetrack there where he's working."

"Linc can have the police arrest him up there."

Rosa shook her head. "I don't want that, not if he doesn't bother us again."

"Think this through, Rosa. You need to consider all the angles."

"I will." She smiled when the horn tooted. "I'll talk to you later." The demure woman descended the steps. Joe stared after her, gripping the chair's edge.

"She reminds you of it, doesn't she?" Annie's voice was soft.

"Every time I see her." He drew in a deep breath. "But it's important not to forget."

"Maybe." Annie breathed in the morning air. "But not today. It's too beautiful out."

Today. Mention of the significant date made him go still.

She got up to sit on the thin porch railing. "The weather was just like this fifteen years ago today."

"Yes, it was."

"But it wouldn't have mattered. I couldn't wait to marry you."

He closed his eyes briefly, picturing her in the delicate lace and satin that graced her body. Seeing her eyes brim with love and acceptance, both of which he'd betrayed. The feeling of loss washed over him, threatened to drown him.

Reaching up, she pulled on a tree branch. The yellow forsythia blossoms gleamed in the sun. Several fell onto her. She shook her head to dislodge them.

He crossed to her and brushed the petals from her hair. She smiled, and his hand laced through the thick strands.

From the corner of his eye, he saw the newspaper delivery boy ride by on his bike and, like an NBA player, vigorously toss the *Gazette* to the porch. The loud thud against the front door startled Annie. She tipped backward and he grasped reflexively onto her hair to keep her from falling.

"Ouch," she said as she grabbed onto the railing.

"Leave her alone!" The youthful voice was followed by a slap of the screen door.

Startled, Joe turned.

Matt's eyes focused on Joe's hand in Annie's hair; then he flew across the porch and grabbed onto his father. He said raggedly, "I won't let you hurt her, ever again."

Ever again.

Joe stared at the anger and contempt in his son's eyes. Ludicrously, the phrase *driving a stake through his heart* ran through his head; it couldn't have been more appropriate.

"He wasn't hurting me, Matt."

Matt's gaze swung from Joe to Annie. "Tommy says that's what his mother told *him,* too."

"Tommy?" Annie gulped back a gasp.

There was a long, ugly pause. "I know, Mom." He raked Joe with a disgusted glance. "Tommy heard Dad and his mother talking. He told me all about it that night he stayed over." Like a grown man, Matt held Joe's gaze. "I know what you did to my mother."

ANNIE watched Joe deflate. His strong shoulders slumped, and his six-foot-plus height seemed to dwindle. She glanced at her son, whose stance, on the contrary, had become taller, more belligerent. Her little defender, come to rescue her. It made her so sad her heart ached in her chest.

"Matt," Joe finally said. "We need to talk about this."

"I don't want to talk about it." He looked at his mother. "You okay?"

"Yes. Your father wasn't hurting me, Matt," she repeated.

"I'm going in." The boy turned to leave.

Joe just stood there, like a condemned man, watching his son.

But Annie sprang to her feet and grabbed Matt's arm before he got inside. She tugged hard. "Wait, Matt."

He stopped.

"Come and sit out here for a minute."

"I don't want to."

"Well I want you to." When he hesitated, she said, "As your father can testify, you can't squelch your feelings. They'll surface somehow. Maybe in ways you don't mean, or you don't like."

Matt whirled around. "Aren't you mad at him?"

Thoughtfully, she stared at the almost-man before her. What she said to him could be crucial to his health and well-being for all his life. "I was. For a very long time."

"Yeah, well, so am I."

"That's okay. But you should be mad at the person who left here six years ago, not the one standing before you."

Again Matt scanned Joe with disgust. "He's the same man."

"No, honey, he's not."

Annie could see the deep doubt on her son's face. But behind it, in his Murphy eyes, also flared the need, the *desire* to believe in his father.

She looked to Joe. His expression was stone-cold blank. He was shell-shocked. "Joe, you need to talk to him."

As if coming out of a trance, Joe straightened. "Of course." He focused on Matt. "Is this what's been bothering you for the last few weeks?"

Matt nodded.

"I wish you'd told me."

No response.

"But it doesn't matter. What matters is that you understand what happened. Why it was so wrong." Joe drew in a deep breath, more in control now. "And the fact that I've changed."

Right before their eyes, Matt became a little boy again. He looked down at his feet and kicked his bare toe on the porch decking. "I read about it."

Joe tensed again. "You did?"

"Uh-huh. There's sites on the Internet."

"Oh, Matt," Annie said. "I wish you'd talked to *me*."

He didn't look at her. Instead, he raised his eyes to his father. "It says men don't change easy. It's inside them. How do we know you won't turn back into that man again?"

For the first time in the five months he'd been back, Joe's face revealed doubt. Annie remembered Linc's comment. *He struggles with the Jekyll and Hyde idea all the time.* From somewhere inside her, the need to help him surfaced.

When he still didn't answer, she intervened. "You're right, honey, abusive men don't change without a lot of help. Maybe if your dad explains what he went through when he left here, and the years of help he got, you'll believe he *has* changed."

Matt's expression was torn. "Do you believe him, Mom?"

He takes his cues from you, Annie, Linc had warned her.

Annie studied Joe. She got a flashback of him, on this very day, fifteen years before, dressed in a black tux and an irreverent smile. Clearly, he was so different now from that cocky twenty-two-year-old. "Yes, Matt." She locked her gaze with Joe's. "I believe he's changed."

JOEY, please don't hurt me. . . .
Your wife has a dislocated shoulder and severe bruising. . . .
You flirted with him. . . . I told you what would happen if you ever flirted with him again.
Your father's just grumpy because he's tired. . . .
Daddy, don't . . .

Joe forced the voices out of his head—they'd been there all morning, given free reign by Matt's accusations—as the noon sun beat down on him and his son. They sat under the umbrella table on the deck, partly shaded by that and the large oak whose branches hung over the railing. "So, what do you think?" Joe asked.

"It's better, I guess." Matt pushed away the last of his sandwich. Joe could tell he'd had about all he could handle. Though Joe insisted they take breaks, where they tossed around a baseball, Matt showered and Joe took a short walk to clear his head, he'd insisted on a marathon discussion with his son. But now it was over. Matt had to digest what had been said. He couldn't take in any more until he did.

"Let's stop now, buddy. I made my point. You've got a lot to think about." He reached over and squeezed Matt's shoulder. The only bright spot in this whole ugly thing had been that Matt didn't shrink from his touch, as Joe had thought he might. That and, of course, Annie's part in the morning. She'd given them time alone, but also partaken of the discussion when he asked her to, explaining her own long road to mental health. "I want to say one more thing, though. I think you should go for some counseling."

"Me? Why?"

"So you can say some things that you might not be able to say to me or your mom."

Matt's nose scrunched up. There were a few freckles on it, like Annie's. "I couldn't talk to a stranger about this."

"How about to Linc, then?"

"Linc knows?"

Joe nodded. "He knows the whole story."

"I guess I could talk to him."

"Good. I'll set something up."

Matt pushed back his chair and stood. "I'm going to my room for a while."

Joe nodded, suddenly overcome by a deep sadness. The results of his abuse had been so far-reaching, it threatened to level him. "Thanks for listening."

Matt shrugged. "It's okay." He turned, just as Annie came to the doorway. Matt took a few steps, then pivoted around. "Will, um, will I see you tonight? For practice?"

Forcing a smile, Joe said, *"Wild horses couldn't keep me away."*

Matt grinned at the phrase. Thought a minute. "Okay. I'll try to *lose this chip on my shoulder* by then."

Joe felt his body relax at the conciliatory retort. For three weeks, his son had refused to trade sayings with him and Faith. He watched as Matt hugged Annie, then disappeared into the house. Drained, Joe leaned into the cushions of his chair and stared at her. It was the first time they were alone since Matt had stumbled onto the porch this morning.

"I hope I did all right," he said softly. "I wasn't ready for that little ambush."

Her smile was sincere. "Oh, I think Billy the Kid handled it just fine."

"Do you, Belle?"

She looked after Matt and nodded. "I do. He'll be all right."

Joe wasn't so convinced. "I don't know. It's tough to come to grips with the fact that your father's a batterer."

Annie stared at him for a long time, then she whispered, "A *recovered* batterer. His father's a *recovered* batterer."

Joe just stared at her, unable to believe the absolute certainty in her tone. As the soft June breeze bathed them in its warmth, on their wedding anniversary, Joe marveled at the gift he'd just been given by his ex-wife.

TWENTY-EIGHT

———

RONNY sat in his bedroom, playing with Doc's homemade video game that ran circles around any professionally made game he'd ever seen. Margo had been impressed, too, when Doc had sent her a copy. She and Doc even talked on the phone about it.

Ron thought about calling Margo tonight, or Linc, but he'd been hanging around all day waiting for Lily to call, and he wanted to keep his phone line free.

His gaze landed on a picture of his mother, and his heart clutched. She hadn't been happy since the Indy. First of all, his grandparents were on her case big-time about letting him go to the race with Tucker, and in general about the way she brought him up. Finally, Ron himself had told them to leave her alone.

But more than that was bothering Bonnie Parker. It was as if some life had been sucked out of her. Over the weeks, Ron had remembered similar behavior from the time his dad died. Even at seven, he'd sensed the phony front she'd put on then. Like now. And he remembered hearing her cry, the same as he'd heard her a couple of times this week.

He didn't know why, though. Any more than he knew why Lily was acting so weird. *She'd* been an ice maiden lately. She'd stopped returning his calls a week before graduation, and when they were together, she wouldn't let him touch her. He asked to

see her tonight to straighten things out, but she said she'd call if
she could see him.

He wished he had a guy to talk to about this. Linking his
hands behind his head, staring at the ceiling with its faint plaster
swirls, he thought about Tucker. Ron could talk to him. They'd
shared lots of things these past few weeks, besides working on
the race car, which had been a real kick. Tucker had told racing
stories, but also talked about his own life, growing up without a
dad, like Ron had.

The only thing was, Tucker seemed sad these days, too. Ron
frowned. Tucker was sad. His mom was sad. He wondered
if . . . the phone rang, dragging him from the line of thinking. He
was glad. Bounding off the bed, he reached it on the second ring.

"Hello."

"Ronny?" It was Lily.

"Lily? Are you okay? You sound upset."

"I'm not okay." Her voice cracked. "I'm . . ." She broke off,
started to cry. "I'm . . . Ronny, please, come and get me."

"Get you? Where are you?"

"I'm at the lake. At Maze's cottage." Before he could respond,
she added, "There was a note in my locker to come here. . . . I
thought it was from you. . . . Loose . . . and Maze . . . they aren't
being nice, Ronny."

Ron froze. She was with Loose and Maze? Those guys had
been acting crazy for weeks. Ever since Mr. Johnson was hurt.
Loose had yelled nasty things to Lily in the hall, and he'd left
filthy notes in her locker. Sammy said Maze had pushed him
around when he was hanging out at the drugstore. They'd left
Ron alone, except for the glaring looks Loose sent his way in the
cafeteria.

Suddenly, Ron heard pounding in the background. ". . . Open
up, bitch. . . ."

"Lily?"

"Oh, God, no, they woke up."

"Woke up? Lily what's going on?"

"Ronny, please, come . . ."

". . . spread your . . ."

"Lily?" He panicked. *"Lily?"*

"Ron—"

The phone went dead. For a second he stared at it. Shit!
Dropping the receiver, he crossed to the dresser, found the

keys to his father's Harley that he kept tuned and ready to go in the garage, and bounded downstairs. He tore out of the house, jumped on the motorcycle, and turned the key. Its engine growled to life. Fast, he sped out into the dark night. It was strange being on the bike after so long. He forced himself to slow down. Officer Pratt would love to catch him driving, and nobody'd believe him about Lily.

Tucker would.

The thought stayed with Ron as he drove out of the town limits, where, once on the open road, he let it rip. Staring into the oncoming traffic, the headlights hurting his eyes, his mind whirred with thoughts. Lily was in trouble. Maze and Loose were with her. And they were dangerous. He knew it in his gut.

As he neared the turnoff to Doc's cottage, he realized he couldn't take on those two, especially if they were carryin' their weapons of choice—knives. He hadn't even *thought* to bring his, he'd been without it for so long. And suddenly Ron was afraid.

Oh, God, Ron wished his father were alive.

He glanced at the road leading to Tucker.

But maybe . . .

"HOW much farther is it?" Tucker asked, concentrating on the winding lake road; the pitch-black night was broken only by the beam of the headlights of Doc's Mustang. Tucker's heart thrummed in his chest.

"About a half mile." The kid's voice was hoarse with worry.

He couldn't reassure Ron. He was still reeling from the unexpected visit. Tucker had been asleep—dreaming about Beth. When the kid pounded on the door, Tucker threw on jeans and a T-shirt and, once he'd heard the story, a light jacket. Together, they'd flown out the door. "You sure your mama isn't gonna know you took the bike? I wouldn't want her worryin'."

"No, she's out on a date with that Becker guy. She said they were going to a late movie after dinner."

Forcefully Tucker pushed the thought from his head. He had more to worry about right now. Later he'd consider what the woman he loved was doing with another guy tonight.

Ron said, "I'll kill them if they hurt her."

"Hang on, son, we're almost there." Tucker hadn't thought about calling the police until he and Ron were on their way to

Maze's cottage. Then, he realized he'd left his cell phone back on his dresser. He was afraid to stop to call and lose time.

They pulled into the driveway in the back of the posh house on an acre lot facing Glenora Lake. Ron bolted out of the car before Tucker cut the engine. They hustled around front.

"Wait, Ron." Tucker grabbed the boy's arm just as he lifted it to pound on the wooden front door. "Let's take a look inside, first." He nodded to a bank of floor-to-ceiling windows facing the water.

He and Ron ducked into the shadows and crept to the windows. The blinds were open, revealing the interior. Sure enough, they were there. Loose lounged in a chair, his foot draped over the arm of it, a glass of booze in one hand, a joint in the other. He was staring at Lily, who sat on the couch, looking small and fragile.

Another boy appeared in the doorway. His swagger was enough to alert Tucker, even if the girl hadn't gasped. Maze carried some rope—and yanked on it menacingly. Lily backed up in her chair.

And Ron went ballistic. "No-o-o . . ." he shouted and began to batter the window.

The three people in the house stilled. Maze and Loose whirled toward the windows. Lily started to cry.

Tucker noticed a screen door to the left. "This way."

They ran to the door, pulled it open and were inside the garage, then the kitchen, in seconds. Tucker heard voices to the left and raced toward them with Ron behind.

Loose and Maze were at the window, their backs to Tucker and Ron. Tucker was thanking his lucky stars for the surprise edge this would give them when Lily gasped again.

And Maze and Loose circled around.

Each boy held a knife in his hand. Their faces were wildly animated, their eyes glassy. Their bodies had an unnatural edginess to them.

"Well, well, well, if it isn't Batman and Robin." Maze laughed and wielded his knife. "I'd like to carve me up some fuckin' bird right now, wouldn't you, Loose?" He crouched, narrowed his eyes. "Shall we take care of the dickheads?"

Loose's eyes gleamed brightly. "Looks like these boys need a lesson, Maze my man. Just like good ol' Johnson."

Tucker kept his mouth shut and assessed the situation. "Lily," he said inching toward the girl. "Get outside."

Lily froze.

"Now!"

She scrambled off the couch and out the living-room door.

"Ron, take off your jacket and wrap it around your arm." As Tucker did the same, he watched Maze and Loose come toward them.

They lunged simultaneously.

From the corner of his eye, Tucker saw Maze tackle Ron just as Loose dove for Tucker. Tucker did a quick sidestep, and Loose banged headfirst into the wall. The knife clattered to the floor and Tucker reached for a straight chair next to him. Lifting it high, he hit Loose on the back and the boy slumped into a heap.

A crashing behind him made Tucker whirl around. Ron had fallen back and hit his head hard; Maze hurled himself on top of him. Tucker flew across the room into Maze, knocking him off Ron. Maze fell to the floor, still clutching the knife. Tucker straddled him, and gripped his hand. He yanked on it, but the knife didn't budge. Tucker got a quick glimpse of the boy's eyes up close—they were frenzied, and his face was flaming. The kid was high on something, giving him unusual strength. Tucker was as strong as a bull, but Maze held him off.

With a huge surge of strength, Maze bucked, and Tucker fell off of him to the floor. The boy towered above him on his knees, and raised the knife. Tucker rolled to the side just as the blade came down, slicing the edge of the beefy part of his hand. He cried out and rolled completely away.

A huge metal object came down on Maze's head and the boy slumped onto the rug. Lily Hanson stood over him, holding a bloody statue that had graced an end table.

In the background, Tucker heard the whir of sirens.

MUCH as she had that night five months before, Beth flew into the police station just past twelve. Like last time, Linc accompanied her. After the cops had called him, he'd found her at the movies with Roman. All they knew was that Tucker and Ron had been involved in some kind of incident at the lake with Loose and Maze, but they were all right. Still, her heart beat a frantic tattoo of worry.

Pushing the door to the holding area open, she halted. Again, just like before, Tucker was seated at the table sipping a cup of coffee. His face was bruised, and he had a bandage wound around his hand. Scanning the rest of the room, she saw her son sitting on a couch; plastering an ice bag to his forehead was Lily Hanson. Both kids looked up, as did Tucker.

Ron stood. "Mom, we're all right. Don't panic."

"I'm not panicking." Giving Tucker a quick once-over, she crossed to Ron. "Are you sure you're okay?" She studied him. "That's a nasty bump."

"I'm all right. Tucker's hand is hurt, though. He should have it looked at."

Linc had gone to Tucker and sat down with him.

"I'm fine," Tucker grumbled "It's not very deep." He grinned, and the pain in Beth's chest eased. "I don't need no doctorin'."

"What happened?" Linc asked.

Ron automatically looked to Tucker. Like he might to his dad.

Tucker smiled affectionately at her son. "Apparently, Maze and Loose got our girl Lily here up to the lake on false pretenses—that Ronny was there waitin' for her. They had . . . ah . . . unhealthy motives in mind. She called Ronny, who went charging out like some knight in shining armor. He stopped along the way to pick me up."

Beth stared at him as if he was speaking Greek.

"Anyway, we got all set to rescue the little lady. After a scuffle, seems she coldcocked one of the scoundrels with a statue of Aphrodite."

Ron smiled. Lily gave a watery grin. Linc chuckled.

And Beth realized she loved Tucker Quaid. For what he'd done for her son—she was sure he'd been instrumental in the rescue. And for lightening up the charged moment to calm everyone down.

She reached up and hugged Ron. "I'm just glad you're all right."

"I wouldn't be if it wasn't for Tucker," he said hoarsely.

Beth glanced over at Tucker. He looked sore and tired. He winked at her, then got up and headed to the coffeepot, moving slowly, without his usual athletic grace. He made a solitary figure who had nobody to care about him as much as she cared about Ron, as Linc and she cared about each other.

Until now.

In that moment, it became crystal clear to Beth that that part of The Menace's life was over.

Squeezing Ron's hand, she stepped away and crossed to Tucker. His back was to her so he didn't hear her come up to him. When he circled around, he was so surprised to see her close, the coffee sloshed onto his hand. He jolted from the hot splash of liquid. Beth took the cup from him, and set it aside; reaching for a napkin, she wiped the spill from his hand.

Then, not letting go, she pulled him to her.

In front of Lily, Linc and Ron, she enveloped Tucker in the biggest, best hug she'd ever given anybody in her life.

Then, taking his hand again, she pivoted and looked at her son. "Ron, I have something to tell you."

THE cocoa was hot and steaming as his mother took the pan from the stove and poured it into mugs which had been his father's. They were Glen Oaks track mugs with a sleek race car on the front. It reminded Ron of Tucker's Jag.

His mother faced him; her pretty brown eyes narrowed when she got another good look at his face. Still dressed up from her date in a red skirt and top, she scowled. "You sure you don't want more ice on that?"

"The damage is done, Mom. It is what it is."

She took in a deep breath. She hadn't gotten the chance to tell him what she wanted to say at the police station. Officer Pratt had interrupted them, but it didn't take a rocket scientist to figure out where she was going.

Picking up his cup, he sipped the warm chocolate brew. It took him back years; he thought of all the cocoa he'd shared with his mother like this. She'd always been there for him. "This is about you and Tucker, isn't it?"

She nodded. He noticed the sadness was gone from her eyes.

"You haven't been straight with me, have you?"

"In some ways, not. I meant what I said a few months ago about there not being anything between me and Tucker. There wasn't then, except some feelings we were both trying to . . . quell."

"But you couldn't."

She shook her head. "Instead, they've grown."

"I could tell. Tonight. You were as worried about him as you were about me."

"Oh, honey, no one could ever take my affections away from you."

Ron rolled his eyes. "I know that, Mom. Geez, whadaya think I am, a baby?"

"No, honey, I don't. But I want to be sure you know that nobody could ever change what I feel for you." She hesitated. "Or what I felt for your dad, either. I loved him very much."

"Do you . . . um, like . . . feel the same way about Tucker?"

"No, I feel very differently about Tucker than I did your father. But I do love him, Ron."

He drew in a deep breath. The demons battered in his brain to get out. Insecurity. Fear. Old grudges.

"What are you thinking?"

"Nothin' much."

She gave him her best stern-mother look. "Ronny, you've got to have faith in yourself that Doc's and Tucker's attitude toward you has nothing to do with me."

"I know it here," he said pointing to his head.

"Well, you need to understand it here, then." She laid her hand over his chest. "Think about the time and attention they've given you. I know it had nothing to do with me, but you've got to find that answer in your own heart."

"What are you gonna do now? I mean, about Tucker?"

"I don't know, exactly. I know what I'm *not* going to do. I'm not going to force this relationship on you too fast." She stared at him hard. "But I'm not giving him up, either. I lost one man I loved to death. I'm not going to lose another without a fight."

"Old Bonnie Parker surfaces, hey Mom?"

Her smile was good to see. "Maybe." She reached over and grasped his hand. "I love you, honey. I'll always love you. But life's so short." She glanced at the picture of his dad on the counter. "We both know that. And you've done a wonderful job of turning yours around. I just hope you can . . ." She drew back and didn't finish. She glanced at the clock again. "It's late. Let's go to bed now and sleep on this. There's no hurry in making any decisions tonight."

Bed sounded good to Ron. He stood and stared down at her. At the woman who had been there for him for every single second of his life. Through all the shit he'd pulled and all the trouble he'd gotten into. He owed her, big-time.

"I love you, Mom. Thanks. For always being there for me."

"I love you, too. And you're welcome."

He left her then, but the vision of her sitting alone in the kitchen, by herself, with only his father's picture backdropped behind her, stayed with him for a long time.

TWENTY-NINE

MARGO hadn't seen Philip since her disclosure to Jack the Thursday before. Now, as she strode into the CEO's office where Philip was standing by the window staring out and one of the company lawyers sat off to the side, her pulse raced. She realized it was *Showdown at the OK Corral* time.

Well, she of all people, the engineer formerly known as Ma Barker, was up to it. Dressed somberly in a black suit and crisp white blouse, she nodded to Jack when he looked up from his desk. "Hello, Margo."

Turning quickly, Philip stared at her. She'd expected some kind of response—anger, guilt, disbelief. Instead, his face was blank, his eyes a flat blue. Cordially, he said, "Margo." His voice was frigid, that of a man facing a divorce lawyer or a doctor with bad news.

"Philip."

The lawyer gave her a terse greeting. Jack looked troubled. His face was taut with stress, and the shadows under his eyes betrayed sleeplessness. She was sorry such a good man had to deal with this offensive situation. He indicated the chairs. "Let's all sit down."

Both Margo and Philip sat, as they had so many times in this very room, on the chairs facing the CEO, next to each other.

Jack addressed Margo. "For the purposes of expediency and

to make this as comfortable as possible, I'll outline your charges and Philip's response to them. Is that all right with you?"

"Yes."

He picked up papers from an open folder on his desk. "First, you contend Philip behaved inappropriately in Boston. Philip denies the charge. He did confess that while you were there, he told you that he felt you two were getting too close and he wouldn't spend as much time with you anymore, that it wasn't good given the fact that he's married."

"That's not—"

Jack held up his hand. "Please, let me finish. You've had your say, Margo, and he deserves his."

Nodding, she forced her clasped hands to relax.

"As for the charges that he held your work over your head, perhaps caused or allowed some of these deadline/attention things to happen, he states that the contrary is true. Because of the fact that he cares about you—and he doesn't deny that—he's tried to cover for you."

Jack looked even more weary. "In general, Margo, Philip's position is that he acted ethically." The CEO sat back in his chair. "As you can see, his stance is contrary to the statements you made."

When no more was forthcoming, she spoke. "I'd like to ask some questions."

"Go ahead."

"Did Philip say why I'd jeopardize my career if none of this is true?"

Jack nodded. "I think he should answer that."

Philip faced her. "I have no idea why you'd turn on me like this. We've been close for eight years. As I told you in Boston, too close. Was that it, Margo? We got too close, and when I wouldn't take it further you couldn't handle it?"

"How can you say that? You know it didn't happen that way."

A muscle in his jaw leapt. "Of course it did. And I told you I was sorry, but Sally and the girls were too important to me to jeopardize my relationship with them—for you."

"I can't believe this." She looked at the ceiling. "That isn't how it happened at all."

Philip shot Jack a look of male bemusement. His big, powerful shoulders shrugged underneath navy wool. "I don't know what else to say, Jack."

"Margo?" Jack's voice was kind, but unhappy.

"I don't know what else to say, either, except I'm sticking to my facts. Philip has sabotaged my work. Period."

Jack looked to the lawyer, who finally spoke.

"Then there's nowhere to go with this but to put a memo in each of your files documenting the complaint. If either of you is ever involved in this kind of thing again, it will be there as prior evidence."

She cocked her head. "I can see your point." She faced Jack. "But I'm meeting with my own lawyer tomorrow. If her advice is to drop it, I probably will. If not"—she stood and smoothed down her skirt—"I guess, as they say, I'll see you in court." Turning, she walked to the door.

"Margo?" Jack's voice held traces of exasperation. "I haven't finished yet."

She pivoted. "Yes?"

"I want to tell you something else." He glanced at the lawyer, who nodded.

"What?"

"I'm offering you the vice presidency of engineering."

That took the wind out of her sails. *"What?"* She just stared at him. "Why? After all this, I thought . . ."

Again the lawyer spoke. "Yes, I'm sure you did. And I'm sure your lawyer would have a field day with that news. The job's yours, if you want it."

Your lawyer would have a field day . . . She addressed Jack. "Let me get this straight. You're offering me the VP of engineering so I can't prove any discrimination on your part?"

"Of course not. I'm offering you the VP of engineering because, as I've said openly and documented, by the way, you've had an impeccable record at CompuQuest up till now, and you're the best choice for the job."

Ah, life. It was so strange. For years she'd dreamed of this moment and how happy she'd feel. Instead, the whole thing was tainted. For some reason she thought of Linc. What would he do with this turn of events?

He'd tell you to tell them to fuck off.

She smiled.

"Margo? Are you happy about this appointment?"

She shook her head. "No, Jack, I'm not happy about this appointment."

He blew out a heavy breath. "I think we can put this unfortunate misunderstanding behind us, if we all try."

Unfortunate misunderstanding? Oh, brother! "How long do I have to decide?"

"Decide?"

"If I want the vice presidency?"

Jack's eyebrows arched. "Oh, well, take as long as you like."

"Fine. I'll let you know." Margo gave the two men one last look and strode out of the office.

Geraldine wasn't at her desk. Margo was glad she didn't have to face the woman. She needed to think about what had just transpired in Jack's office. She wished she could call Linc. Get his take on it. But she wouldn't. She needed to work this out by herself, like a lot of things lately.

Funny, though, she didn't feel so alone anymore. She felt centered, as if she had roots. As if she had . . . help.

Linc? God, maybe.

Nah, it couldn't be that.

"HI, babe." Linc spoke into the telephone and frowned at the receiver. "If you're there, please pick up."

No answer.

"All right. Then I'll have my say this way. It's damned stupid that you won't talk to me. I love you. I want to know if you're all right. How can you cut me off like this?" He paced his office. Swore. "All right, I know it's been tense between us. But we can work it out." He waited. Then heard a *b-e-e-e-p*.

"Shit!" He looked at the phone. "Well, I'm not giving up."

He punched redial.

"This is Margo. Leave a message."

"This is Linc, *babe*." The endearment was less tender this time. "Don't you get it? I'm not giving up. I love you. We can work this out. I need you in my life, Margo. We need each other." He kicked an innocent wastebasket he happened to walk by. "Okay, okay, I know we haven't been able to do this the right way since I became a minister. But breaking my arm has given me a lot of time to think. I've decided we've been going at it the wrong way. We need to . . ." He thought for a minute. *B-e-e-e-p*.

The curse was worse this time. Apologizing to God for his language, he pressed redial again. "You're not getting rid of me,

Margo. I was saying we need to commit to each other. We were meant to be together." He swallowed hard. "I think we should make love again. We both know why we've been holding off, and it's stupid. You can't take me away from God. And I can't browbeat you into accepting Him. We're old enough to make good decisions and . . ." *B-e-e-e-p.*

Linc pounded the phone on his desk before he called back. "This is the last time! Look, we can have a long-distance relationship. You don't have to live here. Stay in the city. Keep your job and your fancy apartment. We'll just be together when we can." He knew time was running out. He gave a quick prayer to God and ended with, "Marry me, Margo. I know we can make this work."

Linc stared at the phone as it gave another *B-e-e-e-p.* He replaced the receiver with a soft, "Please."

WITH a why-not-stay-and-take-them-for-what-they're-worth attitude, Margo accepted the vice presidency of engineering at CompuQuest. Dressed in an off-white pantsuit with a black silk shell underneath and high black sandals, she drew in a deep breath before she entered Philip's office. This was her first official top-level executive meeting since she'd taken the job.

And she felt good, really good, about that and a lot of things. It seemed like some burden, or some long fight to keep something at bay, was finally gone. The thing with Philip? Maybe. But she sensed it was more.

"Good morning," she said as she stepped in and found the men assembled around the huge oak table, much as she had that day she'd been here after their Deliverance weekend.

"Morning, Margo." Philip didn't look up from the file he was reading. He'd been treating her like The Invisible Man for the past three weeks, which was just fine with her. Then he scanned the six men at the table. "We're just waiting on Riley, right?"

The others nodded, welcomed Margo and chatted among themselves as they waited for the meeting to begin. Perfunctory remarks were addressed to her, but it was obvious she wasn't one of the boys.

You'll never *be one of the boys,* Linc would say with a cocky perusal of her body. Just the thought of his sexy looks made her flush.

I think we should make love again.

Marry me!

Margo hadn't seen or talked to him in almost a month. He called religiously, left her messages that were either devastatingly tender or so hot they made her ache.

Dumb, really dumb, she thought as the meeting began and she listened to the men discuss the latest products. Sure, she'd made some progress; she'd been thinking long and hard about her hangups with religion, as Linc had asked her to do, and she'd been doing a lot of reading. But she was still a far cry from believing she could ever be a minister's wife. However, when the distribution manager went into his usual harangue about impossible deadlines, she couldn't get her mind off Linc's latest call.

Why won't you talk to me? I think you need me. . . . I just have a feeling a lot's going on with you. . . .

Finally the meeting ended, and when she was gathering her things, Philip looked down the table. "Margo, could you stay a second?"

"All right." She glanced around, thinking she should ask someone else to stay, remembering her conversation with her own lawyer. . . .

He was wrong in what he did. You can see that, can't you? Margo had been adamant.

So had her lawyer. *Of course he was wrong. And believe it or not, most cases that come to me are hidden harassment like this; they're almost impossible to prove. My advice is to take the vice presidency and wring out of them what you can, then move on.* The woman had laughed. *And make sure you get a sizable raise. Money is great comfort.*

"Margo?"

She smiled perfunctorily. When she took the job, she knew working with Philip was one of the cons on her list. She thought of the thirty-thousand-dollar raise, compensation package and stock options she'd demanded and gotten. "Yes?"

He walked over and closed the door.

Not a good sign. But she'd be damned if she'd jump like a skittish colt around him. When she was fifteen, Ma Barker was eating guys like him for breakfast.

"I thought we should have a talk."

"I'm not so sure that's a good idea."

"Of course it is. Since you decided to stay."

"All right."

Giving her his most boyish grin, raking his hand through his perfectly cut hair without messing it, he said, "I'd like to put the past behind us. Start over."

"Why?" She folded her arms over her chest and watched him.

"Because we have to work together. Because we both made mistakes."

Say you've made a mistake, her practical side warned. *Even if you don't mean it. It'll go a long way in soothing things over.*

"The only mistake *I* made, Philip, was not reporting my suspicions sooner. Not getting some kind of proof."

"Jesus Christ, Margo, it's not like this was some kind of plot. I like you. I wanted more. I took a gamble and it didn't pay off."

"You just don't get it, do you?"

"I get that I might have been too up-front in my feelings for you. My marriage was in trouble, I was lonely. . . ."

She laughed at that. According to office gossip, he and Sally were having a second honeymoon. She came to town a few times a week for lunch or dinner, he took her on business trips, and the guys teased him constantly about his new wedded bliss.

And her treatment of Margo—sweet and innocent as before— revealed that Mrs. Philip Hathaway didn't have a clue to what had gone on. If Margo didn't know better, she'd think she'd dreamed the last five months of harassment.

"So, think we can be friends?"

She stared at Philip.

Play the game. Soothe feathers. What do you have to lose?

Your integrity, Linc would say.

"No, Philip, we can't be friends. We can be colleagues and work together, but I've got real friends, and you don't have a clue what that means."

Male pique suffused his classic features. "The minister, right?"

"And others, yes."

"You know, you're a coward."

"What?"

"You're a coward. You venture out into the real world, but you keep Grayson and those other buddies of yours as a safety net. As soon as you get scared or unhappy or lonely, you go running to them." He picked up a file. "Why don't you just move to Glen Oaks for good and forget the life you have in New York?

You're not happy with it anyway. Not really." He opened the file. "I've got work to do."

She didn't respond. She just stared at him, then turned and strode out of his office. Ignoring Geraldine, who treated her with barely concealed disdain these days, she sought solace in the elevator.

Once alone, she was suddenly faced with the truth.

In so many ways, Philip was right. She wasn't happy with her life. Since Linc had gotten hurt, she'd been thinking about priorities and what was most important to her. And she'd admitted that the people she was closest to, the people she wanted to spend her time with, were those she saw the least.

I wish you'd come back here to live. . . . God's not so bad.

Ronny's plea echoed in her mind all the way to her office. She loved him, she loved them all. But go back to Glen Oaks? Make a life there? With Linc? With God as a part of it?

Could Ma Barker really do that?

SHE'S not coming back, is she?

No answer.

Linc sat alone in a pew and stared at the cross behind the altar. The unique church scent of wood and incense surrounded him.

It's time to give up, isn't it?

Silence.

Damn it, God, answer me.

Prolonged silence. Well this was just great. Even God deserted him.

Oh, ye of little faith.

Linc breathed a sigh of relief.

I'd never desert you, Linc.

Like she has.

You're not going to get that out of me today.

Why?

I work in—

—mysterious ways. I know.

I will say you did the right thing with Jane.

I hated to hurt her.

Jane will be fine. I got my eye on this nice manager at the electronics plant for her. She wasn't for you, buddy.

Is anybody?

No trick questions.

He held up his uncasted arm. *My arm's better.* That *was a dirty trick, you know.*

You needed to slow down.

You're right. I did.

God took a moment of contented silence.

And thanks for what you've done for Rosa. And Annie.

You're welcome.

Is Bethy gonna be okay?

Bethy's gonna be just fine.

Linc stood. *Well, thanks. I'll talk to you later.*

He got to the sanctuary door when he heard, *Linc?*

Huh?

You'll be just fine, too. Trust me.

He smiled back over his shoulder at the cross. *That's good enough for me.*

ONE of the things Linc liked best about sitting on the altar before services was that he got an eagle-eye view of the entire congregation. As the organist played the introductory hymn, he scanned his people. God had a full house today. Every pew of the small sanctuary was occupied, which was good, because nearly everybody in Glen Oaks needed to hear the sermon today.

His sister sat in her usual seat about ten rows back to the left, next to Ron, who was flanked by Lily Hanson. Both Beth and her son looked happier than he'd seen them in a long time, and Linc knew that the past six months had brought them even closer than before. Ronny's eyes kept darting over to the left side of the church where Tucker sat with Doc and Gerty. Ron and Tucker had gotten tight since the incident with Maze.

Both Loose and Maze were being prosecuted for kidnapping and assault, and Linc had asked God this morning to help him find a way to break through to the boys. He'd never forget what it was like to be a teenager alone in this town and in trouble. He and Joe were getting together tomorrow to talk about what they might be able to do.

Behind Beth, Annie sat with Faith and Matt. Little Belle Star looked happy today, too. Linc felt a pang for Joe, though, who'd chosen a pew in the back of the church, alone. He'd come in after

Annie but hadn't joined her and the kids, or even his mother and Suzie.

Linc smiled and nodded when he caught Rosa DeMartino's eye. Sitting with her two children, and Anita Camp, Rosa smiled back. Linc hoped he'd made the right decision about not prosecuting Sam, at Rosa's request. She'd asked him to hold off after Sam had called and said he was residing in upstate New York and begged her and the kids to come to Watkins Glen to live. It was obvious he wanted her away from her support system. Rosa had refused, telling him she was staying in Glen Oaks and had a restraining order against him. She'd informed him that Linc would institute prosecution if he came back and threatened her. She'd also told him he could only see her or the kids if he got help first.

Sam had refused. Like most abusive men, Sam would not go for help. Nor would he recover. Joe Murphy was an exception.

Joe had flown up to see the man, but Joe didn't think their talk had done any good. Rosa seemed sad sometimes, but healthier and certainly more content. She was practically running Annie's summer dance program, which gave her much-needed self-confidence. And, of course, all the other women in the self-esteem group were supportive.

The hymn ended, and Linc stood to give the invocation, followed by the doxology, the children's sermon, and the prayer of joys and concerns. Then he began the sermon. "The title of today's talk is *Forgive Me Not*." He smiled at the sea of attentive faces before him. "Would you all turn to page forty-five in your pew Bibles while I read God's words on this subject? It's a familiar story, about the townspeople throwing stones at the adulterous woman."

Linc read the scripture and then turned calm eyes on the congregation. "What do we have to learn from this lesson on forgiveness? I'd like you all to call to mind two things: someone who has harmed you and someone you've harmed. It can be through direct actions that you've hurt someone, through negligence, through old grudges, through the inability to accept that someone has changed, or through fear. Now think about the stones you cast against this person: unkind words or even looks, inner resentment that can be felt every time you're around him or her, of your cold unwillingness to forgive. Those stones hurt more than real ones. Those stones leave more scars."

Then Linc went on to discuss the opposite, about needing others to forgive you. Finally he came to the last point. "Equally important is the need to forgive yourself for what you've done. Just as God asks the townspeople how they expect Him to forgive them if they don't forgive others, I ask you how you can forgive others if you don't forgive yourself." Linc gave them his best stern-minister look.

"Can we change this pattern? Of course. Forgiveness can go a long way in doing that. Forgive me and your friend or mother or sister for what they've done, now, today; forgive little and big slights and, forgive yourself for having done these things to others. It's time to throw *away* all the stones. God wants you to do this." He grinned at the congregation. "I know. He told me."

Linc sat down for the choir's hymn. Just before they began to sing, he heard God's voice. It was loud and clear. *Remember your own words, Linc. Forgive yourself.*

THIRTY

ON Sunday, at noon, Tucker popped the hood of his Jag and
stuck his head under it to investigate the rattle he'd heard coming home from church. He smiled, thinking about the Jag. Five
months before, this car had brought so many changes to his life,
and no matter what happened now, he'd never regret it. The early
summer breeze filtering in through the open bay bathed him in
warm weather. For the first time in a lot of years, he was looking
forward to the coming months.

"Car's lookin' good," he heard from the front of the garage.

Tucker's head snapped up. "Yeah, kid, it's as good as new."
Playfully he narrowed his eyes on the boy. "Don't have no knife
on you, do you?"

Ron grinned at the question. "Nah." He shuffled into the
garage, appearing young in baggy denim shorts and an Indy T-
shirt. Jamming his hands in his pockets, the boy studied the Jag,
then met Tucker's eyes. "I never said . . ." he scanned the garage.
". . . I mean, I never told you I was sorry about what I did to the
car."

Tucker straightened, gripping the wrench. "This comin' from
your uncle's sermon this morning?"

"Sort of. Other things, too."

Intrigued, Tucker set down the wrench and leaned back

against the side of the Jag. Crossing his arms over his own Indy T-shirt, he cocked his head. "Wanna tell me about it?"

Ronny held his gaze. "I was a shit about everything."

"You had reason."

"Not really. I just didn't know it, then."

Tucker nodded, feeling his heart swell at the reiteration of the fact that Ron did not hold him responsible for his daddy's death. That had gone a long way to helping him forgive himself. Hrrmph. Guess he'd listened to Linc's sermon, too. "You already told me this, kid."

"Yeah, well I wanted to say it again."

When Ron just stared at him and didn't say any more, Tucker asked, "Wanna stay around awhile and hang out? Doc's out in the boat with Gerty, but they won't be gone all day."

"No, Lily's waiting in the car. Her and Sammy and me are spending the day with Mr. Johnson at his cottage. The police found out that Loose and Maze had sabotaged Mr. Johnson's car. He's really lucky to be alive."

"How's he doin'?"

"Good. The physical therapy's really helping. Lily loves playing with his baby." Ron rolled his eyes. "Women."

Tucker chuckled.

"I gotta ask you something."

"Shoot."

"I want the truth."

"Scout's honor."

"Oh, yeah, I believe that one."

Sober, Tucker said, "I'll never lie to you, Ron. I promise. You can trust me."

The boy's eyes were wide with belief. "My mom? I wanna know . . . if you . . . if your . . ." He swallowed hard, his Adam's apple bobbing. "How do you feel about her, man?"

Tucker had talked to Beth on the phone every night since the incident with Maze and Loose. She'd told him she'd spoken frankly to Ron about her feelings for Tucker, and she'd made it clear she wasn't giving up on a relationship with him. Tucker had told her in return that he wouldn't do anything to jeopardize Ron's state of mind now, and they needed to hold off for awhile. But he wasn't giving up either. He'd tried to take solace in the hope they gave each other, but it was hard waiting to be together.

At Tucker's long hesitation, Ron shook his head. "You said you'd be honest."

"I love your mother, Ron."

"You mean it? Sometimes guys say that to chicks . . ." Ron didn't finish the thought. He didn't have to.

Tucker bit back a grin, wondering what Beth would think about her son calling her a *chick,* much less what she'd think about him coming out here asking after Tucker's intentions.

"I mean it." Tucker eyed him. "But we didn't lie to you, either. My feelings for her have nothin' to do with you."

"I know that. Lily said it was a stupid thing to think in the first place."

"We all do stupid things."

Ron shrugged. "I guess I should go."

Tucker nodded. "Thanks for comin' out here."

Slowly, Ron crossed to him and stuck out his hand. Tucker clasped it. They held on tight. Ron said, "My mom . . . She's home alone now. The diner closes at two on Sundays."

"I'll keep that in mind." He wondered how fast he could shower and drive to town.

Tucker watched Danny Donovan's son turn and leave the garage, his step light, his bearing easy, like an ordinary seventeen-year-old's should be. Just before he got out of sight, he turned back.

"So . . . I'll be seeing you around, right?"

"You'll be seein' me, son. That's a promise."

THE dream came, bathing her in its erotic shroud. Tucker was in her bedroom, sitting on the edge of her bed, brushing back her hair.

Turning to the side, she grasped his hand and brought it to her breast. His moan was loud and lusty and so sexy it made every part of her body hurt. She arched into his palm.

His touch intensified as he flicked a thumb over her bare nipple. It was her turn to moan. She felt his hand slide lower, caress her stomach, which he leaned over and kissed.

"Please . . . more," she whispered into the dreamy darkness. A male chuckle.

His hand went lower. He cupped her boldly.

She cried out. "Tucker!"

Then his mouth was at her ear. "Wake up darlin'. You're killin' me, here."

From outside of the dream, she could see her head move back and forth on the pillow. "No, no. Don't want to wake up."

Butterfly soft kisses on her cheek. A mouth on her neck.

She raised her hand and clasped his nape, anchoring him to her, trying madly to hold on to the dream.

It was the smell that woke her. The woodsy, just-applied, *very real* smell of aftershave.

She opened her eyes. "Oh, my God."

He drew back. His gaze was filled with an odd combination of lust and amusement. "Sweetheart, if you're this sexy asleep, I can't wait to get my hands on you when you're awake."

She glanced down her body, naked beneath the slipping sheet. Then she looked back up at him. Never in her life had she wanted a man more. "I . . ."

Standing, he dragged his blue and white striped dress shirt out of his navy pants. His big hands released one button on the placket, then two. "The door was unlocked. You should be more careful. No tellin' who'll come in and find you in bed, all lazy and warm, in the middle of a Sunday afternoon."

"Careful?" Her mouth went dry when the entire set of buttons was undone. Better than a Chippendale, he shrugged out of the shirt slowly. A mass of curly dark blond hair drew her gaze like a magnet. It dropped lower when his hands went to his belt.

"I locked up the house, of course," he said matter-of-factly.

Jingle, jingle. The belt was unfastened.

"And the bedroom door's locked, too, just to be safe."

"Safe?" she whispered hoarsely over the audible rasp of a zipper being undone.

"Hmm." Plop. Plop. Shoes hit the floor. "And I closed all the blinds and unplugged the phones."

His pants dropped to his feet revealing navy blue silk boxers. "We're all alone, Mary Elizabeth. Just you and me."

His thumbs hooked into the waistband of his shorts, he gave her an I'm-yours-baby look. She knew she should ask him something, but she couldn't think straight, could only stare at the road map of muscles rippling his chest, cording his arms and bare legs. All of him was lightly dusted with the dark blond hair, as if God had sprinkled it himself in just the right places.

"Don't stop there," she whispered achingly.

"Your son came to see me today." He eased the Calvin Kleins down an inch.

She swallowed hard. "Do I have a son?"

He chuckled and the sexy sound made her toes curl.

Another inch was bared. Oh, God.

"He asked me what my intentions were with you."

Her gaze flew to his face. "And you told him?"

"Not about this."

Her gaze dropped to *this*.

One more inch and he stopped. "Look at me, darlin'."

"I am, Tucker, oh, I am."

"Look at my face."

Reluctantly her gaze traveled up his body. She took pleasure in the way it flushed as she perused it.

His voice was husky as he said, "Before we do this . . ." He stared at her. "I want you to know I told Ron that I was in love with you, Beth."

"Tell me."

He smiled. Dropped his shorts, and stood before her eloquently aroused. After giving her a minute to look her fill, he whipped back the sheet, took his own sweet time letting his eyes travel over the contours, dips, and curves of her body, then placed a knee on the bed.

Finally, he covered her with his weight; he drew her arms up so they bracketed her head and linked his hands with hers. "I love you, Beth. The kid's okay with it now, but even if he wasn't, I didn't plan to let you go. I want to marry you." He bumped his middle with hers, giving her a sample of his impressive anatomy.

She bumped back. "Yes."

"Yes? Just like that?"

"Uh-huh. Don't take no time at all for Bonnie Parker to make up her mind, Mister."

Just before his mouth closed over hers, he whispered, "Good. Maybe we can work on a little brother or sister for Ronny."

Sexily, Beth smiled. "Ronny would like that."

Tucker smiled back. "So would The Menace."

"THIS is Margo, leave a message."

"Come on, honey, pick up." Sneakered feet propped up, Linc lounged back at his desk and stared at the wall, at the cross she'd given him. No answer. "Aw, hell, where are you at five o'clock on Sunday night? Do you realize you haven't talked to me in a month? I miss you, Mary Margaret."

Still no answer.

"You know, I feel like I'm having an affair with your answering machine." Under his breath, he murmured, "Is this like cybersex?"

He could swear he heard her chuckle. Geez, he was really losing it.

"I love you, damn it, and I'm not letting you go. I'll storm down to New York, throw you over my shoulder and drag you back here if I have to. Like I did when you and that freaky guy in college were planning to go cross country."

"I remember that." Her voice was husky.

"Oh, thank God." She'd picked up. "I'm mad at you, Margo."

"I'm sorry."

Something was wrong here. "You sound funny."

"You look funny sitting there with your feet up on your desk talking to an answering machine. The new jeans I bought you fit great, though."

His feet hit the floor with a thud, and Linc whirled around in the chair. His jaw dropped.

"Close your mouth, Rev, or you'll catch flies." Full of sass and dressed like sin, she lounged in his open doorway. Dusk was falling, and he devoured the sight of her. Black pants to just below her knees gave way to an expanse of shin and ended in three-inch mules. A leopard-skin Spandex top hugged her curves.

He wondered how quickly he could get the outfit off of her.

"Why have you been avoiding me?" he asked softly.

She sidled inside and closed the door. "It's a long story."

Standing, he walked toward her. Probably because of the look on his face, she backed up to the door. When he reached her, he snicked the lock and braced his hands on either side of her head, palms flat against the wood.

Then he took her mouth. It was a hot, sexy kiss that had her whimpering. His last thought before irrationality claimed him was that at least he still had the touch to send her up in flames.

The kiss went on a very long time. When he pulled back, her eyes were slumberous, her body soft and pliant.

"Come on, baby." He drew her to the couch. "Sit."

She sat.

He dropped down next to her. Taking her hand, he held on tight. "What's going on? You got me dyin' here."

"I'm sorry," she said sincerely. "I had a lot of thinking to do, and being with you confuses the issues."

He scowled. "What are the issues? What's been happening?"

"I quit my job."

"What?"

"I quit CompuQuest."

"Why?"

"I don't know where to start."

"I got all night." *The rest of my life.*

She tapped her do-me high heels on the floor. "You were right about Philip."

Son of a bitch. He forced himself to remember he was a man of God. And her stricken look softened him. "I'm sorry, sweetheart. I didn't want to be right."

Sighing heavily, she just stared at him.

"Did he force you out?"

"Nope. As a matter of fact, Jack Sheer asked me to reconsider when I handed in my resignation yesterday."

The information hurt. She'd made monumental decisions without consulting him. But hell, he got what he wanted so why did he care? "Start from the beginning."

She lay back on the cushions. He noted the smudges beneath her eyes and the lines of stress around her mouth. "It started just where you said it did. The pressure was all very subtle."

Still holding her hand—and *please God let me keep my big mouth shut*—he listened to her tell him about the remarks Philip made, the actions he took and the culmination which, ironically, led to her appointment as vice president of engineering.

"That's exactly what you wanted, Margo. I can't believe you threw it back in their faces."

"Neither could they." She sighed. "It feels good, though."

"Why'd you do it?"

"Because I realized I didn't want that life anymore. Good people like Jack Sheer are trapped by it. Even he can't do the right thing in a situation like this. It's an empty life. And unfulfilling."

Linc rubbed her hand with his thumb, noting the cut she had on her middle finger. He wondered how she'd gotten it. Oh, God, this was lame. He wanted to know every single thing there was to know about her. "So, where do we go from here?"

Her whole body tensed. "I'm not sure. I gotta tell you something else, before we decide."

Stoically, he readied himself for the emotional blow. *Please, God, let me handle this okay.*

"I . . . um . . ." She gave him a soulful look. And then, shockingly, her eyes filled.

He'd only seen her cry once before, when he'd told her he was going into the ministry. And, for the first time, Reverend Abraham Lincoln Grayson did not know what to do. He did not know how to give comfort to the woman whom he loved, next to God, more than anything else in the world. "Margo?"

She linked their fingers. "I heard your sermon this morning."

It was the last thing he expected. "What . . . where . . . I didn't see you."

"I stood behind that big bulletin board just outside the sanctuary."

The picture of her in this get-up, almost in church, blew him away. "Why did you come there?"

She smiled. "Do you know, I've never heard you preach before."

"What did you think?"

"You were wonderful. Inspiring. I'm sure you saved a lot of souls today."

"What about yours?"

He waited for her to say she didn't have a soul to save.

She didn't say it.

"Margo, tell me straight where your head's at. I can't deal with this any other way."

Drawing in a deep breath, she smiled through her wet, spiky lashes. "I love you, Linc."

"Aw, baby, I love you, too."

"I . . ." She gulped in a breath. "I want to be your wife."

"Oh, Mar—"

She put her fingers to his lips. "Shh. Let me finish. You need to know something else. It's about . . ." She paused as if heralding an important announcement. "It's about God."

Blood swam in his head. His vision blurred. He was, quite simply, in shock.

"You know that time you asked me to think about God?"

Somehow he managed to say, "Uh-huh."

"I did. And then, when you got hurt, I . . ." She shook her head. "This is so stupid, but I talked to Him."

His heart stopped beating, and his breath backstopped in his throat. His own eyes filled. Never in his whole life had he ever expected to hear her say those words. He wondered if God was mad at him because he didn't have faith enough to believe that this would one day happen.

"Actually," Margo went on. "He talked to me. Twice."

"W-what did He tell you?"

"That He never abandoned me. That life is full of evil, but He wasn't the one to do all that to me."

"Do you believe that?"

"Honestly, I don't know. But I'm willing to think about it. Work it out in my mind." She hesitated. "If you'll help me."

He couldn't speak past the lump in his throat.

"Linc?"

Finally he was able to say, "I'll help you." He soothed a hand down her hair. "Do you realize what a gift you've given me?"

She shook her head.

"That you'd think about making peace with God . . ." Linc was overcome with emotion. Because he admitted, for the first time, that they probably wouldn't make it if she didn't at least try to effect some reconciliation with his God.

"Linc, I'm not there yet. But I'll try. I want to share your life, not just tolerate it. So I'll work hard at coming to some terms with Him."

Linc's smile was broad. He could barely contain it. *God will take care of the rest,* he thought. But he didn't say it. He didn't want to push his luck.

She drew in a deep breath and tried for a real smile.

Intuitively, he knew to lighten the moment; so he stood and pulled her up with him. Slowly, he bent over and caught her behind the knees.

"What the hell are you doing, Jesse?" Ma Barker was back.

He was glad. He swung her over his shoulder like a sack of potatoes; she wiggled furiously. His whole body responded. Just for good measure he slapped her nicely exposed fanny. "Shut up, Ma."

She giggled. Her body relaxed against him as he strode to the bedroom.

Just as he opened the door, he whispered mentally, *Thank you, God.*

Just as he closed it, he heard, *You're welcome, son.*

"HURRY," Margo begged as he dropped her on the bed, none too gently, and dove on top of her. She could hardly wait until he was inside her.

His answer was to tunnel his hands through her hair and take her mouth. The kiss was carnal and consuming. They'd been apart too long for tenderness.

Her hands slid up under his shirt and she raked her nails down his back. A long, low, sensuous moan escaped him. When they were young, she used to drive him nuts with her sexy ministrations. His lower body, no longer young but definitely at attention, jerked into her. "Witch," he mumbled against her lips, biting the lower one, soothing it, then tracking his way to her neck with tiny little nips along the way. She was squirming by the time he buried his face in her hair. He inhaled her scent, uttered "Mmm," and continued back to her throat.

She slid her hands inside the waistband of his jeans and kneaded his butt.

Suddenly he was gone—standing, and dragging the shirt over his head. She lay where she was and enjoyed the show. She whistled saucily as his bare chest came into view. "You're in great shape, Rev."

"Right now I'm ready to go off," he said, his face flushed, his hands unsteady. He kicked off his sneakers, cursed when he had trouble undoing his jeans, then dropped them and boxers in one motion.

"Yeah, you are," she chuckled when she got a good look at him. Her voice was full of female pride.

He threw himself back on the bed and his hands went for the hem of her leopard shirt. Without finesse—it ripped—he yanked it over her head. "Aw, shit, I'm dead meat," he said when he saw her black lace demi bra. His gaze flew to hers. "You did this on purpose." He'd been a sucker for black lace all his life and she knew it.

"Uh-huh."

He slipped off her shoes, then slid down her pants. When he

saw the matching lace thong, he groaned. "Fuck it, Margo. You tryin' to give me a heart attack?"

"How about a hard-on like you've never had?"

He kissed the black lace, slid his finger inside and fingered her. "You're wet. For me. I love it." Before she could answer—she was too busy moaning—he stripped her of the underwear and covered her, naked skin meeting naked skin for the first time since she was twenty-two and leaving for grad school out west because he'd decided he was going to divinity school.

They'd both cried through the whole thing.

She pushed away the memory of all that loss. Their bodies melded. For a long, precious moment, they reveled in the feel of each other.

Then he kissed her again, working his way down her body, suckling her breasts in just the way she'd always liked. He nuzzled her stomach and his mouth closed over her. "No, Linc, together," she said just as the spasms began.

Dimly she heard him whisper, "That's it baby, come for me." His sexy baritone destroyed her. Sights, sounds and colors all exploded in her head, and she had to close her eyes to tolerate them. When the tremors finally subsided, he kissed her stomach. "You're so beautiful like this. I almost forgot."

Linc crawled up her body, bracing his arms on either side of her, and said hoarsely, "I've got about two seconds of sanity left." He started to pull away, reaching toward the nightstand for a condom. She stopped him.

"I've got protection in there."

She raised up on her elbows. "I don't need protection from you, Linc." Grasping his hard length, she slid her fingers lovingly and sexily up and down. "Come inside me with no barriers. Please."

He sucked in a breath at the picture she made, at the import of her words. Without saying anything, he turned her to her side, scissored her legs, inched his hips forward and locked his eyes with hers. Then he plunged into the only woman he'd ever really loved.

His world went dim. His head felt light and his body wound so tight it thrust mindlessly into her. He heard her say, "Ah, Linc. Yes . . . hmm . . . oh, geez . . ." Then she began yelling and begging.

It was the last thing he was conscious of as an explosive climax hit him so hard his mind went numb and his body witlessly battered into hers.

A long time later, when he finally could, he opened his eyes and saw her face was wet. She raised her hands to his and wiped moisture off his cheeks that he didn't even know was there. "It's a miracle, Linc."

He nodded. "I know." Her gaze was somber, reflecting his own. "I'm never letting you go again, you know that, don't you?"

"I don't want to go again. Ever. No matter what." She hesitated. "I trust you. I know this can work out."

"Thank you for that."

Later, nestled spoonlike with her under the covers, he silently thanked God for bringing Margo back to him.

He thought she was asleep when she mumbled, "Hey, Rev, remember how we used to do it in college?"

Grinning, he eased her over and pressed her face into the pillow. He slid his arm around her hips and raised her lower body up, his hand cradling her intimately. She spread her legs and his erection pressed against her. As he slipped inside her, he whispered, "This way?"

"Hmm."

"Yeah, I remember." He began to move and before rational thought fled once again, he vowed he would always remember— how he loved her, how he lost her, and how she came back to him and completed his life. Then he stopped thinking altogether.

WIPING away the steam from his shower, Joe looked in the mirror. For the first time in five and a half years, he approved of the man who stared back at him. Linc was right in his sermon this morning, it was time to forgive himself. He'd taken a long run after church and stayed for hours in the park, thinking about his life, both where he'd been and where he was going. As he lathered up and glided the razor over his face, he realized this was the last step to healing completely. He'd been a monster, but Hyde was gone. For good.

The blade scraped his cheek; he tilted his chin to shave his throat, his heart full. Things were going to work out. His children had accepted him. And he and Annie had a truce.

Gray eyes stared back at him honestly. *You want more from her.*

"Yeah, well," Joe said aloud as he wiped off the excess lather. "You can't always get what you want." He'd try to be happy with what he had. It was a skill he'd learned during recovery.

Leaving the bathroom, he strode into the bedroom and drew out a pair of gray Polo shorts and a matching T-shirt. He wanted Annie all right, physically, emotionally and psychologically. But he'd never get her back. So he *would* be happy with what he had.

His gaze dropped to the message pad next to the phone by the bed. Taylor had gotten him a date with one of her straight friends in the industry. Saturday night, six o'clock. She'd called earlier and ordered him to be there.

And Joe had said yes. It was time to get on with his life.

The doorbell rang, chasing away the flutter of sadness that accompanied that thought. Shrugging into a navy bathrobe, he padded to the front door. He was shocked to see his ex-wife standing on the top of the staircase that led to his apartment.

"Hi." She was dressed in the long baby-pink sleeveless dress she'd worn in church that morning. Its slim cut accented her dancer's body but made her look taller. Freckles dotted her fair skin, and he remembered how he used to tease her about them. When she'd get mad, he'd end up kissing every single one. There *had* been some good times. "Joe? What are you staring at?"

"Your freckles."

She swiped her nose self-consciously. "Can I come in?"

"Here?" Never once had she been to his apartment. It somehow seemed intimate, even to him.

Glancing over his shoulder, she frowned. Her eyes rested on his bathrobe and wet hair. "Oh, sorry. Is someone here?"

"No. No one's here." He was fumbling like a boy calling his first girl. "Sure you can come in." He stepped aside and let her enter. "Sit down."

She moved gracefully to the couch and sat on the edge. Her eyes were drawn to his chest, which was exposed through the open V of his robe. Odd, it made him blush. "I'll just get dressed," he told her. And collect myself, he thought as he scrambled into the bedroom.

Annie's heart was beating wildly in her chest as she watched Joe's retreating back. It wasn't that she was afraid of him, though. Afraid of being alone with him. She was nervous about what she'd come to tell him. To distract herself, she scanned the apartment. It was small but meticulous. She'd noticed the same thing about his office and car and even the way he dressed. Joe was very careful about everything these days.

Her gaze landed on the coffee table. Several magazines were neatly stacked. A catalog had been tossed on the top. Peering up at her, right under the title *Men Undercover*, and logo, Exclusive Underwear For Men, was a full-blown picture of Joe. Instead of lazing on a couch, like the shoot she'd seen with him that day in New York, he was lounging on a bed. Gray-striped sheets backdropped him. He was slouched against an oak headboard, his arms linked behind his head. He was naked, except for a pair of silky gray boxers that emphasized his trim waist, his muscular thighs. Patterns of dark hair whorled beautifully across his bare chest. And on his face was a smile sexier than Pierce Brosnan's.

She picked up the magazine. Her finger outlined his head, his jaw, his shoulders.

"Annie? What are you . . . Oh, Lord."

Slowly, she peered up into his blushing face. He'd put on gray shorts and a matching T-shirt with black sandals. He seemed healthy and happy and—she glanced down at the catalog—sexy. She held it up smiling. "You look . . . terrific."

His blush deepened. He shrugged. "It's embarrassing."

"It's honest work."

His eyes flashed with the memory of the time in New York. *You always land on your feet, don't you Joe?* She knew now that had been a gross misstatement. The road to health had been rocky and treacherous, and Joe had paid a high price to recover. It was there in the sadness of his gray eyes every time she looked in them.

"Thanks." He took a seat across from her. He was always careful not to invade her personal space. She wondered if he learned that in his counseling sessions. "Why did you come here?"

It was her turn to blush. She felt it creep up her neck and chin. "I have something to say."

He tensed.

She rushed on to add, "It's . . . good."

Visibly he relaxed. She felt bad for having this power over him and wielding it.

Stop it. It's water under the bridge. And you had cause.

She did, but she was tired of living in the limbo of retribution.

"I was wondering if you might want to come over for dinner tonight."

His eyebrows rose. "To your house?"

"Yes."

"Is Faith cooking?" He grinned. "Not that I don't like peanut butter and jelly."

"No, Faith's not cooking." She smoothed her hands down her dress. Suddenly her palms were clammy. "Actually, both kids are going to supper and a movie with Rosa."

He stared at her blankly. "I don't understand. You want me to come over to your house for dinner . . . with just you?"

She nodded. Felt foolish. "Um, if you don't want to, it's okay."

"I want to. I just don't understand. . . ." His eyes narrowed on her. "Does this have anything to do with Linc's sermon today?"

"Partly." She drew in a deep breath. "I told you before I believe you've changed, Joe."

"That's not the same as forgiveness."

"I know. That's why I'm here. To tell you I *do* forgive you."

Slowly his eyes filled. He closed them and rubbed them with his thumb and forefinger. When he was composed, he met her gaze again. "I don't know what to say. I never expected your forgiveness."

"Well, you have it if you want it."

"I want it."

"I'm glad." She scanned the room nervously. "So, I thought it might be a good idea if we had some alone time to talk. To kind of get to know each other better. You know, to get to know the people we've become."

He swallowed hard. "I'd really like that, Mary Anne."

His use of her formal name relaxed her, made her smile. "So would I." She stood.

So did he. "What time should I come?"

"About seven?"

"Fine."

They walked toward the door. She opened it, but turned back. She had flats on and he was a good foot taller than she. He looked big, but . . . breakable. And she realized she truly didn't fear him anymore. "So, I'll see you later."

He nodded. She could tell he was still overcome with emotion. Her own throat felt tight. Staring into his world-weary face, she gave him a small smile.

He returned it.

Then, in a gesture as natural as summer rain, she reached up and encircled his neck with her arms. He froze for a minute, then gently wrapped his arms around her, and as he'd done so many times, lifted her into his embrace.

Somehow it felt right. Like a new beginning.

Just what the minister ordered.

EPILOGUE

———

UNDER a canopy of clear blue September sky, punctuated by fluffy white clouds that looked like cotton candy, Ron leaned over into the shiny new car and tightened the strap on Tucker's safety harness. Hordes of people buzzed in the stands, waiting for the much-publicized September Exhibition Race to begin. Race driver legends that hadn't come to compete were in the crowd—even The King, Richard Petty.

Grinning, Tucker ruffled Ron's hair. "The harness is tight, kid."

"Just wanna make sure." Ron ducked his head out and looked at the track where his father had died. He tried not to let on that he was worried. At almost eighteen, he knew today was different from ten years before. It was just that sometimes, he did fear losing his *new* dad.

"See you in the pit," The Menace said cockily.

"Ah, no, you won't."

Tucker nodded to Ron's red and white jumpsuit, which matched his own. "You're part of my crew, Ronny."

Shaking his head, Ron shrugged. "I'm gonna go sit with Mom during the race."

Through his safety glasses and chin strap, Tucker smiled. "Good idea, son." He reached up and grasped Ron's wrist with his gloved hand. "Tell her not to worry. I'm gonna be fine." He leaned over conspiratorially. "I plan on seein' that little brother or sister we're gonna give you in seven months or so."

Ron sputtered and Tucker laughed. This was the first Ron had heard about a new little tyke in the family. As Tucker drove off to the starting lane, Ron shook his head, his heart squeezing tightly in his chest. He was gonna have a kid brother or sister. One he could watch over and keep safe, away from the trouble he'd gotten into. "Now, don't that beat all," he mumbled as he watched Tucker maneuver into place.

"Geez, kid, you even sound like them Southern boys."

Ron turned around and smiled at Margo. Dressed in a long Menace T-shirt—Doc and Tucker had gotten them for the whole *family*—Ron cast a glance at the name written on the front. "Yeah, well, *Mary Margaret,* I could do worse."

Margo smiled radiantly and wrapped her just-beginning-to-bulge belly with her arms. Now *her* he'd known about.

"The twins givin' you trouble today?" he asked.

"I tossed my cookies again this morning. They're already hell-on-wheels, I tell you."

As they walked to the edge of the pit, Ron shook his head. "You got names picked out?"

"Of course. We're calling them Frank and Jesse James."

"Well, if you'd take your husband's name like you're supposed to . . ."

"Never see the day, kid."

When Linc and Margo got married that summer—just after his mom and Tucker—they didn't want to rush anything. She'd kept her place in New York and did some consulting in computer design but had spent more than half her time in Glen Oaks. When she was here, she ran the racing video game business she'd set up with Doc.

They were just about to head for the stands when someone tugged them back.

Ron pivoted.

Doc's complexion was rosy and his eyes sparkled with energy; given that *everybody* was watching out for his diet and exercise these days, he was the picture of health. "Tell your mama Tuck's gonna be all right, boy."

"I will, Doc." Ron glanced over to the pit. "Where's Gerty?"

"She went up to sit with your grandparents."

"No shit, are they here?"

"Yep. She's tryin' to coax 'em down to sit with the rest of the family."

Ron looked all the way back to the stands. Sometimes, if you had enough faith, and trust, the pieces just fell into place. When he reached the box seats, he found his mother sitting on the bench. She wore shades, and the sun beat down on her hair, which was getting longer. Like she used to wear it. She had on her Menace T-shirt, with *Mary Elizabeth* etched on the top left. Uncle Linc was next to her, in his racing shirt, too. God, they all looked like the freakin' Brady Bunch.

And it felt damn good.

Margo climbed over his mother and plunked down in Linc's lap, giving him a big smooch right on the mouth.

"Have you no shame, woman?" Linc asked, coming up for air.

"None."

"I've got my reputation to think of." His protest was weakened by the fact that he was nuzzling her neck.

"Screw your reputation." She kissed him again.

He whispered something in her ear that Ron was glad he couldn't hear. Sex between adults boggled his mind; despite that, seeing Margo and Linc together made him feel warm right down to his toes.

Flanking his mother on the other side, he put his arm around her. "Tucker's fine, Mom. He said to tell you he's gonna be all right."

"I know he is. Nothing's going to take him away from me now, Ronny."

"Away from *us,*" Ron corrected. Then, with a glint in his eye, he added, "All three of us."

Beth grinned. "He told you?"

"Uh-huh."

"How do you feel about it?"

"Feel about what?" Linc had settled Margo next to him and held her hand like some teenager.

With pretended disgust, Ron snorted. "We got a regular baby boom happenin' around here."

Linc's eyes lit up. He grabbed his sister and hugged her. "Oh, Bethy, I'm so glad."

Margo reached around Linc for an embrace of her own. "Way to go, girl. Now ours'll have playmates." Her eyes twinkled. "Just like us."

"Oh, Lord," Linc said. "Imagine the trouble they'll get into."

Ron shook his head. "I'll keep all three of them in line." He rolled his eyes. "And if Lily can tear herself away from that college she went to, she can help me with them."

Who would have thought—Lily Hanson enrolled in SUNY Brockport to become a Math teacher. Mr. Johnson was really proud.

There was a rustle in the stands as a group made its way up to them. Now *there* was a posse if Ron ever saw one. Matt Murphy and Tommy DeMartino, wearing The Menace shirts, too, clomped alongside their two little sisters. Ron used to be jealous of their family. Now, he was gonna have a sibling of his own— and cousins to boot. Behind them, Rosa DeMartino followed, trailed by Annie and Joe. The kids sat a few rows up, and the adults took the seats behind his mom.

There was a round of warm hellos.

Annie and Joe looked good in their Menace shirts, too; Annie's sported *Mary Anne,* her full name, like Mom's and Margo's. Studying them, Ron didn't think he'd ever seen Annie happier, or Joe more relaxed. He didn't know why they'd split, but he'd been thinking all summer they were heading back together.

Joe reached out, took Annie's hand and just held it. It was almost a reverent gesture.

Annie squeezed his back, then nodded to the track. "So, how much longer?"

"Any minute now," Beth told her.

Annie touched his mother's shoulder.

"I'm okay," Beth responded to the silent query.

Just then, a loud voice came over the speaker for the spectators to stand to sing the national anthem. Rising, Ron looked out at the packed bleachers, at the newly refurbished track where he'd spent a lot of the last summer with Doc and Tucker. He smiled. He had his own secret, which he'd keep to himself awhile. Mr. Johnson was helping him apply to design schools. Though he loved the race, Doc's side of it was more interesting. He stared at the fourth turn where his father had crashed. And designing was safer. Now, he knew how important that was.

The introductions over, the announcer spoke the most famous words in racing lore. "Gentlemen, start your engines!"

Ron grasped his mother's hand as Tucker took his place on the pole and led the other cars out onto the track.

Two hours later, when the checkered flag came down right behind number thirty-one, Ron was still holding her hand.

The Menace had won the exhibition race, but Ron knew *he* was the luckiest person at Glen Oaks Race Track that day.

Author's Note

Trust in Me was a challenging book to write because it deals with difficult subjects. Believe me when I say that I understand the issues here are deep and significant ones, not easily worked out. I also realize that not everyone will agree they should be dealt with as I have dealt with them. Yet for me, the story was an uplifting one to tell, too, because all of the characters grow and change and are able to deal with their personal demons to become better, happier people. At its heart, *Trust in Me* is a book about redemption, and how it *is* possible to make up for past mistakes, and how it *is* possible to let go of guilt. All six characters need to leave their pasts behind, and forgive themselves for their mistakes or weaknesses—not an easy task.

The crux of this book is friendship, something I've always believed vital to adult contentment. The six main characters help each other to find happiness. In my life, I've been blessed with close friends, and I know personally how these very special people make a difference in my life. Also important in the novel are the relationships between parents and children. I've seen firsthand how the love of a mother or father can turn a child around, or vice versa. Adults play major roles in kids' lives, sometimes when the kids don't even know it. And finally, the book is about that unique relationship between a man and a woman. It makes me smile to think how these couples find each other, some after years of separation, and are able to overcome guilt, insecurities and old resentments to be together.

I hope you enjoy reading about Linc, Margo, Beth, Tucker, Joe and Annie—and one special boy, Ronny—as much as I enjoyed writing about them. Drop me a note to let me know your impressions at kshayweb@rochester.rr.com, or at P.O. Box 24288, Rochester, New York 14624. Also, visit my website at www.kathrynshay.com.

And now, a special excerpt from the newest novel by
Kathryn Shay . . .

AFTER THE FIRE

Available November 2003 from
The Berkley Publishing Group

"OH my God, the ceiling's coming down!" It was all Captain Mitch Malvaso got out. In seconds, a crushing weight slammed him into the floor, face first. As he hit the concrete, he thought of his sister Jenny, who was also in the warehouse, slapping water on the fire that caused the collapse. "Please God, don't let her die," he murmured. Then the world went black.

When he awoke, outside in the bright sunshine, he startled. Immediately, he felt raw, lacerating slices of pain on the back of his legs. Burns. Through his bunker pants.

Sucking in a breath, he slitted his eyes and forced them to focus. The first thing he saw was that the fire, which had blazed like an angry monster, consuming Sinco Automotive's five-hundred-square-foot warehouse, was out. Black smoke still curled from the building, where several companies of the Hidden Cove Fire Department had been called to the four alarm blaze.

Were some of his men still inside?

He took inventory. He was lying on a stretcher, his airpack removed and his turnout coat off. Then things crystallized.

And reality hit him—where was Jenny?

When he tried to move, the burns scraped raw. He let out a long low moan and consciousness momentarily dimmed. Then, he became aware of sirens and shouting, and people barking out orders. He shifted, and his breathing escalated with what now felt like torture. He caught sight of his sister, lying on a blanket off to the left. He managed to yell, "Jenny, you okay?" but it came out like a rusty saw on wood.

After worrisome seconds, she inched up onto her elbows, groaning with the effort. "Yeah. I'm okay." As if she'd been awakened from a deep sleep, she looked around. "Oh, God." She scrambled to a sitting position. "Shit, that hurts," she spat out but came up on all fours and crawled over. Kneeling above him, she said, "Mitch, oh, God, Mitch are you all right?"

He drew in a breath. "I'm burned. But okay." He reached out and gripped her hand, which was streaked with grime like her face. "You sure you're okay?"

"I guess."

Someone approached them. A medic, Jimmy, from Engine Twelve. "Hey, you two doin' all right?"

"Yeah." Mitch surveyed the scene. Several smoke eaters lay on stretchers, the ground or blankets. Some coughing, some too still. Medical personnel were tending to a few, left others alone.

Jimmy frowned. "Don't worry, Captain, we're working on getting your brother outta there."

Both Jenny and he gasped. "Our brother?" Mitch said. "Zach's not here, he's on the night shift this week."

All three Malvaso firefighters worked at the same station, he on the elite Rescue Squad, Jenny on Group One, and Zach on Group Two of Quint/Midi Seven, housed at fire department headquarters.

The young medic's face blanked. Then he said, "Mitch, Zach showed up here when he heard about the fire on his scanner. He barreled inside when he realized the Red Devil was out of control and you two were in there."

"Son of a bitch." Mitch gripped the medic's arm. "You know anything else?"

"The men that've been rescued said he pushed them out of the way when the wall started to cave on them after the ceiling fell on you guys."

Mitch struggled to get up. He couldn't. "Fuck, I can't move."

"You're burned bad. We did some work on you already, but others were hurt worse so . . . we're gonna take you to the hospital right now."

"No, I won't leave here until I know Zach's okay."

"Mitch—"

"No!" He reached out again for his sister; she flinched when he made contact with her arm. Burns reddened her skin. "Get Jenny some help. Do what you can for me, but I'm staying."

His heart in his throat, Mitch transferred his gaze to the building, watched the smoke circle like a lazy cat along the flat roof and wondered if his baby brother was alive.

FIFTEEN minutes later, they still didn't know what was happening with Zach. Jenny sat stiffly beside Mitch, ignoring the pain that danced along her upper body like electrical sparks. She simply stared at the warehouse where her brother was still inside. They'd done some preliminary burn treatment on both her and Mitch, but since Mitch had dug in his heels and there were so many casualties and life threatening injuries, they were allowed to stay here and wait.

It had been the worst fifteen minutes of her life.

"You okay kid?" Mitch asked in that tone which always made her soft. The oldest of all five of them, he played the father role much of the time.

"Uh-huh." She stifled a sob. As one of ten female firefighters in the Hidden Cove Fire Department, about a hundred miles north of New York City and west of the Hudson, Jenny was tough. But this . . .

The fire had been routine; five trucks had arrived within minutes of each other. Three of the crews had mounted an interior attack when the ceiling fell, complete with beams and searing plaster; several firefighters had been trapped. Apparently they'd rescued her and Mitch's crews. Now, special teams were digging the rest out.

She rubbed her eyes with her thumb and forefinger.

"Does it hurt bad, baby?" Mitch asked.

"No. Yeah. I guess." She looked down at him, and smoothed back his hair. "You?"

"Like a bitch." Mitch coughed and sputtered. He'd removed his SCUBA gear—his air had run out because he'd been in the warehouse longer than her—while waiting to be rescued. Consequently, he'd inhaled a lot of smoke.

Again she nodded toward the warehouse. "Mitch, Zach's still

in there . . . Do you think he's . . ." Jenny's eyes focused on the structure. There were dead smoke eaters in there and out here. She just prayed Zach wasn't one of them.

Though her brother rode through life on a short fuse and chased after too many skirts for her taste, she didn't know what she'd do if something happened to Zach. All three Malvaso firefighters were close—since childhood they'd stuck together against their other brother and sister, and the world in general. What if . . .

Her hand crept out to the side. "Mitello?"

They only used their given, Italian names when things were really bad.

Mitch found her hand, clasped it. "Yeah, Genevieve?"

"If he gets out of there . . ."

"*When* he gets out of there."

"When. We're going to do things different. All of us."

"What do you mean?"

"I wanna have a baby."

Her brother chuckled, then choked like a rookie eating his first smoke. His voice came out in a wheezy rumble. "Better find yourself a fella first."

"What would you do different, if you had the chance?" Pain turned her voice raw. "I know you haven't been happy with Cindy."

"No, I haven't been happy. And my kids need help."

"Promise me, when this is over"—she gripped his hand tighter—"you'll do something about all that. You'll make your life better."

"Okay, I promise."

She glanced back at the warehouse. "Zaccaria, too. He's gotta get his act together. We'll help him."

Momentarily, Mitch closed his eyes. He looked like he was struggling to stay conscious. "All right. The three of us, we'll do better. We'll live better lives."

Just then a shadow came over them. Both she and Mitch looked up and when she saw who it was, Jenny's eyes started to tear. "Oh, God, Grady."

Her best friend in the world, and coworker on her crew, crouched down. Despite the cast on his arm, which had kept him off the line and out of harm's way for this fire, he clasped her to him. She buried her face in his big safe chest. "I just heard and came over." He knelt to hold her more securely. She felt a hand in her hair. Soothing her, he said to Mitch, "What's going on?"

"Zach . . ." Mitch cleared his throat. "He's in there."

"What?"

Jenny heard Mitch mumble an explanation.

Grady said, "Son of a—" but stopped. Stilled. His body went taut. Jenny drew back; he was staring at the building. She turned to see two firefighters stumble out. Both were covered with layers of grime and white dust.

One held on to shoulders, the other on to the feet of an HCFD smoke eater.

She tensed. Though she couldn't make out who they carried, Jenny knew in her heart it was her brother.

He looked dead.